LIKE THE AMERICAN ~~~~~~
YESTERDAY, THESE BRAVE EXPLORERS
CHALLENGE A HOSTILE NEW WILDNERNESS

America 2040—Volume 2
The Golden World

CAPTAIN DUNCAN RODRICK—
With steely strength and unwavering courage, he has
completed the first leg of his historic mission in space.
But now he faces new dangers from a strange world of
awesome proportions—and his decisions alone mean
survival or death as a fierce attack threatens the colony
. . . and a captain must choose between honor and
love.

LT. JACQUELINE GARVEY—
Lovely and sensual, she has given herself willingly to
Duncan Rodrick, only to find that sharing his bed does
not mean she possesses his heart . . . and that revenge
is as strong a feeling as desire.

AMANDA MILLER—
The attractive, intelligent medical director for the
mission, she tries to lose herself in her work, but she
cannot heal the pain of wanting a man she can never
have . . . or of a marriage gone bad.

America 2040—Volume 2
The Golden World

ROCKY MILLER—

No one doubts the courage of this strong, quick-tempered officer, and no one guesses the ambitions that make him a dangerous rival for control of a world.

THERESITA PULASKI—

The most powerful Soviet leader aboard the Russian star ship, she has a dream she would kill for . . . and a fate that put her face-to-face with terror and the unknown.

JACOB WEST—

He pilots his scout plane *Apache One* with the same breathtaking skill his Indian ancestors used, galloping their pintos across the great American West, and his special bravery can mean life or death to a woman . . . and a world.

SAGE BRYSON—

She is the most beautiful woman among the pioneers, her classic face and perfect figure like a magnet for lustful men, but the partner she chooses is not a man, not a human, at all.

American 2040—Volume 2
The Golden World

THE ADMIRAL—

Stronger, faster, and more intelligent than any man on the ship, his craggy good looks and gentle manner make him beloved by many . . . but cannot make this robot human.

CLAY GIRARD—

A high-spirited teen who began as an orphan stowaway finds that the future is his on this new world . . . and so is the girl he loves.

CINDY McRAE—

Young and attractive, she is coming to womanhood with a new world at her feet . . . but she alone senses the hostile force that will come to threaten them all.

Bantam Books by Evan Innes

AMERICA 2040

AMERICA 2040
BOOK II

THE GOLDEN WORLD

Evan Innes

 Created by the producers of
**Wagons West, White Indian, and
Children of the Lion.**

Chairman of the Board: Lyle Kenyon Engel

BANTAM BOOKS
TORONTO • NEW YORK • LONDON • SYDNEY • AUCKLAND

THE GOLDEN WORLD
A Bantam Book / September 1986

Produced by Book Creations, Inc.
Chairman of the Board: Lyle Kenyon Engel

ISBN 0-553-25922-9

Published simultaneously in the United States and Canada

PRINTED IN THE UNITED STATES OF AMERICA
KR   0 9 8 7 6 5 4 3 2 1

THE GOLDEN WORLD

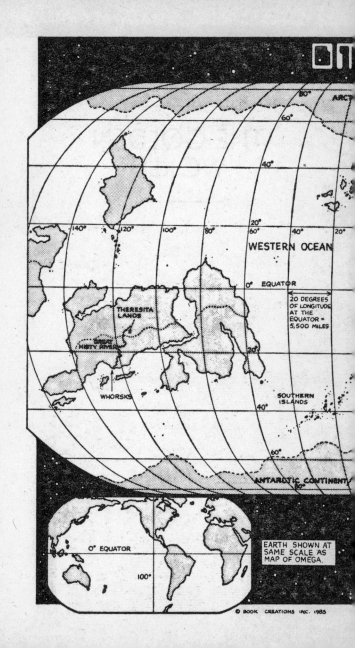

OT

80° ARCT

60°

40°

20°
140° 120° 100° 80° 60° 40° 20°

WESTERN OCEAN

0° EQUATOR

20 DEGREES
OF LONGITUDE
AT THE
EQUATOR =
5,500 MILES

THERESITA
LANDS

GREAT
MISTY RIVER
20°

WHORSKS

SOUTHERN
ISLANDS
40°

60°

ANTARCTIC CONTINENT
80°

0° EQUATOR

100°

EARTH SHOWN AT
SAME SCALE AS
MAP OF OMEGA.

© BOOK CREATIONS INC. 1985

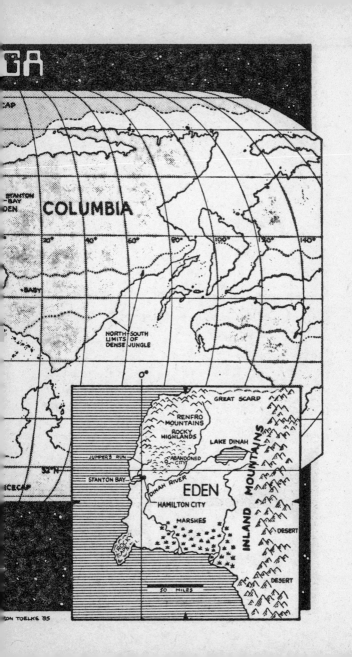

GA

ICECAP

STANTON
BAY
EDEN

COLUMBIA

20°   40°   60°   80°   100°   120°   140°

BABY

NORTH-SOUTH
LIMITS OF
DENSE JUNGLE

0°

32° N

ICECAP

GREAT SCARP

RENFRO
MOUNTAINS

ROCKY
HIGHLANDS

LAKE DINAH

JUMPER'S RUN

ABANDONED
CITY

STANTON BAY

DINAH RIVER

EDEN

HAMILTON CITY

MARSHES

ROCKY

INLAND MOUNTAINS

DESERT

DESERT

50 MILES

ON TOELKE '85

PROLOGUE

From the journal of Evangeline Burr, official historian, the Spirit of America

On this 4 July, 2043 we began the day with a moment of silent prayer or contemplation, depending upon the personal beliefs of the members of our company. Everyone was relieved when Captain Duncan Rodrick did not call a holiday to observe the birthdate of our country. We can honor what President Dexter Hamilton has called "the crowning achievement of governmental experiments."

Although the *Spirit of America* has been a scientific and technological masterpiece and a safe home for our journey through space, we are tired of breathing recycled air, drinking recycled water, eating artificial proteins, and having to make do with rationed fresh fruits and vegetables from the ship's gardens.

The *Spirit of America* bears the scars of the dangers we have faced during our long journey. Just yesterday the captain allowed me to view the starship's exterior, as seen from the sensors of a scout ship returning from an exploratory mission. I was shocked. The large, curving plates of the hull are blistered and pitted. All the paint has been seared away from the multiple jutting rocket engines and the pods that house the scout ships. The large letters that once proclaimed proudly that our ship was indeed the

Spirit of America have been obliterated, but we don't need a painted name to remind us of our mission.

After almost three years in space, we have our goal in sight—a beautiful planet, four times larger than Earth. To see our new home, we merely use our personal screens, walk through a lounge, visit the observatory, or—as I have done no fewer than three times—obtain permission to visit the areas near the outer hull of our ship and look with naked eyes through one of the thick, polarized glass ports.

We can also see that odd sun, 61 Cygni B. Our new sun is farther away from our target planet than old Sol is from Earth, but she's larger and appears as a swollen, bloated, orange-flaring disc of unusual beauty.

To say that we face an uncertain future would be nothing new. But when I think about what was facing the billions on Earth when our ship rocketed away, I count my lucky stars—and there are plenty of them to count from space. I must soon begin to record and preserve the shocking facts given to me by Captain Rodrick as to the reasons behind President Dexter Hamilton's decision to use the dwindling resources of the United States to build this great starship: Soviet Premier Yuri Kolchak suffered from a rare terminal disease and was determined to see a Red world or a dead world before his own death. Hamilton's choice was a grim one. He had either to stand aside and let the communist forces occupy all the world except the United States or contest the communists. Kolchak had promised him that the end result of American resistance would be nuclear war.

So, more than anything else, the *Spirit of America* is Dexter Hamilton's creation. He had it built to keep the spirit of freedom alive in the face of a threat of nuclear war. We colonists are charged with keeping the American way of life alive in space, no matter what happened on Earth after our takeoff.

When we left Earth, two other starships, the Russians' *Karl Marx* and the Brazilians' *Estrêla do Brasil*, were making preparations for takeoff. With our communications out, we don't know the whereabouts of those ships or their intentions. There are billions of stars in our galaxy, and in theory, many of them will have habitable planets. Perhaps the Russians and the Brazilians will find their own planets, but I have heard many people, including some of our officers, speculate that the Russians might want to carry the old Earth war into space. Should they follow us here to the Cygni system, I know we will be ready.

I also feel confident that our huge new planet is going to be friendly to us. Today, eleven light years from Earth, over a thousand passengers who represent all civilized skills and all scientific knowledge are busy preparing to join our scouts and scientists, who have already proven that our new planet is quite friendly to human habitation. We are all eager to begin. We have the tools, the knowledge, and the expertise to build a technology and do whatever it takes for Captain Rodrick to return this vast starship to Earth with her raw materials, food, and most important, a message of hope.

I

OMEGA

ONE

The *Spirit of America* was big. She was the largest object ever to be lifted from a planetary surface by rocket power, or any other power, unless one believed the theory that Venus had been flung out of the planet Jupiter or that Earth's moon had been spun off from Earth's mass during planet formation aeons past. She was a complicated collection of millions of parts, mechanical and electronic, and Captain Duncan Rodrick knew that in any mechanical or electrical system lay the foundation of Murphy's Law: If something can go wrong, it will.

Humankind's eternal task, when dealing with machines, was to see that the malfunction didn't occur at a crucial time . . . such as when landing megatons of mass balanced on the pillars of fire of one hundred rockets.

"Systems check," Rodrick ordered in his laid-back, informal command voice.

"Communications operative," Lieutenant Jacqueline Garvey said.

"Computers operative," said little Japanese-American Emi Zuki.

Ito Zuki, Emi's husband, spoke from his seat directly beside his wife. "Navigation system operative. Landing sequence programmed."

Chief Engineer Max Rosen's voice came soft and lazy to Rodrick through the communicator. Rodrick had come to know and value Max Rosen during the years in space, and he knew that Max's tone of voice indicated tension.

"Rocket engine firing system armed and ready," Rosen reported.

Rodrick smiled. He could almost picture Rosen's face, screwed up into its perpetual expression of pure agony.

"Hull cooling system operative," said the electrical engineer, Sage Bryson.

"Weapons system armed and ready." Lieutenant Commander Paul Warden, the old jock, was stationed behind the thick armor plates of the *Spirit of America*'s weapons control center, ready to blast any threatening entity with beams, rays, projectiles, and rockets.

It was easy, Rodrick thought, for some to forget that a ready weapons system was an integral part of the landing procedure. After all, Jack Purdy, chief scout, had been down on the planet's surface for over twenty days, and a sizable group of passengers had already been shuttled down to join him. These two hundred plus people, who now sat on a low, grassy hill to watch the ship come in, were another indication of Rodrick's innate cautiousness. The *Spirit of America* had never been landed. Should anything happen on the way down, there would be a solid core of people safely on the surface, to assure survival of the colony.

All this was going through Rodrick's mind as he heard Paul Warden's voice reporting the status of the ship's weapons systems, and thinking of Warden in weapons control made Rodrick feel better. He liked the man, drank with him on occasion, called him, with affection, the no-neck monster because Warden was built like a wrestler, with a thick chest, big arms, and highly developed deltoid muscles, which made it look as if his head sat directly on his shoulders.

First Officer Rocky Miller, whose function it was to stand ready to fill any position on the control bridge in the event of emergency, looked at the captain out of the corner of his eye. Miller was taller than Rodrick, and more muscular; he spent long hours in the gym. Rocky Miller had not agreed with the captain's decision to land two hundred selected people by scout ship. As he let his eyes swing swiftly over the array of instruments, he was thinking that Rodrick had the looks of a man who had been spooked. Rodrick, Miller felt, put up a good front, but at times during the trip out, the captain, in Miller's opinion, had been on the verge of losing his judgment in tight situations.

Rodrick allowed a few seconds to pass. Jackie Garvey crossed her long legs and looked up at him. She felt that she knew the captain better than most; one aspect of their mission was the understood but unstated order that women of childbearing age were to breed children. It had seemed logical, in the beginning, that she was the perfect choice for the ship's bachelor commander. He winked at her, but her answering smile was questioning. Things had seemed so promising early on, and then something had gone wrong. They had been very good together, and then nothing.

The bridge, although not spacious, was never crowded. The ship had been built to fly herself. The bridge crew consisted of Emi Zuki, computer programmer; Ito Zuki, her husband and astronavigator; Jackie Garvey, ship's communicator, and the first officer, Rocky Miller, on standby. His wife, Dr. Amanda Miller, was usually on the bridge during interesting maneuvers, but she and the bulk of her Life Sciences staff, including the medical unit, were now on the surface.

There was one other figure on the bridge, a tall, slim, handsome individual in United States Navy white, his chest resplendent with ribbons, his back stiff, a cap adorned with admiral's gold pulled rakishly low over his piercing, unblinking eyes.

Rodrick swiveled his command seat. "Admiral?" he asked.

"Sir!" the admiral snapped.

It was difficult to remember, sometimes, that the admiral was one of Dr. Grace Monroe's "boys," that those dark, piercing eyes were not really alive, that the impressive figure was built of synthetics, that the brain behind those eyes was Dr. Monroe's greatest achievement. An electrical lead seemed to emerge from the admiral's rear pocket. It was attached to Emi Zuki's main computer terminal.

"How do you read?" Rodrick asked.

"All systems at optimum efficiency, sir," the admiral said.

The admiral had been proven invaluable. His lightning-fast brain, more than a computer, could be synergically meshed with the ship's computers. Rodrick had come to depend on the admiral as one more check on the ship's computer system.

"Put me on all-ship's circuit, Lieutenant Garvey," Rodrick said, and when Jackie had pushed the proper buttons, he took a deep breath. "This is the captain. In three minutes we will fire retro-rockets preparatory to landing. Please position yourselves in your gravity couches at this time."

During the stressful times, two things belied Max Rosen's attempt to be cool and casual—his face and his Space Service uniform. During preparation for the landing, Max's uniform had given up the fight and now looked as if it had been slept in for days. Max's ability to perform a negative miracle on the uniform was only one of his qualities that Dr. Grace Monroe found fascinating, especially since millions of dollars had been spent in research to develop a fabric that would withstand long wear in cramped quarters. In less than one hour, starting with a fresh uniform, Max could prove that all those millions had been wasted.

As Max watched the digital countdown clock display its ever-changing numbers, he ran long fingers through his black, unruly hair, managing to muss it even more.

Grace was standing by at a computer terminal. After a bad start, when Grace's menagerie of robotic entities had thoroughly annoyed the chief engineer, he'd come to respect her more than any other person he'd ever known. There were times when he wondered which he liked most about her: her intuitive intelligence or her mature beauty.

"You look like you could use a drink," he growled, as the clock counted off the seconds, and around him, the engine-room servomechanisms clicked and hummed in readiness.

"I feel as if I need a drink," Grace said.

Rosen was a tall, thin, dark, strong-nosed, wiry-haired Jew. His heavy beard gave him a five-o'clock shadow all day long, and his black hair was just beginning to be peppered with gray. On him it looked almost distinguished. He'd worked with Harry Shaw from the beginning in the development of the Shaw Drive, which propelled the starship through time and space.

In contrast to Max's disheveled state, Grace Monroe looked as if she'd spent the past few hours with a makeup, hair care, and fashion expert instead of at Max's side as they checked the computations again and again.

Grace was in her mid fifties. Her mature, full-bodied beauty was set off by her mauve suit, accented at the throat by a paisley scarf. Once, when she'd entered Rosen's engineering sector dressed impeccably, he had growled, "Don't you have any work clothes?"

"These are my work clothes," she'd told him.

Max sighed, wished for that drink, then looked down as something rubbed at his shin. The thing was catlike in appearance. In fact, Cat, one of Grace's robotic creations, had been experimenting of late in growing hair, and the attempt had not been totally successful. Cat looked to Max like a blue Tinkertoy feline with hog bristles protruding from its odd, elastic body, composed of material that Dr. Monroe had developed when she was head of Research and Development at Transworld Robotics, Inc. back on Earth.

"Damned Cat," Max growled, but there was no fury there, as there once had been. True to Grace's design objective, Cat had pulled the ship out of the fire for them, almost literally, by altering its shape to allow for close-quarters repairs of the rocket-firing system when the *Spirit of America* was falling rapidly into a sun.

The digital clock now showed less than one minute to go when Captain Rodrick's voice came over the communicator. "Chief, any problem if we go on hold for thirty minutes?"

Rosen looked at Grace, agony on his features, wondering what had gone wrong.

"It's just that the light isn't right down below, Chief," Rodrick said.

Rosen snarled and rolled his eyes helplessly. He knew that a filming crew was on the planet's surface, waiting to record the *Spirit of America*'s landing for posterity.

"No problem," he said, but his face showed disagreement. Putting off the landing to wait for better light for recording the event didn't rate a very high priority with him.

Grace laughed and began punching buttons. Rosen put the retro-firing on hold, then took Grace's arm and said, "I offered you a drink."

Cat at first led the way, soaring in the nulgrav, zero gravity. The spin had been taken off the ship so that there was zero gravity in all sections now. Cat had learned to flatten its body into a soaring contour, but Max, lacking Cat's abilities, lengthened his stride, opened the door to his quarters, followed Grace inside, then used his foot to deftly block the robot. Cat scratched on the metal of the door for a few seconds and then, rejected, slunk off down the corridor, its body turning black with sadness.

The ship's boozery made a decent gin. Max's quarters, in contrast to his person, were tidy. He mixed, handed Grace her covered cup and straw. He'd used a liberal quantity of the fresh orange juice squeezed from fruit grown in Amando Kwait's on-board gardens. Max sipped and then exhaled noisily. His smile showed no sign of tension as he looked at Grace. She was still standing.

"You gonna sit down?" Max asked.

"I think I'll sit down," Grace said. She'd learned during the past two and a half years not to be put out by what some considered bluntness on Max's part. She took the chair that served as the acceleration couch.

"You gonna sit down or stand up all day?" she asked, humor lighting her brown eyes.

Max growled. He had never had time to get married. He had been a brilliant young man in a hurry, and he'd hurried himself right into the most fascinating work, helping to design and test the components of the huge space stations that had been lifted into space on bellowing rockets. When he had been called to California to work with a young genius named Harry Shaw, he'd thought his life was complete and could never get better. Now he had hopes that his life *would* get better because he'd met a woman named Grace Monroe.

Intellectually she was superior to most men, and Max's initial response to her had been almost openly hostile; he was the kind of genius who felt, without admitting it to himself, that one genius around any given installation was enough. At first he'd felt that just because Grace was the topmost authority on the new breed of thinking computers, which utilized amino-acid units for data storage, it didn't give her the right to come messing around in his engineering areas and, by God, certainly not the right to turn her eerie menagerie of robots loose on his ship.

Max prided himself on being an opinionated man, but he was not so self-centered that he didn't realize that an opinionated man does not hold opinions, they hold him. Change came hard for him, but it had taken Grace only a few weeks to begin to break through to the sensitive, warm human being under Max Rosen's outer crust.

There in his quarters, waiting out a half-hour hold so that the light would be right for pictures, Grace's mental powers were not foremost in Max's mind. He saw a mature, lovely woman sitting on his acceleration couch, her classic face in repose. He swallowed, let his thoughts surface, thoughts that he'd been indulging in only in privacy: He liked looking at her. He liked hearing her talk. He liked being around her. He liked working with her. She had proven to be a good team worker. She challenged him, all right, but he was a man who liked challenges. The skull sessions they had during slow times were, to Max, more stimulating than good booze.

He *knew* that the mass of weight that was the *Spirit of America* was going to behave and sit itself down all in one piece, but there was just the odd chance— And he'd never even tried to tell her how he felt about her.

"Grace," he began, "I just want to say—"

She looked at him with an expectant smile.

"I just wanted to say . . . that I appreciate your help."

"Thank you."

"That wasn't what I wanted to say," he muttered, so low that she could barely hear.

She waited.

"I—" He swallowed. "Hell, we make a fine team, don't we?" he demanded belligerently.

"I think so," she answered, a tiny smile twitching at the corner of her mouth.

He was, he knew, acting like a lovesick kid. He was, he told himself as he almost turned and left the suite, too old to get involved in the mating dance of the juveniles. He was a man who always faced reality. He swallowed and, instead of leaving, took two steps toward her.

"Damn it, Grace," he said. "I'm out of practice for this sort of thing."

She had the feeling that if she spoke he'd run for it. She didn't want him to run. She tilted her head to one side and looked up at him, a smile on her full lips.

"Oh, hell," Max growled. "Stand up."

She put her drink down slowly, not taking her eyes from his. He took her hands and helped her up, and she went into his arms. Her eyes closed as his lips found hers.

"I've been wanting to do that for a long time," he admitted after a few moments.

"Well, it took you long enough," she said.

"I want you to *feel* my heart," Max said in amazement. He put her hand on his heart. It was beating rapidly.

"Thank you," she whispered.

He raised his bushy eyebrows in question.

"For feeling that way about me," she explained.

He grinned. There was an element of pleased disbelief in him, but mostly there was a gladness that she, so lovely, so sophisticated, could be in the arms of an old bear of an engineer who certainly was not the prize catch of all time.

"Want to get married?" Max asked.

"What do you think?"

"Yeah, I think so," he said, pulling her more tightly into his arms. "How much time we got?" he asked, knowing that she was facing the wall clock.

"Enough for you to kiss me a few more times," she said, lifting her face.

Now his heart was really going crazy. He felt first hot,

then cold. His breath was short and rapid. He looked into her eyes, and what he saw there, dreamy and beautiful, caused him to gasp.

"Whew," he exhaled.

"Yes, whew," she said.

He felt weak. He moved with her in his arms to lean her against a wall so that he could press himself closer. Their lips meshed. The door opened with a crash, and a boxy, noisy apparition rolled in, preceded by the streaking Cat. The squat robot on wheels spoke in a softly modulated but obviously nonhuman voice. "Emergency. Emergency."

"Doc!" Max yelled. "Get the hell out of here!"

Doc was another of Grace's "boys," a medical robot. Doc could complete a physical examination and come up with a diagnosis in less than three minutes.

"Do not be alarmed," the medical robot said, rolling to seize Max in its tentacles, one of which wrapped around Max's arm. "You seem to be in a state of excitation, but it is nothing to worry about. I will administer a mild sedative."

Grace was laughing so hard that her sides hurt. Doc produced another extension, tipped by an injector that misted medication painlessly through the skin.

"No, Doc," Grace gasped, as Max tried desperately to fight off the tentacles. "No sedative."

"If you say so, Grace," Doc said, but he was checking blood pressure and temperature and beginning a quick EKG.

"Get these monsters out of here," Max wailed. "Damn it, Grace—"

"Doctor," Grace said mildly, "that will be all." She was wiping tears from the corners of her eyes.

"I advise you to lie down and relax," Doc was telling Max. "A good rest—"

"You may leave, Doc, and take Cat with you," Grace ordered.

Max was glaring at her as the robots left. "Now Max—" she began, but couldn't keep back the laughter.

"Did you program that rolling bucket of bolts to keep an eye on my vital signs?" he asked her.

"Guilty," she said.

"Damn it—" he began.

"Because I care for you," she interrupted.

He felt his anger melting away. "Now where were we?" he asked, moving toward her.

She pointed toward the clock. Max rolled his eyes toward the ceiling. It was time.

TWO

Jack Purdy, chief of scouts, sat on fresh, green grass with his long legs crossed under him. He had a bush of blond hair in need of cutting, and a thin, intense face. He had taken the first scout ship down from the *Spirit of America* to the surface of the big planet, and against orders, he'd removed his space armor to breathe air that had not been recycled and to go for an exuberant swim in the ocean, which, from his vantage point atop a low hill, extended endlessly into the distance. He'd had to spend twenty days quarantined, alone on the surface—that is, except for other scouts who had recently landed by the spot on the sand dunes where he'd set up his survival tent. The visitors were envious because they were in space armor and he was not.

The time alone, especially the nights, had been good for Jack. The dark circles of grief that had been under his eyes ever since the death of his wife, Dinah, and his best friend, Pat Renfro, of the virus on the planet were gone, merged into a good tan.

Dr. Mandy Miller sat on the grass next to him, shading her eyes to look up into the sky.

"You'll hear *Spirit* before you see her," Jack said. "When Max opens up one hundred rockets at max power, she'll bellow like nothing you've ever heard."

But the sky, to Mandy, was fascinating. Their new

sun, 61 Cygni B, a K7-class star, emitted a light that appeared far more orange than the familiar, yellowish, G star that was old Sol. The sky's blue was deeper, darker than an Earth sky, and the few clouds took on a soft, silvery look. The grass on which she sat was the deepest green she'd ever seen in vegetable matter. In the distance, behind them, a line of trees near a watercourse gleamed with iridescent yellow blooms as big as her two hands.

"Look," Jack said, tapping her on the arm. She lowered her eyes. A small herd of antelopelike creatures, the males with long, curved, silver horns, had emerged from the trees and were grazing toward them. They were about the size of an Earth goat, their coats a lustrous orange-tan. They seemed not to notice the humans congregated on the hilltop. The little grass eaters did not seem, to Mandy, to be alien at all, and yet they were native to a planet over eleven light years from Earth. As head of Life Sciences, she had run tests on blood taken from one of the animals by Jack Purdy, and those tests had astounded her. The difference between the blood of those orangish-tan alien animals and an Earth dairy cow was so minor as to be almost indistinguishable.

For centuries scientists and writers had speculated about life among the stars, and some of them had been rather inventive. Then an Earth expedition lands on an alien planet, and the first life form to be seen was hydrocarbon based, had eyes like an Earth deer, and the same methods of synthesizing protein from amino acids as a cow.

The meat eaters that preyed on the little antelope were graceful feline types with pleasant heads, sleek, streamlined bodies, and greenish-tan hides to blend with the native vegetation. The only truly alien-looking creature to be seen by the expedition to that date were the scavenger birds, several of which were sitting patiently in the trees along the creek. They were the size of an eagle, featherless, with slick-looking, leathery skin, and blunt heads equipped with teeth rather than a beak.

A sudden commotion among the antelope took Mandy's thoughts away from parallel evolution on two planets so far from each other. A small, black, definitely not alien dog had dashed toward the antelope, causing a moment of panic among the animals before the herd bull discovered his courage and ran, head low, silvery horns a threat, to send Jumper the dog scurrying back to his master, Clay Girard.

Clay was sitting with the McRae family, close beside his foster sister, Cindy McRae. Clay and Cindy, twelve years old when the *Spirit of America* left Earth, were nearing sixteen.

The little antelope chased Jumper to within a few yards of the McRae family and then turned, his short tail jerking, to rejoin the herd. Big Stoner McRae was roaring with laughter at Jumper's expense.

Stoner had already tramped over a few square miles of the new planet. He was a big teddy bear of a man who had once been a very good professional football linebacker with San Diego—the kind of gentle, easygoing, big man who, just below the surface, has a solid steel core. Stoner had been chosen for the expedition because he was the best mining engineer on Earth. Stoner and his wife, Betsy, hoped to see their daughter, Cindy, and Clay Girard married someday. For the moment, Clay and Cindy were content to be best friends.

Dapper Clive Baxter, the ship's head chemist, sat with his wife, Ellen, near Mandy Miller and Jack Purdy. Ellen was a petite woman, even smaller than Clive. She was the starship's head dietitian, all business and quick movement. Clive had become more active in the ship's social life since helping to uncover the identity of the undercover Russian terrorist who had created havoc on the trip from Earth. Mandy suspected that the small, mustachioed man had developed political ambitions.

"Any time now," Jack Purdy said, checking his button-watch. It was almost too warm for the long-sleeved uniform. The scientists had determined that the planet was rotating on a tilted axis, like Earth's, and the current season at this location on the new planet was late spring. Jack thought that summer here might be rather warm.

From far off, seeming to come at them from all directions at once, there was a rumble like low, distant thunder.

"Come on down, baby," Jack whispered at the sky. "Come on down."

A scattering of very high silvery clouds had moved in directly over them from the sea. They blocked the view, so no one could see the starship as the sound of thunder grew into a throaty roar of multiple rockets.

Jack had picked up a habit from his wife. As the rumble of the *Spirit of America*'s engines grew and seemed to shake the ground, he crossed his fingers. He knew that it was a tense time aboard ship.

Down in the armored cubicle that was the heart of the *Spirit of America*'s weapons-control system, Lieutenant Commander Paul Warden was the loneliest man on the ship. He braced himself in his couch and felt first the sharp tug, then the g-forces of deceleration, as the retro-rockets fired, slowing the ship so that she began her plunge down toward the planetary surface. The knee he'd injured sliding into second base in the Army–Space Academy Service championship game in 2023 gave him a twinge, just to let him know it was still there. The knee did that under g-forces or when he had to sit in the weapons-control room for long periods. He shifted when the rockets stopped firing and he was weightless again.

Warden was not a large man, but his body showed the benefits of years of participation in athletics. At forty, in the prime of his life, he was tautly muscular of arm and thigh. Pumping iron had built the muscles in his shoulders and neck. His quick smile was thought by some to be dopey or lopsided, but those who knew Paul knew that he was very intelligent and that his smile indicated a genial, people-loving personality.

Warden had specialized in armaments at the academy and had been required to take the usual technical and engineering courses. He was glad of it, because that ancient knowledge was still floating around his unconscious somewhere to give him a foundation for a new and surprising ambition to further his technical learning. He didn't even try to hide the reason from himself; he knew that he was hitting the books because of Sage Bryson.

Paul Warden had been attracted to her from the first

time he saw her. But Sage seemed totally uninterested in conversing with an old jock, preferring instead to talk only of her shipboard experiments in electrical-field theory. Warden always functioned on the firm basis of a winning attitude, but he knew that he faced one of his greatest challenges in trying to win the serious attentions of a strong-minded woman who, in her youth, had won several beauty contests.

Electrical-field theory wasn't his idea of fun, but if that was what it was going to take to interest Sage, he could learn about it. It was a price worth paying.

As the ship lost speed and began to spiral downward, Warden pictured Sage in his mind the way she'd looked just yesterday. She favored an old-fashioned lab smock for work because its shapelessness tended to diminish, if not totally conceal, the curvaceous body that she seemed to consider a bane. She wore her dark hair in a casual bun at the back of her neck and never wore makeup. Her skin, however, had a golden glow, and her almond-shaped eyes were so green that they made Paul Warden's good knee go as weak as his bad one. Her full lips with their natural blush appeared in his dreams at night.

He had found her in the lab yesterday.

"Buy you a cup of coffee, lady?" he'd asked.

"Oh, hi, Paul," she'd said, just before hiding her face in the opened repair hatch of a field generator.

"Hey, lady," Paul had said. "Testing, testing. Is there anybody there?"

"I'm very busy," had been her reply.

"Hey, come on. All work and no play."

She had shown her face. "Paul, some other time. I'm very busy."

"Maybe you need something stronger than coffee," Paul had said, with that dopey little smile. "Come along and we'll get you around a cool, tall drink."

"Paul," she'd said. "Just leave me alone, please?"

Yes, he had himself a challenge, he was thinking, as the first of the ship's main rockets began to grumble, low, then stronger, in preparation for planetfall.

* * *

From the couch in her own quarters, Evangeline Burr had heard the first low rumble of the main rockets firing. She had been working on what was to be the official history of the voyage of the *Spirit of America*.

Evangeline—no one had ever been close enough to her to give her a nickname—was a short, soft woman, tending toward brief periods of overweight. When she gained weight, some men thought it made her cuddly, but she'd always go on a stringent diet and get back to her one hundred pounds. She had heavy, red hair. Her round, pretty face relaxed quickly from her usual studious look into a wide, toothy smile. Not quite forty, Evangeline had been perfectly content with her nice apartment in Wilmington, North Carolina, and reconciled to occupying it alone. She had always wanted to marry and raise a family, but she just didn't seem to attract men—except when she put on weight. She hated carrying extra pounds on her small frame, so she worked at staying thin and contented herself with her job and few friends.

She had been the most surprised person in America when she had been asked by President Hamilton's scientific adviser to make the trip with the *Spirit of America*. Not that she doubted her knowledge of library science. She knew she was good in her field. With a few lightning touches of her long, well-manicured fingers she could make a library-records computer sit up and sing out esoteric research materials. She was a loner and had never entertained any ambition of moving from her job as librarian at the University of North Carolina at Wilmington, a secondary university always in the shadow of the main branch at Chapel Hill. She had almost turned down the chance, but Presidential Adviser Oscar Kost had won her over by telling her that the *Spirit of America*'s library would have to be the most complete ever assembled, all electronic, with every bit of the filed wisdom of the ages readily accessible. A staff of hundreds of people had been working to collect the knowledge of man, from the first crude marks on baked clay tablets to the scientific papers and novels published a few days before the ship's departure. With her staff of three and the finest computers in the world—perhaps in the universe, since they were no longer on "the world"—she had fascinating, challenging work, enough to last her a lifetime.

As the ship began its plunge into atmosphere and the rockets bellowed louder, she thought about the captain's own private library, and the shocking, confidential information it contained about the Russian Premier pushing the world toward nuclear war. Evangeline knew humankind. She knew that there had never been a weapon invented that had not been used, and she tended to look upon her ship's library as the last remaining record of humankind's greatness and evil. She would guard that information with her life.

Evangeline wondered how the Russians aboard the starship *Karl Marx* had felt upon leaving Earth. Had they been relieved to leave cold, stern, poverty-stricken Russia and the threat of nuclear holocaust? Or had they left with both anticipation and regret, as she had? And where were the Russians now? Grace Monroe was working to perfect a language-translation machine, and she herself was studying Russian; were both she and Dr. Monroe subconsciously expecting the Russians to appear in the Cygni system?

It was interesting speculation, and it continued even as the rockets fired again and the entire ship vibrated and the *Spirit of America*'s outer hull began to heat.

The *Spirit of America* was the sum total of all technical skills and knowledge. Every discipline of science and every branch of knowledge had been required to build her, and Captain Duncan Rodrick wished, more than anything in the world (other than that the magnificent ship continue to function), that all the men and women on Earth who had had a part in building her could see her now, at her moment of glory.

She did continue to function, and function perfectly. When the speed of her descent began to heat her hull, the cooling system automatically moved cold air to the needed areas. The bellow of the hundred rockets continued, the engines gulping the fuel at an impressive pace. She was lowering much slower now.

The admiral was on the bridge, noting hull temperatures, stress, and fuel consumption, and nodding in satis-

faction. Ito Zuki was calling out speeds and altitudes. With
rockets thundering, the ship lowered herself into the silvery, high-altitude clouds.

When the ship burst through the high clouds, the two
hundred people on the hilltop started a spontaneous cheer-
ing, but the hurrahs died in their throats and were replaced by a reverent silence as the *Spirit of America*
thundered down, down. She was so huge. None of them
had ever seen her from below, and her size was awe
inspiring. It was impossible for anything that big, that
massive, to ride a few slender fingers of fire down to a safe
landing.

Mandy Miller had instructed her medical staff to supply earplugs for all because the volume of the ship's multiple rocket engines firing could do severe damage, even
though the hilltop was two miles from the flat, hard earth
that had been selected as the ship's resting place. Even
through the earplugs the noise was a growing, cracking,
roaring thunder, which allowed no other thought than the
ship, the ship. She was seared and pitted by space, but
she was the most impressive sight ever seen by any of
them.

The *Spirit*'s landing seemed to take forever. Surely it
was impossible for her to get bigger, and bigger, and
bigger, but she did, and Jack Purdy realized that her
sheer size misled him to estimate her to be lower than she
was, for she kept coming, and her shadow covered them.
Now little whirlwinds began to form on the open ground
where she would land, and the reflected exhausts of her
engines began to make a wind across the hill, and with it
came the scent of burning rocket fuel and heat. Dust
swirled, and the smaller vegetation and loose, dead grass
billowed up into the fires of the exhausts, and the very
earth seemed to burn underneath her as she settled into
the gigantic dust cloud and seemed, for a moment, to
disappear.

The dust settled slowly. There was a silence. She was
down.

The impact with the ground of the new planet had
been so gentle that Max Rosen had to check his instruments to be sure she was solidly down. He sighed, let his

agonized face relax, looked over at Grace in her usual place at the computer console, and gave her a grin.

"You, sir," Grace said proudly, "are the greatest."

"The *Spirit* did it," he said.

On the bridge Jackie Garvey uncrossed her fingers.

Rocky Miller said, "Congratulations, sir. Excellent landing."

Ito Zuki reached over and squeezed his wife's hand.

Duncan Rodrick had a grin on his face, and he turned to look for Mandy, only to remember that she was outside, already on the surface.

"All right, my friends," Rodrick said. "Secure systems. Mr. Zuki, after we cool off a bit, you may take a quick tour outside to get a look at things, and then I want you back here, to begin a final check of the instruments."

"Yes, sir!" Ito said.

"Mr. Miller, you may begin your preparations. We have at least eight standard hours of daylight left. Let's see how many shelters we can offload in that length of time."

"Aye," Rocky said, thinking irritably that it was unnecessary for the captain to repeat orders he'd been studying ever since they had left Earth.

"Captain," Max Rosen's voice said on the communicator, "permission to open the outside vents."

"Permission granted, Chief," Rodrick said.

It took a full ten minutes for the circulators to replace the ship's air with the fresh, unpolluted air of the new world. After breathing recycled air for these years, the members of the ship's company had become accustomed to the flatness of the air, the burden of slight, almost undetectable odors it carried. The fresh air was, at first, almost a shock.

"Hey," Jackie Garvey said, beaming, as the control bridge filled with fragrant, sun-warmed air with a hint of the smell of the sea, "you can get drunk on this stuff."

THREE

The events that immediately followed her assassination of Russian Premier Yuri Kolchak would always be hazy in Theresita Pulaski's mind. Only two moments were vivid: running for her life down the hallway as she listened for the muffled explosion of the bomb she had planted under his bed, a roar that had reverberated along the corridors of the ancient Kremlin, where she had spent nights and hours and days of suspense, and of love, with Yuri; and the feeling of great weight when the rockets fired and she was lifted upward to the Russian starship *Karl Marx*. She did not remember the small details, the conversations, her first reaction to space, because she had killed the man she loved. That it had been necessary to prevent Yuri from ordering a nuclear strike against the United States did not lessen her grief or guilt.

She accepted her welcome aboard the *Karl Marx* as her due, although she herself had forged the order that stated that Yuri Kolchak's last wish had been to have her included in the great galactic adventure. As a military marshal of the Soviet Union, she was assigned suitable rooms. Later, she found that the second officer had been put out of his quarters to make room for her.

She spent most of her time sleeping while the ship's crew made last-minute preparations. In sleep she could escape the roar of the explosion and the worry that Yuri had had time to realize her betrayal.

Days after departure from Earth, when she finally decided that it was time for her to become a part of shipboard routine, she removed the marshal's insignia from her uniforms. So it was that she appeared in the officers' mess in an unadorned off-white skirt and the tunic of the female officer of the Red Army.

She had eaten little since that fateful night in the Kremlin, and she'd lost some weight. It made her look the part of a woman who had lost the man she loved.

When she entered the mess, Captain Fedor Novikov leaped to his feet and hurried to meet her. "Your chair is waiting, comrade," he told her. "We are pleased that you are feeling better."

She was seated to the captain's right. Looking around, she saw that most of the officers were quite young. Eight of the twenty people in the mess were women, four of them in the uniform of the Soviet Space Service. The other people, she found, were officers' husbands or wives.

"Comrade Marshal," the captain said, "we were just discussing the news from home."

Novikov had been handpicked by Yuri Kolchak to command the *Karl Marx*. Theresita had ordered and thoroughly examined his security check herself. It was natural for Novikov to be friendly toward her. They had both been Kolchak supporters—she his most trusted military adviser and lover, Novikov a young protégé. They had suffered a mutual loss with Yuri's death.

"I'm afraid I'm a bit behind on the news," she said.

"Comrade," Novikov said, "you will be pleased to know that the glorious Red Army took only thirty-six hours to demolish the defenses of the capitalist stooges in West Germany and France." He smiled. "But I would guess that comes as no surprise, Marshal, since you probably had a hand in the plans for such an operation."

Indeed, she had helped to formulate the plans for a swift thrust of armored columns in a three-pronged attack designed to slice West Germany and France into three isolated pockets of resistance. Yet she felt no satisfaction; in fact, she lost what little appetite she had. Were the fools so determined to have the nuclear war that had been Yuri's last wish?

She nodded to the captain. Her plan had depended on reaching the channel ports in thirty-six hours. So it had worked.

"Is it over, then?" she asked.

"The few remaining French units surrendered this morning," Novikov said. "The Red Star flies, at last, over all of Europe."

"What was the reaction of the Americans?" Theresita asked.

A young officer laughed. "The Americans? What can they do?"

Captain Novikov smiled indulgently. He was a young, vital man, Theresita was thinking, no more than forty-five. He had the same strong face, the same coarse, black hair and strong nose that had made Yuri such a handsome man.

"I don't think the Americans will contest the outcome," Novikov said. "After all, the old alliances between western Europe and the Anglo-Americans were discarded long ago. And, after all, the Americans have had their little victory in South America."

Theresita was saddened. That "little victory" had cost the Soviet Union its entire Pacific Fleet and the lives of hundreds of thousands of men.

"I have only one regret about being aboard ship," another young officer said. "I won't be there to see the airborne armies drop into England."

Theresita looked quickly toward Novikov, her face flushing in shock. "Surely they haven't—" She paused. *Not England*, she was thinking. *Surely they would not be so stupid*. The Americans might accept the envelopment of West Germany and France, but they would react to an invasion of England; the link between those two nations of English speakers was too ancient, too close. Even though Great Britain had become a tiny, helpless island-nation, there was a kinship between them and the Americans.

"No, not yet England," the captain said, shrugging. "Why bother?"

But Theresita knew the purpose: The invasion of the

British Isles would be an exercise for the Red Army. The Royal Navy would be used to blood the Soviet navy, and it would be taken out relatively quickly through the use of submarines and missiles.

"To take England," she said, "would be to declare war openly on the United States. The Americans would be unable to use conventional means to prevent the invasion, so they would use nuclear weapons."

"England would not be worth the risk," Novikov said.

"We'll move on Japan next," said a young officer.

Theresita smiled. "The Americans are so closely linked with Japan economically and industrially that they would fight. They have sufficient forces in the Far East."

"But they would be at the long end of a supply line, which could be easily broken," the young officer said. "This time we will be fighting in *our* backyard, as they were in South America. Then, too, they have problems of their own in their own hemisphere."

Theresita nodded.

"Brazil knows that the United States Navy was severely crippled by the South American war. The American victory was not without losses. Brazil is moving into the smaller South American nations, while making belligerent statements against the United States."

Theresita went back to her quarters thinking, *Stupidity, stupidity.* The old men in the Kremlin, smarting over the defeat in South America, had had their revenge in taking West Germany and France. Couldn't they now be satisfied? She turned on her viewscreen for the first time since coming aboard. On one channel was a recording of the latest newscast from Moscow. She saw the face of President Dexter Hamilton. She had met Hamilton, had talked with him face to face. When he had stated that the United States would continue to offer total and unqualified support to both Great Britain and Japan, she believed him. He had not backed down from Yuri, even when he knew that Yuri was unbalanced and would push the nuclear button.

Marshal Mikhail Simonov, the old man, followed Hamilton on the screen and promised that the Americans would be punished for "their treachery in South America."

So, after all, the Kremlin had learned nothing from their close brush with the final disaster. They simply did not understand that the United States had been pushed into a position that allowed no further retreat.

The world was almost totally Red. Communist arms and communist promises had long since won all those undeveloped nations, which, back in the twentieth century, had been called the Third World. Now, with Germany and France occupied, the Red Star flew over all the world except Australia, Sweden, Israel-Egypt, the British Isles, Canada, Japan, and the United States. (And South Africa, of course, that nation of mad dogs, sitting behind their tank traps, with every antitank gun armed with a tactical nuclear warhead.) Black Africa would not be able to overrun the last white enclave on the continent without Soviet help, and the Soviet Union would not risk another exchange of nuclear weapons for as poor a prize as South Africa.

From the time Theresita had realized that Yuri Kolchak intended to use strategic nuclear weapons, she'd begun a study of the English-speaking peoples. She had been impressed by their deep love of freedom, which was reinforced by her own deep feelings for her homeland, Poland, which had been overrun by the Russians in the mid-twentieth century. She had come to realize that few Anglo-Americans subscribed to the notion that they would be better off Red than dead. She knew in her heart that President Hamilton had not been bluffing when he had stated that he'd use any weapon in America's arsenal to avoid becoming a part of a worldwide Soviet.

As the days passed and the *Karl Marx* moved slowly outward toward the fringe of the solar system, Theresita began to feel that she had accomplished nothing more than the purchase of a little time by killing Yuri. The viewscreen informed them of crisis after crisis, threat after threat. Perhaps, she began to think, the pessimists who said that man had always been and would always be a self-destructive, death-seeking creature were right.

Gradually, she was able to form mental scar tissue over the open wound, the festering trauma of what she had been forced to do. She allowed herself to become a part of the day-to-day routine of the ship. At first the colonists were wary of her. They knew that she was a marshal of the Red Army and had once been the second most powerful person in the Soviet Union. However, as the days passed and she made it a point to talk with more and more people, some of them seemed to be able to forget that the big, well-formed, attractive woman had once been at the very peak of the power pyramid.

Government had always been a corps of elitists with little regard for the masses. The Revolution had been fought to change that, but for many, including the scientists aboard the *Karl Marx*, it seemed that nothing much had changed except the faces at the top. The people were considered to be too stupid to participate in any important decision. Personal freedom and individual initiative still eluded those who desired them. There were individuals aboard the *Karl Marx* who felt secretly that one of the chief goals of the expedition should be to change the system that put all power and all decision-making in the hands of an elite.

Soon people began to find that Theresita Pulaski was a good listener. She showed no interest in becoming a part of the rigidly structured cadre who ran the ship. Committee leaders began to come to her for an impartial viewpoint on problems. She did not actively avoid the ship's officers, but she didn't seek them out, either. Captain Novikov was the only officer with whom she talked regularly, and that at his initiative. Their conversations tended to dwell on the glory days when Yuri was reorganizing the political and power structure of the Soviet Union, taking more and more of the power onto himself. Those had indeed been exciting days. The younger, healthy Yuri had been a visionary. At the time it had seemed that anything was possible.

Novikov was a hard-core Kolchakist, proud of his mission to establish communism among the stars. Theresita guarded her thoughts when she was with him. She did not tell him that the form of government being exported aboard the *Karl Marx* bore little resemblance to the ideal communism that had been dreamed of by the ship's namesake.

When she ate in the officers' mess she sometimes felt

as if she were back in the Kremlin's War Room, for she heard the same bellicose statements and the same hard-core disregard for the individual.

The ideology that had brought Earth to the brink of nuclear disaster was aboard the *Karl Marx*, complete, unalterable, waiting to be planted in the virgin soil of an alien planet. Since the officers and their political advisers held the power, she did not, at first, even consider mounting opposition to them.

People were slow to reveal to Theresita that she was not the only one on board who aspired to better life in their new home among the stars. For a long time the old habits held: If someone made a statement that even implied criticism of the government, he was given a cold, angry stare.

But then one day, while Theresita was watching the newscast in one of the colonists' lounges, a mild-mannered chemist said, "It seems that they will not be content until they can use their nuclear bombs." No one glared at her. No one got up to leave.

A young girl, not more than twelve, asked Theresita on another day, "Why does there always have to be war?"

"Hush," her mother said quickly.

"There doesn't have to be war," a physicist said. "Where we are going, there need never be war."

There were good, intelligent people aboard, Theresita found. The selection process had worked well. The physicist was right. There need be no war among the stars. Where they were going, why should there not be a certain amount of personal choice and freedom in the building of the new society?

Only one thing stood between the exceptional people aboard, scientists all, and a more lenient, more pleasant way of life: the power structure. If the colonists established a society based on individual freedom, the political cadre would be out of work. What would the officers do? They would no longer hold important positions. They would fight to hold onto their power.

"Would you really like it to be different?" she asked the small group gathered before the viewscreen.

Many looked uncomfortable. One woman said, "Very much so."

Perhaps Theresita didn't make her decision at that very moment, but that moment was the beginning. Could she make it different? Was it time for a historic change? Perhaps, she told herself, all the hard years of pain, hunger, and conflict since the Revolution of 1917 pointed toward one end, to give the people aboard the *Karl Marx* the background, knowledge, and desire to break with the past and build a truly ideal society on a new world.

When contemplating a way, one must know one's enemy. Theresita had two groups of adversaries: the officers and the Communist party advisers. She began to spend more time with the officers. She listened to their personal problems, from the most junior lieutenant up to the captain, for Novikov, too, found Theresita to be a good listener.

Although he was obligated to consider the opinions of the political advisers in certain matters pertaining to the running of the ship, Novikov was the man whose responsibility it was to make all final decisions. He was a hard man, a cool man. He would be a worthy opponent. She considered ways to get him on her side.

Novikov was much concerned about Russian pride. The American ship had gone into deep space first. He was determined that the *Karl Marx* would atone in achievement for the head start of the Americans.

"We have always taken the lead in space," he told Theresita one evening over tall, cool drinks mixed with ship's vodka. "When we put the first artificial satellite into space, we used mathematical calculations done by the space prophet, Tsiolkovsky, in the 1880s. Not only did Tsiolkovsky anticipate and solve almost all of the engineering difficulties of spaceflight, he told us, before man had flown an airplane, that liquid fuels would put the first vehicles into space."

"That's very impressive," Theresita said. However, being a Pole, she was not always ready to believe it when a Russian said that Russia was first. But after some research, she found that Novikov was right about Tsiolkovsky. Much impressed by one of the space pioneer's statements she'd read, she had the engineering shop engrave it on brass and presented the plaque to the captain for hanging in his quarters.

> EARTH IS THE CRADLE OF THE MIND, BUT ONE
> CANNOT LIVE IN A CRADLE FOREVER.
> *Konstantin E. Tsiolkovsky*

She had some hope that the captain, hard-core Kolchakist that he was, might see the double meaning of the quotation. If she could win the mind of Novikov, the others would not be difficult. If she could make the captain see the failures of the rigid, joyless system that had brought the world to the brink of extinction, the rest would be easy.

The *Karl Marx* had been in space for a matter of weeks before the Russian lightstep probes, which had been launched to find habitable planets for the ship's passengers, flashed back into the range of their radios. Theresita had been invited to be on the bridge when the messages came. The tension was evident. After all, the *Karl Marx* had left Earth without a definite destination, and the information sent back by the probes would have a tremendous effect on the lives of all those aboard.

There was obvious disappointment among those on the bridge when the first probe's information had been received and displayed on the screen. A class G-star, much like Earth's sun, was all alone in space.

"So much for the theories of the astronomers," Captain Novikov said.

"We'll have the results of the other probes in a few minutes," Theresita said.

"We needed more time," Novikov said. "We should have sent out a half-dozen probes, more. Unlike the Americans, we were not short of rhenium."

She did not tell him that there had been no more time, that Yuri Kolchak had been near death, ready to begin the final war, and wanted the *Karl Marx* safely away before the bombs began to drop.

A message from the bridge told them that the information from the second probe had been received.

"There is a difficulty, Captain," the computer operator said. "Problems with the decoding."

The captain walked forward to lean over the computer operator.

"Sorry, sir," the operator said. "There has been a malfunction of the coding equipment on the probe. The data from the probe's sensors is lost."

"Damn," Novikov said. But there was one more probe. The signal from the last probe arrived within minutes of that of the second, was decoded, and once again the viewscreen was filled by the glare of a star, and once again that star was a lone star devoid of a planetary family.

"So now we are without a destination," Novikov said, wiping his brow. "Get me ground control."

The communications officer bent forward, but before he could touch his console a red light began to flash. He laughed. "They're thinking about us, too, sir. There is a call from ground control coming in."

"Put it on the screen," Novikov ordered, expecting to see the face of the chief ground controller. Instead he saw a printed message, which had to be decoded.

"Urgent. Urgent," the message read when decoded. "Enact contingency plan D."

The message meant nothing to Theresita, but Novikov went stiff, and his neck reddened. He was motionless for long seconds. He cast one harried look toward Theresita.

"What does it mean?" she asked.

Novikov turned away. His voice, when he spoke, was lower than usual, seemed to lack the usual bright, harsh snap of command.

"Navigation," he said, "begin positioning and firing for return to Earth orbit. Engineering, stand by for course alteration and rocket firing."

"We're going back?" Theresita asked, stunned.

"Ship's communicator, when navigation is ready, alert all personnel to stand by for deceleration." He smiled sadly at Theresita. "This is going to take some time, Marshal Pulaski. You might want to wait in your quarters."

She left the bridge feeling uneasy. The three probes had found them no planets, but the *Karl Marx* had plenty

of fuel and could journey to survey dozens of stars and still
have fuel for a return trip to Earth.

Theresita was to learn the truth soon enough. Novikov
joined her in her quarters within minutes and went directly to her bar to pour himself a large, straight vodka.
He drank deeply and then poured another vodka and
drank again.

"There is more to this than simply being recalled
because the probes didn't locate a planet," she ventured.

He wiped his mouth. "As you are aware, the *Karl
Marx* is a well-armed ship. We have lasers, missiles, projectile weapons, nuclear warheads."

She felt suddenly ill.

"Under contingency plan D, the *Karl Marx* is to
assume a position that will give us a clear range of fire
with all weapons at the American nuclear missile space
stations," Novikov said.

Theresita's sick feeling changed instantly to a cold
fury. "What have the fools done? Have they invaded England or Japan?"

"There is no word."

"And we are to abandon the future, leave all space to
the Americans, to die with those senile old men in the
Kremlin?"

Novikov's eyebrows shot upward in surprise. "I did
not hear that statement, Comrade Pulaski."

"So you are going to go back?"

"Of course. I have my orders."

FOUR

Duncan Rodrick had purloined Jack Purdy's scout ship, *Dinahmite*, leaving the chief scout to act as communicator for the other scout ships, which were deployed over an area roughly the size of Australia on mapping and survey flights. Rodrick had wanted to get a look at the new country from the air. He'd been too busy during the landing of the *Spirit of America* even to look at anything but the landing site. He had *Dinahmite* hovering at one thousand feet over the bay near the landing site. The bay, he was thinking, would offer protected anchorage to water vessels to be built later.

Rodrick had intended to go up alone for just a few minutes, but as he prepared to take off, Clay Girard watched with such longing in his eyes that Rodrick had said, "Wanta come along, Clay?" And Clay had leaped at the opportunity, bringing Jumper along as a matter of course.

Below them it looked as if the *Spirit of America* were being ripped apart. Various cargo hatches were open, and a swarm of men and women, each with a preassigned duty, were operating a variety of machines. The hull plates and girders of the ship had been removed in four places— the ship had been so designed—and already the tractors were pulling the inner shells of the colonists' quarters through the gaping holes. The metal cubicles rolled easily;

several were already in place. The new town to be formed had been carefully planned back on Earth. Each family knew where its first dwelling would be located from having studied the town layout.

Removing the quarters intact from the ship served two purposes: It gave the colonists comfortable shelter until larger and more luxurious homes could be built, and it opened up vast areas aboard the *Spirit of America* to be filled with cargo for the return trip to Earth.

An automated well driller had tapped into sweet, pure water at reasonable depths, and there was the little stream that came into the bay on the rocky, northern side in a spectacular little waterfall. These waters were also sweet and pure and could be used for drinking until the wells were drilled and plumbing hookups made. Electricity would come from the ship's fusion-generator plant.

"Look, sir," Clay said, tapping Rodrick on the shoulder and pointing.

A large, self-propelled drilling rig was pulling away from the landing site and heading toward the rocky highlands inland to the east. "Good," Rodrick said. "They're not wasting any time." The colony needed oil first and foremost, not as fuel but as building blocks for the plastics to be used in permanent construction and the thousand and one other items that would be needed.

It was all going well. From the productivity of the last few hours, Rodrick felt confident that the colony would be settled before the end of the next day, and then they could all get down to business.

A small trail of dust at a distance of about one mile south of the bay caught Rodrick's attention. He focused the scout's long lenses and saw the sun gleaming off the admiral's white uniform. Gliding next to the admiral, on sets of tracks that had been self-mounted, was the six-foot, eight-inch TR5-A robot called Mopro, Grace's Mobile Overt Protection Robotic Operator.

"Rodrick to the admiral," Rodrick said into the communicator.

"Admiral reporting, Captain. Over."

"How does it look?"

The admiral and Mopro, who packed more firepower

than a whole company of infantry, had requested permission to make a reconnaissance of the area immediately surrounding the landing site.

"Sir," the admiral said. "You have picked a location ideal for defense."

Rodrick chuckled. Of course he'd picked a location ideal for defense. Rodrick was quite satisfied with his selection of a landing site. So far the only large life indications picked up by the scout's life sensors had been in the subtropical jungles of the twin southern continents of the western hemisphere. Here tall, ice-bound mountains cut off a peninsula from the continental mainland and would be a strong deterrent for anything coming from the east. There was ocean to the south, west, and north, with the great desert beyond the coastal mountains in the northwest.

"All is quiet," the admiral said. "We are just completing our circuit of the landing area."

"What life forms have you seen?" Rodrick asked.

"Aside from those already noted, sir, no animal life," the admiral said. "However, we have observed several species of insects. I think that Dr. Kwait will be pleased. The insects seem to perform the function of pollination, just as bees and butterflies do on Earth."

"Keep up the good work, Admiral," Rodrick said. "Rodrick off."

He pushed the scout upward. "Well, Clay, it's time we took a look at our little Eden, isn't it?"

"I'd like that," the boy answered.

The land chosen by Rodrick for the first settlement was an almost square, blunt protrusion from the planet's largest continent. North of the landing site, the north-south coastline faded away slightly toward the east. In the distance was a range of coastal mountains with the distinctive peaks of dormant volcanoes. Past the mountains the coast turned eastward, back toward the bulk of the continent. To the south the coastline ventured westward to end in a large, rocky cape at the southwest tip of the peninsula. The southern coastline of the peninsula was low, with saline marshes extending inland in bays. Two major rivers emptied into the sea through the coastal marshes, one river having its source in a large lake about two hundred miles inland from the west coast on a line to the north of the landing area. The other came from the massive inland mountains, which very effectively separated the peninsula from the continent proper, with peaks reaching to a height that made the Himalayas and the Andes lesser mountains.

The river that had its headwaters in the large inland lake meandered to within a few miles of the landing site before curving back to the south. Halfway to the lake, the river was joined by a smaller stream, which had impressed Jack Purdy with its fishing possibilities. It came down from the coastal mountains. Rodrick piloted the *Dinahmite* to the northeast, following the river to the big lake. A brisk wind was blowing over the lake, and it was large enough to form four-foot waves.

"Quite a body of water," Rodrick commented.

"It's beautiful," Clay said. "I was just thinking, Captain. Remember when Pat and Dinah were in the *L'il Darlin'*, going down to, well, you know, to crash?"

"I remember, son," Rodrick replied. He knew that Clay had been extremely fond of Pat Renfro and Dinah Purdy.

"Remember Pat said we should name a river or something after them?"

"So we will," Rodrick said.

"I think Dinah would like to have that lake named after her," Clay said.

"Well, it has a certain ring. Lake Dinah."

"And maybe Pat would like those mountains named after him."

"Pat's Mountains?" Rodrick asked. "No. Doesn't scan. How about the Renfro Mountains?"

"I like that."

"And let's not forget Dick Stanton," Rodrick said. "Of course, we can't just go around naming things arbitrarily. We have a committee that will want to have a say in the decisions. But I'll see to it that our friends are remembered. Let's see. We've got a lake for Dinah, mountains for Pat. How about the bay by the landing site? Stanton Bay?"

"I'd vote for that," Clay said.

Rodrick kicked the *Dinahmite* upward and guided her at top speed to the east, then slowed the cruise over the rugged, ice-bound peaks of the tall mountains. To say that they were impressive was a definite understatement. Future generations of mountain climbers would have plenty of challenges.

A low flyover of the coastal marshes to the south spooked thousands of multicolored seabirds into flight. At times their vivid rainbow colors made a solid palette of beauty below the scout ship. It seemed that nature had squandered all her color on the seabirds; to Rodrick's eye, it seemed that there was a wide range of color even in the same species.

The rocky cape at the southwest corner of the square peninsula soared up at least five hundred feet from the sea that surrounded it on three sides, and fell off gently inland to the marshes.

The *Dinahmite* flew a random course as Rodrick headed her home. He made detours to look at individual land features such as the valley of the large western river, then made a right-angle turn westward over the rocky highlands. Clay was very interested in these highlands because he'd heard Stoner McRae talking about making his first expedition among them. Stoner was in charge of a group that would be responsible for locating deposits of useful minerals and metals for mining, and he was eager to get started. But, like all the other members of the expedition, he first had to get the colony settled off the ship.

It was rough country below. The area was arid—patches of sand studded with sparse brownish-green growth alternated with ridges and canyons and buttes of gray, sharp-angled rock. Even an all-terrain crawler would have to pick a way through the badlands. Clay was examining the ground closely in the starkly beautiful highlands when he thought he saw something with straight lines and sharp outlines. He caught just a glimpse of it, off to the south, and then the ship was past. He hesitated to speak, but he finally said, "Captain, could you reverse course and take us just about two miles?"

"See something?"

"I don't know," Clay said uncertainly. *Dinahmite*

turned and went back at a slower speed. Clay saw only the jumble of rough, rocky country, a few stunted trees in dry washes. Rodrick made a couple more sweeps, but he wasn't flying a careful search grid using the ship's instruments.

"I guess it was nothing," Clay said, but it nagged at him, that glimpse of sharp right angles and lines. There are few straight lines in nature. He knew enough about navigation and the instruments aboard a scout to make a mental note of the approximate site of the area where he'd seen *something*.

The temporary town was being assembled at the head of Stanton Bay. Rodrick was already thinking of the bay by that name. A grove of wide-spreading trees had been incorporated in the somewhat flexible town plan, and the gleaming, metallic housing modules from the *Spirit of America* were being placed among them even as the earthmovers cut streets and cleared undergrowth. A few of the quarters climbed the slope of the grassy knoll from which Clay had watched the *Spirit* land.

The view from the town site was magnificent. The land sloped gradually down to the sandy beaches of the bay, and rose to the north into the knoll. One could just see, in the far, far distance, the blue haze that was the huge line of inland mountains, the blue topped by a crown of the white snows. The heavily wooded coastal mountains to the north were much nearer, and to the south the land undulated toward the open plains.

The weather was perfect. Anyone who didn't have a definitely assigned duty post aboard the ship was outside, working to position as many temporary dwellings as possible before nightfall. The training back on Earth at Desert Haven was paying off.

Communications Officer Jacqueline Garvey was in charge of laying temporary power lines so those colonists who would spend the night in their new quarters would have lights. Paul Warden was helping to offload one of the huge building machines that would, once petroleum was available, begin to formulate and mold pre-formed plastic walls for building. The plastic would be made by a new process, developed on Earth within the five years prior to their departure. It was a "smart" plastic, with the property of absorbing heat from cold air and radiating it uniformly to the inside of a building, or reflecting heat when the outside air was warm. Tiny power cables built into the plastic walls would allow residents to light their homes with glowing, color-adjustable, soft light.

Mandy Miller's Life Sciences section was the largest single group aboard ship. None of Mandy's staff had drawn work assignments, but they were as busy as anyone, their work aimed at prevention of unpleasant surprises from this alien environment. Within hours after the landing, sample specimens were pouring into the *Spirit*'s labs. Marine biologists had found life forms in the sands of the beaches and in the surf and were engaged in netting operations from inflatable boats to sample the free-swimming marine life. Entomologists were roaming the woodlands and grassy areas near the landing site, armed with nets and capture boxes. Twelve different varieties of soft-winged insects of vivid color had already been identified, and two species of pollinating insects much like bees were being dissected in the labs. The beelike insects had no stingers.

The arrival of a team of scientists hauling a cage on a crawler drew a crowd of curious people who were getting their first look at one of the carnivores that preyed on the silver-horned antelope. The cat—it could not be called anything else—was young, big footed, and wide eyed. It had the long, sharp teeth of the carnivore, but looked like a cross between a kitten and a teddy bear, and the women wanted to cuddle it, until it lifted its lips, gave a very businesslike growl, and shot a paw out to rake long claws against the wire of the cage.

Another team had taken one of the scavenger birds with a stun ray, and the bird, revived in a lab, perched itself unconcernedly in its cage and watched all movement with cold, reptilian eyes. Zoologists quickly but tentatively placed the scavenger bird low on the scale of evolution and compared it to the first flying reptiles on Earth. The reptilian characteristics of the scavenger sent teams in search of other reptiles, and before the day ended three very ugly and quite primitive lizards were aboard ship for examination. One lab was a squawking, fluttering area of noise as a dozen different seabirds in their vivid colors protested their captivity in a cage.

Mandy Miller was in the lab running tests on the blood of the carnivore kitten when her husband stormed in, his uniform streaked with perspiration, his face glowering.

"Did you see where they put our quarters?" he demanded.

"No, I haven't been off ship," Mandy said calmly, "except just to sniff the air and take a look this morning."

Rocky whipped out a plan of the town, spread it on a worktable, and stabbed a finger at a spot. "Right here," he said. "The people on either side of us have a view of the bay. We're directly behind this line of trees, and because of the lay of the trees, the quarters to our left are ten feet closer than they're supposed to be."

Mandy was conducting an important blood-count test. She sighed. "Is it all that bad?" she asked. "I mean, after all, when we build permanently—"

"Yes, damn it, it's that bad!" Rocky yelled. "I think Duncan Rodrick deliberately ordered them to put us where we couldn't have a view."

"Oh, Rocky—"

"Don't 'oh, Rocky' me," he snorted. "I'm going to see the captain."

She watched him leave the lab, her face set in grim lines. It was getting worse.

Mandy sighed. Rocky had never been able to get along with his commanding officers, and the only reason he had been given the post of first officer was because the government had wanted her so badly to head Life Sciences. They were a package deal, she had told the recruiters; if you want me, you have to take my husband.

Sometimes she wondered if her own relationship with Duncan Rodrick had made things worse between the captain and Rocky. Not that she and Dunc had done anything dishonorable—unless a fond friendship with strong sexual undercurrents between a married woman and a single man was dishonorable. . . .

She also wondered whether her marriage had suffered because she admired Dunc so much. No, she decided, her relationship with Rocky had always been difficult, a parent-child one, really. And Rocky's secretly hoarding uncontaminated water for himself when the ship's supply had been poisoned— Well, that had done irreparable damage to the way she felt about him.

The first officer caught Duncan Rodrick as he and Clay were dismounting from the *Dinahmite* after their sightseeing flight. "I'd like a word with you, Captain," Rocky said curtly.

"Thanks for the ride, sir," Clay said, snapping his fingers to Jumper and making himself scarce. He found Cindy watching the electrical crew hook power into the McRae quarters, with his own little room attached, and they sneaked away to explore the clear creek just a hundred yards from the quarters. The creek ran over beds of polished rock, clear and sparkling. Jumper eased the tension of a long flight in the scout and the heat of the day by dashing ahead to fling himself into the water. He ran up and down on the slick rocks in the shallow water, splashing and yapping in invitation for Clay and Cindy to join him. It took them only a few seconds to take off their shoes, roll up their pant legs, and do just that. The creek was to become their, and Jumper's, favorite place. By default, the creek was to be named Jumper's Run.

"What's on your mind, Commander?" Duncan Rodrick asked Miller when Clay was out of hearing.

"I want to lodge an official protest concerning the location of my quarters," Rocky said, standing at attention.

"Protest noted," Rodrick said. "Now, if you'll explain why?"

"You'll see better what I mean if you'll take a look," Rocky said.

The first-officer's quarters, larger than most, nestled among a group of trees. The spreading limbs shaded most of it from the sun. Rodrick thought it was a very pleasant setting. He looked at his first officer and waited.

"By moving it twenty feet to the south," Rocky said, "we would not be deprived of the view of the bay."

Since there were no windows as yet in the metal rectangle, Rodrick didn't see the point in Miller's objection.

"And I want you to note, Captain, that the house on

the left is ten feet closer than the prescribed two hundred feet." The layout of the town allowed for plenty of growth. Each quarters was assigned one acre of land.

Slightly exasperated, Rodrick asked, "How can you tell?"

"I measured it," Miller said indignantly.

"Mr. Miller," Rodrick said, "it would seem to me that you'd have better things to do than waste your time worrying about a house being ten feet too close to you. Now if you want to see the bay, I'd suggest that you use a mover to shift your quarters twenty feet to the right. But not until the rest of the quarters are situated."

Rodrick turned and walked away. Rocky glared after him, eyes squinted. The captain's anger told him that he'd been right in thinking that Rodrick had ordered his quarters to be located behind a tree. He didn't understand what he'd done to make the captain dislike him, but if that's the way it was going to be, so be it. This was a new world, and on a new world things could change.

Amando Kwait, the African agricultural expert, had joined a zoological team in order to have a firsthand look at the country. He was a man with a feel for the soil. The semiarid areas near the landing site pleased him. The dry, virgin soil supported several varieties of plant life, including a grass that seemed to prefer higher areas, such as the rise to the north of the town. In areas where the grass was exposed to full sun, it grew lushly, and tightly, and so close to the ground that it would, with a minimum of care, make a perfect lawn.

Amando had, in his storage banks, seeds for every useful plant on Earth, and many for which no uses had yet been discovered. In practice, he would go very slowly in trying to adapt Earth vegetation to the new planet, for he remembered the ecological disasters of Earth, such as the innocent importation into Florida and Louisiana of the Far Eastern water hyacinth, which soon clogged the waterways of those states, and the kudzu vine, which became the plant that ate the South, spreading with incredible speed from the highway embankments where it had been thought to be ideal for holding the soil of steep cuts and embankments in place.

If at all possible, Amando would try to develop, alter, or perhaps crossbreed local vegetation to adapt it to other uses. Earth crops would be test grown in certain confined areas at first.

If he had been pleased with the semiarid uplands, he was ecstatic about the river valleys. The soil there was so rich, so loamed by the endless centuries of growth and decay, that seeds, he knew, would sprout almost overnight and eat the nutrients of the virgin earth to grow to record yields.

Amando filled many specimen bags. In a pack attached to his back he carried a miniature sun-powered analyzer. Before he touched any new species of plant with his bare hands he ran tests, and after checking at least a hundred different varieties for toxicity or irritants, he began to think that something was out of whack on this big, new world, for of the hundred varieties of plant life, not one had so much as a bad smell. He had not even found a plant with protective spikes. Roots and tubers from the low, marshy areas along the river gave off pleasant aromas when dug and sliced, and his preliminary analysis indicated that a few of them might just be edible.

On relatively even ground the small, two-passenger crawler that Amando had drawn from the equipment park purred along, its hydrogen-burning engine making a muted mutter on front-wheel drive alone. The Hughes crawler had been the standard vehicle for military use and industrial exploration for two decades, and although there were constant minor improvements, the basic design had not been changed since a stripped-down scout model had been used by the first Mars expedition to traverse the burning, boulder-strewn sands of the red planet.

The scout model was the smallest of the three standard models, had the same power plant as the four- and six-passenger models, and, like the larger models, had the horses to become a cargo carrier with the addition of articulated, nonsteerable trailer units. A complicated control panel allowed the operator to add power to the rear tracks and, when utilizing a cargo train, call on the additional power units in the trailers.

Amando pushed a button, which lowered the windows and retracted the fleximetal top, so he could bask in the new planet's sun and enjoy the cooling breeze created by the vehicle's considerable speed.

The crawler sped along smoothly. On uneven terrain, Amando could activate automatic levelers, which, with hydraulic hisses, would elevate the individual tracked units on the downhill side to level the vehicle. There were also laser spikes in the rear track, which could burn holes in solid stone to allow the insertion of sharp spikes to pull the vehicle up grades to forty-five degrees. If Amando were to encounter soft sand, he could activate paddles that allowed the crawler to "swim" through soft sand, deep mire, or open water.

On a short tour near the home base, Amando had no reason to activate the vehicle's computerized navigation system, or the weapons system, which consisted of twin-laser cannon and a wicked, automatic projectile gun system that could spray hundreds of shots per second in any direction.

The crawler came up out of the lush, rich river bottomlands to the semiarid flats, which stretched back toward the landing site. The sun was low to the west, and the orange quality of its light made for a spectacular sunset over the ocean, with long streamers of blood-red stabbing upward. Never had he seen such vivid colors, never more beauty, and just as the sun's disc disappeared into the watery horizon, a glow of deep emerald green flushed the entire western sky. The glory of it filled Amando's eyes with tears of appreciation.

For a long time Amando had questioned his decision to become a member of the *Spirit of America* expedition, feeling that his place was on Earth, working to ease the terrible famines that ravaged his native continent. Now that he had seen the beauty of this world, he knew that he'd made the right decision. Many of the native tubers, grasses, and fruits offered him hope. The lawnlike, deep-green grass might be the answer to the grazed-out grass-lands of Africa. And the soil was so fertile that, given one growing season, he could fill the considerable storage areas opened up on the ship with foodstuffs for the Earth.

The crawler arrived in the town just as darkness came suddenly, leaving the sky overhead studded with billions of unrecognizable stars. A notice was being broadcast that all hands were to board the ship and find seats in the various lounge and assembly areas. Amando's quarters had not yet been removed from the ship, being far down inside near his gardens, which would not be removed until he had finished his testing and had begun to transplant desirable Earth varieties into the fertile soil.

When the entire colony was gathered before viewscreens, Duncan Rodrick reported on their first day in their new town, their new country, their new world. He congratulated them on work well done. Then team leaders reported the findings of the various scientific disciplines. All reports were very positive. The next day's assignments were reviewed and altered as conditions warranted, and those whose quarters were already in place and supplied with power left the ship to spend their first night on the new planet.

Duncan Rodrick had dinner alone and then joined a medium-sized group in a meeting room. The committee was made up of geographers, geologists, and cartographers, with representatives from other -ologies and disciplines. Evangeline Burr, the ship's librarian and historian, was chairwoman. She followed strict procedure in getting the meeting started. A reading of the last meeting's minutes took five minutes.

"At the close of our last meeting," Evangeline said, "we were, once again, discussing possible names for our new planet. Before we return to that subject, let me say that we're honored to have Captain Rodrick with us this evening. Do you have anything that you'd like to say to the committee, Captain?"

"Nothing official," Rodrick said. "I'm just an interested observer. I think the committee is doing a fine job. I've looked over the list of possible names for the planet, and there are several worthy suggestions on the list. I might suggest that you, as a committee, set yourself a goal to come out of tonight's meeting with at least three names:

for the planet, the peninsula—which we are beginning to consider 'our country'—and for the town. If we don't come up with something soon, we're all going to fall into habits of calling things by some nickname. I find myself thinking of this planet, for example, as Big Boy, and that's not a very dignified name."

There was a general chuckle. Clive Baxter said, "I know exactly what you mean, Captain. I ran into Clay Girard and Cindy McRae today, wet to the waist. Clay said they'd been chasing crayfishlike things over in Jumper's Run. They'd given that name to the little creek."

"That's exactly how many places got their names in colonial America," Evangeline said. "I think Jumper's Run is a lovely name for our creek."

There were a few murmurs of protest.

Clive Baxter laughed. "Just to prove to ourselves that we can make a decision, I move that we make the official name of the clear, rocky creek near the town Jumper's Run."

"Do I hear a second?" Evangeline asked. The motion was seconded and quickly passed, over two brief objections.

"Madam Chairwoman," Rodrick said, after the laughter had subsided, "if I may intrude again, strictly unofficially?"

"Of course," Evangeline replied.

"We lost three members of our group at Cygni A," Rodrick said. "The aforementioned Clay Girard, who seems to get around, was reminding me just this afternoon that we should name some significant geographic features after them."

"Hear, hear," someone said.

"Clay knew Dinah Purdy and Pat Renfro well. He seems to think that Dinah would have been honored by our naming the large inland lake to the northeast after her."

"Let's see a map," someone said, and Evangeline projected a map. The committee was in a decision-making mood, and within five minutes not only the lake but the eastern river that had its source there had names, Lake Dinah and the Dinah River. The coastal, wooded mountains became the Renfro Mountains, and the bay was now officially Stanton Bay.

"And now," Evangeline said, "let's move on. The names we're considering for the planet are New Earth, Earth Two, Hamilton's World, Troy, Elysium, Shaw—in honor of Harry Shaw—and Columbia. I suggest that we try to narrow the field even more."

It was done. One by one, negative votes eliminated Shaw, Elysium, Troy, and Earth Two, because it could be perverted to Earth Also.

Clive Baxter, the leading proponent for New Earth, had the floor. "I'm not saying that Dexter Hamilton is not a great man, but let's look back into our history. When our ancestors came to America, they began to name places for royalty: North and South Carolina, Virginia, and Georgia, for example. Our government has no royalty, and I see no reason why we must carry on the tradition of naming places and geographic features after our so-called great men. We need a simple name. Whatever we call the planet, sooner or later it's going to become, if not for us, for our children and their children, The World, or The Earth. Might as well call it New Earth from the beginning."

"I agree with Dr. Baxter," said a distinguished geologist. "We're going to avoid the evils of politics here. Let's not give the name of a politician to our new world. However, we have a chance to right a great historic wrong done centuries ago to a brave and brilliant man. I speak of Christopher Columbus, who braved the Atlantic, quelled a mutiny, and sailed on to discover a continent which, for inexplicable reasons, was named for Amerigo Vespucci, an obscure merchant who didn't even set foot on a ship until five years after Columbus had discovered the New World. I vote strongly that we right that long-past wrong and honor the great explorer, Christopher Columbus, by naming our planet Columbia."

The discussion was long and often heated. Several votes were taken, and the two remaining names in consideration, New Earth and Columbia, were caught in an exact tie.

Evangeline Burr said, "Is there anyone who would like to change his or her vote and break the tie?"

"No," Clive Baxter said, glaring at her. "It's up to you. You have the tie-breaking vote."

Evangeline knew that feelings were running deep. She sighed. "I admit, my friends, that I am a coward. I don't want to alienate any of you. May I put forward a compromise?"

"New Columbia?" Baxter asked.

"No, not that," Evangeline said. "I've been thinking since the reports from the investigative teams began to come in that we are so very, very lucky to have found this planet on our very last chance. We didn't have enough rhenium to explore other possibilities. It's such a warm, friendly planet. There are no dangerous wild animals. There are no snakes. There are no stinging scorpions, and most unbelievably, no biting insects have been discovered to date. The weather is beautiful. The land is beautiful. The soil is rich, the water pure and sweet."

"She's going to suggest that we call it Heaven," Clive Baxter said.

"I'm going to suggest that we consider naming our planet Eden."

"Well, it makes sense," someone said.

"Are you going to be Eve, Evangeline?" Baxter asked. "And wear a fig leaf?"

"Not in your presence, Dr. Baxter," Evangeline said, blushing. "Shall we vote?"

Eden. Duncan Rodrick liked it. He nodded his approval and put in his two cents worth again to say that, in his opinion, Eden was an excellent name.

"Maybe for the country, but not for a planet," Clive Baxter objected, and immediately picked up supporters.

"Just so we can have some progress, then," Evangeline suggested, "do I hear a motion to name our peninsula Eden?" She did. Eden it was, for that area between the high, snowy mountains and the sea.

The battle was joined once more. Another compromise had a majority feeling that Dexter Hamilton should be honored in some way. The town on Stanton Bay became Hamilton City and would, as the days passed, become just Hamilton, in Eden, by Stanton Bay.

New Earth or Columbia? The discussion raged on

into the night. A name for the planet would be selected before the meeting ended.

News of the stalemate had been spread by the ship's grapevine. All meetings were open meetings, and people gathered in lounges to watch the debate. Petitions were quickly written and signed, some supporting the New Earth proponents, some the Columbia proponents.

Max Rosen and Grace Monroe had been busy all day. It was Max's responsibility to mothball the ship's power units, rockets, and the Shaw Drive for future use. When colonists, alerted to the great debate, began to call engineering requesting further viewscreen hookups so that they could watch the meeting, Max growled and, at first, complied. After the fourth interruption of his work he looked at Grace and asked, "What the hell's going on?"

"I don't know," she said, turning on a screen to hear a learned scientist talking heatedly, his face red and earnest. Max listened for a few minutes. New Earth or Columbia.

"I was named to that committee," he growled. "If we're going to get our work finished, we're going to have to do something about this. You want to go with me?"

Grace smiled. "I wouldn't miss it for the world."

Max stalked into the meeting room, his uniform mussed and oil stained, his hair standing in all directions. "Evangeline," he growled.

"The chair recognizes Chief Engineer Max Rosen," Evangeline said.

"You monkeys," Max said, "are getting the whole ship upset, forcing people to take sides, and what's worse, you're keeping me from my work. I think both of your names stink. New Earth sounds like something out of a cheap science-fiction story, and if you want to name the continent or an ocean Columbia, do it, but there's only one name for this big ball we're on, because, as you all know, it was our goddamned last chance. If this planet hadn't been livable, we'd all be breathing recycled air right now instead of creating all kinds of hot air about what we're going to call her. She's Omega. The last. Our last chance."

Max turned, grabbed Grace's hand, and led her out. She looked back over her shoulder at Duncan Rodrick and smiled. Evangeline Burr giggled. Other women, and then Rodrick, and then the men joined in the laugh. The motion was passed.

At last, the committee members could get to their beds. There was another day of work ahead, to make the town of Hamilton, on Stanton Bay, habitable, to get everyone off the ship and into land quarters. Most of them were pleased with the night's work: A lake, a river, a bay, a range of mountains, a town, a country, and a planet had been named, along with a pleasant, clear, rocky little creek. And, by dawn, Jumper's Run was dropping its crystal waters into Stanton Bay near Hamilton City in the country of Eden on the continent of Columbia on the planet Omega—the last chance, and a glorious one, where not even the bees had stingers.

FIVE

"Well, Clay," Stoner McRae said as the crawler rolled and rocked over uneven ground, "you flew over the area. Which direction shall we take?"

They had traveled seventy miles on a line northeast from Hamilton, and the first low scarp of the highlands was no more than a mile ahead. They'd made fast time across the rolling plains, but now the terrain became drier, more uneven.

Clay had not been able to get out of his mind the conviction that he'd seen something that was too smooth, too regular in its angles to be of natural origin. He had been doing some mental calculations, based on his memory of *Dinahmite*'s navigation instruments. He pointed.

"It looks as if there's a break in the scarp there, Stoner," he said. "And then there's some interesting-looking country almost straight ahead."

After the crawler found a sandy, dry opening in the low cliffs, which led to a very rugged plateau, Clay oriented himself on a distant peak of the big mountains and pointed Stoner in that general direction.

It was slow going, partly because of the broken, barren, rocky terrain, and also because Stoner often stopped the crawler to take volcanic-rock samples, which Betsy, Cindy, and Clay carefully labeled and put into a bag.

Each hour Clay reported their position to the control

center on the *Spirit of America*. Once he spoke to Duncan Rodrick, who asked him how the badlands looked from the ground. Most of the time during the morning he was talking to the scout pilot Renato Cruz, whose radio call, like his scout ship, was *Apache Two*.

They had lunch in the shade of high cliffs, which marked yet another scarp as the highland rose. They had to detour far to the south to find a break in the line of cliffs, and the going was tough—so tough that the usually silent hydrogen engine of the crawler whined in protest, and the jerks and jars became more severe for the passengers. The crawler clawed its way up a scree slope of fifty degrees inclination and burst over the top with a jar that caused both Cindy and Betsy to cry out as the vehicle slammed down. It was that jar, Clay decided later, that had put the radio out of action. When he tried to call in on the hour, he could not reach the ship, and when he tried to receive, there was nothing—not even static.

"Shouldn't we turn back?" Betsy asked. "Without radio contact, they'll be worried about us."

Clay felt that they were quite near the area where he'd seen the unnatural straight lines. "Stoner," he suggested, "let's look over the next ridge before we turn back."

Stoner was a man always willing to see what was over the next hill. They found a dry riverbed and followed it into a deep, narrow canyon, ending in a staircase of jumbled and broken rock, which had once been a waterfall. It was so steep that Stoner made everyone dismount while he backed the crawler away and came at the incline at a higher speed. The big machine slewed and slid on the first try and almost overturned as it slid back toward the foot of the slope, making Betsy catch her breath. Clay saw that Stoner was prepared to leap off the crawler if it started to tip, but its low center of gravity and spinning gyros kept it on its tracks, and the second time, with greater speed, it reached the top of the slope. Then Stoner threw down lines to make the climb easier for Clay, Betsy, and Cindy.

The crawler sat on a barren, smooth, windswept surface of fractured rock. Behind them, they could see all the way to the coastal areas, although details were lost in the haze of distance. Before them was a saucer-shaped valley. The cliffs directly in front of them fell vertically at least two hundred feet and were even higher on the northern side of the valley. It was about three o'clock, Omega time, and long shadows were beginning to form on the western side of the valley. Betsy gasped in surprise, for extending from the shadow of the towering cliffs was a staggered grouping of what could only be buildings—all straight lines and square corners, story piled atop story next to the cliff, their height lessening in steps as they extended toward the dry riverbed. Few details were visible, but it appeared that the buildings were ornamented with carvings, for the walls of the upper stories looked smooth, while below they took on a complexity.

Stoner reached for binoculars. He could distinguish a carved image on the lower wall of one of the buildings near the dry river. "Wow," he said.

"Don't just 'wow' me," Betsy said. "What is it?"

Silently he handed her the glasses. "Check the lower wall of that building nearest the riverbed," he said. His face was screwed up in question, because it was hitting him now. That was a *city* down there. That was a city built by someone with intelligence and some sense of beauty. It was obviously a deserted, dead, even ancient city, and that brought up so many interesting questions that he tried to concentrate on the most important: Who, or what, had built that city and then left it? And why had they deserted it?

"It has wings," Betsy said.

"I thought so," Stoner answered.

"It's—it's—quite manlike," Betsy said.

She lowered the glasses, her face white, and looked up at Stoner. Cindy and Clay tugged on the glasses, and Clay gave in.

"That's stone construction," Stoner said. "They had to have some kind of metal tools."

Clay had his turn and saw a thin, graceful figure carved into stone, a flying figure with spreading wings. The legs and head, although possibly stylized, were humanoid.

"The way in must be at the south end, through the canyon," Stoner said.

"Let's not go down there," Betsy said. "Let's go back and get some company."

Stoner turned the crawler around to point toward the south. "There's no danger. It's been deserted for a long time. See the sand heaped up against the walls?"

"Stoner, let's not," Betsy begged. "We don't know what's down there."

Clay, of course, was all for going. When, with some difficulty, the crawler reached the dry riverbed, he leaped down and scouted a route; there were four dry falls leading into the valley, each of them a challenge for the crawler. It was after five o'clock when they emerged into the open floor of the valley, scattering a herd of silver-horned antelope. The dead city was directly in front of them, and up close, it was more impressive than they'd imagined.

The crawler sped through the grass, hit a roughly circular area of discolored grass, and sank quickly down into the sand as if the ground had suddenly collapsed under it, but because of its speed, the crawler was quickly out of the depression, with only the back end of the treads sinking down before gaining solid ground again.

"What happened?" Cindy asked, looking back. There was an oval depression behind them where the ground had caved in.

"Just a sinkhole," Stoner said, his eyes on a grouping of statuary that was half-buried in sand beyond a low, intricately carved fence, which had obviously been built for decorative purposes. He stopped the vehicle at the opening in the low fence directly in front of the statuary, and Betsy forgot her nervousness.

The carving was exquisite, so realistic in tan, marblelike stone; it seemed that the two spaniel-sized carnivores attacking a male silver-horn were alive. Behind the realistic stone group, the buildings rose, and it seemed that every available surface of the first-story walls was carved.

"Stoner, we need trained archaeologists here," Betsy said.

"I know. We won't move anything, but we can look."

Clay ran to get a closer look at a carved wall. Behind

hunting scenes featuring the native carnivores and the little silver-horned antelope were tall, thin, manlike beings with large, round eyes and hands that had only three fingers opposing a thumb. "Stoner," he said, "it looks like they tamed the cats and used them for hunting."

Stoner had little prickling feelings running up and down his spine. The impact of the implications of the obviously ancient city was just hitting him. He knew that scouts had flown over every land mass on Omega and that their sensors had picked up life signals on most land masses, but none corresponded to manlike beings with wings. That opened the door to eerie speculation. There was something about the long-dead city that made him apprehensive. He knew that Cindy and Betsy were feeling it, too, because they stayed close to him as they walked over shifting sands to stand before an ornately carved wall. The building material was native stone, a tan, rather attractive sandstone. Being soft, it showed weathering, so that many of the carvings were blurred by erosion. But the bas-reliefs on the smooth, evenly jointed walls gave them a picture of alien life that was fascinating.

The wall had been separated into panels to show different scenes. Some were landscapes, trees of three different types, all done in a simplified, stylized way. One variety—already being called umbrella trees for their perfect symmetry of branches and shape, a semicircle almost straight across the bottom—were of a size, and of a perfect contour.

Silver-horned antelopes and the small cats that preyed upon them were well represented. Smaller, unidentified animals were also pictured. And, in the central panel of the wall, there was a huge thing that caught Stoner's attention: Between two trees, from an opening in the ground itself, there emerged a large, evil-looking head and a powerful, muscular neck. Its mouth was open just enough to expose a huge set of teeth. If the mouth had been closed, the head would have been cone-shaped. On the outside of the cone were row after row of blunt, forward-pointing projections.

"I hope," Betsy said, "that thing is either mythical or extinct."

"Wouldn't want to run into it in a dark alley," Stoner agreed.

Clay had been leading the way. He entered a sand-clogged street and waited. All the first-story walls were decorated with either objects from nature or simple, decorative motifs of stylized flowers, trees, and four-pointed stars. The opening on the upper stories was blank.

"Stoner," Clay said as the others caught up with him, "there aren't any stairs. Do you suppose they flew up to the second story?"

"Good question," Stoner replied.

"We'll let the archaeologists determine that," Betsy said. "Let's go."

"We're going to have to spend the night somewhere," Stoner said. "It's too late to get back to Hamilton. This is as good a place as any."

"I will not sleep here," Betsy stated firmly.

"Okay," Stoner replied, still feeling uneasy. "We'll set up camp away from the city."

"Let's go do it," Betsy said.

Stoner agreed. He ran a finger along a joint between two large building blocks, then looked around. There was a dark opening in the wall near them. "Let's just take a quick look inside."

He led the way. Sufficient light came from the entryway and some high, square openings, which must have been windows, to light the interior of a large room. The floor was stone, drifted over by the encroaching sand. The walls were nothing more than the inside planes of the building stones. The ceiling of longer and, probably, Stoner thought, thinner slabs of the same stone was supported by regularly placed pillars of stone. At one corner of the large room, which took up the entire ground floor of the building, there was a rectangular hole in the ceiling. Stoner dug in the drifted sand below the opening.

"Look," he said. "This looks like wood residue. I think there was a staircase here. Judging from the holes in the sides of the door opening over there, I'd say that there was once a wooden door. Since there's no sign of metal, they probably used wooden pegs and maybe leather hinges."

They examined the interiors of several more buildings

at ground level, finding nothing of interest, before Stoner boosted Clay up through the opening in the ceiling of a large, ground-floor room; then Clay secured a line around a stone pillar so that the others could join him. They had moved closer to the cliff, where the buildings were higher. The dust of centuries lay on everything, so that when they walked, they left tracks.

They climbed to the fourth story. All rooms were empty, the walls unadorned until, at the very top, they entered a section that had been partitioned off with smooth stonework into three oblong rooms. It was in the center that they found the only representations of the former inhabitants of the city other than the one carving of a winged man they'd seen on the wall of the building nearest the dry river.

In the center room, illuminated through an opening at either end, the walls were covered on two sides by similar scenes. In one a group of sticklike humanoids knelt in a circle around a cone-headed beast emerging from the earth. The beast had a silver-horned antelope in its jaws.

"Well, there you are," Stoner said. "That thing is one of their gods, and probably just as unrealistic as some of the gods early Earthmen dreamed up."

"Ugh," Cindy said.

"They have offered the silver-horn as sacrifice," Stoner went on.

The other wall showed the sticklike people cultivating a field, working in a row with what looked like a primitive hoe.

"Stoner, it's getting late," Betsy said, made uneasy by being high up in a building that had been built only God knew when.

Stoner reluctantly led the way back toward the crawler. "There was no violence here," he decided. "They left peacefully. Every building we've checked was systematically emptied. If the end had come by war, disease, or some violent natural occurrence, there'd be artifacts everywhere. My guess is that the climate changed. That river used to run with water. When the rains stopped they simply moved on."

"To where?" Betsy asked.

"Good question."

Jumper, who had been made quite unhappy when he was left on the ground floor as his friends and master disappeared through a hole in the ceiling, was feeling better, scouting the way. He halted suddenly, froze into an attitude of discovery, then began to bark. Clay went over next to the wall of a building and saw that Jumper had discovered a small burrow.

"There may be something in there with teeth, boy," he told the dog. "Come on."

Jumper whined and began to dig. Clay reached down to pick Jumper up just as the dog's frantic digging unearthed an object with an ancient, green patina. Clay pulled Jumper away and yelled, "Hey, Stoner!"

The object was an axhead of hammered bronze. Stoner whooped and showed the metal to Betsy. None of the rock samples he'd taken that day had been encouraging so far as traces of metal were concerned, but he had the proof in his hands now. "There's copper and tin," he said. "And where there's copper and tin, there have got to be other metals."

The Americans on Omega were an elite group. Each had been selected for achievement in his or her individual field, and even in an era when robots and computers had produced a twenty-hour workweek for the majority of people in the United States, high achievers still followed the ancient rules of success. One simply did not make it to the top of his or her field by working a twenty-hour week, or even an old-fashioned forty-hour week. Everyone chosen for the *Spirit of America* expedition was aware of the basic time management rule, that there are only so many hours in a day, and the important thing is how one uses those hours.

It seemed a blessing, therefore, to have an extra ten minutes in each hour on Omega, adding up to an extra four hours daily. And since the ship had landed just as Omega's summer season was starting, the long days gave almost eighteen standard hours of good daylight. The problem was that the human body was used to a day of twenty-four sixty-minute hours, not a day of twenty-four seventy-minute hours.

Of course, each specialist wanted to spend time working exclusively in his or her specialty field. But everyone had work assignments outside the specialty field. There were times, such as during the construction of the smelter on the Dinah River, when there was a need for ordinary physical labor, and at such times research and exploration had to be interrupted. To make up for the time taken away from their own work, scientists and technicians often burned lights in the laboratories into the early hours of the morning, and then got up after inadequate sleep to continue construction, or woke in the predawn hours to do extra work.

Amando Kwait, for example, always got an early start on the day, whether he had special extradisciplinary responsibilities or not. Today he had his own staff busy, working in the ship's gardens or testing botanical samples and gathering others, so he linked up with Paul Warden, who was taking a cartographic crew across Jumper's Run to the north. Amando wanted to cover as much territory as possible, gather samples at random to get an overall picture of Eden before planting food crops.

Paul was in a good mood, in spite of the fact that once again, just last night, he had been brushed off in a cold, almost crude way by Sage Bryson. He'd then had a talk with a friend of his, Grace Monroe, who knew as much about the human brain as anyone living and, being a woman herself, a lot about women in general.

"Yes, I know Sage," Grace had told him. "Isn't she a lovely woman?"

Paul, his face going red, confessed that he did, indeed, think that Sage was lovely, more than lovely, leading Grace to smile and say, "Why, Paul, I think you've made your choice."

Almost everyone knew everyone else. The ship had been a small world for the long voyage, and there had been no little speculation regarding the unmarried members of the company. When an unmarried couple paired off and stayed that way for any length of time, it was said that so-and-so had made his or her choice.

Warden flushed deeply, and his half grin became an east–west smile. "I have. She hasn't."

"Well, she couldn't do any better," Grace assured him.

"I can't figure out whether she dislikes just me or men in general," Paul said.

Grace didn't tell Paul, but she suspected that there might be something in what he'd just said, for Sage had been given plenty of opportunity by the ship's bachelors to socialize as a pair, and she had always refused.

"She'll come around, Paul," Grace said, not at all sure, but wanting Paul to feel better. He was, in Grace's opinion, one very sweet man.

As Warden drove the crawler through Jumper's Run, stirring up silt from the creek's rocky bed, he remembered Grace's words and prayed that she was right. He had Sage Bryson so deep under his skin that he was beginning to itch.

It was a beautiful day for exploring. Climatologists, who had begun their study of the planet's weather patterns while the ship was still in orbit, had concluded that the coastal area of Eden would receive between twenty-five and forty inches of rainfall annually, mostly during the winter months. Summers—the ship had landed in what proved to be the area's late spring—would be dry, with temperatures not more than ninety degrees Fahrenheit at midday, with cooling ocean breezes coming from the great western sea. Winters, the climatologists predicted, would be mild, snowless, and relatively brief, considering that Omega's year was four hundred twenty-five Earth-days long, making for thirty-five-day months.

As Paul Warden steered the crawler up the slope from Jumper's Run in the early morning, the temperature was seventy degrees, the sun pleasantly warm, the almost purple sky cloudless. No one aboard was in much of a hurry. Paul would stop the crawler when Amando wanted to take a closer look at a plant or when the mapmaking team wanted to apply the sensors of their automated, computerized instruments to the surrounding terrain.

They moved quickly into a wide plain of undulating tall grass, studded with the beautifully symmetrical umbrella trees. Paul aimed at a small grouping of three trees in the near distance. A herd of silver-horned antelope moved casually aside, splitting to let the crawler move past them on its almost silent hydrogen power.

Lynn Roberts, not yet thirty years old, short, bronzed from her time spent under sunlamps aboard ship, was in charge of the mapmaking team. She had not seen the silver-horns before. "They're so beautiful," she breathed.

Paul obligingly stopped the crawler, and the silver-horns, after checking them out, grazed on, some within a distance of less than a hundred feet.

"They're not afraid of us at all," Lynn said.

"That's because we haven't started eating them," said her partner, George Evans, a Minnesota man, still in his twenties but acknowledged to be among the best survey-ors on Earth.

"No one would eat anything so beautiful," Lynn said.

"There were beautiful animals in Africa, too," Amando commented. "There are few left, if any." He let his thoughts wander sadly, remembering when the communists took over and began to use hunger as a weapon to force the tribes to their will and as a way of reducing the trouble-some population surplus. Those who were hungry ignored the conservation laws, and beautiful animals had been eaten.

"We've got a fresh chance here," Lynn Roberts said. "We ate synthetic protein at home and on the trip out. We can't start killing just to stuff our stomachs with natu-ral protein."

A herd bull decided that the grass was more desirable a hundred feet away. He lifted his head and pranced gracefully toward a new spot, moving in a determined straight line until he approached a spot of grass that was of a slightly lighter color than the rest. He made a wide, careful circle around the browner grass, and as his harem followed dutifully, each of the silver-horns circled the lighter grass. Amando did not take particular notice; it was not unusual, in a grassy plain, to see spots of different color. He could see several of the small, lighter-colored spots from the crawler.

They sat in silence, watching the silver-horns. Warden moved the crawler toward the trees, where a family of the as-yet-unnamed meat eaters lolled in the shade, the bones of the night's kill attracting a dozen of the leathery scavenger birds not a hundred yards away.

There had been a lot of discussion about the catlike carnivores. The young one that had been brought to the ship for study had no patience for men and was quite belligerent when approached. Paul Warden had been asked to determine the reaction of the carnivores to man in their own habitat. He stopped the crawler again and, his stun gun set on full charge, walked purposefully toward the trees. The greenish-tan animals looked at him until he was within fifty feet, and then they rose one by one and faced him. He was ready to stun the entire family, adult male and female and two yearling cubs, with the beam of his gun.

"Scram!" he said, waving his arms. The male's ears jerked forward inquisitively, and then, with a yawn, he turned and started to walk slowly away, the others following. Warden kept walking, moving faster than the animals. The male, the size of a healthy cocker spaniel, stopped and pointed his short ears at Paul and opened his heavily toothed mouth to make a mewling, purring sound. The female and the cubs kept moving, but the male held his ground, managing to look quite bored with it all, until Paul was only ten feet away.

"Well, boy, what's your decision?" Paul asked the animal, stun gun at the ready. "We're going to be here for a while, you know, and we don't mind you staying around as long as you don't decide that we look good to eat."

While the scientists in the crawler watched tensely, the animal yawned again, made that mewling, purring sound, and took padded, feline steps toward Paul, long tail pointing straight up into the air. Paul, quite nervous, started to use the stun gun to put the cat to sleep for a few minutes, but on a hunch he held his fire. The cat wasn't all that big, but its teeth were big enough, and there were smooth, powerful muscles rippling under that greenish-tan hide. But Paul still didn't fire, and the cat came to within four feet of him, sat down, and looked up with big, yellow, cat's eyes.

"Want to be friends?" Paul asked, wondering if the animal was sizing him up for dinner. The cat made a purring sound and fell heavily, with a soulful grunt, to his side and lay there looking up fetchingly.

"I'll be damned," Paul said. He swallowed hard, stepped forward, knelt. "Easy old boy," he whispered, and put out his hand to touch the animal's head.

The cat purred, and Paul ran his hand down the smooth hide to the lighter-colored belly fur and rubbed. A tongue like sandpaper rasped across his arm, and the purring increased. He looked back toward the others on the crawler and shrugged, and the cat, deprived of rubbing, reached up and licked his hand.

The rest of the family came drifting back, and Paul was soon surrounded by four big cats, the two young ones butting him with their heads to get their share of rubbing.

Lynn Roberts got off the crawler and came forward. The four animals looked at her, yawned, mewled, and one of the young ones frisked toward her, spooking her a bit, until the cat started rubbing against her leg. Soon all of them, including Amando, were squatting on the ground, scratching feline ears and rubbing smooth bellies.

"I'll be damned," Paul said. "The bees don't sting, there are no snakes, and the wild animals like to have their tummies scratched."

The male carnivore decided that playtime was over. He stood, shook himself, growled a growl that got everyone's attention, licked Paul's hand, and led the family away, past the carcass of the night's kill, where the scavenger birds hissed, and then led a parade around a lighter spot of grass, which was in his line of march.

"They acted almost as if they'd seen men before," George Evans commented.

Warden had been puzzled. It just wasn't natural for wild beasts to be so tame. But Evans's suggestion had not occurred to him. He stood, looked around, and shivered in spite of himself. It was all too idyllic to be real.

They loaded up and moved on, making two stops for the mapmaking crew, one for Amando, who saw a magenta-colored flower not in his collection, and then they climbed a long, gentle slope to another flatland of grass and stopped once again for the mapmakers. The three mapmakers' instruments were set up on tripods at a precise separation, a button was pushed, and the instruments did the rest. Then Lynn and George went to swivel the two end instruments. Lynn was walking directly toward an area of lighter grass.

Paul was still contemplating George Evans's remark about there being other men, and his own reaction to it, a reaction that had him wanting to look quickly over his shoulder. He was looking toward the south when he heard Lynn's one agonized scream. He turned, his hand going for his laser weapon, just in time to see Lynn in the jaws of a nightmare from his youth, a thing with white flesh and sawteeth in a pointed snout. Lynn's arms flailed for a moment, and then the muscular, snakelike neck of the nightmare creature flexed, and Lynn's blood spewed forth. With a quickness that was almost as frightening as the appearance of the beast, the pointed, toothed head disappeared, taking Lynn down with it. Dust flew, and there was a concave hole from which the dust arose for a moment, and then there was nothing.

Amando Kwait, not more than twenty feet away, had seen it all. "She walked into the circle of lighter-colored grass," he cried out to George. "The ground seemed to explode under her, and then the thing seized her."

"We've got to get her out!" George Evans called frantically.

"It's no use," Warden said. "It's no use." He'd heard the snap of bones, had seen the gush of blood, had seen the jaws of the beast close, driving the huge teeth through Lynn's body.

Now they knew. Even the biblical Eden had had its serpent. This, their Eden's serpent, had teeth, teeth that exploded upward from the ground itself.

Paul immediately got on the radio. He knew that there were many teams working in the field, and the areas of lighter grass were common sights. He gave warning. Jackie Garvey, on duty aboard ship as communicator, passed the warning along to all field units. "Look for areas of grass lighter than the surrounding grass and avoid them."

*   *   *

The McRaes and Clay left the abandoned city in a mood of celebration. There were almost four hours of daylight left. "We'll check out the area under the north rim," Stoner said. "My guess is that there's water there. Should make it a nice place to camp."

There was water, and a quick check on the crawler's analyzer showed that the water was safe for swimming. Cindy and Betsy changed into their swimsuits behind the crawler, and then Clay and Stoner joined them in the water, which, after the pleasant, warm day, was deliciously refreshing.

Even as they splashed around and Cindy and Clay played chase with Jumper, a pair of the handsome little carnivorous pussycats came down to drink at the far side of the pool, seemingly not very curious about the noisy humans.

They all dried in the sun, changed, and started making camp. Clay helped set up two tents on the grassy margin of the pond, and then he and Cindy gathered dead, fallen limbs from the umbrella trees nearby. Clay got the fire going and soon there was a smell of synthasteak grilling.

With nothing to do but wait, Clay suggested a walk. Cindy was the only taker. They started off down the dry riverbed, with Clay, at Stoner's suggestion, checking along the bank for artifacts. They were even with the crawler when Stoner called out, "Hey, Clay, how about turning on the beacon just in case anyone is looking for us."

The beacon, separate from the malfunctioning radio, sent out a homing signal coded to identify that particular crawler. It had a limited range, and that was reduced even further by the high cliffs surrounding the valley.

Clay walked along the riverbed, which was only twenty-five to thirty feet wide, and Cindy followed him. Two hundred yards down the river a small herd of silver-horns grazed. Clay started walking idly toward them, past a roughly circular area of grass that was lighter in color, and glanced at it, seeing nothing of interest there. There were several of the lighter areas of grass ahead.

"Let's see how close we can get to the silver-horns

before they spook," he suggested. Cindy was walking to his right, watching the silver-horns.

The herd buck lifted his head and gazed at them, and then went back to his grazing.

"Brave little beggar, aren't you?" Clay said.

Jumper had just seen, or smelled, the silver-horns. He showed indications of going after them, and Clay told him to heel.

"They don't seem to be afraid of us at all," Cindy commented.

"I'll bet if we could catch a young one, we could tame him," Clay said.

The lighter circle of grass was twenty feet in front of them, directly in their path. It was wide enough so that all three of them, boy, girl, and dog, could walk across it abreast.

SIX

Lieutenant Jackie Garvey lifted her coffee mug, took a sip, then frowned. The coffee had gone cold and stale. She shoved it away, rose, stretched. The ship's clocks were still set on Mountain Standard Time, but her body wasn't. She, like most, was having a bit of trouble adjusting to Omega's longer day.

Outside, Hamilton was beginning to settle down for the evening. Jackie had the ship's ears on and had used powerful visual equipment to try to spot the different varieties of birds that had begun to sing from the trees around the town at dusk. Unlike the seabirds, the land birds were drab in color, and their songs, although quite birdlike, were just different enough to give the early evening an alien feel.

She swung the visuals toward the distant, inland mountains. On the tallest peaks, the champion of which was five thousand feet taller than Earth's Mount Everest, iced rocks protruded harshly from the eternal snows. The thirty-four-thousand-foot peaks would be almost as hostile to humans as was space itself. And yet, she felt, someday some young men and women would climb them and look down on this new world from its top and claim it as their own.

She closed off the optics and ran a systems check. The ship was humming along nicely. Power-plant monitors showed blank, with the rockets and the Shaw Drive put nicely to bed by Max Rosen, to await an awakening that would not come until plants had been built to manufacture rocket fuel and the exploration teams found metals.

It had been a long watch. Omega's seventy-minute hours had crawled. When the signal bong sounded and the access hatch to the control bridge opened, she looked up quickly, pleased with the thought of having company, and was doubly pleased when she saw that it was Duncan Rodrick.

"Good evening," she said. "I was just about to put on some coffee."

"Sounds good," Rodrick said, walking to stand beside her to check the ship's log quickly.

"Busy day," she said. "Poor Lynn."

"Yes."

She looked at him. His eyes were still on the log. The rigors of command and the times of tension had not changed Duncan Rodrick. To Jackie, he looked the same as he'd looked the first time she met him, during those days when the *Spirit of America* was still diagrams and figures on Harry Shaw's plans. For a mature man, he looked amazingly youthful. There was about him at all times an air of laid-back alertness, like a panther at rest, or like an athlete at ease, prepared at a second's notice to spring into all-out action. His blond hair, cut full, showed no sign of thinning. At first glance, a stranger might take him to be just a very relaxed fellow, a man always ready to smile and say something pleasant, a likable, all-American boy-man who, given the chance, might look good in a full-color ad for shave lotion or a particular brand of brandy. But when Jackie had made the contact with Rodrick more personal and stood close enough to look into his eyes, she'd seen unwavering confidence. There was more than the handsome, youthful, pleasant outward appearance. Behind those hawk's eyes was someone very intelligent.

"I haven't seen much of you lately, Dunc."

He caught her eyes, looked away quickly, and that glance, his avoidance of her smile, aroused her puzzlement yet again.

"Things have been pretty hectic," he said. "And they're not going to get better for a while."

He had given her the right to be informal with him when they were alone, not by words, but by actions, during the first months of the outward trip. Now he was almost indifferent to her, it seemed. But in that assumption she was mistaken.

Rodrick's primary reaction to Jackie was guilt, with a bit of regret. He regretted that he'd moved so swiftly in courting her during those first few months of the journey. There was a limited number of choices for any single person aboard, and in the first warm flush of their relationship, he had given Jackie reason to think that their alliance might become permanent. In the group of people aboard the ship, for every man there was a woman. He felt guilty because now Jackie's choices were extremely limited; many singles had paired off while he'd taken up her time.

There were moments when Duncan Rodrick frowned at himself in the mirror and wondered if his mother had had any children that lived. Here he was, a young man, just forty-six years old, not having reached half his life expectancy—a one-time loser at marriage and practicing to be a tragic figure in love with another man's wife.

Things would have been more simple back on Earth: Stealing a fellow-officer's wife would, at worst, have merely moved him from near the top of the always clogged promotion list to the bottom, a price he would have paid gladly to have Mandy Miller as his wife.

Jackie, a mature personality, a good officer, had never openly talked of marriage, but the assumption had always been there during their brief intimacy. She was well within her rights to expect permanency, and doubly so in view of the situation.

Jackie was, when one looked at it logically, more beautiful than Mandy Miller. She was younger, more lushly formed, and available. He and Jackie were the obvious match. She had let him know in no uncertain terms that she liked him. She was emotionally stable. She was service through and through. She'd always be a strong woman, and together they'd probably make beautiful children.

Each applicant for the ship's complement had been tested for childbearing potential, and it was understood that each woman aboard would have several children. This, for some who had been exposed to decades of zero-population-growth propaganda, was a welcome departure; to be able to have as many children as one wanted, without guilt, was one of the new freedoms of living on the huge planet.

It all counted in Jackie's favor, but it had been two years since he'd visited her in her quarters.

Her expression didn't change at his lame excuse of being too busy to socialize, although she felt a stab of pain and anger. Once again she'd opened herself to him in friendliness, and once again her overture had been rebuffed. She tried to tell herself that he really was so busy, that there was still plenty of time for them to get back together, but she wasn't listening, and as she stood to make a fresh pot of coffee, a tiny bud of resentment that had been with her for a long, long time began to grow.

Rodrick began to roll various reports onto the screen. Things were moving so swiftly that it was difficult to keep up. And it was difficult to adjust one's mind to the scale of Omega. The smaller continent to the east of Columbia had a land mass twice the size of North and South America combined. Everything was big on Omega. For example, the meteorologists' surveying scout ships had measured hundred-foot waves in the area of tropical storms.

The astronomers were hard at work measuring Omega's rotation, orbit, and relationship to her neighbors in the B system, and already the ship's machine shop was making new mechanisms and faces for all nondigital clocks to conform to the seventy-minute hours of Omega and the thirty-five day months. It was going to be an interesting adjustment. Did one celebrate his birthday by Earth time and Earth's calendar, or by Omega's time and calendar? He made a note to tell the techs to keep one chronometer on the bridge of the *Spirit of America* on Earth time, just as a reminder of their mission.

The preliminary reports on the oil-exploration team were very encouraging. They'd located likely oil-bearing deposits on the first day, and the automated drill rig had been operating since that discovery.

The geologists had determined that Omega was a living planet with a molten core, but aside from that, she didn't seem to obey any of the rules. Omega's core was smaller in proportion to her size than Earth's. Metals, the scientists predicted, were going to be very, very scarce. The planet's crust, however, was thicker in proportion to her size than Earth's and formed of rocks of lesser density. But the most vital speculations, in Rodrick's mind, had to do with the nature of Omega's molten core: There were no logical reasons why a planet four times the size of Earth had two-tenths of one percent less gravity. One had to assume that there were virtually no heavy metals in the molten core, that the core was made up mainly of molten silica. Consequently, there would be little or no heavy metals in the crust.

Thus it was that Omega's livable gravity was a mixed blessing, allowing them to move about normally—even just a little bit more spritely—but making it quite uncertain whether there would be the metals needed to begin to build the manufacturing plants necessary to civilization as they knew it, and to refuel the ship with rhenium for the trip home.

One thing was in their favor, Rodrick knew. The accidental discovery, during the trip out, that the ship could take lightstep with much less rhenium than first theorized, would allow them to make the trip back to Earth with an amount of fuel tons less than originally believed needed, and the trip would be cut to next to no time through the ability to lightstep from planetary orbit.

Rodrick would be following Stoner McRae's expedition with great interest, because the trained geologist would be able to gather much information about the possibility of minable ores by a survey of the exposed igneous rock of the barren inland highlands.

After checking the last report on the screen, he said good-bye to Jackie and headed for the scout ships. He wanted to investigate the scene of Lynn Robert's death. Rodrick glanced guiltily at the coffeepot, still percolating, before he left the bridge.

*　　　*　　　*

The warning had been broadcast that there was something very mean and nasty on Omega, after all, and was acknowledged by all field teams except one—Stoner McRae's. There was a possibility that McRae had heard the warning on his communicator. However, when the check-in call from Stoner was thirty-five minutes overdue, Jackie began to be concerned. She asked the scout communicator to put his ships on alert to try to spot the McRae vehicle, but the scout ships were scattered all around the globe, none of them near the rocky highlands. She started trying to reach Duncan Rodrick after forty-five minutes.

Rodrick had just arrived at the scene of Lynn Roberts's death and was on hand when, suddenly, the dry earth in the concavity into which Lynn had been pulled stirred and ejected, with some force, her disjointed skeleton. Paul Warden fired a laser into the concave pit with no apparent results.

Death, especially such a bizarre death as Lynn's, seemed so out of place in this pleasant, friendly land. Rodrick looked at the clean-picked bones and berated himself for having been so lax. He had let Eden lull him into being off guard. That danger had come from a totally unexpected direction was no excuse. He went to the scout he'd flown to the scene.

"Captain," Jackie said, "Stoner McRae's party is an hour past their last report time."

"Put as many scouts as possible over the area," Rodrick said.

"Yes, sir. That's being done. There'll be a scout in the general area within a half hour."

Rodrick was nearer than a half hour to the badlands. He told Jackie he was going airborne, destination the highlands, and contacted her again when the scout was shooting at top speed toward the east. "Recall all exploration parties except the oil-drilling crew," he ordered. "Send the admiral and Mopro to Paul Warden's location on the first available air transport. I assume that everyone except McRae's party has been warned?"

"That's affirmative," Jackie said.

Rodrick closed circuit with Jackie, called Paul Warden's crawler, and got an immediate answer. "Paul, I want that thing," Rodrick said. "What's your opinion of the chances of taking it alive for study purposes?"

"Cap'n, we saw about five feet of head and neck, sort of bullet shaped. It looked damned powerful."

"Okay. Then alive only if it can be done without danger. Mopro and the admiral are on their way to you. Mopro's heavy armament should be a match for that thing, whatever it is."

"Cap'n," Warden said, "Dr. Kwait wants to speak with you."

"Yes, Amando?"

"Captain," Amando said into the communicator, "the light-colored areas of grass seem to be in definite patterns in this area—one roughly every half acre. I've noticed that the silver-horns very carefully avoid the areas. We've seen a whole herd skirt around the edge of light-colored areas, giving it a wide berth of at least five yards. We have some lengths of high-tensile cable in the crawler. I think that we can fashion a trap, a noose, and then use a silver-horn for bait."

"Sounds good," Rodrick said. "Just be very careful."

"Don't worry," Amando answered. "I saw what that thing did to Lynn Roberts."

Rodrick turned his attention to the badlands below him and flipped on all the scout's sensors. It was getting late, and he was beginning to feel a gnawing of worry when, suddenly, the scout's radios picked up the coded beat of a beacon. He was twelve miles from the crawler at that point.

Jumper was so eager to chase the silver-horns not more than a hundred feet away that he was quivering and looking up pleadingly at Clay, who had to tell him repeatedly to heel. Jumper's heeling consisted of a taut, quivering pose a few feet out in front of Clay. The dog was no more than five feet from the edge of the light area of grass when Rodrick's scout, moving at top speed, flashed across the valley. Clay and Cindy, eyes on the silver-horns, didn't see the ship or know it had passed until they heard the sonic boom. The great, dull explosion of sound stopped them in their tracks, but the scout was already out of sight.

Jumper, thoroughly frightened by the boom, scampered back to cower at Clay's feet. The little herd of silver-horns was shocked into a stance of heads-up motionlessness as their limpid eyes searched for danger.

Rodrick had had just enough time to see the human figures against the blurred color of grass. He felt the tug of g-forces as he turned, stressing the capability of the scout, and felt his pressure suit fill and squeeze to keep the blood from being forced from his brain. Then he did a bit of very tricky flying. As his scout cleared the western rim of the valley he could see two people within ten feet of the light-colored grass. He flipped on the scout's wailer, and the burst of sound alerted Clay and Cindy to stand still. Rodrick, still flying very fast, braced himself, kicked in retro-rockets usually used only in space, and slammed the scout to a halt. Rodrick performed a trick very few pilots could have brought off, using the retro-rockets to kill a speed of over six hundred miles per hour and bringing the craft to hover with the hydrogen-powered jets all in a matter of scant seconds. He flipped off the wailer and clicked on the hailer and said, "Clay, Cindy, don't move. Stand exactly where you are."

The amplified human voice convinced the silver-horns that something was going on, and the herd bull threw his head high with a snort and led a panicky flight. That was too much for Jumper. The movement sent him streaking directly across the danger spot.

It all happened quickly: The earth erupted, and a great, dead-white *thing* whipped a coned snout that missed Jumper by inches. It whipped back and turned to point a pair of recessed, gleaming red eyes at Clay and Cindy. Then, with startling speed, it jerked back into the now-disturbed sandy earth.

Rodrick had seen the thing, and it was recorded on the scout's cameras. "Clay, I want you and Cindy to stay exactly where you are."

Clay was not about to move, unless it was away from that thing that had erupted from the ground. He whistled to Jumper, who had been outdistanced quickly by the silver-horns, and the dog came trotting back. The scout landed nearby, and they boarded, making it just a bit crowded.

Rodrick's first impulse was to chew Stoner out for not returning to base immediately after his radio had failed. He had not had time to notice the city, which was now in the dark shadows of the western cliffs.

"What the hell is going on?" Stoner asked, as Cindy leaped down from the scout, followed by Clay, Jumper, and the captain. He saw Rodrick's grim face and advanced to meet them. The sonic boom, the wailer, and Rodrick's highly amplified voice on the hailer had startled Betsy and him, but neither had been in a position to see Jumper's narrow escape.

"Stoner, you know the rules about staying in contact," Rodrick began, still tense from almost having lost Clay or Cindy or both.

"Wow, Stoner," Clay said, too excited to keep quiet, "did you see that thing?"

"Just a minute, Clay," Rodrick said.

"But, Captain, you don't understand," Clay said. He pointed and added, "Before you chew us out, take a look over there."

Even in dark shadow Rodrick recognized the city for what it was. He experienced the same shock and asked himself the same questions that had occurred to Stoner earlier in the day, then walked quickly to the scout and activated the radio.

Rocky Miller had taken over the duty on the bridge. "Commander," Rodrick said. "I want a red alert issued now." He waited until he heard the hooting of the ship's alert system. "I want all parties still in the field to drop what they're doing and return to base, and I want all citizens aboard ship."

Well, Rocky was thinking, *he's finally panicked, and all because some underground animal killed one person.* He did not, however, voice that opinion.

"My orders are, Mr. Miller, that all personnel will spend the night aboard ship, under red alert. Mopro and the admiral will patrol outside the ship. Confirm."

Rocky repeated the orders, thinking how uncomfortable it was going to be for the colonists. Their quarters had been set up on the surface. They'd have to bed down as best they could in the open spaces and lounges.

"I have located the McRae party, and all are safe," Rodrick continued. "I will take a quick look around, then fly cover for their return trip. In the meantime, all exploration flights are canceled for tomorrow."

"Question, Captain," Rocky said.

"Go ahead."

"Is the oil-drilling team to come in, too? They're down to oil-bearing shale now, expecting a strike at any time."

"*All* parties, Commander," Rodrick said.

He had had all the surprises he wanted from Omega. He'd learned, at the cost of a life, that there was more to peaceful Eden than met the eye. And the presence of that dead city raised questions that would have to be answered before he'd send any more field parties out. He could tell by the looks of those odd buildings in the shadows, by the smell of it, by the feel of it, that this big, beautiful planet was not going to be as easily tamed as it had first appeared. That city over there in the shadows was old, very old. Intelligent beings capable of building that city centuries in the past could now be capable of almost anything.

The alert came just as George Evans was pulling a very reluctant silver-horn yearling toward the dusty concavity from which Lynn Roberts's bones had been ejected. Thin cables of high tensile strength had been rigged into a noose, which lay around the hole. One end of the cable was attached to a sturdy umbrella tree, the other end to the winch at the front of the crawler. The crawler's engine was running, and Amando Kwait was standing ready to jerk the vehicle backward, to close the noose quickly. Paul Warden was standing by with explosive rounds in the chamber of a high-powered projectile rifle.

Amando relayed the red alert. Evans stopped pulling on the rope tied to the silver-horn's neck. Warden yelled, "It'll only take a couple of minutes." He wanted that thing. He didn't want it alive. He wanted it dead. He'd heard the bones crunch, seen the blood squeezed out of Lynn's body.

Evans nodded and pulled the little animal toward the hole. As the silver-horn's front feet were pulled into soft dirt, the animal began to bleat pitifully. It struggled and fell and lay in the cavity. Nothing happened. It scrambled to its feet and ran in the direction of Evans, leaping from the hole to stand, breathing hard. Its bleat was so sad that Kwait killed the crawler's engine and went over to turn it loose. The antelope scampered off.

"I guess it wasn't hungry," Paul Warden said, looking moodily down into the disturbed area.

"We can come back and dig the thing out," George Evans suggested. He still could not accept what had happened. He had seen a member of Mandy Miller's medical staff put Lynn's bones into a body bag, but he still couldn't accept it. He'd loved Lynn. He had chosen her, and she'd promised to give him her decision that very night. He'd been sure that it was to be a reciprocal choice. Now she was dead, her flesh eaten by a nightmare thing from below the ground.

Duncan allowed himself one good look at the ancient city. He walked along sand-clogged streets, seeing the somewhat crude but expressive carvings in stone, admiring the excellent stone jointing. He agreed with Stoner that the winged figure carved in the wall was probably some mythical figure and that the carved sticklike figures were more representative of the former inhabitants of the city.

"They must not have had much to eat," Cindy commented.

"Funny how that one piece of statuary out by the wall is so realistic, as are the animals in the carvings," Betsy said.

"While the carvings of the people seem almost child-like," Rodrick said. "Stick figures."

"There's a bit of flesh on the limbs of that winged one," Stoner reminded them.

"A god," Betsy said. "A flying god."

"Then they weren't made in the image of their god,"

Stoner remarked. "They must have suffered from low self-image."

"My parlor psychologist," Betsy said.

In each of the sanctuaries, as they began to call the upper, middle rooms, carved scenes showed stick people kneeling in worship as that horror from the depths of the earth accepted a sacrifice.

"Why would they worship that thing?" Cindy asked.

"Because it is powerful, deadly, and mysterious," Stoner said.

"Some early people on Earth worshiped volcanoes," Betsy added, "because they were an elemental force beyond people's control and understanding."

"I'm glad my God doesn't look like that," Clay commented, remembering the dead-flesh look of the thing, its burning, tiny eyes.

Betsy looked thoughtful. "I think we'll find the answers to these early people and what was important to them when the archaeologists, anthropologists, and paleontologists begin their research. There are fossils on Earth; there are probably fossils and other clues here. We can learn something about these people in that way."

"Maybe," Rodrick said. To date the archaeologists, anthropologists, and paleontologists had turned up nothing, but they'd explored only a limited area in the two days of work on the planet. He knew that sooner or later Omega would reveal more of her secrets. His main job was to see to it that she didn't demand a price in human blood.

Juke, the entertainment robot, rolled into one of the big bays emptied by the removal of the quarters. It was now crowded with people who had been called back to the *Spirit* when the captain issued the red alert. Juke rolled around bedrolls and sleeping bags, family groups and pairs. A large viewscreen had been installed on one bulkhead, and a science-fiction thriller was being screened. The colonists hooted when an insectlike alien threatened the hero and heroine, cheered when the thing was zapped by the heroine.

"Down in front, Juke," someone yelled. Juke found a

spot against a bulkhead and watched the hero zap thousands of evil insect beings and win his reward, a quick kiss from the heroine and a fast ride into the sunset aboard his own rocketship.

A squad of volunteers entered the bay bearing large quantities of liquid fresh from the ship's stills and were cheered roundly. Mandy Miller, in her office, seeing the scene on her own viewscreen through Juke's sensors, turned to Duncan Rodrick and said, "They're taking it very well."

Back in the bay Juke rolled up to a family of four and said, "You know, I was built in a small town in the West."

"How small a town was it, Juke?" asked the boy of the family, with a sly wink at his sister to show that he knew he was playing straight man.

"It was so small," Juke said, "that our one heavy industry was a four-hundred-pound Amway distributor."

In Mandy's office Rodrick grinned and shook his head.

"I don't know where he gets them," Mandy said.

"Wherever it was, he should have left them there," Rodrick said. He'd stopped in Mandy's office to get the results of the ship's coroner's examination of the remains of Lynn Roberts. Mandy had told him that they weren't quite ready and offered him a drink. He had accepted, and now his glass was empty. The coroner had called to say that the report was being printed and would be delivered in five minutes.

"I haven't even spent a night on the surface yet," Mandy said, as they waited.

"We'll be back out there soon," Rodrick answered. "I just don't want to take any chances. I need to know what happened to the people who built that city."

"That concerns you more than that thing that lives underground, doesn't it?" she asked.

"The big worm doesn't show signs of great intelligence," Rodrick said. "True, it builds a nice trap, but the native wildlife seems to be wise to it. My concern there is just how many of those traps exist. I've got a team studying low-level aerial photos, and there's an astounding number of discolored areas. It's amazing that someone wasn't killed before poor Lynn. The spots are all around Hamilton and wherever there's grass for the silver-horns to graze."

"I talked briefly with Dr. Kwait earlier this evening," Mandy said. "He thinks one of the things can be trapped."

"I don't want to risk any personnel," Rodrick replied. "I'm going to use the admiral and Mopro tomorrow. We do need to get one of the things alive, if possible—dead if not. Then we'll know better what we're up against. I'm going down to see Grace Monroe when I leave here to discuss it with her."

Mandy reached for her drink to hide her moment of disappointment. It was comfortable sitting here and talking with Duncan. They never seemed to have any time to talk.

An enlisted crew member brought the coroner's report. There wasn't much information there that Rodrick didn't already know. The only new information was that the marrow had been very efficiently removed from the bones. Very tough tendons were still attached in a few places, but otherwise all flesh had been removed. He shared the report with Mandy. She shuddered as she read, and Rodrick had the desire to go around the desk, take her in his arms, and tell her that it would be all right.

He controlled his urge and stood. "Thanks for the drink."

She didn't want to be alone. Rocky was on duty on the bridge until midnight. "I've finished here. Mind if I tag along? I have been intending to see Grace all day." That last was a lie, but on the way down she'd think of something to ask Grace.

Three levels down, at the very core of the ship, Grace was about to be kissed. She had gone down to help Max Rosen in engineering as soon as she'd heard that all colonists were going to spend the night on the ship. She had a special dinner planned for two, and the sooner Max finished his work, the sooner he'd be able to come to her quarters.

Mainly, the problem was cooling and ventilating the large bays where the colonists were bedded down. She ran figures through the computer for Max, estimating the caloric heat output of sleeping bodies. Max fed the figures into the climate control center. The colonists never thought about the fact that the comfortable temperature and circulating fresh air didn't just happen naturally. It was also necessary to install temporary water fountains and deploy a great number of emergency chemical toilets.

Max supervised from his office and, everything finished, ran his fingers through his mussed hair and grinned. "You look like you need a drink," he said.

"I happen to have some premixed in my quarters," Grace said.

Max rose and held out his hands. She put her hands in his, and he pulled her to her feet. "I can't wait that long for this," he murmured, and his lips had just touched hers when the soft bong of the opening door jerked Max's head around to see Juke roll in.

"Excuse me, Grace," Juke said. "I just thought I'd better report that morale seems to be very good."

Max's face was contorted with pure agony. "Get out of here, Juke," he growled, while Grace was trying to swallow her laughter, her nice neck straining with the effort, her cheeks bulging. "This is getting to the point where it isn't funny, Grace," Max moaned.

"Well, if you have no further instructions for me, Grace," Juke said, "I will leave you with this thought: When fortune tellers serve instant tea, what do they read?"

Max reached for a heavy wrench and threw it to clang off the door as it closed rapidly behind Juke.

"I'm s-s-s-so—rry," Grace sputtered, making a great effort to stop giggling. She reached up and put her cool, smooth hands on his cheeks. It had been a long day. His beard was a sharp stubble on her palms. She drew his head down to hers, and her lips parted. The bong sounded, and Duncan Rodrick said, "Sorry, gang."

Max rolled his eyes and turned. Mandy Miller was looking at Grace with wide eyes. Grace winked and, unseen by the men, gave Mandy the thumb-and-finger circle for okay. Mandy smiled widely. Grace Monroe had chosen.

"I checked your quarters and lab, Grace," Rodrick said, "and figured you'd be down here. Your boys are the ones to get us one of those damned underground things. I know Mopro can fry the thing or blast it apart, but can Mopro and the admiral capture one alive?"

"Mopro isn't designed for grasping or holding things," she answered. "But he's very powerful. Given time I could give him new arms. And a tension spring across his back, I think—"

"I don't want to take that much time," Rodrick said. "I want the area to be safe so the scouts can go out looking for whoever built the city the McRaes found. We need the oil team drilling again. Amando wants to get some crops planted as quickly as possible."

"Let me say this," Grace mused. "I'd put the admiral in an arena with a full-grown rogue Bengal tiger with no concern for his safety. Also, he's lightning fast. He could easily stay out of the thing's way. With the right equipment, I think my boys can do the job."

"What will they need?" Rodrick asked.

"I'd say the best idea is the original one—the noose. If the admiral can get the noose around the outside of the creature's snout, Mopro's strong enough to pull it out of the hole. Then I guess it might be possible for the admiral to help guide it into some sort of a cage."

"I think I'll go out and talk it over with the admiral," he said. "Anyone care to come along?"

Rosen looked at Grace. "No, thanks. I'm off to find a private corner where I can kiss this woman without some robot busting in."

Grace laughed and pulled Max along, to go with the captain.

Rodrick looked at Mandy. "You might as well come along. You haven't had much fresh air since we've landed."

In the brief walk down to engineering and then outside, Duncan had found that it was more than pleasing to have Mandy by his side.

Omega's two moons were in one of their rare double-full phases, hanging just over the eastern mountains, casting a discernible double shadow. The admiral, forewarned, waited for them just outside the hatch. The air was summery and balmy, and salty with an ocean breeze. Grace clung to Max's arm and breathed deeply. Mopro's bulk was half-hidden in shadow. Mandy listened as Rodrick

talked with the admiral as if the robot were human, then
listened to the admiral's suggestions with respectful interest. The admiral seemed eager to tackle the job and suggested that he could rig a central noose secured four ways
to keep the beast anchored in one spot.

Grace said, "Stay out of its reach, Admiral."

"I will, Grace," he promised. "But I don't think the
thing could do me any harm, short of soiling my uniform."

"Stay out of its reach anyhow," Grace said.

Rodrick looked at the two moons. Interesting patterns
on the larger one. Full moons. Lovers' moons. He could
just catch a hint of Mandy's light perfume as she stood
beside him.

"I'll get back to my patrol, Captain," the admiral said.

"I've got a drink waiting," Max said. He took Grace's
hand, squeezed it. "Captain, how'd you like to perform a
marriage?"

"Right now?" Rodrick asked.

"This minute," Max said.

"Max is impetuous," Grace explained, grinning.

"Eden is a country of laws," Rodrick said, with mock
solemnity. "First you have to get the license."

"Damned red tape," Max growled.

"You can't rush it," Mandy said. "It's an important
event. You two are very well liked. Everyone will want to
come. You can't just say you're going to get married and
not make *plans*."

"Plans I got," Max said, his leer evident to Grace in
the bright moonlight.

"Max, take out the papers. Do the planning. When
we get things organized a bit, a big wedding will give us
our first holiday," Rodrick said.

"It'll give us something to celebrate," Mandy added.

Max grunted and led Grace toward the open hatch.
Mandy lingered for just a moment.

"We already have something to celebrate," Rodrick
said, wanting to hold her with him for just a little longer.
"Did you get the report that Stoner found a piece of metal
today?"

"Yes, isn't it wonderful?"

"You two coming?" Grace called from the hatch.

"In a minute," Mandy called back.

The admiral and Mopro disappeared around the curve of the ship's hull.

"It's so beautiful," Mandy said, sighing, lifting her face to the moons. Her head-high pose accentuated her mature breasts. With a sound that was almost a moan Rodrick moved quickly to take her in his arms, and in their mutual hunger and haste her teeth bumped his lip, hard, before their lips found each other. The kiss lasted only seconds before sanity came to them at the same instant. The parting was as mutual as the coming together, and neither of them could speak. Mandy started walking toward the hatch at the same instant Rodrick took a step. Such a short kiss, and so overwhelmingly complete. Such a short kiss, but long enough for Rocky Miller to reach a conclusion.

Rocky had been notified at his post on the bridge that Rodrick was going out the main hatch. He'd noted the light on the panel when the hatch was opened and then, idly, for lack of something better to do on a boring watch, he clicked on the ship's night eyes and was interested to find that the captain was not alone. His eyes narrowed when he recognized his wife. He heard the sappy talk about marriage from the bear, Max Rosen, and was about to turn the night eyes off when Rosen and Grace Monroe went back into the hatch and left Rodrick alone with his loving wife.

He wasn't even surprised by the kiss. He thought, *Well, so that's it.* He should have known it all along, the way Mandy had been acting. He regretted that he hadn't activated the cameras. It would have been nice to have some solid evidence when the time was right, but he'd probably have other chances to get that.

In the two and a half years of the *Spirit of America* voyage, he'd had time to talk with key colonists. Many were people of faith, all of them family people. Even the unmarried ones were family oriented. Good people, all. If push came to shove, they'd be on his side when they found out that from the very beginning the great Captain Duncan Rodrick had been screwing his first-officer's wife.

SEVEN

When one hundred rockets fired simultaneously, it was as if the *Karl Marx* had been struck by a giant fist. Theresita's body was slammed backward into the acceleration couch. For a few minutes it was difficult to breathe. A wisp of her hair fell over one eye, and she had to struggle to lift one hand to brush it away. Her arm had become a mass eight times its own weight.

There would be other retro-firings. The ship would be slowed, then steered into a long curve, which would eventually reverse her direction and send her back toward Earth.

"All personnel," the captain's voice said. "You will have only ten minutes before the next retro-firing. Please do not venture far from your assigned place."

Theresita, feeling a furious helplessness, got up and paced the floor. To her surprise a soft bell announced that she had a caller. It was Fedor Novikov.

"We have only a moment," he said. "I come because of our common loyalty to our great leader. Before we fired the rockets, I contacted ground control." He removed his cap and ran his fingers through his thick hair. Even in the climate-controlled atmosphere of the ship, his hair was damp with perspiration. "They would give me no explanation about our change in orders. I was told to keep radio

89

silence. All broadcasting stations in the Soviet Union have now gone off the air."

"Perhaps the bombs are falling already. . . ." she said.

"No. The Americans are still broadcasting. They have ordered total mobilization." He made a futile motion with hands. "If there is further information, I will share it with you."

"Fedor," she said, as he started to turn. "You don't want to go back."

"What I want personally is not the point," he answered. "I am a soldier of the Soviet Union, and I have my orders."

"If the bombs fall, there will be no Soviet Union," she said softly. She could sympathize with Novikov; she knew his type well. He had been trained from childhood to obey. The Red Army had been his life since he was twelve years old. Yet she could sense a reluctance in him. He knew as well as she that taking the ship back to participate in a nuclear war was a waste.

"Fedor," she asked, "how many missiles would it take for the Americans to destroy the *Karl Marx*?"

"One direct hit at the hub of the wheel," he said. "We'd be dead in space, our weapons systems useless, air leaking into space."

He was searching desperately for a way out.

"If I, as a marshal of the Soviet Union, give you a direct order, will you obey?"

He looked at her with dead eyes. "You know as well as I that on board this ship I am the ranking officer."

"Then what do you want?" she demanded. "My blessings in this madness? If you're asking me to agree that we should take this great ship, with one thousand men, women, and children, to her death, you will not have it."

He stiffened. "Women have never understood honor," he said.

She spat. "Honor! Honor, the way men see it, will be in the finger that pushes the button to send the bombs rocketing down from the space stations. Where will your honor be when the last child dies of radiation sickness? Will it be with the Americans aboard the *Spirit of America* when they return from space to find a sterile world? The entire universe will be *theirs*, then, Fedor. Theirs and their children's, and their children's children, and a thousand years from now those Americans who own all of space will remember the Soviet Union as the country that started the last war, the war that killed our planet. Is there honor in that?"

"There is nothing I can do," he said miserably. Then he left.

Nor was there anything she could do; she was only one woman—it was not her fault that the ship was turning back. It was not until after the next course correction, which lasted five minutes, that she felt the cold anger build up. She had been wrong to blame Novikov. There *was* something she could do.

Her bell announced another caller. She was suddenly very popular. This time it was Anton Emin, a bear of a man who was a heavy-construction expert. He was in his mid-thirties. She knew him from several conversations in the lounges and had shared a drink with him and his sturdy, smiling wife. Ordinarily, his eyes showed laugh crinkles. Now his face was grim.

Behind Emin, to her surprise, was reedy, frail-looking Ilya Salkov, a young lieutenant in the engineering section. And Pavel Simonov, a crusty, grim-faced electronics engineer.

There was no room for all three of her visitors to sit. Theresita stood, too, leaning against one arm of the couch. It was Anton Emin who spoke first. "Ilya has told us that we are going back to Earth."

She nodded.

"We have come to you, Comrade Marshal, to ask you to tell us why." His effort to be officiously respectful of her rank only seemed to emphasize his size and strength.

She kept her face expressionless from long habit. In the Kremlin, one never displayed one's personal feelings. It took her perhaps three seconds to decide what she was going to say.

"All Soviet broadcasting stations are silent. The ship has orders to go into position to attack the American missile-launching space stations." She gave them the news bluntly, forcefully, throwing it into their faces as a challenge. If they were merely curious, that would be the end of it.

"I feared as much," Lieutenant Salkov said, his thin face going pale. He looked toward Anton Emin, who, obviously, had been selected as the spokesman.

"Comrade Marshal," Emin said, "sometimes I have felt that you are not like the others." His face went red. He was Russian, not accustomed to talking openly. Treason was serious.

"Am I different because the *others* are male?" she asked, not willing to make it easier for him. If anything was to be done, it would take great bravery to do it.

"Damn, Anton," Pavel Simonov said forcefully. "Speak. We are dead either way." After this outburst he glared at Theresita, but his face was pale, too. He swallowed. "Comrade Marshal, we must stop the captain from going back."

"The three of you?" she asked.

"There are others," Emin said, regaining his courage. "And we hope that you will join us. Perhaps if you spoke with the captain—"

Make up your mind, she was thinking. *Are you willing to do something, or do you just want me to stick my neck out?* Aloud she said, "Ah. Four of us. And others. What others? The crew is a well-trained military unit. The security forces are well armed." She let contempt come into her voice, for she knew that talk was cheap. Before she joined, or led, any incipient mutiny, she had to know it would have some chance of success.

"Only security is armed," Salkov said. "Many of them would not fight against comrades. They, too, have husbands or wives and children aboard."

"Going back is useless," Pavel Simonov growled. "By doing so, we abandon the future and all of space, leaving both to the Americans and the Brazilians."

"Did these splendid ideas come to you just now?" she asked.

"No, comrade," Emin answered. "My ideas did not come to me suddenly. From the beginning there have been those among us who were determined that things were going to be different on a new world."

"Ah," she said. But she was thinking, *Perhaps they are men.* "There has never been a successful resistance in the Soviet Union. We, those in power, have had the guns, the personnel. Those who have power and influence will keep them. The officers of this ship would kill all of us to keep their positions, even in the face of a nuclear war. Party Commissar Boris Bely always carries an automatic pistol, which shoots soft-tipped bullets at a great muzzle velocity. He has only to hit a man in the arm or leg to kill him. Do you think *he* will relinquish power easily? The officers and crew have sworn oaths to obey orders. The security people are almost all KGB, trained to kill."

"Then you are not with us," Pavel Simonov said. "Can we at least have your neutrality? We would dislike having to hold you incommunicado or to harm you."

"You? Harm me?" She laughed. "Step back, you two. Pavel Simonov, you stand here."

Puzzled, they obeyed.

"Now, Pavel," she continued, "I want you to harm me."

Pavel laughed uneasily.

"I want you to hit me," she insisted. He made a feeble motion toward her face with one hand, which she avoided easily, hitting him in the stomach as she twisted away with her right foot, just hard enough to bend him double.

"So you are going to take over the ship?" she asked.

"Damn you," Pavel said, panting. "I won't hit a woman."

"There are women in the security force," she said. "And I assure you that they are just as deadly as the men." She leaned close, thrusting her face into Pavel's. "Can you kill a woman to save your life, and the life of the ship?"

"We won't have to kill them," Pavel said. "Ilya and I will break into the armory. We will use stun guns."

"Stupid, stupid, stupid," Theresita said. "If you start this thing, you had better be prepared to finish it, to kill. You had better be prepared to kill the security force, because if you try to stand up to them, they will take a terrible toll. You will have to kill the captain and Boris

Bely and many others. If you leave them alive, they will kill you without hesitation."

Emin's face was white. "If that is what we must do, we will kill them."

She sighed, sat down. "Tell me about the others you mentioned."

Yes, treason came hard—even to a Pole. She listened, spoke, doubted, hoped. It would be untrained idealists—a few of the scientists, another young engineering officer, and one woman marshal—against men and women trained to kill. But she remembered Pavel Simonov's words: "We are dead either way."

If she had to die, she preferred to die trying. She had no desire to die in her quarters, gasping for breath, after the *Karl Marx* was holed by an American missile.

If there were to be any chance of successful mutiny, it would have to be done quickly, before the ship complied with orders and became yet another weapon in the Soviet arsenal. Theresita's first step was to confer privately with the young engineering officer, Ilya Salkov. He had assured her that he was expert enough to operate the Shaw Drive, with some assistance from knowledgeable scientists.

She had to assume that the crew would be loyal to Captain Novikov, and so she had to be sure that there'd be enough skilled manpower left after the necessary killings to navigate, operate the computers, rockets, the Drive, all the complicated multiplicity of systems that made up the ship. Most of the scientists who had designed and built the *Karl Marx* were aboard, and she was assured that the ship could continue to function without any of her crew.

The security force would be the greatest danger. Personnel would be on duty at assigned posts throughout the ship, and there were, at all times, two-person security teams roving at random.

In organizing her strike forces, she assigned the engineering areas to Lieutenant Salkov, since he was the one most familiar with that part of the ship, and he had hopes of convincing at least two of the engineering junior officers to join him.

Theresita felt that she would need to be in a dozen places at once, which was impossible, of course. Her most important point of attack was the bridge, where duty and honor would force Captain Novikov to resist if he had half a chance. She had the feeling that Fedor Novikov had almost invited her to take over the ship, and she was sure in her own mind that, given an out with which his precious honor could live, the captain would be useful alive. His knowledge and his leadership ability would be great losses.

During a sleepless twenty-four hour period she selected her strike teams, gave them brief instructions in the handling of weapons, and told them over and over, "Do not hesitate, comrades. To succeed, you must be totally merciless. No pity. No warning. No hesitation."

Only in engineering would two officers be given a choice, and only because Lieutenant Salkov assured her that he *knew* the two men, *knew* they would elect to join the mutiny and send the ship outward toward the stars and her rightful destiny.

When Theresita and two others accompanied Ilya into a restricted area to perform the first overt act of insurrection against the government she had sworn to uphold and defend, she actually felt ill. A lifetime of training told her, "Fool! You are wrong!"

There were always two security guards on duty at the armory. Theresita knew them by name. They were young, sunny Russian lads who, while on duty, were all business.

She left her team behind, hidden by the bend of a corridor, and approached the guard post. Her weapon, a small but deadly automatic, was in her skirt pocket. The two young men snapped to attention as she said good morning.

"Good morning, Comrade Marshal," said the ranking man. "Are you lost?"

They were not at full alert, she saw, but they were suspicious because the armory was in a deliberately isolated part of the ship near the engineering areas. One didn't just happen to pass by the armory; one had to be headed for the armory to get there.

She continued to walk toward them, and just as she

was near enough to be sure that her tiny weapon would be effective, the ranking man put one hand on his weapon and said, "What can we do for the marshal?"

She smiled. Both men were now very alert. Neither, however, had unslung his weapon. Theresita's hand moved as fast as she could make it move, and even then she almost muffed it because, as she saw the handsome young eyes widen in surprise, she hesitated. The corporal, the second to die, had his weapon off his shoulder and was swinging it around when, after the quick burst of the first shot and the instant death of the first man, she aimed the weapon at his forehead.

"No," he whispered, even as her weapon flashed.

She had killed before. Once, as a young Red Army major, she had led the eradication of a group of two thousand Italian nationalists who, unarmed, had foolishly gathered in secret to plot rebellion. There had been women and children there. Killing the very young ones had bothered her a bit, but nothing in her career, with the possible exception of having to kill Yuri, affected her as did the last, pleading word of that young guard. The word was still ringing in her ears when Lieutenant Salkov dashed down the corridor and burned open the door of the armory with a torch.

Inside she chose for herself one of the same death-spraying automatic rifles that she had used so long ago to slaughter the Italian nationalists.

She was committed now—she'd killed two of her own.

She paused for one look at the young soldiers who lay in their own blood outside the armory door. She shook her head. *So*, she was thinking wryly, to hide the real pain, *after all these years I find that I am not a good communist*.

Such a thought. Such a time to think it as she dashed down the metal corridors, intent on delivering more death. So she had ceased to be a good communist loyal to the party and the Soviet Union, but had she betrayed the communist philosophy? No. Because she had killed and would kill, regardless of number, for the greater good of the survivors on board the *Karl Marx*. Death of the individual was justified by the greater good of the survivors.

The great Lenin himself had taught that it was proper for millions to die to ensure better conditions for the survivors.

Salkov and the others were behind her, with electric carts laden with weapons.

"Go, go, go," she urgently whispered to them as she let them pass.

She had selected the crusty electronics engineer, Pavel Simonov, to be her accomplice on the bridge. He was waiting at the appointed place. Two by two, the teams were hurrying to their appointed places. The hour had been carefully chosen, based on the ship's routine. The late-night watch would be handing over the bridge to the captain's watch, and thus a double crew of officers would be congregated in one small killing area. The commissar Boris Bely would also be there. Bely affected an officer's uniform without insignia of rank and wore a weapon at his side.

She forced herself to walk calmly beside Simonov. "Once more," she said. "What is the first thing you do?"

"I kill the commissar."

"And then?"

"I start to my right and begin to kill the others as quickly as I can move the muzzle of the weapon."

"And the captain?"

"I leave him to you."

"Are you all right?" she asked, for his face was pale, and he was perspiring.

"I am not accustomed to this. I will do my job."

"Good."

They had arrived. She halted at the door, took a deep breath, pressed the button. The door was locked, of course.

A voice came from the speaker in the door. "Identity and purpose?"

"Marshal Pulaski requests permission to enter the bridge for observation and a cup of the captain's coffee." Her voice was calm, very friendly. The door clicked. She nodded to Simonov and kicked the door open. They rushed through the hatch together.

There were thirteen people on the bridge: the captain, the commissar, and eleven officers. She held a stun gun in her left hand, her automatic rifle in her right. The stun gun was for the captain. She would put him out of action, and harm's way, while Simonov's fire caused a moment of delay on the part of the others.

Captain Novikov was standing in front of the complex control console. The third officer, who was being relieved of the duty, was in the act of rising from the command seat.

Success depended on exact timing, on instant action. Even as she used that fraction of a second required to aim the stun gun at Novikov she knew that it was going wrong, because Simonov's rifle had not yet spoken. It did not surprise her to see that Boris Bely was the first to react. The commissar made a dive for the floor, reaching for his weapon at the same time. When Simonov's weapon began to chatter quietly, it was too late. She discarded the stun gun, and as the officers recovered from their surprise and began to react, death sprayed the bridge, starting from right and left and coming toward the center with men and women being flung backward by the force of the high-velocity bullets.

That familiar thudding, whining sound of a projectile passing close by her ear was followed by a small explosion on the hatch behind her. Pavel Simonov had not done his job: He was not moving swiftly enough; he was overkilling, leaving some of his assigned targets free to bring their weapons into action. Another round clipped a piece from the shoulder of Theresita's uniform.

Fedor Novikov—she'd deliberately lifted her finger from the trigger of her automatic rifle as she'd swept the muzzle past him—was reacting very slowly. The fire was coming from her right. Where was Boris Bely?

What was wrong with Pavel Simonov?

An explosive round missed her, angling upward to blast against the bulkhead near the ceiling. The captain had leaped for cover behind the command chair. Men and women were down, killed instantly or dying. It had all happened in split seconds. Flesh had been mangled, had blossomed with the impact of the deadly, explosive bullets. And Pavel Simonov was dead, falling even as Theresita began to search desperately for Boris Bely.

It was suddenly quiet.

"Fedor," she said, "I don't want to have to kill you. Throw out your weapon."

A movement to her right triggered her survival instincts, and she fell, rolling, using Simonov's body for cover, sending a burst of fire toward the origin of the shot that had almost killed her. She caught a glimpse of Boris Bely's frightened face as he ducked into the communications room.

"Your weapon, Fedor," she said.

"I cannot," he answered, his voice sad, dull.

"Fedor, come with us to the stars," she implored. "The stars. Come with us. You know as well as I that it means death for all if we go back to Earth. Throw out your weapon. Be with us. Be our leader."

"I am going to stand up, Comrade Pulaski," Novikov said.

His head showed, then he was erect. She got to her feet carefully, holding her weapon at the ready, for his sidearm was still in his hand, muzzle down. He looked around with stunned eyes. "All of them? Did you have to kill all of them?"

"It was necessary," she replied.

"But you have lost, comrade," Novikov said.

"Will you join us? Will you be our leader?"

"You forget that we are a suspicious and cautious race, comrade," he said, and there was a great sadness in his voice. "You have lost." He was looking toward the communications room. She jerked her head for a quick look at the closed door.

"Tell me quickly what you mean." Her urgency left no doubt in Novikov's mind that he had to speak, and speak quickly.

"Surely, as a marshal of the Red Army, you must know that all sensitive installations, and all such weapons of war as our nuclear submarines and space stations have self-destruct capability to prevent them from falling into the hands of the enemy."

She felt faint for a tiny moment.

"Boris Bely has his finger on the button." He slowly put his sidearm into its holster, then ran a hand over his lined face. "I'm sure, knowing you, that your mutiny was efficient and prepared and that the ship is now in your hands. But with Bely in the communications room, it was all for nothing."

"Why didn't you warn me?" she grated. "You invited me to take over the ship. You didn't have the courage to say it openly or to disobey your precious orders, but you were hoping that I'd do exactly what I've done."

He sat down weakly in the command chair. "But I thought you were different. I thought you would have the leadership and the inspiration to do it without . . . this." He looked around the blood-splattered bridge, then shrugged. "Well, no matter," he said loudly into the transmitter, so Bely could hear inside the locked communications room. "You have only two choices now: You can lay down your arms, and we will then obey our orders and go back to join our countrymen in their fight." He looked toward the closed door and called out: "Would you care to state her other choice, Comrade Bely?"

Bely's voice was tense, pitched high. It came to her from the speakers of the communications system. "The second choice is total destruction of the ship and everyone on it," Bely said. "Give the captain your weapon, traitor."

Theresita knew that Bely was not bluffing. She knew his type. He would be totally loyal, to the point of fanaticism.

"All I have to do," Bely continued, "is move one finger. Small charges will detonate the rocket fuel, causing explosive decompression throughout the ship. You will not be alive when the nuclear warheads detonate. You must call upon your fellow criminals to lay down their arms."

Theresita had made her decision instantly, but she pretended to be indecisive for a few moments before speaking. With a sigh, she bent and put her rifle on the deck. "There is nothing else I can do," she said. "I cannot, however, reach all of my force by ship's communicator. To prevent an early alarm, many areas of the ship have been isolated. I have laid down my weapon. I will go to them and explain the situation. They will obey me."

The captain moved, somewhat reluctantly, to pick up the rifle. As he straightened, his eyes met hers, and in his there was regret. At that moment she hated him. He didn't want to go back. But he didn't have the courage to do what was right.

"Let her go to talk to the other traitors," Bely said, his voice more confident now.

She found that a few, like Pavel Simonov, had died from indecision and hesitation. But the ship was in her hands. The security forces had been eliminated, along with most of the crew. And Ilya Salkov had been correct in thinking that he would find sympathizers in the engineering section—he had five young officers with him when she found him making his way toward the bridge.

"We have won, Comrade Marshal," Salkov said, but there was no joy in his voice. He had blood that was not his own on his tunic.

"Not yet," she said. "Is there, in the ship's armory, a Zhukov?"

Salkov's eyes widened, but he did not question her. "Yes, of course."

"Quickly, then," she said. Salkov departed on the run. She examined the pale, strained faces of the five young officers. "You choose to go with us to the stars?"

"Yes, Comrade Marshal," one said. The others nodded.

"Damage in the engineering section?"

"Nothing serious. The ship is fully operational."

"Who of you is familiar with the communications room?" she asked.

"I, Comrade Marshal," said a young lieutenant with a small cut on his cheek. "I am assigned to electronic maintenance." He was young, not over twenty-one.

"Tell me the effect on the ship following total destruction of the interior of the communications room."

He thought for a moment. "We would, of course, be cut off from all communications with the Earth. We would have to rewire and improvise an in-ship system, using an alternate power supply. If the destruction is confined to the communications room, none of the vital functions of the ship will be affected."

Ilya Salkov came pounding up the corridor, the deadly Zhukov slung on his shoulder. The weapon had been named for one of Russia's great military heroes of the mid twentieth century. She took it, and a set of earplugs, from Salkov. She was quite familiar with it—she'd used it against British-built tanks in Kenya. It was a sweetheart of a weapon, no heavier than a standard assault rifle, and it fired a rocket-propelled, shaped charge, which could pierce the heaviest armor and devastate a confined area. And Bely had himself locked in a room with a door that was metal, an inch and a half thick, counting a hollow core.

If the junior officers knew of the ship's self-destruct system, they gave no indication of it, and she had no intention of telling them. She was going to take an enormous chance: She had no way of knowing whether or not the destruction of the communications room would automatically set off the charges of the destruction system.

She had gone too far to stop now and allow the captain and Bely to take the ship back to engage in a mutually destructive war.

She pushed the button to the door to the bridge. "Pulaski," she said. "It is arranged."

She heard the door click, and for the second time within minutes she burst through.

Seconds later the Zhukov made a hissing roar. There was an instant smell of burning rocket fuel. The small projectile easily pierced the metal of the communications-room door. The door hurled toward her, almost intact, on the wings of a booming explosion and slammed into Captain Fedor Novikov, crushing him against the unyielding bulkhead. For a moment Theresita couldn't hear, although she'd protected her ears with the plugs. But there were no titanic, rending, destroying explosions from the fuel storage areas.

She let the spent Zhukov fall to the deck. It clattered in the silence. She walked to Novikov's crushed body. His face was untouched.

Anton Emin was standing in the door when she turned. Denis and Vera Ivanov, members of the ship's medical staff, had arrived with him. Vera, a small, dark woman, began to make the rounds of the dead bodies, kneeling beside some, shaking her head.

"I want you to remember this," Theresita said. "I want you to look around and mark it well. Perhaps some of them would have chosen to be with us, but for the good of all, we could not risk giving them that opportunity. Just remember that we have purchased our chance to live, and to reach the stars, with the lives of others. Remember that we have a solemn responsibility to those who had to die.

"We must never forget. And we must so construct our new world that such needless waste will never be necessary again."

EIGHT

The admiral and Mopro, robots that needed no sleep, made their preparations during the next night. Grace Monroe and Max Rosen, who did need sleep, quickly had their dinner and went to Grace's lab—they were both of a kind to put business before pleasure.

Max appropriated a pipeline-cleaning apparatus from the petroleum engineers. The bullet-shaped machine was designed to travel under its own power inside a pipeline, and its cleaning brushes could be adjusted to pipes of different diameters. Grace and Max removed the drive for the cleaning brushes and inserted into the nose of the machine a powerful light and two minicameras. They had a bit of a challenge adapting the machine control system to remote, so it was after eleven o'clock before they were satisfied. The pipeline cleaner was now a remote-control camera on wheels that could be lowered into a hole to record an underground creature's whereabouts and behavior.

Mopro had self-mounted his most effective tracks, larger than those he normally used, then had worked with the admiral to weld sharp, long spikes to the tracks. With Mopro's considerable weight bearing down on the tracks, the spikes would dig deeply into the ground, giving the big TR5-A robot enough traction to win a tug-of-war with a front-line war tank. He was ready to haul the creature out of the hole.

Stoner McRae stayed up late, too. The capture attempt had been scheduled so he and the captain would be present. He knew that the admiral and Mopro were readying their equipment in a bay out near the scout pods, and when he had completed his own preparations, he made his way there. He was followed by a small, big-wheeled, self-propelled machine, which obeyed a remote that he carried in his right hand. He found Max and Grace with the two robots.

"This is a mobile signal generator," Stoner said. "We use it to measure underground formations. It's effective down to a couple of hundred feet. I made a few adjustments so it'll give us a definite echo if the signal hits a burrow."

"That'll be useful," Grace said. "We need to know as much as possible about those creatures before the boys try to lasso and hog-tie one of them."

Max explained the camera apparatus, and the admiral showed off his four-way snare. The humans decided to get some sleep while the admiral and Mopro loaded the equipment on an all-terrain cargo carrier and spent the early morning hours locating a nearby herd of silver-horns. The admiral used a stun gun to capture a young buck, and then they were ready. It was well before dawn.

Duncan Rodrick found himself very popular that early morning. His breakfast was a series of interruptions as dozens of people volunteered to join the hunt for the underground killer. But Rodrick had already chosen the capture crew on the previous evening, so they would be ready. Paul Warden had been named to prepare a heavily armed security squad.

Paul and four others in protective armor reported to the cargo crawler soon after dawn, and Paul blushed with pleasure when the camera crew joined the cargo carrier in their own small all-terrain vehicle, for the crew was headed by Sage Bryson. He went over and grinned up at her.

"Glad to have you with us," he said.

"Thank you," Sage said coldly.

She was still smoldering from an incident that had occurred the previous night. She had put in her bid early to be part of the day's effort and had waited until past nine o'clock before learning that a man with far less experience in recording important events had been chosen for the camera crew. She had accosted Duncan Rodrick in a corridor, fortunately finding him alone.

"Captain, I'd like to ask you to reconsider your assignments for the recording crew," she had said politely.

Rodrick knew Sage only slightly. Whenever she took her turn at the captain's table she was always withdrawn and polite.

"Many people volunteered," he said. "We can't have everybody out there."

Sage seemed to draw herself up to stand taller. "Did you find something lacking in my qualifications?" Like everyone aboard, she had skills in more than one field. She was very good at holographic recording and not only could explain the workings of the complicated equipment, but could repair any malfunction.

"No, no," Rodrick said quickly. "You are highly qualified."

"I can only assume, then, that you chose a lesser qualified *man* for reasons of my sex."

He was silent for a moment. "It's going to be dangerous out there," he said. "And if we succeed, we're going to have to haul this thing—whose strength we can only guess—into a capture cage. I chose the team for strength."

"That, sir, is a sexist attitude," Sage replied, her face red with anger. "As it happens, I can bench press ten pounds more than the man you picked for a job for which I'm more qualified. Please expect a protest to be filed immediately."

She turned to walk away. Rodrick's face was dark. "Ms. Bryson," he said, his voice no longer friendly.

She halted and turned to face him.

"I don't take kindly to threats. Do what you feel that you have to do, and I will do the same. I will assign my people as I decide without any unsolicited advice and—"

He was interrupted by his communicator.

"Captain," Rocky Miller said, "there's been a small accident, nothing serious. The man you assigned to direct the camera crew took a fall off the cargo carrier. The medical people want to check him out."

"Thank you, Mr. Miller." Rodrick spoke into his communicator. He looked at Sage sternly. "What I said still goes, Ms. Bryson. Now, if you're still eager to be on this operation, I suggest that you report immediately to Commander Warden."

"*Thank* you, *sir*," Sage spit out.

She was still steaming about being second choice when Paul Warden came over to greet her.

"Sage," Paul said, "I want you to keep the camera crew well back. Use your long lens."

"I don't need to be told my job," Sage said.

Paul flushed. "I don't want anyone endangered." His voice hardened. He loved the girl, but this was service business. "You will set up your cameras no closer than one hundred feet from the snare site, and you will not come closer under any circumstances." He turned without waiting for an answer.

Sage's face was white with her anger. She was afraid that she was going to burst into bitter tears, and that possibility angered her still further. To think that that no-neck man really believed that she would choose him made her slightly ill. He was just like all the others, the men who had slobbered after her ever since her hormones had dictated early bodily development and nature had refined her face into the kind that made beauty-pageant judges rave. During high school and college she had believed that it was triumph to parade her body in the latest, scantiest bathing suit before crowds of gaping men.

She had her aunt Martha to thank for her enlightenment. Her father's sister had devoted all her time and talents to becoming one of the most celebrated writers in the United States. "They're exploiting you, Sage," Aunt Martha had told her in that cool, logical, loving voice. "You're prime meat on display."

She had been so naive then. "I don't think so, Aunt Martha," she'd protested. "They judge talent heavily, and poise, and the ability to converse intelligently."

"A talking robot can converse intelligently," Martha had said.

"But I have a chance at a movie contract—"

"Great," Martha had responded bitterly. "Then they

can display your fine tits and sweet little ass all over the world. Sage, you're more than bosom and butt. You graduated at the head of your class. You were offered full scholarships to six schools. You can be anything you want to be. You can make a contribution to this messed up world."

When she was nearly raped by the director of her first picture, a picture she refused to finish, she began to realize her aunt's wisdom. She gave up her movie contract, entered the Massachusetts Institute of Technology on a scholarship, and completed a four-year degree in just under two years, her master's in another year, her Ph.D. in record time—all while publishing articles in scientific magazines and winning class honors by holding the only perfect marks ever recorded at the school.

She had been looking for new fields to conquer when she'd been approached by a representative to Presidential Scientific Adviser Oscar Kost. She had come very close to turning down the chance because of that unwritten but understood requirement to marry and bear children. But she had signed on anyway because the voyage would be an uncertain, possibly dangerous adventure. She fully expected that there would be casualties on a new world. Those casualties would be mostly male since men fancied themselves to be the only ones capable of facing critical situations, leaving her, by choice, an odd woman out of the mating game.

But to date, casualties had been almost equally divided as to sex.

Furthermore, the endless months of being cooped up on the ship with not only the single men lolling their tongues at her but a few of the married ones as well had made her question her decision to accompany the *Spirit* into space.

Duncan Rodrick had decided that it would be safe to allow the colonists off ship during the day, so now there was a sizable crowd to watch the two-vehicle expedition leave the ship.

One of the well-wishers was Tina Sells, who had celebrated her sixteenth birthday only two weeks before the *Spirit of America* had landed on Omega. Tina, the daughter of Tony and Trisha Sells, building engineer and architect respectively, thought that Dr. Grace Monroe was the most beautiful and the most intelligent woman she had ever known. She'd spent a lot of time with Grace during the outward voyage and had become fascinated with Grace's robots and the amazing skill and breakthrough knowledge that it had taken to construct them. Since she had shown not only interest but a certain talent, Grace had encouraged her. Tina was, Grace felt, especially receptive to the admiral, so at Grace's suggestion Tina, in addition to her regular schooling, had become a private student of the admiral's in computer science.

When Grace came out of the ship Tina joined her and said, "I wish I could go along."

"You can watch on the screens," Grace suggested.

"You'll be careful, won't you?" Tina asked.

Grace smiled and kissed the pretty little girl on the cheek. She was so lovely, a youthful flower with exceptional promise both in beauty and ability. "I'll be *very* careful."

Grace watched with a fond smile as Tina approached the admiral and Mopro. The admiral smiled at her, standing straight and tall and handsome.

"I think you're so brave to go after that horrible thing," Tina said.

"No problem," the admiral replied confidently. He was, after all, only four and a half years old. He had matured during the voyage, true, but for the first time in his short life he was the very center of attention for many people.

"I don't want you to get hurt," she said.

"I won't. I promise," the admiral said. He grinned and reached up to pat Mopro on his armored head. "My little buddy will take care of me."

"You do that, Mopro," Tina said.

Mopro displayed his answer on a moving band across the upper part of his massive head. "We shall overcome."

Stoner, standing near enough to hear the exchange and see Mopro's answer, wondered if Grace had programmed a sense of humor into all of her robots.

When everyone was aboard, the vehicles moved out. The expedition didn't have to go more than a few hundred feet from the outskirts of Hamilton to begin to learn some disturbing facts about the underground monsters. Stoner deployed the mobile signal generator, and the echoes that bounced back from below the surface showed that the area was literally honeycombed with burrows of four to five feet in diameter. The depths at which the burrows had been dug varied considerably, from five to ten feet below ground near the surface traps constructed by the beasts to an almost uniform fifty feet for long traverse burrows. Stoner soon began to think of them as tunnels because they were so perfectly constructed, as round as a pipe, as straight as if lasered in places.

But the most astounding thing didn't show up on Stoner's small screen for a while: A tunnel he'd been following with the signal generator suddenly sloped downward from fifty feet to over two hundred feet, out of the range of the generated signals.

"Those things would make great miners," he told Grace wonderingly as she watched the image of the tunnel fade into nothing on the screen.

Warden was disturbed by the extent of the tunnels. Some went directly toward Hamilton and, presumably, under the town. There was nothing to prevent the monsters from surfacing in a street to nab some unsuspecting victim. He relayed that information to Duncan Rodrick, on control.

"They tunnel through solid rock?" Rodrick asked.

"As if it were butter," Warden said.

Rodrick asked Emi Zuki to project the pictures he had taken with his scout ship's cameras near the dead city onto the screen. He stopped at the frame with the monster's neck and head at its greatest extension, then asked Emi for enhancement of the picture to a larger size.

Rocky Miller was acting as communicator for the four scout ships assigned to fly cover for the hunters.

"Rock, what do you think?" Rodrick asked. "How does that thing cut perfectly circular tunnels through solid stone?"

So he's calling me Rock, now, Miller was thinking.

He put his emotions aside and examined the enlarged head and neck. "Not with those teeth it's showing," he said.

"No," Rodrick said. "Funny teeth. Sharp and curved backward near the front, blunt and heavy near the back."

"Let's see it with the mouth closed," Miller suggested. Emi complied.

"Looks like the business end of an auger drill," Rodrick said.

"Those toothlike protrusions on the outside of the snout are very much like the serrations on a drill head," Miller agreed. "But what's that line just about three feet back from the snout, the sort of fold that goes all the way around the neck?"

"Good question," Rodrick said. "And there are two openings of some kind just aft of that line."

"Well, we'll know soon enough," Miller said.

"Let's hope so. If that thing starts boring, or drilling, it would make noise."

"I see what you're getting at," Miller said. "Want me to give orders to implant listening devices around the ship and the town?"

"Please," Rodrick said. "I don't like the thought of one of those things surfacing in the midst of a work crew."

Jackie Garvey took Miller's place as scout communicator. She replied to the captain's pleasantries in a crisp, formal voice, using as few words as possible.

An alert came not five minutes after the first listening devices had been put into place, their long probes extending down into the ground. Rodrick amplified the sound on the speakers. Coming from a tunnel angling toward the edge of Hamilton from the east, it was faint at first, and the computer said it was originating at a distance of just under a mile from the listening post. The sound was in two rhythmic pulses. It sounded as if something dry and hard was being scraped against a corrugated surface. It grew gradually louder, approaching the town. A crawler was positioned directly above the origin of the sound. It was moving steadily at a rate just under five miles per hour through a section of tunnel fifty feet below ground level.

Rodrick relayed this new information to Paul Warden, who positioned his armed squad. Mopro used his laser to sink holes for four strong steel stakes to which he and the admiral attached their capture harness.

The high tensile cables used were capable of supporting ten tons of weight. On each cable was strung a motorized, in-line winch. Once the snare had been secured around the neck of the beast, the synchronized winches would tighten, under the admiral's control, and the band of almost indestructible flexisteel used as a noose would close tightly, hopefully to snag behind the toothlike projections on the thing's head. By tightening the two cables on one side and giving slack at the same time to the other two through use of the in-line winches, the beast would be pulled from its burrow.

Grace Monroe's heart went out to the frightened, bleating silver-horned antelope used as bait. But she also felt pity for the underground creature, which was only satisfying its need for nourishment. The Americans had seen just its head and neck, and there was bound to be a sizable body attached, with a constant need for food.

What might it eat? The signs pointed to dirt and flesh. An unlikely combination, but this was, after all, an alien planet, and even some burrowing worms on Earth took nourishment from the soil.

Max had jury-rigged a camera onto a pipeline crawler that could be driven down into the creature's tunnel, so they could watch for the beast's approach. The crawler's camera, which had already picked up what appeared to be a smooth, glasslike lining inside the tunnel, now showed what looked like a shadow on the wall at the extreme edge of the reach of the lights.

"Let's take a look," Max said. He stopped the crawler, turned it. The lights reflected glaringly back from the glazed walls of a small chamber. The cameras quickly adjusted themselves to the light. The fume detector was registering a strong emission from the contents of the basin. On the screen, the basin appeared to be filled with something the color of dark mud.

They saw the beast at the very edge of the light beams. In the pictures Rodrick had taken near the dead city, the beast's eyes had been small, glowing red. As this one emerged into the light far down the perfectly straight tunnel, its eyes were huge, reflecting light yellowly, and then, as the distance continued to close, the eyes began to contract, until, in the full beams of the lights, they were half-inch circles, glowing coals of malignant red.

"I think it's angry," Grace said, for now the audio receivers were bringing to them, in addition to the frantic, rhythmic scrape-scrape of the creature's movement, a chilling sound, a combination of hissing, grinding, gurgling.

"Grace," the admiral said, "I think we should move everyone back."

Paul Warden was thinking the same thing. He gave orders. Sage Bryson had moved her camera crew to within ten yards of the excavation and was seated high on the saddle of an extended boom, shooting down into the excavation.

"Sage, move back about five yards," Warden ordered, and when Sage did not comply immediately, he yelled, "That's an order, Ms. Bryson!" The boom rolled slowly backward. The coned snout of the beast was very distinct on the screens now.

"You move back, too," Max told Grace. "I'll join you as soon as I get a sample of the substance on the wall of the basin."

The admiral was obviously in communication with Mopro on their private frequency, because the big robot rolled up to stand at the edge of the excavation. The admiral was positioning the noose around the opening of the tunnel.

"Everyone stand by!" Max yelled.

Mopro's fingers opened at the tips, exposing his deadly, rapid-fire guns. His chest plate became an outlet for a laser cannon. The admiral was half-crouched, tense, ready.

"Here it comes," Max said.

Grace cried out as the beast below put on a surge of incredible speed, and on the screen, she saw its powerful maw begin to open.

It all seemed to happen at once. The backside of the pipeline crawler shot up out of the tunnel and the cargo crawler flew backward as Max and Grace abandoned their equipment and ran. Paul Warden and his men crouched, weapons ready. The admiral and the powerful head and neck of the beast seemed to shoot up from the excavation at the same time. The small antelope was catapulted about twenty feet, and the admiral, using all the more-than-human power of his legs, flew through the air, with the gaping maw of the beast within inches of his body.

Mopro caught the powerful, tubular neck with the full blast of a stun gun, and with a hissing bellow the head of the beast reached its greatest extension, the teeth snapping shut with a crash to miss the admiral by a margin so fine that Grace's heart was in her mouth. Then the dead-white flesh of the powerful neck was squeezed by the flexisteel collar, and even as he landed lightly on his feet, the admiral was operating the winches, snapping the high-tensile cable into tautness.

The convulsions of the beast shook the ground, causing the edges of the excavation to begin to cave in. The cables sang with tension.

"We've got him!" Paul Warden yelled.

Suddenly the beast was still. Only the head and neck were visible. The flexisteel collar had closed tightly just behind the fold in the neck.

"Shall I bring him out?" the admiral asked.

For a moment Paul Warden didn't answer. He was awed by the sheer malevolence of the thing, and he, like the others, was getting the smell of it, the sickening stench of rotting flesh. Evil, tiny, red eyes darted back and forth. The exposed neck, dead-flesh white, pulsed. The mouth opened, exposing the huge, back-tilted front teeth and the broad, flat, crushing back teeth. A hiss, which was mixed with a nauseous gurgle, made Grace back up a few more steps.

"Bring him out," Warden ordered.

The admiral shortened two of the cables, let the other two out as the winch motors whined and began to smoke with the resistance being put up by the beast. And then the ground seemed to explode upward from the excavation and the twenty-foot length of the monster was yanked from the tunnel.

It looked like a huge grub. The tubular body writhed,

and Grace saw immediately how the thing moved itself along its tunnels. The midportion of the body seemed to lengthen and contract. When underground, the thing would, by that movement, push the head forward as the midbody lengthened. The scraping sound was created as the beast slid over rock. Then the midbody would contract and scrape, as the rear portion was drawn forward. There was not a great deal of flexibility in the body, however, for the creature's struggles moved the rear end of the body only in a small arc.

"Capture cage!" yelled Paul Warden. The four men of his squad put away their weapons and ran to offload the cage, made of the strongest metals ever alloyed, big enough for two elephants in tandem.

The creature closed its mouth. The hissing roar ceased. The red eyes seemed to calm. The admiral was standing ten feet away from the creature's suspended head when it turned its neck and clipped one of the high tensile cables in two as if it had been made of string and, with lightning swiftness, faster than the fastest strike of the quickest Earth snake, lashed the powerful neck to catch the admiral just as he reacted and began to leap backward. The teeth closed on the admiral's thighs, the mouth covering his legs from knee to groin, and as Grace Monroe screamed a belated warning, she heard the crunch of metals and plastics followed by the clatter of Mopro's automatic weapons.

Paul Warden watched in astonishment as high-velocity, metal-jacketed rounds chipped small fragments off the dead-white skin of the slug. Mopro was giving the creature eight barrels of automatic fire, and the bullets sang off the thing as if striking solid stone, causing a bit of excitement as people dived for cover, with whining ricochets zinging off into the distance.

Before Warden could react past drawing his laser, Mopro was falling into a kneeling squat and the joints of his knees were opening, and two armor-piercing, high-caliber rounds blew the slug apart in the middle in a roar of explosive sound.

The back portion of the separated slug jerked and writhed. The front part was stunned for a moment, falling to thud onto the ground, the admiral still in its jaws. Mopro rolled rapidly, and the searing beam of a laser began to smoke and cut the stonelike skin just behind the creature's head. As the band was severed from the body, the jaws relaxed and the admiral dragged himself out, a puzzled look on his handsome face, his legs totally useless. He drew himself away from the gaping mouth by digging his fingers into the dirt, halted at a distance of five feet, and turned to look in wonderment at the dead beast.

Mopro spun his treads, sped to the admiral's side, and bent ponderously to pick him up on his thick, powerful arms.

"My God," Max breathed.

Grace recovered from her shock and ran toward Mopro and the admiral.

"I'm sorry, Grace," the admiral said, smiling at her from Mopro's arms.

"Damage report, quickly," Grace snapped.

The admiral looked at her, a smile on his face. His reply was slow in coming. "No . . . damage, Grace," he said. His voice was weak.

"Your electrical system, Admiral. Check it, please."

"I . . . no . . . fine," the admiral said.

"Max!" Grace shouted. "My toolbox!"

Max, seeing the seriousness of her face, went toward the crawler at a dead run.

"Put him down, Mopro," Grace said gently to the big robot. Mopro laid the admiral tenderly at her feet. She knelt quickly and began to tear at the admiral's shredded trousers, unable to remove them over the mangled legs. Max was back with her kit. She grabbed power shears and began to talk at the same instant. "Max, use the laser scapel. Vertical incision just below his left ear, one-eighth-inch depth, three inches long."

Max went to work. Grace cut away the obscuring trousers and used the power shears to tear and rip at the tough material of the torn skin.

Paul and Stoner stood at a respectful distance. "If that had been a man," Stoner said, "he'd be dead."

"I'm through the skin," Max said. "There's an RD 33 atomic power pack exposed."

"Good," Grace said, still ripping and cutting, into circuitry now, pulling out and tossing aside tiny assemblies of microchips. "We're all shorted out down here, draining all the power away. Splice in an RD 33. There are several in the kit."

Max looked inside the neatly arranged kit, stabbed for a power pack and tool, and began to work, his big, blunt fingers surprisingly quick.

"Can he die, or something?" Paul Warden asked.

"We can lose him," Grace replied, still working frantically. "The redundant power packs are in his legs. The massive short circuits are draining all power from his brain."

"Ready to splice," Max said.

"Nuclear bond for good contact," Grace said, and Max plunged into the kit for a tiny bonder. There was a sharp spark of power and then another, and the admiral said, "Very good work, Chief Rosen. Thank you."

"Can you help me now, Admiral?" Grace asked.

"Certainly, Grace," the admiral said calmly. "I have power restored to my brain."

It had been very, very close. A few seconds longer and all that was the admiral—that unexplainable, unexpected personality that made him what he was—would have been gone. Now the race was to save all the data that had been so laboriously stored in the memory chambers built into his chest.

"So far no data has been lost, Grace," the admiral said. "If Chief Rosen would lift my head so that I can see . . . My sensors are dead below the waist."

Rosen propped up the admiral's head and shoulders. "I would say, Grace," the admiral said, "that the drain is at the main junction in the left hip joint."

Grace used the power shears relentlessly.

"You're not being very neat, Grace," the admiral said.

"Look who's being a critic," she snapped. "I wasn't the one who thrust a pair of perfectly good legs into that damned thing's mouth."

She exposed the metallic bone of the hip joint, probed, and yelled, "Ouch," as sparks flew and she jerked her hand back. Then she ripped out a mass of wiring and tiny electronic objects. "How's that?"

"Separate the leads to that area, and we've got it," the admiral said.

She closed off and insulated the bare leads.

"Very good," the admiral said. "Now, Grace, would you please cover me? I feel quite exposed."

"What have we got here, a modest robot?" Max asked.

The look that came over the admiral's face caused Max to clear his throat in embarrassment. Robots were not supposed to have feelings, but, by God, this one did. He patted the admiral amiably on the shoulder.

The admiral was transported back to the ship on a litter carried by Max and Stoner. A small crowd had gathered near the main hatch. As Max and Stoner lifted the admiral down from the crawler, Tina Sells rushed out. She seized the admiral's hand.

"Oh, Admiral," Tina cried, "I told you to be careful. Are you hurt badly?"

"It isn't all that bad," the admiral said with a stiff upper lip. Grace, walking beside him, almost giggled when he actually bit his lower lip, as if to keep from crying out in pain. He had superb sensors to assess damage, but he could not feel pain.

"I'll stay with you," Tina said. "I'll help you get well."

Grace's urge to giggle left her. There was a sincerity in the teenage girl's voice that alerted her. When Tina turned her face toward her the girl's eyes were wet. "Grace, is—is—"

"He's fine," Grace said. "The damage is in nonvital parts. We'll install a set of new legs, and he'll be like new." But she was thinking, *Good Lord, we have a modest robot who seems to be developing human emotions and a girl in love with him.*

NINE

Max Rosen was beginning to believe that he was destined never to have a moment alone with the woman he loved. Since the admiral was an important part of the colony's defenses, Grace worked night and day to repair the damages. When she was not in her lab working on and with the admiral, she was in some other lab assisting in the tests and biopsies of the giant slug.

With the admiral out of action, Mopro was attached to Paul Warden's team, and working together, they killed three more of the underground beasts within five miles of Hamilton. There would be no further attempts to capture one of the things—they were far too powerful, far too deadly. But after three fairly quick kills—with the beasts lured to the surface not by sacrificing one of the pretty little antelopes but by having the pipeline crawler invade the beasts' burrows—all further attempts were fruitless.

Random checks with listening devices showed a surprisingly dense underground population, and the densest concentration of the slugs was in the hidden valley of the dead city.

"Maybe the damned things ate everybody," Stoner grouched, unhappy because he was not free to go roaming in search of minerals.

The information that poured out of the ship's labs regarding the slugs was intimidating and astounding: For the first time, humans had encountered a life form not based on the complex, oxygen-burning carbon molecules. The rocklike skin of the slugs was just that, rock. Its compound was based on silicon dioxide, the basic ingredient of common sand, which was elasticized by a binding enzyme that had the chemists shaking their heads. An analysis of stomach content—if the interior of the slug could be called a stomach, being mainly a rock-hard tube that exuded acids so virulent that an entire new chemistry could be founded on them—showed that the slugs drew sustenance from the very rocks of the planet.

"The damned things *are* miners," Stoner said. "They crush rock with those massive back teeth, using the forward, pointed teeth much as we would use a pickax."

That was how the underground beasts were named, "miners," for the name began with Stoner and spread to the scientists in the labs and then to others.

Stoner was vitally interested when the analysis of stomach contents revealed minute amounts of iron, zinc, copper, and, in the last miner to be killed, a slightly radioactive acid soup, which indicated the presence of uranium somewhere down there along the beast's burrow.

It was Grace Monroe who uncovered the last secret about the miners. She had the admiral up on his feet on a pair of slightly improved legs, ready to join Mopro and Paul Warden in their hunt for more miners.

"Grace," the admiral commented, "it would be very helpful if we had at least one more of the pipeline crawlers."

She'd been so busy that she'd forgotten all about the sample that Max, sitting in the crawler, had taken from the wall of the tunnel. She sent the admiral to the site of the latest stakeout, where he retrieved the sealed tube containing the sample. When Grace opened it in the lab, the stench was overwhelming, and it took her only a few minutes to know why. She called Duncan Rodrick and Max to her lab.

"Whew, what stinks?" Max asked in his blunt way. Then he saw that Grace had been crying. "What's the matter, honey?" he asked, and the tenderness in his voice caused Rodrick to smile to himself.

"You're smelling the decay of animal fat," Grace answered.

"Knowing what it is doesn't make it smell any better," Max said.

"Human fat," Grace added quietly, and had to wipe her eyes quickly.

Max sobered and reached for her hand. Rodrick cleared his throat.

"Crudely rendered," Grace said. "Remnants of hair, small bone chips, blood, but mainly congealed fat."

"They don't eat—?" Max paused. He felt a little queasy.

"Apparently not," Grace said. "I estimated the amount of the . . . fat in that basin." She had to swallow hard. "It's almost all there, about all you'd expect to be able to render from a . . . woman of Lynn's size."

"I don't understand," Max said. "We had assumed they needed flesh for nourishment."

Grace turned to face Rodrick. "I've written a report on this creature's brain. It's a complex organ. The ratio between brain and body size is comparable to that of the dolphins of Earth."

"Are you saying that miners might have a relatively high level of intelligence?" Rodrick asked.

Grace shrugged. "Any conclusions would be premature, but Stoner has been doing charts of the tunnels. Their complexity is impressive. They never come near to or cross any other tunnel. How can the miner dig a tunnel that runs absolutely straight and level for, in one case Stoner has found, ten miles? And I'm sure you've noticed that since we've killed four of them, they can no longer be lured to the surface. In fact, not one miner has been heard within ten miles of Hamilton since the last one was killed."

"You're thinking that they have some way to communicate a warning?" Rodrick asked.

Grace shrugged again. "I don't think we should continue a policy of extermination until we've done further study."

Rodrick nodded thoughtfully. "Since we can spot their traps so easily, I think we can get the teams back to work." He paused, considering. "All right. We won't go after them if they don't come after us. We'll keep our defenses up, and if they leave us alone, we'll leave them alone."

Following the bloody mutiny on board the *Karl Marx*, the experienced personnel pulled long duty hours until others were trained to replace those who had died. Theresita Pulaski, with her marshal's stars back on her uniform, was in command, although she insisted that she be called comrade marshal rather than captain. She was out of her depth when it came to operational technicalities of a complicated mechanism like the *Karl Marx*, and she designated young Ilya Salkov to be her second in command and to be at her side constantly.

When a smooth routine had been established, the overworked survivors were able to relax a bit. It was then, in a new spirit of freedom, that the discussion groups began to form. The main topic was the destination of the ship. There were adventurers who wanted to pick a star at random and lightstep to it. With the huge supply of the metal rhenium aboard, the *Karl Marx* had the ability to lightstep through time and space at least a dozen times— all they had to do was bombard a small amount of the metal with antimatter molecules to propel themselves instantly across mind-boggling distances. Surely, the adventurous ones insisted, a dozen planets would yield at least one that conformed to the narrow range of living conditions necessary for man.

Most of those aboard, however, were conservative and resistant to change. They distrusted any departure from the plan that had been pounded out mainly by the dead Premier Yuri Kolchak: In the event that the three probes sent out by the Soviet Union did not find a suitable solar system, the expedition would proceed to the one planet known to have free water and an oxygen atmosphere. To Yuri Kolchak and his advisers and spies, who had infiltrated the American work crews and learned the information, the obvious solution was to simply take the planet of the 61 Cygni system away from the Americans.

"That would mean that we have not left war behind us," said the bearlike Anton Emin.

There were others who were sick of war and blood,

and they spoke up vociferously. Killing, they said, should not become a part of the new civilization among the stars.

But as the long months passed and the feeling of space seeped into the consciousness of those aboard the ship, they began to appreciate the enormous distances involved, and the thought of roaming for a long, long time through those vast, hostile stretches of nothingness became a gnawing dread.

"Perhaps we wouldn't have to fight," Anton Emin said. "Perhaps we could work with the Americans."

"For how long?" asked Denis Ivanov. Denis was a physician who came from a proud heritage. His ancestors had been among the original Bolsheviks who first went to battle against the czar's oppression. "You know the intolerance of the Americans. They would not allow us to live in peace. They would not even try to understand our system of true socialism. No. If we go to the planet where the Americans are, it will be best to fight first, while we are still strong."

"We will go to them in peace," Theresita said firmly, but she was heartsick. The old attitudes were gaining force. "I, for one, favor exploration of other star systems. The cosmos is vast. How much better it will be to have our own planet so that we can develop as we please—without friction, without the necessity of fighting."

"I insist on a vote," Denis Ivanov said. He was backed by others.

Theresita postponed the decision for as long as possible. The year 2040 passed. The ship continued its sublight cruise toward the outer limits of the solar system. And, as the second year passed and icy Pluto's orbit was near, she reluctantly set up the procedure for a secret ballot. She hoped that her sensible talk, backed by most of the Space Service people who had joined the mutiny, had convinced the majority that conducting their own exploration to find their planet was the best course.

The vote was close. Fifty-three percent of those aboard wanted to avoid the 61 Cygni system and the Americans' planet and find a planet of their own.

"Comrades," she told them, on the jury-rigged all-ship communicator, "we must not let this difference of opinion among us cause rancor. We must work together. I ask those who are in the minority to accept the decision and join with us. We live in comfort here on this great ship, and there is no danger of shortages, thanks to our efficient life-support systems. Perhaps we will be lucky and find a planet on our first attempt. If not, we must develop patience."

"Each time we search a solar system," Denis Ivanov angrily told a group of his followers, "we will have to cruise at sublight speed. It will take ten years or more to search the systems of five or six stars, and if they, too, have no planets, what have we done other than waste a decade of our lives?"

A star was chosen. It was not even in the same segment of the galaxy with 61 Cygni. Ilya Salkov and his engineering staff began to make preparations for the big moment, the activation of the Shaw Drive.

The rhenium fuel, cast into three foot-long cylinders, was bulky and very heavy. The ship's architects had placed the storage areas for the excess fuel in the engine room so that refueling would not require laborious movement of tons of heavy metal. Rhenium was an inert metal until bombarded with antimatter, so it had seemed perfectly safe to store the tons of excess fuel in close proximity to the drive room. What the designers of the ship did not anticipate was the field of undefined force, which extended outward from the Drive when it was activated and encompassed the entire ship.

And what Theresita had not anticipated was a second mutiny.

Denis Ivanov and his supporters, in a slashing, surprising display of violence, decimated the ranks of those who had voted to stay away from the 61 Cygni system, took the engineering staff with Ilya Salkov as their prisoners, and overwhelmed Theresita in her quarters while she slept.

"We offer you the same choice that you offered Captain Simonov," Vera Ivanov told Theresita, speaking for her husband and the new mutineers. "We would like to have you with us, comrade."

Having survived the bomb she'd used to kill the man

she loved, and having escaped certain nuclear war and lived through a mutiny against heavy odds, Theresita was not going to stand on principle to the point of throwing her life away. "Thank you," she said. "I accept your generous offer."

Under guard, she talked with Ilya Salkov and his engineering crew. "To stay alive is the important thing now, comrades. Perhaps we can be of some influence later."

"To fly this ship requires technical know-how," Ilya said. "We can refuse to participate in any attack from space on the Americans."

"Such talk will be reported to the committee," said their guard.

"Report it and be damned," Salkov said. "What's to prevent me from programming the Drive to take us to the star that was chosen by the majority?"

The guard, a microbiologist not accustomed to his role as weapon-bearing mutineer, looked uncertain. "There are those among us who are familiar with the operation of the Drive," he said.

"Do as you are ordered," Theresita told Ilya.

When the time came, when the *Karl Marx* was safely out of the gravitational influence of the solar system, there was an understandable air of tension throughout the ship. Ilya Salkov was on the bridge. Theresita, no longer under guard, was observing. The target for their lightstep was 61 Cygni A. The Americans were, at that time, only weeks ahead of them, and there was talk that they might find the *Spirit of America* still in space. With the advantage of surprise, one missile could settle the issue of ownership of the new planet.

But even among the new mutineers there was disagreement. The Space Service officer who had been in charge of weapons control had been killed in the first mutiny. One of Ilya's engineers was now serving in that capacity. As the countdown continued his voice broke in on the communicator.

"I serve notice to all," he vowed in a trembling voice, "that I will not obey any order to fire on the American ship."

"Relieve that man immediately," Denis Ivanov yelled, to no one in particular, although all the self-proclaimed leaders of the second mutiny were gathered on the bridge.

"Whom do you suggest in his place?" Ilya Salkov asked, with a sneer. "Perhaps the nutritional expert from the ship's kitchens?"

"We must take advantage of the element of surprise!" Ivanov said, his eyes a bit panicky.

Anarchy, Theresita was thinking, a grim smile on her lips. With a certain amount of disgust she began to understand why American democracy had never been successfully established elsewhere: The ordinary man didn't have the sense to control his own destiny, much less to make decisions about important matters involving the good of all. He was not capable of handling freedom.

"Comrade Marshal," Vera Ivanov appealed, "you must make that man in weapons control listen to reason."

"Whose reason, Comrade Vera?" Theresita asked.

"You'll have no help from her," Denis said sourly. "She's still unhappy at having been relieved of command."

"Not at all," Theresita assured him. "I feel a certain relief, as a matter of fact. I am happy that you are in command, Denis, so that *you* can decide what will happen if the American ship opens fire on us, with our man in our weapons control refusing to fire on them."

Denis blinked rapidly and swallowed, his face going pale. The countdown was proceeding, in spite of the confusion.

Ilya Salkov and his shorthanded staff did a great job, not missing any checkpoints in the countdown and making the lightstep strictly according to the book. Now the viewscreens showed a different star pattern, although it felt as if nothing had happened.

The navigator was an astronomer who had no practical experience in operating the various sensor systems. It took him a long time to identify two dim stars as, most probably, being 61 Cygni A and B.

"We are too far from them," Denis said impatiently. "What do you mean, bringing us out of lightstep so far from our destination! There will be how many years of cruising to get there?"

"No more than two, comrade," answered the sweating astronomer.

"And which is the Cygni A star?" Denis demanded.

"The one to the left of the screen, comrade," the astronomer said. "At least I'm reasonably certain that it is."

Denis turned, his hands still shaking. "By the name of Lenin!" he snarled in disgust. "He can't even tell us which star is which."

"We can program another lightstep," Vera said. "We're not that close to any object with a gravitational well."

"Salkov," Denis demanded, "is she right?"

"Yes," Ilya said.

"Then go down to engineering and check the Drive and refuel."

"May I have the commander's permission to accompany Lieutenant Salkov to engineering?" Theresita asked.

"I don't give a damn what you do," Denis said.

They found the engineering staff clustered around the Drive control console. "It's good you are here, Comrade Salkov," a young officer said. "We are sustaining quite unusual readings on the instruments."

Ilya stepped to the board and swept his eyes over the instruments. The temperature inside the sealed Drive chamber was high. At first that did not concern him. Temperatures reached almost sunlike highs during the lightstep reaction. Then he looked back at the temperature gauge and felt a jolt of anxiety. Instead of cooling, the interior of the Drive chamber was heating, the gauge moving imperceptibly upward.

"Check the cooling system," Ilya ordered.

"It has been done. The cooling system is operating at maximum."

"Is something wrong?" Theresita asked.

"I don't know yet."

"Ilya," said a young engineer named Ivan, "take a look at the flux gauges in the Drive compartment."

There was a strong magnetic field in the sterile, barren compartment that housed the Drive. Ilya took off his cap and mopped his forehead.

"Air temperature in here is up to eighty-five degrees," someone told him.

"What the hell?" Ilya was stumped. He could think of no reason why the Drive chamber was not cooling, and there was certainly no reason why the cooling system was not being effective in the engineering control room.

On a hunch he said, "Ivan, please give me temperature readings from the fuel-storage areas."

That took a moment. Ivan, young, handsome, came hurrying back, his face tense. "With the cooling systems going full blast, it's still over a hundred degrees in the storage areas, Ilya."

Ilya went to the computer and began to work, his cap tossed aside, his dark hair glistening with perspiration. The temperature in the room continued to climb.

"Ilya," young Ivan said, "at the present rate, the temperature will be critical inside the Drive chamber in just over one hour."

"It is not the Drive chamber that concerns me at the moment," Ilya replied. "There should be nothing but spent fuel left, the residue left after the annihilation process. There is nothing there to cause a buildup of temperature."

"Comrade Ilya," a young, frightened voice said, "the temperatures are rising rapidly in the fuel-storage areas."

A terrifying thought made Ilya squint his eyes. He rose swiftly and ran to a bank of instruments across the room from the main console.

"The radiation sensors are not functioning," he said, tapping their glass covers.

"Ilya," said young Ivan, "the temperature in the fuel-storage areas is reaching toward dangerous levels." Even as he spoke the sprinkler systems responded to the heat and began to release their liquid fire-extinguishing chemicals. The sharp rise in temperature in the storage areas slowed, but it still rose.

"Ivan," Ilya said, "there is a portable radiation detector in the storage area. Get it quickly."

Ivan was back in less than two minutes.

Ilya took the detector and went through the shielded door into the Drive chamber. A sudden realization caused him to grow cold and shiver—he knew that he was a dead man. In the brief time he kept the door open to the Drive room he took enough hard radiation to assure him a quick death. He slammed the door behind him and examined the various dials of the counter. There were enough free electrons radiating from the Drive to cause him to raise his eyebrows in surprise. In that moment he accepted his death and wished only for the time to figure out why the Drive had gone wild. He only knew that streams of anti-matter particles were coming from the Drive housing and causing the stored rhenium to heat up.

Theresita knew that something was terribly wrong, but she did not feel real danger until she saw Ilya's face as he emerged from behind the shielded door.

"You will all put on radiation suits immediately," Ilya said. "And prepare to abandon ship."

No one questioned him.

"It was the surplus fuel," Ilya went on, as he reached for the back of a chair for support. "Somehow it extended the reaction inside the Drive chamber. Now the entire area is acting as a Drive chamber."

Ivan understood. He ran to get two radiation suits and gave one to Theresita, who immediately began to put it on.

"You are all aware of your abandon-ship assignments," Ilya said. He punched up the communicator. "Get me Denis Ivanov," he said.

"What's going on down there?" Denis's petulant voice asked.

"There is a continuing reaction inside the Drive chamber," Ilya said, having to pause to take a deep breath. He was already feeling very weak. "Within a very few minutes one of two things will happen: Either there will be a massive explosion, or the entire ship will be irradiated. You must abandon ship immediately."

"What the hell do you mean?" Denis was demanding as Ilya turned off the communicator.

"They have been warned, comrades," Ilya said. "You and I know that only a small fraction of those on board will find seats on the scout ships. What you do now is up to you."

Theresita pushed a radiation suit against Ilya's arm. "Put it on," she ordered.

"I will not be going with you," he said. He fell, slumping almost instantly into limpness, and as she knelt beside him, his breathing stopped.

"Come, comrade," young Ivan said, pulling her to her feet.

The heavy radiation suit made movement difficult and tiring. She ran as best she could behind Ivan, following him toward the outer rim where the scout ships waited in their individual pods. They ran directly into bedlam. Panicked colonists were fighting to gain access to the hatches leading into the pod areas. Ivan took one look and seized Theresita's arm.

"We will never make it through that way," Ivan panted, his voice metallic as it came through the radiation suit's speaker. "The captain's ship—"

As they made their way around the congested, screaming, fighting people who clogged each hatch, he halted only once, to grab a cutting torch from a storage area. The access hatch to the captain's private scout was programmed to open only to the handprint of the dead Fedor Novikov, but it opened rapidly to Ivan's cutting torch.

"We can take a few of them with us. . . ." Theresita said.

"Let them know there is a ship here, and we'll have to fight to get on it."

"We can't just abandon everyone," she insisted. "We can quietly find six people."

"I will board the scout," Ivan said. "I will give you ten minutes to find six people. If there are more with you when you return, I will blast off without you or any of them."

"Ten minutes," she said. She ran awkwardly back down the corridor. She could hear the panicked screams ahead where passengers fought to get inside the hatch leading to the pods. She was near enough to distinguish individual curses, shouts, and screams when the ship shuddered and there was a muffled explosion from deep inside, near the hub, where the engineering areas were. Then the entire ship seemed to convulse, throwing Theresita forcefully against a bulkhead. Ahead of her a bulkhead bulged outward, then shattered, blocking the corridor. A howl of wind came from behind her, making her think that the hull was holed between her and the captain's scout until her reason told her that the wind was blowing toward the rupture. Fighting against the howling wind, she fell, crawled, and finally reached the hatch that Ivan had opened with his torch and, once inside that bay with the door closed behind her, was out of the wind. She slipped out of the radiation suit and ran as fast as she could run, being hurled forward once by another explosion. Ivan's head was sticking out of the scout's entry hatch.

"Hurry!" he called.

She leaped to the footholds on the side of the scout and clambered up, diving headfirst into the hatch.

She heard the hatch slam shut behind her, and then Ivan was pushing buttons. "I'm going to open the outside lock without decompressing the pod," he said. "Secure yourself in the couch. When we go, we'll go fast."

It took the operation of three fail-safe devices to set off the charges that blew the outer hatch. It exploded outward, and the decompression sucked at the scout even as Ivan activated the rockets, heedless of the damage done to the pod as the scout leaped into space.

G-forces pushed Ivan and Theresita down hard against the couches, but Ivan kept the rockets burning. The rear cameras were activated, and the *Karl Marx*, Yuri Kolchak's answer to Dexter Hamilton's great dream, grew smaller and smaller, the central area near the hub seeming to flake outward like a fast-blooming flower.

"If it all goes at once," Ivan said, "it will take us with it."

It seemed incredible that the *Karl Marx* could explode with enough force to reach them, already miles away, but she didn't question Ivan's comment.

The rockets ceased firing, and the sudden weightlessness sent Theresita forward against her harness.

"Which star is the Cygni A star?" Ivan asked.

She didn't answer for a moment. What had the navigator said? "The one to the right," she said. But even as

Ivan's fingers flew, programming the small rhenium drive aboard the captain's scout, she wasn't sure.

"Here we go," he said.

As the Americans before them had learned, Theresita and the young engineering officer whose last name she did not know learned that Harry Shaw's theories were wrong in some aspects—the rhenium drive in the captain's private scout ship did not detonate when the scout emerged in the primary gravitational pull of a large celestial object. And it was a very large celestial object, a planet of white clouds and golden land areas and purplish oceans.

The scout was driving at top speed directly toward the surface of the planet, the hull beginning to glow red from atmospheric friction.

Ivan panicked. Instead of firing retro-rockets, he tried to slow the ship's deadly velocity by extending the wings; as they popped into position, he realized his mistake. The relatively fragile wings peeled, metal surfaces flaking back and off. Within seconds the surface of the wings glowed red, then white hot, and their disintegrating pieces clanged and slashed at the hull of the scout as, finally, Ivan began to use the rockets.

The sharp bite of the harness caused Theresita to cry out as she was thrown forward. Then she blacked out.

TEN

Life was getting incredibly complex for Duncan Rodrick. The Omega colony was, of course, technically still a part of the United States, and its citizens subject to United States laws. It had been known from the beginning, however, that never in history would a colony be so effectively cut off from its mother country. President Dexter Hamilton, a student of history, had decided that the *Spirit of America* would leave Earth carrying her own constitution, which was based closely on the Constitution of the United States but with provisions for total self-government once the colony had been securely established. In the beginning, though, the captain was to be in sole command until the settlement and building phases were completed.

It was a big job for one person. It was impossible for Rodrick to be expert in all fields, and yet he had to make decisions concerning the work and actions of scientists in every discipline.

Rodrick's primary concern was for the safety of the colony. His ban on field expeditions had created some tension, for all the colonists had been eager to get on with the job and satisfy their curiosity about the immense planet.

After the reassuring visit to Grace Monroe's lab during which they discussed the miners' probable intelligence, Rodrick went directly to the bridge, punched up an all-ship, all-colony circuit on the communicator, and ended the ban for all units. The scout ships and scientific teams began to leave the ship and the town immediately.

But Rodrick still felt vaguely uneasy. He looked at the holographic projection of the planet's globe. There was just so damned much of it; the eight major land masses, of which the continent Columbia was by far the largest, represented four times the land area of Earth, and it had taken centuries for modern man to explore the remote corners of Earth. Furthermore, everything was bigger, taller, or longer on Omega. Even with the aid of the swift scouts and high-tech instruments, it would be a long time before all the hidden secrets of Omega were revealed.

It was difficult for everyone to adjust his or her frame of reference to comprehend the land areas involved. Mandy, whose staff biologists, zoologists, and entomologists were overwhelmed with work classifying, naming, and studying specimens of animal, plant, and insect life, had to envision Earth distance in comparison even to begin to appreciate the size of their new world: On Earth, the largest land mass was the Eurasian continent. The longest straight line that could be drawn across that land mass, roughly from the Rock of Gibraltar to Vladivostok, measured just under eight thousand miles. A line drawn from the point where the equator crossed the western coast of Columbia to the permanent ice cap of the northeastern corner of the continent was over twenty-two thousand miles. From coast to coast at the latitude of Hamilton, the distance was just over ten thousand miles. The smallest continent in the eastern hemisphere, a land mass nestled in the sea bounded by Columbia's east coast and the other two giant continents of the eastern hemisphere, was the size of South America.

Meanwhile, Omega was slowly giving them hints of her totally alien nature—in the matter of the miners, for example, and the enigma of the dead city. Then there were the seas of Omega, vast watery distances, with depths in proportion to the size of the planet. The onshore waters had begun to give up specimens of sea life to the marine scientists. One husband-wife team, without asking permission, had sat down to a candlelight dinner of fresh fish. The fact that exhaustive laboratory tests had shown that several marine varieties were safe for human consumption didn't lessen Rodrick's concern. The long-range effects of eating alien foods of any kind was just one more worry for Rodrick, but there was nothing to be done about that except wait for something to happen months or years down the road.

The ship's supply bunkers still contained huge quantities of food because everything was recycled—but no one wanted to go on eating recycled food forever. Mandy Miller was concerned that foods grown on Omega would be lacking in the trace elements—zinc and iron, for example—that were needed for the Americans' health. Before the ship's own supply of vitamins and minerals ran out, the scientists would have to find a way to obtain them from Omega, either in natural food items, such as the marine life, or in concentrated form. To manufacture food supplements meant the building of manufacturing plants. And the raw material had to exist.

Two days after the work teams were back in the field, the oil drillers hit a large pool at shallow depths. A paper-thin pipeline was rolled out from the ship to the wellhead, and soon the huge building machines, with their own internal factories, were turning out building blocks at a pleasing rate.

The automated building machines were interesting to watch. The software for their computers included a variety of designs, which had been made back on Earth to meet any imaginable conditions in which humans could survive. The home designs for the climate of Eden were open, spacious, and sprawling, and the town was being quickly transformed.

A prefabricated hydrogen reclamation plant was rapidly taking shape on the shore of Stanton Bay, for one of the first needs would be to manufacture fuel to keep the scout ships in the air. Without them, planetary exploration would come to an end, and the colony would be without air and ground transport since hydrogen was the fuel for the crawlers, too.

The colonists had been warned that there would be a return to basics during the early years of settlement. The multiplicity of items that an American could buy, even in the twenty-first century, the century of shortages, would be missing from the colony's early output. The ship's data system held the chemical formulas for hundreds of thousands of different products, and someday those items and more might be made and sold on the new planet.

The drugs and medicines that increased life expectancy were high on the list of priorities. Most drugs could be synthesized by the labs aboard the ship, and factories would be built in Hamilton to manufacture drugs as soon as possible.

It was all Duncan Rodrick's responsibility, with the help of his advisers and the various committees, to choose the proper path and then run like hell. If life-style suffered in some respects, that was only a temporary condition, but comfort and health had to be maintained in order to keep everyone working at maximum efficiency.

The life of each person aboard was precious, but if there had been nuclear war on Earth, each life was doubly precious. If war had killed all humans or created a race of mutants, then the Americans might be the only Homo sapiens in the universe. Also, the colony would need all its human resources to prevent a relapse into preindustrial living standards.

Amando Kwait's semirobotic machines turned sod for the first time in the verdant river valley. Seeds germinated, and it became an evening pastime for people to walk along the banks of the Dinah River and Jumper's Run to comment on the green shoots of wheat, corn, barley, and rye. All the good vegetables of Earth began to grow as if Omega's soil pleased them. Anyone who cared to could stake off a garden plot, requisition seeds from Amando's storehouse, and have his own garden. Flowers began to sprout in beds around the homes. Exploration teams brought back exquisite flowering plants for transplant.

Life began to settle into a routine of work and play. Fish became a part of the diet, and Amando Kwait sampled fruit brought back from the tropical areas of the continent and found it to be delicious. It had been decided to begin to breed a small herd of cattle for milk, butter, and meat, so embryos were being formed in the nutrient fluids of the artificial wombs in the Life Sciences sections.

The zoologists on Mandy Miller's Life Sciences staff had been agitating for permission to mount expeditions into the tropical areas to investigate the huge life signals that were picked up by scout ships. Rodrick asked them to hold off for a while. The intimidating job of surveying and investigating their own huge continent came first.

Animal life was not nearly so varied as on Earth. In general, there were three types of animal life: grass eaters of a half-dozen species; three types of predators, all cat-like; and a family grouping of small grass- and insect-eating rodentlike creatures, the largest species of which was the size of a rabbit. But what the animal world of Omega lacked in variety, the plants and insects overcompensated.

The first child born on Omega came during the time when everyone was concerned with the threat of the miners, and the event passed almost unnoticed. Then there was another and another. A twin boy and girl were named in memory of Pat Renfro and Dinah Purdy. Jack Purdy was asked to be godfather. Somehow, the birth of children gave a sense of permanency to the colony. People who, when referring to home, meant Earth, began to say, "back on Earth," and when a field party finished work and turned the crawlers toward Hamilton, they were headed home.

Clive Baxter, the nattily dressed, diminutive chemist, found Rodrick the next morning in the vehicle park. Rodrick had arisen early to walk down to the bay before sunrise, and the activity in the vehicle park had drawn him to watch the field teams preparing to venture out for the day's work. It was a beautiful summer morning with Omega's sun going to work early. It would be hot, but experience had told them that by early afternoon a cooling breeze would begin to come from the sea.

"Good morning," Baxter said, and before Rodrick could answer, "you're a hard man to find, Captain."

Rodrick didn't answer that.

"Ah, Captain, there's to be a meeting this evening in

the meeting room in Section Two. We'd all be pleased if you could attend."

Rodrick had taken a quick look at his calendar for the day, and he had no meeting scheduled for the evening. "What sort of meeting?" he asked.

"Just a few concerned citizens," Baxter said. "I feel that it's important that you be there."

"What are the citizens concerned about?"

Baxter looked away. A crawler passed, engine humming, treads lifting dust to settle on Baxter's perfectly shined shoes. "I'd rather not say at the moment," he said. "It's not my place to speak for the committee. I'm only one member."

"Well, Dr. Baxter, I have nothing scheduled for the evening. I can stop by."

"Thank you," Baxter said. "Eight o'clock, then."

The scouts began to hit the air in scattered flocks, the entire complement going out, and Rodrick wished that he were up there with them. He wondered again what Baxter's concerned citizens were concerned about, but there was a busy day ahead of him: Allen Jones, the underwater architect, was beginning a survey of the ocean just offshore, using swift, maneuverable underwater craft, which had been most valuable in building underwater cities on Earth. That was going to be very interesting. And scout ship pilots for *Apache One* and *Apache Two*, Jacob West and Renato Cruz, were going to make slow treetop-level flights over the southern jungles near the equator in an effort to find a break in the dense canopy of the jungle for a clue to the strong life signals that were thickly scattered in Columbia's tropics.

Since the miners were no longer fiercely defending their burrows, Stoner McRae, Paul Warden, and the admiral used the camera-carrying pipeline crawlers to explore as many tunnels as possible. Stoner would review the film at night, running it through at fast speed, his eyes peeled for indications of metallic deposits in the stone of the tunnel walls.

Jackie Garvey had drawn the midnight-to-dawn watch. She was finishing her log when her relief, Ito Zuki, came in with a cheerful morning greeting and a craving for coffee. She chatted with Ito for a few minutes and then, yawning, left the bridge, wanting nothing more than a shower and sleep. She lingered in the shower for a self-indulgent period, then turned the water jet to cold, danced in the chill stream, and hopped out refreshed to wrap herself in a huge towel. She turned on the entertainment channel, found soothing music, finished drying her legs, left the damp towel on the carpet, and fell across the bed. She had just closed her eyes when her door bong signaled a visitor.

"Go away," she said softly.

But the call bonged again, insistently, and with a frown she reached for her robe and padded barefoot to the door.

"Hi," Rocky Miller said, smiling. "I hope I caught you before you fell asleep."

"Just barely," Jackie answered.

Rocky produced a thermal container from behind his back. "Hot chocolate, fresh. It'll help you sleep."

"Thank you, but—"

Rocky took a step toward her, bringing his face so close to hers that she took an involuntary step backward, giving him room to slip past her. "I wanted a chance to talk with you alone," he said.

She reluctantly got two mugs, poured the steaming hot chocolate, and sat down on her couch, pulling her robe together as one bare knee tried to peek out. "What can I do for you, Commander?" she asked, using the title to set a military tone.

"We always seem to be on opposing watches lately," Rocky said. "We've never really had a chance to get to know each other."

Jackie's first reaction was to tell him to go away and let her get to bed. The words formed, but for some reason she hesitated. "You pick a hell of a time to want to socialize, Commander," she said.

"Let's drop the service formalities," he replied, with an engaging smile. "I know you're tired. I'll get out of here in a minute and let you get some sleep. I just want to tell you that you have been doing an excellent job."

"Thank you," she said. She had been surprised to see

Rocky at her door. He was a married man, and at first she
had thought that he was there on ship's business. Even
when he started talking in that smiling, friendly way, she
took him at his word. It wasn't a convenient time, but it
was good service policy for a more senior officer to get to
know his junior officer better. She was unprepared for
Rocky's next gambit.

"You look great in uniform," he said, "but in something feminine, like that robe, you're extraordinary."

"Thank you again," she said, standing.

Rocky was not a subtle or a patient man. "And we
have a lot in common."

"Oh?"

"We've both been passed over," he said, his handsome smile a bit crooked.

"I'm afraid I don't understand. . . ."

He rose, finished his hot chocolate at a gulp, smiled
at her over the mug. "Think about it," he said. "I hear
you're quite a tennis player. The courts are under construction. Be finished in a couple of days. I'll give you a
call when they're ready."

She closed the door behind him, and when he was
gone she let irritation and puzzlement show on her face.
Then she shrugged and got into bed. She had not been
passed over for promotion. She did not have enough time
in grade to be due a promotion. He could have meant only
one thing.

Her face flushed. Was it that obvious to everyone on
board? She tried to put it all out of her mind, but it was
difficult. She still remembered Duncan Rodrick's first overture toward her, just after they'd finished the rocket-firing
sequence that had sent the *Spirit of America* away from
Earth. He had smiled at her and asked her to join him in
being the first to try out the ship's swimming pool.

Jackie was a proud woman; she'd held her own all her
life, and the fact that she had been chosen for the *Spirit of
America* expedition was proof that she had done well.
She'd never had any difficulties in her relationships with
the opposite sex. In fact, she had fully understood that, as
a member of the ship's crew, she'd be expected to have a

family after the colony was established. With healthy curiosity she'd checked out each single male colonist even before the ship left Earth. In her survey of available men, she had, of course, looked at the captain, but military thinking had excluded Duncan from her speculations. A full captain, a ship's captain, just didn't fraternize with the junior officers. In Duncan's arms she realized that all the old rules had been left behind when the ship accelerated outward toward the far limits of the solar system.

She tossed on her bed, seeking sleep, trying not to even think about how good they had been together. She felt a great resentment toward Rocky for stirring it all up again. She had just about had her hurt under control. For some reason Duncan had gone, well, not cold, but indifferent, and she'd spent an agonizingly long time wondering why. She was not egotistical, but she knew she was a beautiful woman. He had very definitely enjoyed her company. During the early part of the voyage he had sought her out—not just for lovemaking, but for companionship. He had never totally loosened up with her, she knew, but before the big chill he'd been very comfortable with her—they'd had long talks about things past and future, about his ex-wife, his hopes for a new world, and although marriage had never been mentioned—come to think of it, he'd never even told her that he loved her—it was, at least on her part, understood that it would be Jackie Garvey and Duncan Rodrick together on the new world.

Passed over?

She remembered the look on Rocky's face as he'd used those words. A crooked grin. He'd said, "We've both been passed over."

She shook her head. No. Duncan wasn't the type to go after a fellow officer's wife.

But why was Mandy Miller always on the bridge during times of crisis or interest? Looking back, she could remember a lot of times when she'd seen Duncan and Mandy Miller together, and times when he'd left word on the bridge that he could be reached in Dr. Miller's office. But Mandy was head of the Life Sciences department, a very important department. Duncan would, naturally, have need to consult her on matters in her field.

Rocky's crooked grin, and his words, stayed with Jackie as she fell into that state of near sleep. That grin had the look of a proud man trying to hide his hurt—or his shame. He had said they had been passed over.

She decided, just before falling asleep, that it was possible that Rocky knew something she didn't know. And the last feeling she had before sleep was a shamed anger, a suspicion that she had been used.

Someone was yelling at her. Theresita opened her eyes and saw an endless expanse of the greenest jungle she'd ever seen. There was a roaring whistle in her ears. She couldn't understand what Ivan was trying to tell her. She looked over her shoulder. The hull had been ripped open by a piece of the disintegrating wing. Ivan punched her on the shoulder and pointed down.

"Water—" That was all she understood over the roar of the wind in the slowly expanding hole in the hull, and then she was thrown forward again. The ship slowed. The sound was not so loud now.

"Rocket fuel low!" Ivan screamed at her. "Used too much to slow us." He pointed toward the water. It was a wide river, brown, slow moving. To all sides was endless jungle extending flatly to the hazy horizons.

"This button!" Ivan yelled. "I'm going to use the last of the rocket fuel in the front retros to try to stop us just before we hit the water. There'll be only a four-second blast. When you hear the rockets cut off or we hit the water, push the button. It blows the hatch. Then hit your harness's quick release and get out. The water looks deep."

"I understand," she yelled back.

The water was coming up very fast. Ivan was tense, his finger poised over the rocket-fire button. He had no time to program the on-board computer. He would have to judge the distance himself.

"Brace yourself!" he yelled.

She was jerked violently forward into the harness and things dimmed, but she did not black out entirely. Then there was another jerk forward as the scout's bow struck the water with a mighty splash. A small explosion sounded as Theresita triggered the hatch's quick release, and explosive bolts propelled the metal hatch away. She pounded on the quick release of her harness even as water swirled in with a roar—but she took a deep breath and bided her time, knowing that she could not move against the inrushing water. She reached out and found young Ivan's hand as the water rushed in. The scout sank deeper, and just as the water reached her chin she took another deep breath and looked at Ivan to see a metallic shard imbedded in his throat, and his arterial blood pumping from the jugular vein. He had been hit by a piece of the hatch when it had been blown off. She'd seen enough men die to know that there was no chance for him.

Now the water closed over her head, and she pushed herself away from the couch, pulling upward toward the open hatch. She went out headfirst, kicking upward with all her strength, not knowing how deeply the scout had sunk. She felt a light blow on the back of her right thigh, and there was a stinging sensation there as she kicked upward. The water was brown, no visibility, even though her eyes were open. She seemed to go up and up forever and then, knowing that she was reaching the limit of the usable air in her lungs, she stopped kicking and let her natural buoyancy and the momentum she'd built up carry her upward and upward endlessly until her lungs burned and she fought their spasming efforts to suck water.

There were large areas of blackness in front of her eyes when she at last burst free, coming out of the water almost to her waist, and then gulping life-giving air even as she fell back with a splash.

She tread water with small movements of her hands until she had her breath back. She was almost in midstream, and the banks seemed to be far away. She estimated that the river was at least half a mile wide. Which bank? The current was moving her slowly downstream. It didn't really matter which bank. She remembered the look of the jungle, dark, endless, an almost iridescent green. It had extended to the limit of visibility in all directions. It didn't matter which bank.

She began to swim with a breaststroke, the least strenuous one for her. Her leg was stinging. She floated on her back for a moment and put her hand down. She could feel the cut. Her finger went into flesh for a good half inch, and there was immediate pain in that spot that grew as she began to swim for the shore again. If she was losing enough blood, she might never make it to the bank of the river. And what kind of life was in the murky, brown, muddy waters? Something that would smell her blood and come to feed?

She remembered seeing films of South American fish with huge, teeth-filled mouths ripping and tearing. Crocodiles on the Nile. They had grown fat and brave feeding on the bodies of the dead during the attempted Egyptian uprising. Sharks. No, this was fresh water. But still her imagination stocked the muddy waters with ripping, tearing teeth, and she found herself flailing away in a frenzied crawl that was depleting her energies rapidly.

She forced herself to relax, to float. She felt her thigh. The cut was about four inches long, and deeper in the upper end. She could not feel a large outrush of blood, so there was no arterial bleeding. Blood had shot out into the brown water from Ivan's throat. She hadn't even known his last name. And Ilya was dead. All of them, dead.

She let the current do most of the work and used her strength sparingly to angle slowly toward the bank to her right. The river entered a gentle curve to the left and aided her, bringing her to within swimming distance of the bank. She kicked herself in, then caught an overhanging tree branch. There was no distinguishable bank as such, only a maze of huge trees and massed roots in mud and shallow water. She pulled herself up to cling to the roots of a tree and gasped tiredly, even as she looked around. A crash of thunder followed a vivid lightning bolt, and it seemed that the heavens opened. Rain thundered on the jungle canopy high over her head. Even with the rain dripping down from the roof of foliage, it was hot and steamy. She clung to the tree roots and rested.

A splash from the river behind her caused her to jerk her head around. A very large torpedo-shaped thing leaped in a high arc from the water. A second torpedo shape leaped, and she thought, *Fish*. A third fish left the water, then with an eruption of foam a huge square-tipped, all-teeth thing followed to snatch the leaping fish in midair. After exposing an enormous, ovate trunk behind the square, toothed head, it fell back with a splash that might have been audible for miles.

Theresita tried to crawl up onto the tangled tree roots, wanting to get even her feet out of the water. The emergence of that water monster gave her new strength. The thing came slowly toward her, its body's awesome bulk hinted at by ripples behind the extended neck. She scrambled to her feet and waded, stumbling over the tangled roots, away from the river. She kept going even after she could no longer see the river. She was, of course, soaked, but her clothing did not even begin to dry because the sweat poured from her in the steaming heat.

She had gone, she estimated, a hundred yards when the water that surrounded the trees became shallower. She sank to her knees in mud and fell backwards, pressing her thighs and rump into the soft, warm mud. She struggled back to firmer ground, detoured, and gained soggy ground that gave way under her feet from an accumulation of decaying vegetable matter. The cut on her thigh was packed with mud. She used the side of her hand and her fingers to clean away as much as possible, wincing from the pain.

Off to her left something moved. She froze. The sounds came from deep undergrowth, which began not far from the edge of the river swamp, and they were being made by something big. She had no weapon. She waited until the crashing sounds died in the distance.

A weak sun had burned through the swiftly moving thunderstorm, and she could position it roughly by catching a glint, now and then, through the dense roof of the jungle. All she wanted at that moment were water and a dry place to sit down. She moved on. The sun was to her right, and she kept it there as she traveled a torturous hundred yards through ever-thickening undergrowth. When she came to a fallen tree, she halted, panting, thirsty. She was losing liquid rapidly through her heavy perspiration.

It was a giant of a jungle tree, a full ten feet across at

its fallen base, and it had left a cavity in the jungle floor where its shallow root system had been ripped out. The cavity was half-full of water, which was clearer than the water of the river, the soil being quite sandy under the deep layer of mulch. She didn't even think twice before falling onto her stomach and drinking deeply. The water had the flat, bland taste of rainwater and was, to her, indescribably delicious.

She climbed up onto the trunk of the fallen tree, using the exposed roots as a ladder. The base of the tree, just above the protruding roots, was covered in a soft, gray, mossy growth. The roots made a good backrest as she sat, one leg extended, and protected the injured thigh from contact with the moss by cocking her right knee. She had wetted her neck scarf and used it to carefully clean away the mud from the cut. The cut was no longer bleeding. She couldn't get all the dark mud out of it, but surprisingly it didn't hurt as she tried to clean it, finger wrapped in the scarf.

She put the scarf under her thigh, let it down slowly, and closed her eyes. She had no idea where she was. Perhaps she was on the planet of the Americans, perhaps not, because she still couldn't remember whether the navigator on the *Karl Marx* had said that 61 Cygni A was the star to the left or to the right. She knew only that she was alone, on an alien planet, in the middle of a vast jungle near a wide, brown, slow-moving river.

She thought of the dead—of Captain Fedor Novikov, Ilya Salkov, the boy Ivan, and all the others. And of Yuri.

She found herself laughing bitterly. There was no amusement in her laugh. She opened her eyes and stared up into the impenetrable foliage. A brightly colored bird cocked a beady eye at her. From the direction of the river there came a gargantuan roar, a roar like nothing she'd ever heard before.

She laughed. This was all there was. She was it. She stood up atop the fallen tree. She could see a few yards of tangled undergrowth, and the soaring trunks of the giant trees, the oppressive green of the canopy.

"Here I am!" she bellowed, her throat straining with the effort. "Here I am!" She knew she could very well be the only citizen of the Soviet Union alive. She'd seen the *Karl Marx* die in space and had seen Ivan die with a piece of jagged metal severing his jugular vein. All the killing in the two mutinies had meant nothing, for they would all have died when the ship destroyed herself.

She drew herself up to her full height, standing at attention. "Here I am, Yuri," she said. "Here I am. Look at me. This is Russia. This is your brave new world, your extension of glorious communism among the stars. Look at it, Yuri. Here I am."

She sank down, very tired. She leaned back against the roots of the fallen tree and put the scarf back under the wound on her thigh so that she could stretch out her legs. From somewhere not too far away came a hissing bellow of sound, followed by a shrill, eerie scream of agony. She closed her eyes. At that moment she almost wished that one of the things that bellowed and screamed and crashed through the undergrowth would find and kill her.

Her eyes flew open. She jerked her head, looking right and left. A feeling of devastating loneliness caused a catch in her breathing. For all she knew, she could be the only human on the planet, alone as no person had been alone before. She had never been afraid of death, for she'd faced it many times in many forms, but in the steamy, sodden, heavy loneliness of the jungle, she clasped her arms and a moan of sheer terror escaped from her lips before she regained partial control of her emotions.

If she had died in battle in Africa, her comrades would have done their best to recover her body, give her an honorable burial, and say soldierly things about her. That was the kind of death she had always felt she'd have, a soldier's death. Now she would die, and there would be no one to know that she had even existed.

"To hell with that, Pulaski," she said aloud. She closed her eyes. She would rest, then she would take stock of the situation. She was not totally without resources, for she had herself. She had her low-cut shoes, a pair of ruined hose, her underwear, skirt, and tunic blouse. Add to that the stars of a marshal of the Red Army on her collar and shoulder boards.

"Most probably," she thought, as she started to doze off, "the issue will be decided rather quickly, with infection in the cut on my thigh from the slime of the riverside swamps."

ELEVEN

Paul Warden had an assignment that was very much to his liking: He became the colony's official guardian against the miners, the great underground slugs. This responsibility gave him a chance to be out in the open air and the freedom to roam the countryside in a fast, lightweight, well-armed, all-terrain crawler, sometimes with the admiral, sometimes alone. He had located all of the miners' traps within five miles of Hamilton and had marked all of them well. It was up to Paul to maintain an underground monitoring system, so he and the admiral had rigged up a remote listening post aboard the crawler so that Warden could keep an ear on the entire system and still be mobile.

He and the admiral had done a pretty good job hooking all the listening posts into the monitoring station on the crawler, but there was one little glitch in it that they couldn't smooth out, no matter how many times they went over the circuits. It came from a listening probe just east of town and gave out just one little beep at odd intervals. The signal was just enough to kick the needle on the dial and to form an audio signal alarm of about one second's duration. After going over the electronics three times and replacing the listening probe twice, Paul gave up, deciding that the glitch was in the monitor on the crawler.

There were a lot of unanswered questions about the underground things, which Stoner McRae had named min-

149

ers because they were so skilled at cutting their tunnels. Where did they put the dirt and stone that they excavated from their tunnels? What became of the waste products left from their ingestion of dirt, stone, and whatever else they ate? Both Stoner McRae and Amando Kwait were very interested in finding the answers to those questions— Stoner because he wanted to examine the waste for minerals and Kwait because the waste might make good fertilizer or contain some of the metallic trace elements missing in Omega's topsoil. Warden gathered soil samples from the areas around miner traps and delivered them to the labs at the end of each day.

One of the mysteries of the miners was soon solved: Amando Kwait, touring his planted areas along the Dinah River valley, had borrowed the admiral as an escort that day. When Amando was satisfied that his crops were flourishing, growing so rapidly under Omega's sun that he was astounded, he decided to take advantage of the admiral's company and protection to do some scouting on his own. He had access to all the reports turned in by all teams studying Paul's samples, but sometimes facts, figures, soil analyses, and all the scientific data in the world is not worth one good look. He had the admiral drive up the valley as the river snaked and turned, bearing off gradually to the northeast toward the distant shores of Lake Dinah. There would be enough arable land in the river valley to feed the population of Eden, even if it doubled and redoubled several times.

They were moving at good speed through rolling, grassy veld. The heat of summer was beginning to turn the grass more brown. With the crawler moving briskly along, Amando had the feeling he was riding a roller coaster. The vehicle sped up and down the slopes and ridges, and an ant on a peanut-sized crawler driving across a piece of corrugated plastic roofing would, Amando thought, have the same feeling of quick ups and downs. The odd thing about it was that the ridges, or corrugations, stretched east and west as straight as the corrugations in roofing.

"Admiral," Amando said, "I think we'd better stop and take a look."

As he stepped down from the crawler, the first thing

that struck him was that the grass was thicker, taller, and healthier than any grass he'd seen. He pulled up a few stalks and sniffed at the exposed dirt on the roots.

"If you don't mind, Admiral, would you get the soil sample bags and give me some random samplings?"

"My pleasure, sir," the admiral responded. He was enjoying himself. His chest-mounted memory chambers held all of Amando's data on agriculture, but seeing crops growing and digging one's fingers into the dirt helped to bring the information alive.

When Amando had all the samples he wanted, he asked the admiral to drive east along the top of one of the ridges, back in the direction of the river. They were in a rather large depression, extending for miles to the west toward the ocean, bounded on the north and south by rising, rolling hills.

There were no trees of any size in the area of the parallel ridges and troughs, but after a few miles of driving toward the river, Amando could see the line of trees that grew along the river. He was about to tell the admiral they'd gone far enough when, just ahead, the mounds ended, rounding off into the flat, grassy floor of the veld. They did not all end evenly, but none was more than fifty yards longer than the others; it was, Amando thought, very curious. He had another analogy for the area. It was as if giants had plowed perfectly straight furrows extending far into the western distance, throwing up seed rows for planting.

They drove for almost five miles along the flats past the ends of the ridges. The last ridge was not more than a quarter mile from the rise of higher ground. Not well rounded at the end, it had fresh earth showing. Amando approached the fresh earth cautiously. The admiral had a heavy projectile gun loaded with explosive .60 caliber rounds at the ready. Things that dug on Omega had teeth. It was a miner's tunnel, and the freshly dug earth was distributed evenly and neatly in a mounded slope, building up to an older section, which was covered with lush grass. The tunnel was being constructed as the miner brought up fresh earth.

The admiral's listening sensors detected nothing, so

Amando approached and picked up a handful of the fresh earth. It was fine and dry and obviously contained, from its color, pulverized rock from far below the surface. Samples were taken, the find was reported back to control aboard the *Spirit of America*, and the word was out by the time the crawler reached the vicinity of Hamilton. Amando and the admiral were met by a crawler carrying Stoner McRae, Amanda Miller, and Grace Monroe. The crawlers came to a stop side by side, and the conversation was mostly in question form:

Why would the miners transport their diggings for long distances to dispose of them in neat, straight mounds? Why was there only one sign of digging, when it was known from the early survey, before the miners seemed to move away from the vicinity of Hamilton, that there had been at least dozens, and perhaps more, of the beasts in the area? And how did the miners carry the finely pulverized dirt?

Mandy Miller, all curiosity, switched over to Amando's crawler and went back to the ship with him, where she put on a lab smock and helped Amando with the initial analysis. Amando was concentrating on detecting the important trace elements that were missing in the topsoil and was rewarded quickly. Mandy began a series of tests to isolate anything exotic, and she found traces of the same powerful acids that came from the miner's stomach.

"Amando," she said, a grin on her delicate, heart-shaped face, "I hate to be indelicate, but I think you've been digging in a miner's personal latrine." She showed him the results of her testings.

He scratched his head. "But there are massive amounts of material out there, just in that one depression in the veld."

"But only one fresh sign," she remarked. "How long, how many years, decades, centuries, have they been making their deposits there?"

Amando shrugged. "Too bad the acid's in it. It's rich enough in minerals and trace elements to be used as fertilizer."

Mandy said, "It's a minute amount, but any amount of that acid might prove too much for human consumption, assuming that it would be assimilated by your food crops."

"I'm afraid it would," he said.

Mandy ran further tests on several other soil samples from the mounds. She frowned, repeated the run through the analyzer three or four times.

"I think you've got your fertilizer," she said at last. "The acid is biodegradable. These samples show no acid at all. They must be from mound sections at least fifty years old."

Amando, for his own satisfaction, ran some tests of his own. Any soil sample taken from more than a few feet from the end of a mound was acid free.

"They're big," Mandy said. "The stomach cavity of those we killed could hold about a half ton of material at one time. But at a half ton a load—my God, it may have taken generations of miners to build the mounds you saw."

"I will ask Captain Rodrick to assign a scout to check for more areas such as the one near the river," Amando said, grinning widely. He had begun to fear severe shortage of fertilizer, and knowing nutrition as he did, he had envisioned health problems, a kind of starvation in the face of plenty, when the food supplements carried by the ship ran out. Now the problem was solved. That corrugated plain would provide mineral-rich fertilizer for at least a century, and there would almost have to be other dumping grounds such as that one, for it didn't make sense to think that every miner west of the snowy mountains would make the long, underground trip to that little depression.

That one problem solved, the scientists were ready to tackle the next one, which was the continuing glitch in the one listening probe. It took Warden several days to notice that the point from which the sound originated was moving ever so minutely.

"Whoa, there," he said when he realized that the point of origin had moved some twenty feet. He and the admiral drove to the spot east of town where the listening probe was planted. He had charted the tunnels in that area already. But the echoes from Chief Engineer Rosen's sound generator charted out a new tunnel, headed straight toward the nearest house in Hamilton, about five hundred yards away.

"What do you make of it, Admiral?" Warden asked. Like most who came into close association with Grace Monroe's prize robot, he had to remind himself that the tall, handsome man was not of flesh and blood.

"The probe should have picked up the sounds of movement, and especially the sounds of tunneling," the admiral said.

Warden thought so, too. He circled the end of the new tunnel with listening devices and put on a headset to cut out all extraneous sound. At first he heard nothing, and then there was a brief burst of sound, which ceased immediately. That pattern continued for an hour. He got on the communicator to Emi Zuki, sent her a recording of the sounds that came at irregular intervals, and asked her to run a comparison with the sounds on record. It took Emi only five minutes.

"Here's a recording of a miner crawling," she said, and Paul heard the familiar, rhythmic, scrape-scrape sound. Then, from the tapes made by the crawler inside the burrow of the first miner to be killed, there was the sound of deep-down digging.

Study of the dead miners had revealed that the creatures dug tunnels by rotating their heads just over ninety degrees to one side and then back one hundred eighty degrees to a ninety degree–plus position on the opposite side. Toothlike projections of stony skeletal material on the miner's heavy snout formed, indeed, a living drill bit.

"All right, Commander," Emi said. "Listen to this. I'm going to put your glitch, your one burst of sound, on a repeater." Repeated over and over, the sound had the same scrape-scrape characteristics of the digging sound.

"Son of a gun," Warden said. It appeared that an infinitely patient miner, the first to be detected near Hamilton since the fourth miner was killed near the banks of the Dinah River, was boring a tunnel through the relatively soft subsoil one movement of his digging head at a time.

"Hold on a minute, Emi," Paul said, programming

his monitor to go back to the first day the glitch appeared on the scroll. He found it, fed the sound to Emi, and by using the same technique of repeating the one burst of sound, they heard the unmistakable sound of a miner moving through a stone tunnel.

"What we have here, Admiral," Warden said, "is a sneaky one. He came from God knows how far away, moving one half of his body at a time, waiting for a while, with no regularity of timing, and moving the other half." A bit of work on Emi's computer told them that it had taken the miner over forty-eight hours to crawl a distance of less than two hundred feet. He had done it so patiently, inching the front part of his body forward, resting, then bringing the stern up, that Warden knew that there was a brain of no mean ability there underground. How had the damned thing figured out that the sounds of its movement were being detected?

He conferred with the two people who were most interested in the miners, Mandy Miller and Grace Monroe. "What I want to know is what the sneaky so-and-so is up to," Paul said. "He's moving in a beeline toward the nearest house."

"Let's not do anything rash," Grace suggested, highly intrigued. Mandy agreed. If the miner accelerated his digging in an obvious attack on the house, there'd be plenty of time, with Mopro's heavy armaments, to prepare for its emergence.

"I'll keep a good eye on this joker," Warden said.

Paul, at last, had his chance to camp out. He set up a two-person tent under an umbrella tree near the spot where the miner was working so slowly and so patiently.

"What do you mean, you don't know how to build a campfire?" he asked, when the admiral confessed his lack of outdoor training.

It was fun. He felt as if he had been taken a few years back in time to his Boy-Scout leader days. The suave admiral, always eager to learn something new, helped gather fallen limbs from the umbrella trees, pulled enough dry grass to incinerate a buffalo, and got the fire going with his first try. The admiral sat cross-legged on the grass with Warden, proudly looking at the results of his first outdoor lesson.

Warden set his monitor to give a loud alarm if the pace of the digging increased, then crawled into his sleeping bag. The admiral kept the campfire going all night. By morning the underground digger had increased the length of the tunnel by a few inches.

"He's headed up," Warden said, after a study of the night's readings.

On the second evening Max Rosen and Grace Monroe joined Warden and the admiral at the campsite. Grace had brought synthetic hot dogs and buns made fresh from a local, wild grain, which had been cleared for human consumption. Even Max had to admit that eating them in the open air improved the taste of the hot dogs.

It took three more nights before the miner emerged. On each of those three nights the admiral and Warden had company. Word had spread.

Grace was a regular visitor to Warden's camp. She was happy that, now that the fertilizer mounds had been discovered, there would be no more killing of the miners. They were simply too valuable to kill—except in cases of obvious self-defense—and she had a feeling that there wouldn't be any such cases. The miners were showing amazing intelligence.

When Grace and Max arrived that third night, Paul Warden was showing Evangeline Burr, Spirit's librarian, how to build a campfire. The admiral, who had come to the camp ahead of Grace, was assisting in the lesson, but it was Paul who was on his knees beside Evangeline.

Max looked up at Grace as she walked up, winked, and returned his gaze to Evangeline's rump.

"Dirty old man," Grace whispered.

"A connoisseur," Max whispered back.

But that reminded Max that more days had gone by and he still hadn't found time to romance Grace in the manner she deserved and, miraculously, wanted. In all the tumult of Lynn Roberts's death, and chasing and killing miners and spending long hours with Grace in the labs trying to figure out what made the dead-white grubs tick, there just hadn't been time.

"You have done a splendid job," Paul Warden told the librarian as the flames began to lick at the dry wood. "I hereby award you the Paul Warden broken twig medal for exceptional skill in campfire building."

He pushed a broken stick into her blouse pocket and grinned.

Evangeline was smiling up into his eyes. They were still kneeling beside the fire, and it was getting pretty hot, but she was wondering what was so very interesting about Paul's half grin. Actually, it was, on first view, sort of dopey.

"I'll keep it always," she vowed. She moved back from the fire and sat on the grass. Soon there were roasted hot dogs. Max and Grace had moved about twenty feet away so that Grace could lean her back on the bole of an umbrella tree, and the admiral was in the crawler checking the monitors, so it was up to Paul to entertain Evangeline. Not that he minded. She was a rather attractive young woman, maybe a bit closer to his own age than the younger Sage Bryson. Evangeline was much more friendly than Sage, and she knew a little bit about everything, it seemed. She asked him questions about his service career and listened with a flattering attention, her shining eyes on his, which prompted him to search for old tales to make her laugh.

"Did you fill out those marriage papers?" Max asked Grace.

She made a little face. "I'm sorry, Max."

"Don't be. I lost mine."

"Trying to wriggle out of it, are you?"

"We're going to fill them out tomorrow, damn it," he said, "and to heck with waiting until things calm down."

"Have you finished eating?" she asked.

"Yes." He tossed aside the half hot dog he was holding.

"I think if we very quietly move around the bole of this rather large tree, we'll be hidden from the others," she said, with a teasing little smile.

"That's what I like about you," Max said, grinning. "Your brains."

Slowly, smothering giggles—and the idea of Max Rosen smothering a giggle would have astounded everyone who knew him—they eased around the tree. Max checked rather guiltily to be sure that they could not be seen and, with a sigh of pure anticipation leaned to put his arms around her.

"We've got to fill out those papers tomorrow," he whispered, as her lips parted, met his, and he felt his toes begin to curl. "Just got to," he said, breaking the kiss to make more firm contact. He was just letting out a gusty sigh from the wonderful taste of her when something rubbed against his leg, and he quickly put down a hand without breaking the kiss to feel bristly hair and body heat.

Max yelped in alarm and rolled, taking Grace with him. They were, after all, sitting on the grass in miner country, with one of the monsters carefully digging away not too far from the campsite. His first thought was to put his body between the damned thing and Grace so that he ended up on top of her and she was saying, "What? What?"

He leaped to his feet, going for his weapon.

Cat walked toward them, its tail sticking straight up. And behind Cat, on the dead run, came the admiral with his .60 caliber gun in hand.

"Grace," Max wailed.

"Oh, Max," Grace said, trying desperately not to laugh. She was unsuccessful. Cat came to Max and rubbed against his leg. He rolled his eyes and looked toward the fiery heavens. Evangeline and Paul came to see what was going on.

"We're selling tickets," Max announced disgustedly.

"Oh, poor Max," Grace choked out through her laughter.

"Next time I fall in love," Max said, "it's gonna be with a woman who doesn't have any kids."

The spell broken, the hour growing late, Max took Grace and Cat back to the ship, where they were both still living. They'd move into a very nice house, which was almost complete now, when they were married. For a moment, as he sneaked a quick kiss good night, Max was tempted to enter her quarters, weld the door closed against her menagerie, and tell her he wasn't leaving. But they'd discussed premarital affairs, and Grace had been rather surprised to find that Max was a romantic. Besides, they were going to fill out the marriage papers tomorrow.

Evangeline Burr, finding that she was oddly comfortable with Paul Warden, a state unusual for her in the presence of a man when he was not on library business, stayed at the campsite to help the admiral and him watch the fire. Paul himself asked her to stay, telling her that fire watching was an art as well as a duty, and that it took some practice to become proficient at it.

Omega's seventy-minute hours made for a long evening. When Evangeline said that she'd best be getting back and Paul asked the admiral to escort her, he watched her disappear into the darkness with a smile on his face. She was one nice lady, he thought. And, with a little pang of sadness, he wished that Sage could be as warm and friendly with him.

He put more wood on the fire, roasted just one more hot dog for a nightcap, and leaned back against his bedroll to eat it. Eden was, he decided, his kind of country. The nighttime temperature was a balmy caress. The skies were spectacular. The smaller of the two moons hung at first quarter just over the horizon. There were no stinging insects, although colorful, mothlike things flitted across the flickering light of the fire now and then. He was imagining that Sage was sitting by his side, her hand in his, when the communicator paged him. It was the admiral.

"Commander Warden," the admiral said, "I'd like your permission to delay my return to our campfire. The entertainment robot has malfunctioned and is speeding along the corridors, telling the same joke over and over at the top of his amplification. Rather than wake Grace, I'm going to help the RD seventy-seven repair robot with the circuit adjustment. It shouldn't take more than two hours."

"Take your time, Admiral," Warden told him.

Paul made one last check on the monitoring system. The miner obliged by giving him a little blip, one more turn of that drill of a snout down below. The thing was still twenty feet down, and it would take a long time for him to reach the surface with that slow, careful, and almost silent digging. Paul activated his perimeter guard, and invisible beams surrounded his campsite. He turned on the red light of the alarm to warn the admiral when he returned that the guard beams were on. Omega's pure, ocean-scented air and his tiredness made for instant sleep.

He awoke sitting up in one swift movement with his laser in his hands and the monitor alarm going crazy. The miner in the tunnel was moving at top speed, scrape-scraping frantically. Paul flipped a switch to illuminate the area with the crawler's lights and crouched in a ready position, weapon aimed at a circular mound of fresh earth. He was ready to blast away if the miner did anything more than poke his head up out of the hole. But the sounds of the monitor told him that the miner was retreating.

What the hell? He checked the monitor to be sure he wasn't hearing things. The miner was reaching a point near the limit of the range, and then the sounds stopped. Paul edged closer to the fresh earth. He didn't quite understand how the thing had come up through almost twenty feet of subsoil so quickly, but it had, and there'd been an explosion of fresh dirt, which made a little mound around the hole through which the miner had emerged. The hole was not neatly dug, and the amount of fresh earth indicated that the powerful miner had simply pushed his way violently through the last few feet.

Warden got on the communicator. Emi Zuki was on duty. He reported the odd events but told Emi that it wouldn't be necessary to wake the captain or to send any reinforcements. The admiral, monitoring, broke in to tell Warden that he was on his way. Warden edged in closer to the fresh mound of soil, because there was something reflecting the beams of light. The monitor told him there was nothing down there but an empty tunnel, but he approached warily, ready to fire and flee at the same time.

There was only one object on the mound of fresh soil that was glittering, glowing in the bright lights. Paul held his breath and leaned forward and picked it up. It was rather heavy. It reminded him of a sea fan, that delicate underwater plant that extends leafless, feathery arms out-ward from a central stem. He moved out of the direct glare of the spots and examined the thing. When he tried to hold it by one of the irregularly shaped arms, the arm bent. There was a heavy, metallic feel, and the color was a rich red-gold.

He knew that Stoner McRae had returned that evening from an expedition into the inland badlands. He got Emi back on the communicator, and very shortly Stoner was answering in a sleepy voice.

Stoner came awake quickly as he listened to Paul. He was standing beside Warden's crawler within ten minutes, holding metal, heavy metal, in his hands.

"Is it what I think it is?" Paul asked.

"It's gold, all right," Stoner said, holding the multiarmed, feathery formation carefully. He'd seen natural veins of gold removed intact from the matrix rock before; it made for a certain natural beauty. But he'd never seen so complex a vein, so large a vein, with the tiniest veins so fragile that they would bend at a touch.

"This is the way the molten gold formed as it ran into faults in the forming rock," Stoner explained.

What he couldn't explain was how such a cumbersome thing as a miner could so delicately remove matrix rock without disturbing or distorting the delicate gold formation. And neither of them could explain why the miner had, for days, dug so carefully, obviously trying to avoid detection by the monitors, to burst up into the night air violently and leave such a precious gift.

"But it's more significant than just this gold, Paul," Stoner said. "If there's gold, there'll be other heavy metals."

"Rhenium," Paul said.

"Rhenium," Stoner agreed.

TWELVE

Theresita had slept fitfully through a long night that cooled only slightly. She awoke to the first dim light filtering down from high above to find herself still soaked, sticky, and dehydrated. The pain she had expected from the cut on her thigh had not materialized. She climbed down from the bole of the fallen tree, drank from the water puddled in the cavity left when the tree's roots had been ripped from the earth, and then began to push her way through the dense undergrowth.

She had no definite goal; it was just that she'd spent enough time perched atop the fallen tree. She had, during wakeful periods, accepted her situation: She would die; the untreated cut on her thigh would become infected, and that, combined with starvation, would kill her.

If she had been dumped alone into an African jungle, she would have thought about survival. She had been given two weeks of an excellent survival course when her African service had begun, and she'd learned to eat some very odd things. But this was a jungle on an alien planet, and there was no survival manual to tell her which plant roots were edible and which were deadly poison, which fruits would give her body the fuel it needed to function and which would, with some deadly alien substance, stop all functions altogether.

The heat increased rapidly as the sun rose higher in

the eastern sky, and the filtered light made visibility better far down under the treetops. Things were moving in the trees high above her. She saw a variety of birds and once, with a rustle of sound, something larger than a bird passed overhead, masked by the dense foliage.

She had no destination. She tried to keep moving in a straight line, in the southerly direction of the flow of the river, by keeping the glow of the sun to her left. She had to push her way through a great tangle of vines and low-growing, huge-leafed things that retained water on their surface, so that she was constantly wet with that and her own sweat.

She heard a great chattering ahead, the sound quite like that of the African jungles, and then she could see the source of the noise. Birds. Mauve, they stood about a foot high, and they were congregated in and around a type of tree she had never seen before. It had ladderlike branches growing perpendicular to its trunk, and the birds were eating its fruit. Half-eaten fruit lay atop the undergrowth. She picked up one. About the size of a large grapefruit, the exposed flesh had a deep-green color and smelled slightly acidic. She tore away that part of the fruit that had been pecked and pitted by the birds and touched her tongue gingerly to taste. It wasn't bad.

She looked at the fruit, held it out in front of her, and laughed, for she was suddenly reminded of a scene from an ancient English drama by Shakespeare, in which Hamlet, the prince of Denmark, was holding a skull and saying, "Alas."

"Alas," she said.

Her mouth was watering. She had not realized how hungry she was until she'd touched her tongue to the fruit. She had a simple choice: If she didn't eat, she would die; if she ate, she might die faster. She ate.

Tangy juice ran down her chin. The fruit had a seed core at the center, but the flesh was edible from the thin skin to the core. The consistency was figlike, the taste totally unfamiliar, but tart like a citrus fruit. It was very good, so good that she found herself stuffing huge bites into her mouth and then, thinking that the fruit on the lowest branches, which were probably twenty feet off the ground, had not been pecked by the birds, she hitched up her skirt, leaped to seize a low branch, and clambered up until she could reach a large fruit. Surprisingly, there was no pain from the wound in her thigh. But as she ate the fruit, she waited for the pains to start in her stomach. When there were no stomach pains, Theresita began to pluck other fruit and drop it down onto the cushioning carpet of undergrowth.

The birds had quieted when she began to climb the tree, but now they were squabbling and eating again, one of them walking sideways on a limb level with her head to cock his eye at her from a distance of five feet.

"Watch it," she warned. "You might be edible, too."

A quick shower swept over as she was perched in the tree, and she waited it out there, hearing the roar of heavy drops on the canopy above her and then the drip, drip as it began to soak through. When the rain stopped, she had decided that she might just live for a while after all. Her leg wound had formed a good scab. Because the cut had been deep, she'd expected very slow healing, if any. Perhaps, she thought, there was something in the river mud that aided healing. It didn't really matter. It would either heal or it wouldn't.

It was very hot. She had torn her skirt in several places moving the short distance she'd covered. Her hose were nothing much more than runs but would still be useful. She removed them, stuffed both legs full of the fruit, and slung the makeshift bag around her neck, letting the filled legs dangle down in front. That way she had both hands free for making her way through the undergrowth.

Water was no problem. The rain had left clear, good-tasting little pools in the hollow cups of the big-leafed plants. They grew about as high as her head, so that to drink she had only to tilt a leaf and let the water run into her mouth.

She could tell when she was getting close to the river, for the jungle floor, piled deep in detritus, became soggy. She would sink down into the rotted vegetation, and water would spring up in her tracks. Now and then she'd come across a tree so recently fallen that it had not begun to rot into the jungle floor and she'd rest. She made her lunch on one of the fruit and pushed on toward the south, but the river was apparently making a westward bend, so in the late afternoon the sun was in her face when she found another fallen tree and spent the night atop it.

She had a few bad moments when the light awakened her. There just didn't seem to be much point in going on. She doubted if she'd covered a mile the day before, pushing, crawling, struggling through the denseness. And she'd seen the jungle extending in all directions to the horizon as the scout ship fell toward the river. For all she knew, the whole planet could be jungle. She might spend years not seeing anything but omnipresent green and just a hint of the glow of the sun through the jungle curtain.

She added to her menu a large, thin-shelled nut when she saw it being eaten by a long-limbed tree creature, which had a long tail, a body like a cat, and a short snout with crocodile teeth. The nut meat was oily and substantial.

When she was still alive the next morning without ill effects from the things she'd eaten, Theresita experienced a change in her attitude. Living beat the alternative. She would have done just about anything for a bath and then just five minutes of being dry. These would be possible only if she found her way out of the jungle.

She stumbled onto a wide path beaten down into a residue of dead vegetation. A quick examination of the path sent a chill up her spine. On her first day in the jungle she had heard great crashing noises. This path had been pushed through the jungle by something of great weight, big enough to flatten and crush small trees four inches in diameter. Along the perimeter of the path were deep, regularly spaced gouges, which had torn down through the vegetation to the gray soil.

She didn't like the idea of meeting whatever it was that had made the path, but it made for easy walking. It was a relief to be able to walk without pushing her way; it gave her a feeling of accomplishment, for she had covered, she estimated, at least two miles before the path turned directly away from the river.

She selected her place for the night more carefully.

She had no desire to be awakened by something as big as the creature that had crushed its way through the tangled jungle. She climbed the horizontal limbs of a fruit tree and broke off small branches to make a sort of nest, which she found to be quite comfortable.

She crossed another path at midmorning, and she found her first tool. She saw what she thought was a stone half-covered by crushed leaves. Since a stone can be a weapon or a tool, she bent to pick it up. It was rounded on three sides, quite flat, not more than a half-inch thick at the thickest part, and narrowed to a dull edge. It was grayish-white, smooth on the underside, and sandpaper textured on the top. The edge was not sharp enough to be used as a cutting tool but could be made so if she could find something to use as a grindstone.

Now the going was very hard again as she stayed just outside the limits of the river swamplands. Her bare legs were scratched and bleeding. Her sodden tunic protected her arms somewhat, at the expense of many pulls and rips. She was exhausted before the afternoon had been used up. She found a fruit-tree and repeated her nest-building activities from the night before and was asleep, her stomach full of fruit and nuts, before the total darkness came to that world under the jungle's knitted canopy. She came awake with a grunt of pure panic, dreaming that she was falling. She hugged a limb with both arms just as the tree shook violently. She heard the sound of falling fruit, then a dry, grinding sound and the crackings of breaking limbs and twigs.

The darkness was so total that she could see nothing, but she could hear and sense the presence of something very large there twenty feet below her on the ground.

"Stop that, you crazy bastard!" she screamed as the tree shook again. She had to hang onto the limb to keep from being dislodged.

Her voice brought a response, a terrific roar that seemed to fill all available space and echo off the surrounding trees. In quick fear she climbed higher, bumping her head painfully on a branch. She wrapped her arms around a large limb and clung to it as the tree began to shake with a renewed and more frenzied assault. She feared that the tree would fall and that she would fall with it down into that terrible blackness and into the reach of the huge, roaring thing.

When dawn came, her fear increased. She could make out the outline of something as large as a front-line battle tank, and as the light grew slowly she saw a massive, scarab-shaped body with, apparently, no head. Six short, powerful legs, a thick trunk, which ended in a single pointed horn, churned the jungle floor as the thing flung itself at the bole of the tree and collided with a resounding thud and a jar that shook the entire tree. The six legs scrambled, digging, pulling the massive body backward.

The body seemed to have scales. Theresita, as much in anger at herself because of her pounding heart and dry mouth as at the beast, plucked a fruit and threw it violently. It struck the scaled body near the front, and the churning legs stopped moving. The gray body extruded a bony roundness, which was followed by a scaly neck, and then the head lifted toward her to show her cold, glassy eyes and a beak that opened in a challenging roar to expose fields of needle-sharp teeth.

"Ugly bastard!" Theresita shouted, throwing another fruit, which struck the beast directly in its opened, roaring mouth. The roar ceased immediately, but the head jerked spasmodically and the fruit was expelled, followed by an even wilder roar. The head withdrew just in time for the front part of the body to smash into the bole. This time she heard the roots crack and saw the matted ground covering lift at the base of the tree. The damned thing was actually going to push the tree over with a few more charges.

Theresita looked around frantically. Far above her the fruit tree's upper branches joined the tangled canopy. She began to climb. She was hampered by her food supply, fruit and nuts in the legs of her hose dangling from her neck, so she stopped and threw them one by one at the armored monster and then resumed her climbing. She could find more fruit and nuts, but she wanted to hang onto the hose.

The tree's limbs got smaller and the swaying more pronounced as the battering continued far below, but she would not look down. She was at least a hundred feet above the ground when she held her breath and reached out to grab a limb from another tree. She pulled herself onto it and crawled down its slope to the bole of a true giant and rested there, panting as the fruit tree she'd just left began to fall, its limbs breaking with sharp, shotlike sounds. It couldn't fall all the way, since it was held up by surrounding growth. The beast, all six legs churning, threw its tons of weight up onto the sloping tree trunk, and with a groaning, grinding crash the tree fell to crush the undergrowth. The beast toppled off with a thud and scrambled forward, long neck extended, mouth open, searching for her. Frustrated, it roared, dashed around, crushing undergrowth, and after about a half hour, went crashing off into the jungle, until she could hear the crashing no more.

Theresita was over a hundred feet high, and the limbs on her tree grew to an incredible size nearer the ground. There was no way down, so she went up. Crawling along limbs, clinging to smaller limbs and hand-walking, she progressed toward a section of tangled, climbing vines that obscured the huge trunks of several trees. She had to rest frequently. She made her way into the green tangle of the vines, found runners as thick as her wrist, and tested them to see if they would hold her weight. A half hour later she was on the jungle floor, picking up fallen fruit to restock her supply and finding another of the sandpaperlike rocks, which she knew now as scales from the battering-ram beast.

She tapped the two scales together and made a solid clink. She rubbed the dull, narrow edge of one against the sandpapery side of the other, and by exerting pressure, she could see results. The dulled edge began, after two hours' work, to take on a sharpness. She now had a cutting tool. It was sharp enough and strong enough to whittle through a two-inch sapling to give her another tool, a staff that could be used as a light club.

She pushed through the jungle until she found another fruit tree, checked to be sure that there was an avenue of escape from the upper branches, and built her nest high. It was still early, but she had work to do. The wood of the fruit tree was rather soft. She cut off a limb and laboriously whittled off a two-inch section about two feet long, split one end, drove one of the scales down into the split, and bound it there with one leg of her hose. Now she had not only a cutting-edged tool, but a weapon.

She estimated that, at best, she could travel a mile a day through the jungle. She had no way of knowing which direction would offer the most immediate relief. For all she knew she might, by following the flow of the river, be heading into the heart of the jungle instead of out of it. At a mile a day it would take over three months to travel a hundred miles. And if she had two hundred miles, three hundred miles, or more to travel? She shuddered. She was already losing weight. A diet of fruit and nuts was exotic for one day, but she longed for something a bit more substantial.

The river seemed to be the only solution. The next morning she forced her way to the beginning of the river swamp and waded through. She didn't try to keep the mud off the healing wound on her thigh; indeed, the mud seemed to take the sting out of her many scratches.

The river was brown, muddy, and wider than it had been at the site of the crash of the scout ship. The mud flats were more exposed and difficult to cross. She'd have to find a better site. She began, slowly and laboriously, to make her way downstream, staying in the muddy swampland. She sank quite often up to her midthighs in the soft mud and had to struggle out. The going was slow and tiring. The river was making a slow swing toward the west; to her right the jungle seemed to encroach on the fringe of swampland. And then she was walking on matted jungle floor.

There was an almost imperceptible rise, and the higher ground extended to the river, so that for a few yards ahead there was a riverbank. This, then, would be her construction site. Here she would build a raft. She surveyed it and was pleased.

The jungle giants grew down to the water's edge, and among them was a tree laden with the figlike fruit, with the ladderlike horizontal limbs made for climbing. She saw a likely place for a nest site about twenty-five feet up. She was tired, but she made her way away from the river for a few yards, found a tree of six inches diameter, and began to use her "hatchet" to see just how difficult it was going to be to cut down the tree. It was damned difficult, she discovered, with the first lick, the wood so hard that she feared she'd broken her blade. She tried another type, being careful not to strike hard enough to ruin her tool, and the blade chipped away rough bark.

She went to work eagerly and in two hours' time had the tree cut, branches trimmed, and the six-inch trunk cut to a ten-foot length. She dragged the pole back to the river. She had noticed that a certain type of vine often had long stringers going down into the water and that that portion of the vine in the water lost its bark. She cut a length of it to find it flexible and so strong that she couldn't break it. She notched one end of the pole, tied the vine to it, and secured the other end to a tree. She left the pole floating in the river all night. The wood was so soft and relatively easy to cut, she feared that it might absorb water too quickly. But the next morning, it was still floating as high in the water as it had the evening before.

She spent the next two days clearing a work area. The size of the raft she was going to construct was determined by the fact that her hatchet blade dulled quickly, and repeated grindings against the other scale would, she'd found, eventually wear it away. She would have to construct the raft in the water—one of the ten-foot lengths wasn't too heavy, but she wasn't sure she'd be able to move a raft constructed of a dozen of them lashed together side by side.

She had lost track of the days. It seemed that she'd been hot, wet, and sweaty for weeks, instead of merely days. A heat rash formed under her arms and inside her thighs and made life miserable until she began to coat the affected areas with swamp mud at night, to find them feeling much better each morning.

"All we have to do," she told herself, speaking aloud, "is get a few tons of this miracle mud back to Earth, and we'll be rich capitalists."

At first she had thought merely to lash the logs together side by side, but when she had four of them joined, she found that there was too much flexibility, that the logs moved up and down, rubbing against the vines used as lashings. She'd have to cut more poles and lash them at right angles to the runners to give the raft stability. More work, but the raft was taking shape nicely. It was ten feet long and would be over six feet wide when she finished.

She was trimmed down to a weight she hadn't known since she was a teenage girl. She was hungry all the time in spite of plentiful fruit and nuts. One morning as she pushed her way through the undergrowth in search of the last two saplings, she found a small game trail and began to think in terms of meat. She'd have no way to cook it—trying to start a fire in that permanently wet jungle would be pure folly—but she followed the trail anyway. It led into the jungle, where she did not care to follow.

But at night, knowing where the trail was, she could hear some small animal moving down it to the river. Theresita's desire for something substantial to' eat was overwhelming. She overcame her reluctance to go deeper into the jungle and followed the trail for about two hundred yards to find that something had been digging around the roots of the same big-leafed plant that had furnished her with her drinking water for so many days. The roots of the plant were thick tubers, and there was clear evidence that something had been eating them.

She cut one, rubbed the dirt off as best she could, sliced off a piece and touched her tongue to it. It had a raw, starchy taste. For a long moment she was reluctant, then she remembered the fatalism she'd felt when she first ate the fruit. She took a small bite. It was chewy, like the meat of a coconut, and the taste was pleasing. She ate only a little bit, however, and carried three of the large tubers back to her camp. It wasn't meat, but when there were no ill effects, it was a welcome addition to her diet, and there was an unending supply of the tubers all around her.

She lashed the last pole into place that day. Then, knowing an excitement she hadn't felt in years, she put her weight on the raft and crawled to its center. It sank down into the water until water lapped over the logs, but held. "Oh, hell," she said. It needed at least one more layer of poles to support her weight without her sitting in an inch of water all the time.

"Well, what the hell," she said aloud. "Nobody's waiting for me." She went back to cutting down small trees. She almost caught one of the small animals on the game trail and spent the rest of the day being grateful that she hadn't. She was taking a long break, nibbling on a tuber, when she heard little feet on the trail, which was near the tree she was cutting. She froze and reached carefully for her ax and waited as the patter of little feet came closer. She saw movement in the leaves and launched herself full length, bringing the ax down at the point of movement with a force that would have decapitated a steer. There was a sharp cry from the hidden animal. She'd missed. She raised the ax again.

Before she could strike, a fearful odor assaulted her nostrils, and she caught a glimpse of a small, bristly thing of knobby welts and scurrying feet and an appearance so repulsive that all thoughts of eating left her. She scrambled away from the musk sprayed by the fleeing animal. None had hit her, but she had to abandon the tree she'd been cutting and she had it half cut down.

It took eighteen lengths of small tree trunks to lash a layer of flotation at right angles to the long runner on top of the raft. When she stepped bravely onto the raft from the bank, it held her weight nicely and she was high and dry.

She had been giving a lot of thought to the problem of steering the raft. There was nothing to use as a rudder, so she cut a long, slender pole, which she could use to keep the raft pushed away from the bank. She took one day for food gathering, then was ready to go.

She launched the raft just after first light, pushed away from the bank, and was caught in a slow current. The raft tended to turn slowly round and round, but that was not a serious problem. She was moving. The morning was clear, with only a white haze to limit the heat of the sun. Where her skin was exposed, below the ragged, short length of skirt and through the holes in her tunic, it began to turn pink. She had not been exposed to direct rays of the sun since her service in Africa, and she knew the power of those rays on tender skin.

The current had carried her to midstream. The pole was useless for steering because the water was so deep she could not touch bottom. The only way she could get to the bank was to swim, and she wasn't about to abandon so many days of hard work just to avoid a sunburn. She splashed water over her cooking skin until she saw that the raft was heading toward the east bank as the river entered a gentle curve. She kept testing the water for depth, and when she was very near the bank she felt the muddy bottom and began to lean on the pole until the raft moved out of the current and into an eddy alongside a muddy bank. She lashed the raft to trees and waded ashore. The swamp mud began to cool her burning limbs almost immediately.

She slept in a nest in a tree and went to work the next morning building a lean-to on the rear of the raft. The plants that provided water and tubers also provided their large leaves for her thatched roof. When the lean-to was finished it was too late to cast off, so she spent another night in the same tree and pushed the raft back out into the current just before sunrise.

She decided it wasn't all bad, during that lazy day. The raft revolved slowly, riding the center of the current. She decided to keep going, and darkness came without her reaching shore. She drifted downriver, trying to stay awake, but there was a slight breeze over the river, and for once she was almost dry. She dozed off, and when she awoke, there were two moons in the sky, both of them high. In their light she managed to tie up to two trees, and she spent the rest of the night on the raft, sleeping comfortably on a bed of leaves.

When morning came she decided to replenish her tuber supply and took about three steps into the brush before coming face to face with the cold eyes, gaping mouth, and huge bulk of a battering-ram beast. She screamed and turned, skin puckering, already feeling the tearing of those fearful teeth. But there was no movement from the beast. Then she smelled the ripe, sickening odor of decay and saw that the cold eyes were filmed.

Something had torn open that armored body and eaten away a chunk of white flesh large enough to fill a bathtub. The jungle, for yards around, had been torn, uprooted, and tramped down in the battle. She realized she would have a good supply of tools here. She approached the dead beast and tried to pry loose one of the larger scales. Finally, by using her staff as a lever, she broke it loose, bringing a portion of decaying flesh with it.

As she worked, she kept her eyes and ears open— she didn't want to be surprised by whatever was big enough and mean enough to kill a creature the size of a tank. She used the day to make three additions to her raft: First, she constructed two oars. Then she used the largest scale she could tear off the dead animal as a rudder for a sweep, which she mounted through a forked stick at the rear of the raft. With a reserve supply of scales for toolmaking and lengths of green sapling for handles, she pushed off in the early evening. In her idleness, she carved a notch on a lean-to support pole and made it a habit, as the long, slow days went by, to keep track of them in that way. When, after twenty days of traveling, the jungle looked just as dense, the river just as wide and muddy, she began to wonder just what kind of a world she'd found.

She was bronzed now, and no longer had to protect her skin with mud, which she'd kept on the raft for medicinal purposes. Her hair was always damp, hanging in greasy straightness to her shoulders, so one afternoon after she'd sharpened one of her cutting blades to its narrowest edge, she chopped it off in handfuls, as close to her scalp as possible. Her skirt was nothing more than ribbons. Her lacy panties were torn. Her tunic was faded by the sun, and it, like the skirt, hung in tatters.

But she felt so good, she couldn't believe it. She couldn't do much in the way of movement aboard the raft, but she could do calisthenics. She had leaned down to a trimness that pleased her. "Lady," she told herself, holding a leg up in front of her, "keep this up and you can become a fashion model."

She estimated that the current was moving her along at the pace of a leisurely walker, perhaps three miles per hour. In a twenty-four hour day that would be seventy-two miles. When she marked up her thirtieth day on the river, allowing for the time she'd spent on the riverbanks, she guessed that she'd traveled over fifteen hundred miles.

Just how big was this damned jungle?

II

TROUBLE IN PARADISE

THIRTEEN

Duncan Rodrick was notified by Jackie Garvey of the odd presentation of the gold matrix by the miner. Jackie's call came just before his alarm went off, so it took him a few seconds to understand what she was saying. He had not planned to have a captain's breakfast, but he wanted to know more about the events of the night out there by Paul Warden's hot-dog roasting camp.

"Jackie," he said, "see if you can round up the following people for breakfast in my quarters: Chief Rosen and Dr. Monroe, Commander Warden, Dr. Miller, Dr. Kwait, Stoner McRae, and the animal man on Dr. Miller's staff—what's his name?"

"Dr. James Wilson."

"Yes," Rodrick said. "And Miss Burr, from the library." He had found that Evangeline Burr was an exceptional woman. In an era of specialization, Evangeline possessed more interdisciplinary knowledge than any person he'd ever known. And if she didn't have the facts in her mind, she could find them quickly. He'd made a note to himself to start utilizing Evangeline as a bridge between the various scientific fields; there'd been instances back on Earth when a discovery that seemed insignificant in one field would have opened entirely new avenues of speculation and progress in another field if people had but known about it.

He showered quickly. He tried to concentrate on the possible meanings of the miner's actions, but his mind kept going back to the meeting he'd been asked to attend the previous night. He had a few extra minutes after he was dressed while the enlisted men were preparing for a captain's breakfast, so he unhooked what looked like a button from his uniform and put it into his projector. It was actually a little recording device he'd been given by Presidential Adviser Oscar Kost.

"Captain Rodrick," Clive Baxter said smoothly on the screen, "thank you for coming. We won't keep you long."

First Officer Rocky Miller was not shown on the screen at that time, but he was in Rodrick's mind. He'd been sitting away from the conference table. "I'm just an observer, Captain," he'd told Rodrick.

"This Committee of Concerned Citizens has been formed, Captain," Baxter explained, "to consider problems that, because you are a busy man, might have escaped your attention."

"Please continue." Rodrick's own voice came from the speakers.

"You've seen these," Baxter said, indicating an assortment of semitropical and tropical fruit arranged artistically in a basket at his elbow. "And I'm sure you have sampled them and found them to be quite delicious."

Rodrick had merely nodded.

"To the south of us there is a paradise of plenty," Baxter said. "In my talks with Dr. Kwait—whose ability and knowledge I greatly admire—he has expressed concern with the selection of this particular site of settlement."

Rodrick was startled but showed no reaction. To his knowledge, the only concern Kwait had expressed would be of equal concern anywhere, and that was the lack of vital trace elements in Omega's soil.

"While it is rather beautiful here, in a stark, barren way," Baxter continued, "there are those of us who feel that it would have been to our advantage to build the first settlement in that semitropic zone to the south, where the rains are year round, and there is edible, native fruit in plenty."

"Dr. Baxter," Rodrick said with elaborate patience,

"the characteristics of a desirable settlement site were the subject of thousands of hours of consideration by the planners back on Earth. My selection of Stanton Bay fits their top recommendation almost exactly. If you'd care to become more familiar with the rationale behind the choosing of an area such as Eden, the reports of the Earth planners have been declassified and are available in the library." He thought that would end the discussion.

"If I may speak?" said a stern-faced woman whose field was geothermal energy. "We have all studied those reports, Captain. There's just one thing wrong with them. None of the planners have ever been off Earth, and they have not seen Omega's beautiful and fruitful areas farther to the south. We feel that we are within our rights to consider the possibility of, one, establishing a satellite colony—"

"Hold it right there," Rodrick interrupted. "You're within your rights to *talk* about anything. But under no circumstances will this colony be divided."

"As I was going to say," the stern-faced woman went on, "either establishing a satellite colony or an outpost to gather and ship to us the delicious foodstuffs of the south or, two, moving the entire colony to that more favorable climate."

"We can begin to make use of the resources of the entire planet when we've got this planet surveyed and mapped," Rodrick said, "and when we're producing our own hydrogen fuel."

"Yes," Baxter agreed. "But there's this, too, Captain—and please don't for a moment think that this is criticism of the excellent job you've done. However, as you well know, our constitution calls for free elections."

"At a time when the colony is secure," Rodrick said. "I don't think I have to remind you, Dr. Baxter, that it hasn't been two weeks since we lost a member of our group."

"That was a simple accident," an astronomer cut in. Rodrick, try as he might, couldn't remember the man's name. "It could just as easily have happened on Earth, with one difference, the animal being a lion, or a grizzly bear."

"That's one way to look at it," Rodrick said, wondering how *that* had slid past psychological testing. "Gentlemen and ladies, let me assure you that I have no desire to bear the responsibility of command for one minute longer than necessary. More and more I'm leaving decisions in the hands of the various committees. You yourselves sit on many of the more important ones. I'll be the first to ask for, insist on, free elections when the time comes."

"And that time will be long after Hamilton is too well established to be moved," Baxter complained. "Captain, the chief purpose of our asking you here tonight is to give you this petition, which is signed by some few hundred of us. In short, this petition asks that, one, a concentrated study be made of possible town sites in the semitropical south; two, if such an investigation proves, as it surely will, that the southern areas are more habitable and fruitful, then you will call a special referendum and give the colony a chance to vote on the possibility of moving our settlement south before it is too late."

Rodrick took the sheaf of papers from Baxter. He knew that petitions didn't really mean much. Americans were open-minded people, in general, and usually considerate of the other person's feelings. He himself had signed petitions for actions in which he did not fully believe, just to be kind to those who were circulating them. He didn't think for one minute that the solid-minded citizens of Hamilton would vote to uproot and make a difficult, lengthy move.

"I'll read it," he said. "And I will take the matter under consideration." He turned to look at Miller. "Is your name on the petition, Commander?"

"No, sir," Rocky said. "As an officer in the Space Service, I feel that I should not become involved in political matters. Again, I am only here as an observer."

But now, Rodrick heard others arriving in his dining room for breakfast, so he flipped off the projector and replaced the button on his uniform. Neither the small number of people present at the meeting of the so-called concerned citizens nor the petition, which was, indeed, signed by over three hundred people, concerned Rodrick. It did trouble him that his first officer was present at the meeting. Miller was always strictly correct, very, very service in his demeanor in the presence of the captain, but Rodrick thought he'd noticed a change in the man during the last year of *Spirit's* outward voyage. Rodrick had never been a man to encourage familiarity with his junior officers—it just wasn't good policy—but he thought he had begun to build up a good, working relationship with Rocky Miller. Could Rocky have guessed how he felt about Mandy?

He heard voices from the dining room, rose, entered, and was greeted by those gathered there. The table steamed with fresh Omega rye bread, hot, fibrous cereals, a platter of soy-based bacon and eggs, and coffee. He greeted each guest by name, sat down, and asked Grace to say a morning blessing.

Good smells, good tastes, and good companionship combined to drive the unpleasantness of the previous evening from his mind. "Amando," he said as he took his first sip of coffee. "Have you had a chance to locate a site for our first coffee plantation?"

"The subtropical foothills to the south seem ideal," Amando replied. "I'm germinating seeds on board ship."

"Good," Rodrick said. "If someone asked me the one essential ingredient of civilization, I think I'd have to say hot coffee in the morning."

"Captain," Paul Warden said, "you haven't had a chance to take a look at this." The fan of gold, which had been removed intact from matrix rock, had been placed carefully in a glass-topped, velvet-lined box.

"Very nice," Rodrick commented. "It looks almost designed."

"We're going to find metals," Stoner McRae said happily. "We might have to dig deep, but we'll find them."

"That's what I want to hear," Rodrick said, his thoughts flashing back to Earth. The question was never far from his mind. Had Earth been destroyed by nuclear war? Were there people alive on it? He had taken very few people into his confidence by telling them about the imminence of nuclear disaster: Mandy and Rocky Miller, Jackie Garvey, Emi and Ito Zuki, and Evangeline Burr. He wondered if he should expand that list. Then he reminded himself that if word got out that all the bombs in the space stations, submarines, underground silos, aircraft, and low-flying missiles had been used, that Earth was nothing more than a cinder, there'd be no real incentive in the colony to produce the rocket fuel and rhenium necessary to send the *Spirit of America* back. They were Earth's lifeline, and Rodrick wasn't about to forget it.

He asked Paul Warden to tell him all about the events of the night. When Paul was finished, Rodrick said, "All right, let's think and talk about the miners. What do we already know, and what can we project as being true?"

"I think it's obvious," Grace began, "that they are very intelligent."

"Intelligent enough to know we have ears on them," Warden said.

"We're sending impulses into the ground," Max Rosen said, skeptical. "They probably feel them in some way."

"And then figure out what they are?" Warden asked.

"Dr. Wilson," Rodrick said, "you're the animal behavior expert."

James Wilson was thin, fit, and half-bald. His wife, Lola, thought that he was God's gift to the universe, but his teenage daughter, Mickey, wasn't quite sure. James was one of the foremost proponents of starting to grow dog embryos. He loved all animals, dogs especially, and he often made a point of going out of his way just to play with Clay Girard's Jumper.

"I'm impressed," he said. "First they exhibit extreme territoriality, defending their tunnels fiercely against the crawlers, and then, quite suddenly, they disappear. My guess is that there is some kind of communication among them, perhaps on the level of, say, Earth crows, which use scouts and rather elementary communication to spread the warning of danger."

"Let's assume for a moment that they have a high degree of intelligence," Mandy Miller said. "The brain is quite large. We can take it for granted that there is communication among them. They seem to have a highly regulated . . . well, call it society. It's amazing enough that they carry their waste such great distances to discharge it in those neat, straight mounds that Dr. Kwait found. And they chose a depression, as if they were being careful about spoiling the landscape."

"What puzzles me most," Amando Kwait said, "is why only one mound showed fresh earth."

"I've been thinking about the fact that the digging began just after the death of Lynn Roberts," Rosen said. "What connection do the two events have?"

"When drilling in stone," Evangeline Burr said, her voice low at first, then gaining confidence, "the metal drill bits have to be cooled with a fluid, usually water."

"You're suggesting, Miss Burr," Rosen asked, "that the miner was using Miss Roberts's body fat"—Max was not a man to mince words—"as a coolant or a lubricant?"

"I was just thinking out loud," Evangeline replied, rather shyly, bringing an encouraging grin from Paul Warden, who was seated across the table from her.

"Good thinking," Stoner said. "We have only one recorded incident of a miner digging. That came when he had, uh, body fat available. We know that the local wildlife avoids the traps. We know that there's been no activity for a long time in the dumping grounds. Maybe the things can only dig when they have a supply of, uh, lubricant for their drill bits. That would explain a lot of things."

"We could test it out by feeding one a silver-horned antelope," Warden said.

"Let's not kill one of those beautiful animals," Grace objected, committed.

"Maybe we wouldn't have to use a live animal," James Wilson suggested.

"What would you suggest?" Rodrick asked.

"Our own cooking synthetic," Wilson said.

"Or petroleum products," Stoner added. "We could supply them with plenty of our cooking oil, since we've got crude now for synthesizing."

"They'd want it thicker than cooking oil," Grace remarked. "The fat was the consistency of cool butter."

"No problem," Evangeline said.

"Okay," Rodrick said. "Paul, why don't you have the labs run off a supply of a synthetic animal fat, and then you can go out and see if that interests our underground friends."

"I think he should put a basin of it beside the hole at his camp," Evangeline said, then blushed. When Rodrick looked at her, she explained, "A gift in exchange for a gift."

Warden's camp was enlarged that evening. All those who had attended the captain's breakfast were there, along with selected others. The supply of hot dogs was ample, but Paul had to take a crawler and gather firewood at a distance. He was pleased when Evangeline offered to go with him. She sat next to him demurely, in silence, as he drove away from the camp toward the river, where the trees were thicker.

Finally she said, "You must be very proud to have been the one to make this odd discovery about the miners."

"Well, I was just there, doing my job," Warden said, giving her his half grin.

"I would never have been brave enough to stay there all alone," she said, with a shiver.

Paul laughed. "That's not your job."

"No," she agreed.

"You like your work?"

"Very much."

"Once when I was young I decided I wanted to be a scholar," Paul said. "I quickly decided that it required too much time indoors. I've been a dummy ever since."

"You're not a dummy," she said, so quickly and so heatedly that he looked at her without his usual grin.

"Well," Paul said, recovering, "what I mean is, I have my degrees, sure, and I'm a halfway good electrical engineer, but when it comes to theory, like, say, field theory, I'm in deep water."

"Field theory?"

"Electrical. Gravitational, the whole mess."

"There are two very good books on the subject. If you'll drop by the library, I'll get them out for you. Does field theory intrigue you?"

"Yeah, well, you see, there's this woman. She's a whiz at it, spends all her time working, studying, experimenting."

The charm of the night suddenly disappeared for Evangeline. "Oh, you mean Sage Bryson, don't you?" she asked.

"Yeah, how'd you know?"

"She spends a lot of time in the library. We've talked. She's the only one I know who is working seriously on field theory. Actually—" She paused, for what she was about to say could be considered to be critical. She gave a mental shrug and continued. "—at least in my opinion, Miss Bryson is working in a very unrewarding field . . . until there is a new breakthrough. What I mean is, with our present knowledge, field theory has been taken about as far as it will go."

"Yeah, well," Warden said.

She's not the woman for you, Evangeline wanted to say. But she was silent. The crawler entered a grove of trees, and it was the work of only a few minutes to gather enough deadwood to light up half of Eden.

When they were back at the camp, Evangeline separated herself from Paul and joined Max, Grace, Mandy, and Duncan Rodrick in front of a cozily burning fire. She tossed in some of the wood she'd gathered and only half listened to their conversation. Why, she wondered, had she been so upset when Paul had said he was interested in field theory because Sage Bryson was? He was nothing to her.

But he had such a gentleness about him, the aura of steel and velvet, and such an odd, endearing little grin.

She was still musing when Paul came and sat down beside her and asked if she had eaten. He roasted hot dogs for both of them, and she began to join in the conversation. It was then that she remembered something Sage Bryson had said. They'd been chatting idly about people, and Sage had narrowed it down to men in particular and had expressed an almost vengeful distaste for men. Evangeline remembered Sage's exact words: "They are always after me," she had said.

Remembering it now, Evangeline smiled. That was a problem she'd never had. Men were never after her.

But why? something inside her seemed to ask. Then the answer came. *Because you purposely hide when you can and make yourself unattractive when you can't. You starve yourself, keep your legs looking like matchsticks, your breasts tiny. What are you hiding from, Evangeline?*

Perhaps, she thought later, when she was in her own bed, it had been the night air, the feeling of anticipation from waiting for the miner, the flickering campfires, and drinking the ship's gin, which had been made into delicious fruit drinks with a bombing power.

Whatever it was, she had decided there at the campfire with Paul Warden sitting beside her grinning at her to stop hiding. Of course Sage Bryson wasn't the woman for Paul. She was. She, Evangeline Burr, was the woman for Paul Warden, and she'd have to find some way to let him know it.

For Evangeline, that decision was the highlight of that night, and would always be, even though an event of great importance to all followed her interior dialogue and decision.

Grace Monroe insisted on staying at the campsite all night. There was nothing for Max to do but grind his teeth and stay with her. They had not gotten around to filling out the marriage papers that day.

It was Grace who first saw the miner. A flat metal pan full of synthetic animal fat had been placed atop the drying dirt at the entrance to the burrow. She heard the miner coming on Warden's monitor. The two men were sleeping peacefully, and she decided not to wake them until the miner was closer. And then, when it began to creep upward, a movement at a time, she was too excited to waken them.

She saw the dead-white head, and then a length of neck extended slowly, carefully. The great mouth opened, and something was deposited beside the metal pan. She didn't realize until later that she had not smelled the stench of rotting flesh. She watched in fascination as the miner sucked up the fat and backed slowly into the tunnel. Then she woke the men and Warden turned on the lights. This time there was an assortment of metallic ores. Stoner later identified the ores as containing iron, silver, lead, and, most importantly, sulfidic copper. Stoner raced to the lab with the ore samples and the first tests were run on the copper ore. He whooped with joy, reached for the communicator, and called for Rodrick.

"We're going home, Captain!" he shouted.

Rodrick raised an eyebrow. "I'm listening, Stoner," he said. He was on the bridge with Ito Zuki.

"We've got our first batch of rhenium aboard," Stoner said. "It's not much, but it's there."

"In the ore from the miner?" Rodrick asked.

"The copper. Just like on Earth. Sulfidic copper is not the best source, but it is a source. And now that we know there's rhenium here, we can start looking for the molybdenum sulfide ores, where we can expect to find it in greater quantities."

"Thanks, Stoner," Rodrick said, "that is very good news."

Stoner thought the skipper was being very blasé about it. He didn't learn until later that Rodrick had just been on the communicator with Allen Jones, the underwater architect. Allen had been doing some test diving at the mouth of Stanton Bay, using an amphibious crawler as his surface vessel.

"We can't tell yet whether it's a boat or not," Allen had said. "It's in bad shape, but it looks like a boat to me. One thing for sure, Captain, it's made by human hands." Then realizing that he might have used the wrong description, since humans in the form of the people from Earth had certainly not made the artifact he'd discovered in the sands of the floor of the bay, Jones added, "Or whatever."

It was that "whatever" that Rodrick had on his mind when he heard Stoner's good news about the rhenium. That, and the question of how the miners knew that the colonists would want metals as a peace offering . . . and how the silver-horned antelopes knew not to be afraid and how the predatory pussycats encouraged the humans to scratch their bellies. He had talked it over with Mandy, Grace, and James Wilson, who all agreed that the answer lay with the mysterious inhabitants of the dead city. It was they, the scientists had agreed, who had taught the miners, antelopes, and pussycats what people—or "whatever"—

liked or needed, and how they would act. They probably had taken metals from the miners, hadn't eaten the antelopes, and had scratched the pussycats' bellies. Now, it seemed, they had also built boats.

FOURTEEN

Allen Jones's recovery and preservation of the boat from Stanton Bay attracted quite an audience. The object was approximately twenty feet long and ten feet wide, an ungainly shape for a boat. It had a flat bottom and thin sides, which extended upward almost four feet—a very high freeboard for a boat. There were those who argued that the underwater archaeologists had made some mistake in their reconstruction of the boat, perhaps thinking that what might have been a double-planked bottom was actually material from the sides.

Both bow and stern were rounded equally, making it impossible to say which was front and which was back. There was no evidence of oars, no masts for sails. The material was of a wood not yet encountered by the colonists. Carbon dating showed varied results, anywhere from five thousand to five hundred years, making some wonder if the carbon dating test would be valid on Omega.

Everyone had his or her own opinion of the purpose of holes spaced at regular intervals along the sides of what was thought to be the gunwale.

When the boat had been reconstructed and preserved, the saltwater removed from the wood and replaced with a bonding resin to keep it from crumbling into nothing, it was an unimpressive object. Everyone soon lost interest, everyone but Allen Jones and Duncan Rodrick.

"It worries me," Jones told the captain. "It's about as sorry a boat as I've ever seen."

It worried Rodrick, too. Intelligent beings had built that boat and the abandoned city in what was now called Stoner's Valley. Where were they?

The archaeological team in Stoner's Valley soon gave Rodrick more data about the intelligent past residents of Eden. The sands that had drifted in the dead city's streets began to give up shards of ceramic vessels and, in one exciting find, a hammered-gold bracelet, which, they decided, had been made for a child. Carbon datings of decayed wood residue from the city were uniform enough to allow the archaeologists to state that the city had been inhabited up to three thousand standard years ago. Sophisticated detectors searched the entire valley for more metallic artifacts and found several axheads and spearheads. Detectors showed areas where the subsoil had once been disturbed by digging, and excavation turned up nothing more than an area of dirt more siliceous than the surrounding earth. This led to speculation that the area had been used as burial sites for a life form with the same basic life system as the miners and that the intelligent beings who had built the city were a silicon-based life form.

If that supposition was true, it meant that the beings who had expressed themselves in metallurgy, ceramics, and stonework had been as alien to human life as the miners. And, Rodrick thought, a race that had been working metals three thousand years before the *Spirit of America* landed could have made some rather startling advancement . . . if they were still around.

So Rodrick had his worries, but he was not the only one. Max Rosen had problems, too. He had filled out the marriage-license form, and both he and Grace had signed it. Max had personally delivered it to the captain for his signature but couldn't get Grace away from those damned miner burrows long enough to set a date.

Rodrick kept saying, "Look, Max, this should be a big affair. We can make it our first celebration on Omega. Let's hold off until we get things settled down a little bit." So Max went to work on the rocket-fuel plant now that it was certain that there was rhenium on Omega. The plant would be built near the river Dinah in the industrial sector.

Grace, meanwhile, was trying to establish communications with the miners. She and Paul Warden had become the unofficial ambassadors, as well as chief trade representatives, to the underground nation. The population of miners was far greater than had at first been thought. To find a miner, Paul or Grace would put a pan of synthetic congealed fat near a trap—and traps were scattered all over Eden, from the coast to the snowy mountains, from the southern marshes to the northern desert—and the dead-white, evil-looking miner would come scrape-scraping up to slice a neat, round hole in the sod and extend that knobbed cone of a head.

As a result, the supply of metals was growing. Gold was the most common trade material brought up from the depths of the earth by the miners. Grace tried to get the idea across to the miners that she wanted a particular kind of metal by putting an empty pan next to the trap and putting rhenium samples from Max directly beside it. The miners continued to deliver other metals and ores, but aside from minute amounts of rhenium in the copper ores, she got no direct results.

By shifting her samples to gold or iron or copper, she found that the miners' intelligence was not at fault, for she soon had a dozen individuals trained to deliver gold, copper, or iron on order.

"There's just too little rhenium," Stoner McRae decided. "And it's not in easily accessible form, like the gold and other metals."

Since it was obvious that there was communication among the miners, Grace began to try to find out what kind of a system they used. At night she would record the scraping, tapping, and gurgling of the miners, and then the next morning she'd try to make sense of the sounds. She was slowly building up what she thought was a vocabulary for the miners. She was already sure that some of the gurglings had to do with the mating process, for she had recorded several instances in which two miners would slowly converge, gurgle for a long period, frantically scrape for a brief period, and then separate from each other.

Grace finally had to admit that the sounds made by the miners were as untranslatable as the songs of whales and the whistles of dolphins on Earth, and were probably of the same level of communication. Max growled, "Think we might be able to set a date now?"

"Let's do," Grace said, giving him a kiss that was, miraculously, not interrupted for a full two minutes.

Then Captain Rodrick called and asked Max to join him and the two scouts Jacob West and Renato Cruz in the captain's office.

Jacob and Renato were good friends, supporting the old tenet that opposites attract. Although both men were Apache Indians, Jacob was not typical of the Native American stereotype. He hated the outdoors, for one thing. Stocky, round-faced, and cheerful, he held a Ph.D. in physics and had helped to develop a new rocket fuel before deciding to be a shuttle pilot, then scout. He was known affectionately as Chief Sky Flyer, and Jacob, liking the name, used it as his call name on his scout ship, *Apache One*.

Renato, whose scout ship was called *Apache Two*, was moody, silent, and tended toward drink. He spoke often of the injustices done to Indians in the early days of North American colonization. For this reason, his friends called him Sobbing Wolf. It made one wonder whether he had signed on for this expedition as a means of making sure history from the 1600s did not repeat itself four centuries later on another planet.

When Max came into Rodrick's office, he found the men comfortably slouched in their chairs around the conference table, their long legs stretched out.

"Max," Rodrick began after the chief engineer was seated with a cup of coffee in hand, "Jacob and Renato have been trying to get a photo of the big life forms in the equatorial jungles."

"The only thing we've come up with so far is this," Jacob continued, handing Max an enlargement in color of the surface of a body of water. Max had to look closely to see the shadowy form under the water.

"Whale?" he asked.

"I don't think so," Jacob answered. "That's a freshwater river."

"Big," Max said. A scale printed on the side of the photograph told him that the shadowy shape under the water was over thirty feet long.

"Listen to this," Renato Cruz said, pushing a button that activated a recording device. "We recorded it while hovering just above the jungle canopy."

Something big was crushing its way through the jungle. Now and then a sharp snap could be heard, as if some sizable tree had been broken.

"The problem," Renato explained, "is that the big life forms, like the one making that noise, are in the deep jungle, and I mean deep. The canopy is so tight, there's no break in it. We can locate the big boys by life signal and sound, but we can't see them."

"Send someone in on the surface," Max suggested.

"Come with us down there and see if you'll still say that," Jacob said. "Maybe you'll volunteer to cut your way through a few hundred miles of that stuff, but I won't."

"Burn some clearings," Max said.

"We did and set up monitors. Nothing came close to them. And the undergrowth began to cover the clearings in less than a week."

"Jacob wants to put a landing pad on top of the canopy," Rodrick said.

"Then we can push a camera through the canopy on a long probe," Jacob said.

Max's face took on his pained thinking look. "Yeah," he answered after a few moments. "Yeah. You think the treetops will hold the weight, huh?"

"We lifted a big fallen tree from the edge of the jungle and set it down onto the canopy in the central areas," Jacob said. "The tree weighed just over four tons. It sank a bit, but it stayed right there on top. If we had some way to spread the weight—"

"Captain," Max said, "don't plan anything for Sunday after next."

"Will it take you that long to rig something up?" Jacob asked.

"No, that's when I'm gonna get married," Max said. "We can put a grill down on the trees in a couple of days. We'll weld together some steel-mesh dividers. But if you don't want to do it, Dunc, we'll get one of the ministers."

"It's an honor I wouldn't miss," Rodrick said.

"You'll have to ferry the damned thing all the way south slung underneath," Max said to Jacob, who was a little confused from the two conversations.

"Congratulations," Renato Cruz offered.

"Hell, it's nothing. Won't take more than a couple of hours to weld it together," Max said.

"I mean on your wedding," Cruz said.

"Maybe we shouldn't weld it here," Max said. "Maybe we should carry it down closer to the jungle in pieces and weld it there. How much closer could we get to the deep jungle?"

"At least a thousand miles," Jacob said.

"You think Cindy McRae would like to be our flower girl?" Max asked, looking up into the air.

"I think she'd be honored," Rodrick said. "Who do you have in mind for best man?"

"It gets complicated," Max said. "We'll need to figure out a way to be sure to recover that grill. Can't leave that much good steel just rotting down in the jungle."

Max stood and walked to the door, tried to open it from the wrong side, grunted, found the right point, and went out. Rodrick laughed. "I think, gentlemen, that we'd better get the chief married, and quickly."

"Captain," Jacob asked, "have we got your approval on this project?"

"On two conditions," Rodrick said. "First, as Max said, we have to recover that metal. Steel is as valuable as gold on this planet. Second, you're not to go down to the jungle floor without specific permission from me."

"*Apache Two*," Jacob said, rising, "let's go get ready to take us a look at a thunder lizzard."

"You're that sure you're going to see something down there like a dinosaur?" Rodrick asked.

"Whatever it is," Jacob said, "it's big. It shakes the ground when it walks, and it goes through the small trees and undergrowth like a tank."

"Let me know when Max has your treetop landing pad ready," Rodrick said.

Max went directly to Grace's lab when he left the captain's office. He almost collided with Paul Warden, who was coming out of the lab. He grunted a greeting and went into the room to find Grace just focusing an electron microscope.

"What are you up to?" he asked.

"Cross sections of nerve endings in the brain of a miner," Grace said.

"Don't plan anything for Sunday after next," Max said.

"I just don't know what's wrong with that woman," Grace remarked.

Max got a pained look on his face.

"That Sage Bryson," Grace said, her face hidden in the viewer of the microscope. "He's such a nice man, too."

"Hey, Grace—"

"You set the date without asking me?"

"If it was gonna get set, someone had to do it," Max growled, going up to put his hands on the outflowing line of her hips and kissing her on the neck.

"The brain fluid is an interesting series of compounds. If I can ever find out what exactly happens—"

"Turn around," Max ordered.

"Sometimes I get reactions as if the silicon is going to burst into life," she said, turning into his arms, lifting her own arms, putting one hand at the back of his head, fingers moving into his hair. "Couldn't you have decided *this* Sunday?"

He had just found her lips when the admiral burst in, "Grace—" He paused. Max groaned and pushed Grace away. She did not feel like laughing.

"Excuse me," the admiral said.

"Is there a problem?" Grace asked.

"It can wait, Grace."

"Go ahead," Max said in deep agony. "I gotta go build a landing pad for the jungle."

"Watch out for snakes," Grace called as he left.

"Maybe I'll find one that eats robots," Max said.

The admiral looked after Max, his face showing puzzlement. His face should not have shown anything. She hadn't constructed him to be able to express emotion.

"He was joking," she explained. "Now what is this problem that can wait but seems so important?"

"I don't know how to say it," the admiral said.

"By forming words one at a time in some logical order," Grace said.

"You're angry with me because I interrupted your lovemaking."

"A bit irritated, perhaps. Not angry," she said.

"I'm sorry."

Damn it, she was thinking, *he's becoming a teenager*. She reached out and put her hand on his arm. He smiled. Damn, he was handsome.

"I think I need to ask your advice, Grace, on a personal matter."

"I'll be glad to help," she said.

"What is love?" he asked with a serious look on his face.

She'd learned long ago when she was momentarily stunned by a question to borrow time by answering with a question.

"Why do you ask?"

"I realize that it is a question without a simple answer," he said. "I have assimilated all of the material suggested to me by Miss Evangeline, in the library."

"It's a tough question," Grace agreed. "People have been trying to give a concise answer, or a definition, for thousands of years. Is this a new research project or something?"

"In a way," he said. He turned away so that she could not see his face. "Actually, it's about Tina."

"Ah," she said.

"I know I'm not human, Grace."

Not being able to see his face, she could not read the tone of his voice. "No," she said. "You're superior in many ways."

He turned to face her quickly, looking at her intently. "Oh, don't be concerned about me, Grace. I'm not having an identity crisis. I read over your notes, the notes you made during my construction. I'm not supposed to *feel*, am I?"

"No," she said simply.

Grace was accustomed to handling confidences from other people. But, my God, what do you say to a robot who is in love with a lively, pretty adolescent human girl?

She had feared that something like this would happen, and she'd dreaded it. She'd hoped that Tina Sells's attraction to the admiral was much like her own, a fondness for a really nice, gentle, intelligent being, tempered with a knowledge of what the admiral was.

"Do you know what I see the most beauty in, Grace?" the admiral asked suddenly. She shook her head. "I see a beauty of organization in the ship's computer system when I'm plugged in, when the entire system is working. It's complete, whole. The shades of meaning, the splendid conformity of the billions of bytes of data, there's an unseen glow about it, Grace, something that I can't explain, and something you can't see, but it's beautiful. I know that I'm programmed to appreciate that. But then I can also see the beauty of a sunset and beauty in the way you look at me, even though I'm not constructed to do so. Excuse me, Grace, but you're beautiful to me."

"Thank you," she said, her heart hurting for him, for he was looking at her so earnestly.

"When I walk in and you're kissing Chief Rosen, I sense the way you feel. I'm not supposed to feel emotions, but they just seem to sweep over me, to soak into sensors in a way that I can't analyze. Is that love?"

"Yes," she said.

"Please don't misunderstand," he went on. "I am, of course, programmed never to harm a human being. The overt data there relates to physical harm. I can't seem to separate mental or emotional hurt from physical hurt in my mind."

"You're afraid you're going to give someone an emotional hurt?"

"Yes," he said.

"Tina?"

"Yes."

She was beginning to feel a bit better. For a moment there she'd thought that the admiral was going to confess his love for the girl. But he was only concerned for her.

"Why are you concerned?" she asked.

"Grace, she has told me that it doesn't matter that we are not alike." He paused. "This is going to be a bit embarrassing for me."

"If you can stand it, I can," she assured him with a smile.

"She said that I'm the finest, kindest, most gentle person she's ever known."

"I see," Grace said.

"She says that there's far more to love than the physical aspects."

"And what did you say?"

"I told her that she'd feel differently about that as she grew older."

"I think you said the right thing," Grace said. "You've developed some nice sensibilities, Admiral. Would it help if I had a talk with Tina? I think every young girl goes through this. With me it was music and film stars. A young girl can be safely and madly in love with an unreachable public figure. She can let all her passions burn. She can ache and yearn and weep, and down inside she knows all the time that she'll never be in a position to have to resist her strong urges or give in to them. Isn't it the same in the case of Tina and you?"

"Perhaps, Grace, young people are a bit more mature than they were when you were a girl."

Oh, Lord, she was thinking. *He* is *a teenager.* "The younger generation, my dear, has been more mature—in its own opinion—for thousands of years." She knew that she shouldn't have said it. She didn't want the talk to degenerate into a cross-generation conflict. *Good Lord, Grace,* she was thinking, *you should have married long ago and had children, and then you'd be more prepared for this.*

"Actually, Grace," the admiral said, "Tina *is* mature for her age. She's very solid minded. She's intelligent. She is going to be one of the finest minds in computer science. In fact, I'd like to suggest that you take her on as an apprentice, because her thought patterns are much like yours. This problem you're working on now, for example, the effects the various chemicals manufactured in the brain of a miner have on memory chips, would be a good vehicle to use to teach Tina good research techniques."

"Are you changing the subject?"

"No, just a slight diversion."

"Tell Tina to come talk with me. I'll see if she's really interested. I could use an assistant now that you're so busy."

"Thank you," he said. "I agree with you in principle. I think that she's going through a phase and will, as you adults say, grow out of it. In the meantime, I see no reason why I shouldn't continue to be her friend."

"No reason at all," she agreed. She was thinking wryly that at least no physical consequences could come of it. The admiral was made in man's image, but not to *that* detail. Once she'd actually considered giving him all the attributes of a man, but not even her sly sense of humor went that far. But there could be other complications. The admiral's lips, for example, were made of that artificial skin, which, on the surface, was so realistic that it would take an expert to tell the difference by feel. Of course there'd be no moisture, no saliva, in a kiss from the admiral. But a young girl's dreams didn't go much beyond a kiss. She felt a sudden surge of worry. Talk about mixed-up love affairs!

"Admiral, let me be sure I understand," she said. "Am I right in thinking that Tina is in love with you, or that you think she's in love with you?"

"Yes," he said.

"She's told you so?"

"Yes. That's the problem, you see."

"I'm not sure I do see. You are not in love with Tina?"

"No. Of course not," he said quickly.

Good, she was thinking. *Now we're making progress. Now let me see, how do I want to word this?* "Admiral, may I ask a very personal question?"

"Of course."

"Do you ever have a desire to touch Tina? No, let me

make that a multiple question. You see, there's a lot we don't understand about the functioning of that rather miraculous brain of yours, my boy. You were not supposed to have emotions, and you do. You were supposed to be programmed not to harm any human physically, and your own feelings have extended that to not hurting them emotionally. So, have you touched, kissed, or embraced Tina? Do you want to touch, kiss, or embrace Tina? Are you capable of falling in love with Tina?"

"In the order of asking," he said, "I have touched Tina, but not in a romantic way. Perhaps I might put my hand on her shoulder while she is at the keyboard and I'm giving her instructions. I have not kissed her, although she has kissed me on the cheek. I have not embraced her. As for my desires, I am fond of Tina and want to touch her, in the same manner that you sometimes put your hand on my arm. I have no desire to kiss her or embrace her in a romantic way."

Ah, Grace was thinking, *it's all going to be all right*.

"For, you see," the admiral went on, "although I myself am young in years of existence, I am a mature being. Tina is much too young for me."

Whoops.

"I haven't answered your last question, Grace," the admiral said. "You asked if I was capable of falling in love with Tina. The specific answer is no, for the reasons I've just given. The general answer, however, is that I am quite capable of falling in love, have fallen in love, and find that love returned."

Flabbergasted, Grace was silent for a moment.

"Care to go into a bit more detail?" she asked.

"Not at the moment, Grace," he answered seriously. "The woman I love has asked me to hold our relationship in the strictest confidentiality."

The woman I love? "I can see why," Grace said.

"What we must guard against," the admiral said, "is giving hurt to a very sweet little girl."

I can think of a lot of things we should guard against, Grace thought, but she said, "The woman you love is, uh, more mature?"

"Yes, in her thirties. But that is not the matter of

concern now, Grace. Tina is our concern now. Please
don't let her know that I've talked with you, but if you'll
do what you can to get her interested in working with
you—"

"Yes, I'll do that," she said. *How do you give advice
to a robot who's in love with a mature woman who is in
love with him and to a teenage girl who's about to be
jilted?*

"Thank you. Now I must go. I've promised Miss Burr
to escort her and a friend to the beach."

"Have fun," Grace said under her breath as the admiral went out. "Don't stay out late."

The white, sandy beach at the inland tip of Stanton
Bay was a popular place in the late afternoon. It was a
short walk from Hamilton proper through blooming, succulent plants that grew low to the ground and seemed to
spring up overnight in the summer's heat. When crushed
they gave off a perfume that was tangy and sweet.

Evangeline Burr and Sage Bryson wore their swimsuits under absorbent robes. The admiral walked behind
them, alert to any threat of danger, although no dangers
had materialized in Eden since the unfortunate death of
Lynn Roberts, the one and only victim of the miners.
There were no snakes in Eden, no biting insects, and the
succulent ground-cover plants growing in the sandy dunes
at the end of the bay did not have spikes.

Duncan Rodrick, who always believed in playing it
safe, had ordered that a protective net be installed fifty
yards offshore. It was anchored to the bottom of the bay
and was strong enough to keep out something as powerful
as a great white shark, while the mesh was small enough
to prevent entry by a slender sea snake.

The colony's youngsters were out in force, watched
over by their mothers and fathers, who basked in the late
afternoon sun.

It was Evangeline's first outing to the beach. When
she took off her beach robe, her skin was smooth and pale.
She sat down quickly on her towel, for she was modest
and the ship's issue swimsuit was fashionably brief. Evan-

geline filled it to a degree that made her measure up quite favorably with the less self-conscious Sage.

"You're going to need some sunscreen," Sage told her. "You're as white as a Victorian belle."

"Yes," Evangeline said, "I burn rather easily." She spread the sunscreen onto her legs and arms, then tried awkwardly to rub it onto her back.

"You'll never make it unless you're double-jointed," Sage said, laughing.

"Would you mind?" Evangeline asked, extending the tube toward Sage.

"We have a perfectly capable man here for that," Sage said.

The admiral had taken position, standing at ease with his hands behind his back, on a little sand dune behind them. When Sage called to him, he came down, showering sand in front of his feet.

"Would you please do our backs?" Sage asked him.

"Of course," the admiral said. He knelt behind Evangeline and squeezed sunscreen onto his hand, which, to Evangeline, was surprisingly soft and gentle. She blushed in spite of herself. She'd never had a man rub sunscreen onto her back and shoulders, and the fact that the admiral was not really a man didn't keep her from feeling odd.

The admiral was working on Sage's back and doing a thorough job when Evangeline saw Paul Warden come down the slope and over a dune. Paul looked around, saw her and waved, and came trotting toward them.

"Hi, gang," he said, throwing himself down on his knees beside Sage. "How's it going?"

"Hello, Paul," Sage said coldly.

"Admiral," Paul said, "you're doing a great job, but your relief is here." He held out his hand and the admiral put the tube of sunscreen into it.

"Thank you," Sage said as Paul squeezed the tube, "but I've had quite enough."

"You sure?" Paul looked at the colorless gel on his palm as if to ask, *Well, what do I do with this stuff now?*

"Have you had any interesting experiences with the miners, Commander Warden?" Evangeline asked. She had to steel herself to keep from reaching for her beach robe to cover her feminine curves. But then Paul wasn't looking at her.

"Same old stuff," Paul said, not noticing her formality.

The admiral had resumed his post on the sand dune. Evangeline, her eyes hidden behind sunglasses, saw that Paul had a terrible scar, which ran from the tip of his left shoulder across the pectoral. She felt a moment of sympathy. It must have been a very painful injury.

"Hey," Paul said, "let's have a swim, huh?" He was looking directly at Sage.

"No, thanks," Sage said. "You go, Evangeline."

Paul's face fell. He looked at Evangeline, recovering, and winked. "How about it, Vange?"

She got to her feet, resisting the urge to let her shoulders slump to hide the thrust of her breasts. Paul yelled, "Last one in is the last one in," and trotted off.

Evangeline surprised herself as much as anyone when she ran and passed him quickly. Paul really had to pump to catch her. They ran into the water together and high-stepped through the ripples to dive and surface and swim, Evangeline keeping even with Paul all the way, out to the net.

He stopped there, hanging onto a support, breathing hard. "Not bad," he said admiringly. "How come I never saw you in the pool on the ship?"

"I went there late at night," she said.

"Yeah? How come?"

"I liked it that way," she said.

"You do a mean crawl. I was on the swim team at the Space Academy, and you kept up with me stroke for stroke."

"I swam the freestyle sprints in college," she said.

"I'd never have guessed it. And you keep in shape, too."

"It feels good to swim hard," she said. "I'm a little heavy now, but—"

"Heavy? Heck, no. You're just right. What do you weigh, a hundred twenty-five?" She nodded. "That's just about ideal for your height. What do you say we take it just medium fast along the net down to the end and then all the way back to the other end?"

"No racing," she said. "I could stay with you for a sprint, but you'd wear me down on the distance."

"Okay, just smooth and easy."

It felt very good. She felt her muscles begin to stretch, got into the rhythm of it, and when they had finished the outlined course, she fell onto her back in shallow water, breathing hard and deep, looking up at the purple horizon to the west. Warden, also breathing hard, was looking up the beach toward Sage, who was lying on her stomach. The admiral, staunch figure, was standing guard from the low sand dune.

Evangeline saw the direction of his gaze. "Any progress to report in that direction?" she asked, amazed at her audacity.

"She doesn't even know I'm alive," Paul said, and the puzzled look on his face made her want to reach out and touch him.

"You've never been married, have you?" she asked.

"Nope." He grinned. "Same old story. Never could find a woman who would have me."

"Don't do that," she said.

"What?"

"Never underestimate yourself," she said firmly.

He looked at her. "You're big on that stuff, huh?"

"What stuff?"

"Self-image."

"I'm working on it," she said, and with a start, she realized that it was true. Why had she always put herself down, kept her weight so low that she looked almost emaciated? Was it fear that if she entered the competition she'd lose? So here she was, filled out, curvaceous, overweight by her own standards, and she had, at last, entered a competition with two strikes against her.

"Well," Paul said, "I've always had a winning attitude. You can't participate successfully in sports unless you have it, but—"

"But you don't have a winning attitude as far as Sage is concerned?"

"Hard to. I lose too many times with her."

"When you were participating in sports, Paul, did anyone ever tell you about the law of compensation?"

"What you give you get?"

"That's right. Give out good, good comes back. That's stating it at its simplest. Give out love, get back love."

"Well, *that* part of it hasn't worked," he said.

"Perhaps you're forgetting one of the most important aspects of the law of compensation," she said. "When you give in one direction, the return does not necessarily come back from that same direction," she said.

He laughed. "Then maybe there are a half-dozen women returning my love like crazy, huh?"

"Maybe," she said. "Maybe only one."

He looked at her, startled. "You telling me I should start looking elsewhere?"

She wanted to say, *Yes, dummy*, but she didn't. She said casually, "Oh, I'm just talking. Advice is like bitter medicine—easy to give, hard to take, right?"

"I guess so." His grin came back. "Hey, Vange, you're all right. You're a very all-right woman. You understand things." He was serious again. "Maybe if you put in a good word for me with Sage, huh?"

From a very old American short story: *Why don't you speak for yourself, Evangeline?* From her own lips, "I can try."

"Thanks. Look, I've gotta go. I just sneaked off for a while." He stood and shook water from his hair. "Tell Sage I said so long."

"I'll do that," she said.

He ran up the slope, gave the admiral a salute, and was gone. Evangeline walked to sit down on the towel next to Sage.

"So Evangeline has a beau," Sage said.

She blushed. "He's in love with you," she said.

Sage laughed cruelly. "He's just in heat, like all of them." She looked at Evangeline, with a grim little smile on her lips. "I see the way *you* look at him, though."

No, she thought, *it couldn't show*. "I like him. He's a friend," she said.

"Sure," Sage said. "Surrrrrre. Who are you trying to kid?"

"You know, Sage," Evangeline said, finding that she was full of surprises for herself on that sunny, late afternoon, "you not only have a strong streak of cruelty in you, you're rather stupid at times."

Sage's face went taut, then relaxed. "Oh, you're trying to tell me that I should have pity on him, be nice to him."

And, Evangeline thought, as she lay back to enjoy the sun, *you're so very self-centered that you don't even know when you've been insulted.*

FIFTEEN

The jungle on the continent that the Americans had named Columbia covered an area larger than the entire Soviet Union, with the conquered European countries thrown in. It began to grow dense three thousand miles south of Stanton Bay. There at the jungle's edge the two Apache Indians, Jacob West and Renato Cruz, set up their base camp, and Jack Purdy helped them ferry down the steel-mesh squares from the *Spirit of America*. Renato welded the squares together using a molecular bonder.

Duncan Rodrick flew down, while they were assembling the landing pad to be dropped atop the jungle, to get a good look at that southern paradise that Clive Baxter's noisy "concerned-citizens" faction kept talking about. It was, without a doubt, beautiful country. There were shady glades in deep forest, and clear streams, and almost every growing thing seemed to have a fruit or a nut attached to it. But history repeats itself, and every explorer who settled in a tropical paradise where food was easily available was doomed to fail—either lulled by false security or destroyed by sheer laziness. No, the Americans would stay put as long as he was in charge.

Rodrick had started giving Clay Girard flying lessons. Clay would be celebrating his sixteenth birthday soon, and because of the small population of the colony, adulthood would, Rodrick thought, come early to kids like Clay simply because they were needed. Clay handled the scout very well on the approach to the Apache camp, and Rodrick talked him through a vertical landing that jarred teeth only slightly.

Renato and Jacob were just making the final welds. The admiral, well armed, was standing guard. Clay had Jumper on a leash, much to the dog's disgust. The camp had been set up in a natural clearing in a hardwood forest, which extended its vast carpet of green for over a thousand miles north toward Hamilton. Clay didn't want Jumper exploring the woods on his own, for the scouts had recorded a variety of life signals there.

From the air, the jungle to the south was an unbroken deep green. The thought of a band of almost impenetrable jungle extending three thousand miles on either side of the planet's equator had a sobering effect on Rodrick; he wouldn't want to be out there in the midst of it, even without the larger-than-elephant life forms the sensors had picked up.

Clay pitched in to help finish the welding. He was getting to be a good hand with the molecular bonder, and Jacob and Renato were quite willing to let him help so they could stand up straight, backhand their sweat, and have a long drink of cool water.

Jacob showed Rodrick their target area on the map. Jacob had printed, in that vast area of jungle where the only map features were the winding rivers and two areas of connected lakes, TERRA INCOGNITA. The selected area was two thousand miles north of the equator, near the coastline of a vast indentation which, on a sensibly sized continent, would have been called a bay, but on Omega was big enough to be a sea.

"You're going to have to carry the landing grid over a thousand miles," Rodrick said.

Jacob nodded. "It won't be the most aerodynamic configuration ever flown, but if we winch the grid tight against the landing skids, I think I can fly at around three hundred feet with no problem. Take about four hours, we figure, from lift-off to the time I settle down on the treetops."

"But that means you'll have to put the scout with the

grid down onto the canopy. You won't have a chance to feel out whether the trees will take the weight."

"I'll settle in very slowly," Jacob reassured him. "We're mounting the grid to the landing skids with explosive bolts. If I see I'm going to settle into the trees too far, or if the thing starts to tilt too much, I'll press a button and be free to get the hell out of there."

Rodrick and Clay watched the awkward union of scout and grid lift off, then move away, cautiously at first, toward the south. Renato's *Apache Two* scout was flying just below, telling Jacob that all was looking good. Rodrick let Clay lift the captain's scout and then took over, flying in close to Jacob's *Apache One* himself to take a look. Jacob was up to an airspeed of three hundred.

"It's very musical, Captain," Jacob radioed. "The wind whistling through the mesh sounds like a thousand Apaches doing the death dance."

"You've never even seen a thousand Apaches," Rodrick joked, "much less heard them doing a death dance."

"Ah," Jacob said, "but in my dreams—the souls of my ancestors bewail the dirty deal you white eyes gave them."

Sobbing Wolf, better known as Lieutenant Renato Cruz of the United States Space Service, let out a rapid stream of Mescalero. Rodrick was thinking that their Apache-language conversation was being recorded back at control on the *Spirit of America*, and he grinned. The air talk between *Apache One* and *Apache Two* while on patrol or exploration drove Grace Monroe crazy because her "black box," or translation computer, couldn't make head or tail of the language.

"Damn it," Grace had told him and Renato once, "I think it's all made up. I can handle Russian with this translation computer, and if it can translate Russian, it should be able to translate anything."

"I am hurt," Renato had responded, a smile tugging at his lips. Then his voice took on the tone of a lecturing professor. "I have already explained that at the peak of our civilization, before we were overrun by the marauding barbarians from across the ocean, there were fifty-five families of language in the Americas, and to understand, one must group them into five superfamilies. Mescalero is of the superfamily Nadene, subgroup Southern, family Kusan, along with Kiowa Apache, San Carlos Apache, Chiricahua, and, shamefully, Navaho. Now if you—"

"Hey, Cap'n!" Clay yelled, interrupting Rodrick's memories, "look at *that!*"

Clay had been playing with the scout's optics. They were flying at five thousand feet over an area of shallow lakes, large areas of which were covered with large, golden-hued flowers. Rodrick looked at the screen where Clay had enlarged a view of a great, floating flower garden. In the open areas the water was still relatively shallow so that the clear water took on a green tint from vegetation on the bottom. The blooms looked as big as washbasins. But it was not the impressive flowers that had excited Clay.

There was a family of them. The adults were big, barrel shaped, with short, fat legs and a long, flat tail that seemed to provide underwater propulsion. A ten-foot-long neck supported a triangular head shaped like that of an Earth rattlesnake. The three youngsters were frolicking around the two adults, diving and surfacing, flipping the broad, flat tails to scoot forward, walking on the sandy bottom of the lake on their short legs.

"*Apache One*, Rodrick. I'm going down to take a look at that lake just below. Catch up later."

Rodrick hovered the scout at three hundred feet. The noise of the hydrogen-powered jets drew one disdainful look from the two adults, who then went back to grazing on the large, golden blooms of the water plants.

"They're almost like dinosaurs," Clay remarked.

"Put the calibrator on the screen," Rodrick said.

Clay punched up the calibration grid, and with neck outstretched to reach a particularly enticing bloom, the largest of the two adults measured just over twenty-eight feet from the neck to the tip of the broad, flat tail. The young ones were just under ten feet in length, about four feet of the length neck. They were as frolicsome as kittens or otters.

Rodrick was recording the scene on film. They watched until the two adults, apparently having had their fill, turned, stretched out their long necks, and shot away under water, running first on their short legs and then folding their legs against their bodies as they reached deeper water and used their tails as pushers.

"If there's anything that big down there in the jungle, Jacob had better be careful," Clay said.

Rodrick's scout caught up with *Apache One* and *Two* just as Jacob was maneuvering downward, the hover jets flaring. Rodrick hovered nearby. Jacob carefully lowered the large rectangle of steel mesh, inch by inch. The mesh sank into the undulating green canopy of the treetops. He eased off on the power as more and more of the weight of mesh and scout was supported by the trees.

"I'm down," he said, after three minutes of slow, careful lessening of power.

"Does it seem solid?" Renato asked.

"A rock," Jacob answered. "I'm going to rock the baby a little bit to be sure." He used steering jets to rock the scout back and forth. "Doesn't move at all," he reported. "I'm going to get out and loosen the bolts."

Rodrick began to fly small, slow circles around Jacob's scout. Renato, with the admiral, was still hovering, ready to dart in to pick up Jacob if needed. It took only a few minutes to separate the scout from the grid, and then Jacob lifted his craft a couple of feet and placed it to one end of the grid.

"You can come on down and join me," Jacob told *Apache Two*.

Renato put his scout down beside *Apache One*. The admiral jumped out, and he and Renato offloaded equipment, then Renato lifted off alone to go back to the base camp and get the rest. Next, Rodrick put his scout down, and he and Clay joined the admiral and Jacob on the mesh. The sun hit them with a force that made them perspire immediately.

"I'd like to get one look down through the canopy," Rodrick said, "if we can cut a hole without too much trouble."

They moved to the outer edge of the mesh, where a three-foot square had been cut out. Jacob armed his laser and began to cut, careful not to sever a large support limb. Vegetation flared and turned to ashes. He finally cut through one lower limb, a full twenty feet under the mesh, and the laser beam lanced down to sizzle large leaves on undergrowth a full hundred feet below the lower edge of the densely tangled canopy.

The jungle seemed to be in three tiers: the canopy, which was twenty feet in depth, consisting of tangled limbs, vines, and foliage fighting for a space in the sun; a relatively clear layer below the canopy, which was studded by the boles of the huge trees; and then the undergrowth, which grew, in that particular spot, to a height of around twelve feet.

They could not, of course, see much looking down through the hole Jacob had cut in the canopy, but he lowered a camera on a long boom, and then, by watching the portable screen set up atop the mesh, they could see the dim, damp cave below them.

A flock of black and white birds flew within view of the camera, darting in and out among the tree trunks and hanging vines. There was no breeze at all atop the jungle, and they could hear the steady dripping of water collected in the topmost tangle to seep out slowly after each rain.

"We got one of the big life signals within a hundred feet of our present location. No sign on the camera of anything down there, though."

"Well, enjoy your little outing," Rodrick said. "I'll be monitoring your reports. Don't get any foolhardy ideas."

"I'm an Apache brave, not just brave," Jacob retorted.

It was a relief to get back into the scout and turn the cooler up full blast. The outside thermometers were registering one hundred ten degrees. As Clay waved good-bye to Jacob, he saw that Jacob's uniform was already dark with sweat.

"Well, Mr. Girard," Rodrick said, as he started the scout upward, "I think we could steal a couple of hours if there's something you'd particularly like to see."

"The southern islands," Clay said, his hazel eyes glowing, "if that's not too far."

"Very well," Rodrick said, all business. "Mr. Girard, give me a ballistic vector for latitude forty south, longitude twenty west." Clay punched in the numbers. Back on Earth any spaceport would have been programmed into the navigation computer by code number, but the only point programmed into the computers of the scouts on Omega was home, Hamilton base.

"Checklist for ballistic firing, Mr. Girard."

"You want me to do it?" Clay asked, licking his lips nervously. He had not yet fired the scout's rockets.

"You have to learn how sometime," Rodrick said.

Clay went through the checklist slowly to be sure he missed nothing. Then he looked at the captain questioningly. "Any time you're ready," Rodrick confirmed.

Clay pushed the rocket-firing button, and it felt like a giant had kicked him in the chest and pushed him back into his couch. The ship shot upward, tilted, then came into the breath-catching nothingness of free fall and the deep, purple sky before arching over to begin the downward plunge.

Rodrick nodded to himself in satisfaction as it was done perfectly. They strained forward in their harnesses, and suddenly there was the sea below and a large island with others stringing off the northeast and southwest.

"Going on jets," Clay said.

"That's a roger."

"Want to take her now, Captain?"

"No, you're doing fine."

Clay took the scout down to five thousand and did a lazy circle around an island about the size of New Zealand, leaving behind a sonic boom, the instruments registering Mach one. The islands below were beautiful—thickly wooded mountains, gleaming white beaches, lagoons of such clarity that the coral formations and growth on the sea bottom could be seen. Clay slowed as he approached a cluster of smaller islands, went down to five hundred feet, and saw the white, rhythmic lines of surf breaking onto the atolls.

"I never saw the South Pacific, except on the screen," he said. "Must have looked like this."

"Except the palm trees didn't have broad leaves," Rodrick said.

"Someday maybe we can have vacation places down here."

"Sure."

"I want my house to be on that big rock, right there,"

Clay said, tilting the scout to pass a couple of hundred feet over a rocky headland.

Rodrick was working detection instruments. "Nothing larger than a rabbit down there," he said, when the life-sign monitors showed nothing.

"Should we head home now?"

Rodrick checked his watch. "I haven't seen the western continents."

"You're the boss," Clay said.

Rodrick checked the maps and gave the correct latitude and longitude readings to Clay. Once again the rockets fired, and when the vast land area was below their bow, the far western ocean behind them, Rodrick got a quick impression of the size of the continent. Then Clay was going down and down and doing a fast survey run at Mach three toward the east across the thick body of the continent.

"Clay," Rodrick said musingly, "there's enough land area on Omega to make a good life for all of Earth's surplus population and not even make a dent in it."

"Now that we know we don't have to cruise at sublight before activating the Shaw Drive, we could make several trips a year, sir."

"As fast as we could load 'em and unload 'em," Rodrick said.

"All we need is rhenium."

"All we need is rhenium," Rodrick agreed, but he added, in his mind, *and some sane people left on Earth*.

There would be one more requirement, too. There would have to be men and women to come after the first generation of settlers. There was going to be a severe generation gap, because Clay was an exception, one of the few teenagers in the group. It would be a long wait for the babies born during the trip and the ones being conceived and born now to mature.

Rodrick had liked Clay from the first time he ever saw the boy, when Clay had stood up to authority—after having had the guts to stow away—and said, flatly, that he would not let anyone do away with the small dog he'd smuggled aboard. Rodrick had watched Clay go through one of those growth spurts, and now he was man-tall, if still teenager thin. Rodrick felt a closeness to and a responsibility for all of the people of the colony, but he had a special interest in Clay. It had been almost like watching the son he did not yet have mature past childhood and childish things and begin to take on the appearance and, in Clay's case, some of the responsibilities, of manhood.

"Clay," Rodrick said, "have you given any thought to what place you'd like to have in our community?"

"Yes, sir. I've thought a lot about it," Clay answered. "People keep trying to pump science into my brain, but it doesn't seem to take. I do all right on mechanics and math, though, and I do love flying. I'd like to be a scout, sir."

Rodrick smiled. "You have a feel for it. You've got some time to make a final decision, and we're all going to have to be sort of jacks-of-all-trades for a while, but if that's what you want, I'll have Jack Purdy start you on some training."

Clay said, beaming, "Thank you, sir!"

"And if you ever have any problems, Clay, need someone to talk with, my door will always be open to you."

"I appreciate that, sir."

The scout streaked through the thin, upper air at three times the speed of sound. The jungle was below them, cut here and there by wide, lazy rivers.

When the scout blasted over one particular southerly flowing river, it was too high to be seen with the naked eye. At first Theresita Pulaski thought that the sound she heard was thunder, but it had been too sharp, too attenuated. The sky was clear. She leaped to her feet on her raft and shaded her eyes with one hand to scan the sky. She'd heard that sound too often to mistake it. There was an aircraft up there. She was not, after all, alone.

"You! Whoever you are! I am here!" she shrieked, although she knew that her voice would not be heard.

Nothing was left of Theresita's uniform but the thickest seams of her tunic and the waistband of her skirt. Her shoes were still wearable, and for that she was grateful. There was no reason to be modest, there on that great, brown jungle river, and there were times when she drifted totally in the nude, lying in the shade of her lean-to with her head cushioned on leaves.

Her thoughts and memories were her only company, and she'd taken to talking aloud. Somehow the sound of a human voice, even that of her own, did something to bring that green, damp, often roaring jungle down to manageable size.

She had not heard another aircraft. Several times she'd seen river dragons, as she had come to think of the huge underwater serpents. Once one had leaped after a fleeing fish quite close by the raft, close enough to splash her when it fell back with the fish in its mouth, but so far none of them had threatened her. And on shore one day, when she was experimenting with making clothing from the big, tough leaves of the low-growing plants of the jungle floor, she had witnessed a frightening battle between one of the tanklike tree crashers and a creature out of prehistory, a thing as huge and as deadly as tyrannosaurus rex himself. Although the battering creature knocked the bigger, taller, more agile creature off its feet several times, the outcome was preordained. The long neck of the killer would lance down, and sparks would actually fly as tooth met scale, but each tremendous blow of the huge head, driven by a thick, powerful neck, cost the tanklike creature scales and flesh until, finally, Theresita watched as the predator ripped and tore with tooth and claw to expose the white meat and eat a bathtub-sized portion, leaving the rest.

She ate some of the white meat herself and became violently ill, vomiting throughout the night as her raft drifted southward. She was weak and very thirsty the next morning. There were times, when she hadn't been able to steer the raft toward the bank, that she'd had to drink the river water, and although it had a muddy taste, it hadn't hurt her.

There was a sameness about her existence that gradually deadened her senses and drove her to spend the long, sweaty, steamy hours lying on her back and remembering every incident of her life, every conversation, every word. She would tell herself aloud that there was no way she could remember when she was four years old, back in Poland, but she did, and her memory was, at times, so accurate that she wondered if she were already insane. And then one morning she said, "Theresita, there are low mountains off to the right."

"It can't be," she answered herself, "I am actually dead, and have gone to hell, the hell of the Christians, perhaps."

"Don't be an idiot, Theresita. Your eyes are not lying. The jungle rises there; you can see a horizon. There, over the trees. Hills. Wooded, green, jungle still, but hills. And the river is moving faster, you've known that for days."

And a day later: "Theresita, the river is narrowing. The banks are high over there. Look, you can see mud and reddish earth where the bank has given way."

The low mountains were closer. They paralleled the river to the west, and on a very clear day she thought she could see, far in the distance, mountains of great height. But then the inevitable, swift, hard-hitting thundershower blotted out her view and peppered her naked body with rain. She used the rain to wash, catching it in her hands, rubbing her bronzed body briskly.

The character of the jungle itself was changing: The canopy was not as densely matted, and here and there a giant tree found freedom for its topmost branches and actually towered over the canopy. The showers that had kept her thoroughly wet for weeks and weeks had become much less frequent, and as the days passed and the river ran between high banks covered with profuse growths of vines and flowers, she began to see trees along the bank. And it was not as hot. She knew that she had traveled an incredible distance, something on the order of three thousand miles on the river.

Another mighty river joined the one she'd come to think of as her own, and the stream widened again, so that in midcurrent, the banks were a full mile away on either side. She awoke one morning and was thrilled to see an area of lushly grassed plains studded with huge, spreading trees. Theresita began to use her sweeps to bring the raft to ground on a sandy beach, wanting to set foot on that grassy, beautiful land, to be able to walk for the first time in months without pushing herself through rank undergrowth.

She wore only a skirted arrangement of big, flexible leaves and a halter strung from a length of raveled cloth, the last of the waistband of her skirt, hanging around her neck. The Slavic darkness of her skin had been baked by the sun into a golden, tawny brown.

"Damned jungle," she said, turning to look back up the river where, in the distance, the low-hanging clouds on the horizon spoke of the steaming, sweaty, always sodden hell she'd endured for so long.

"But what do we eat?" she asked herself.

The jungle's fruit and nuts had been her sustenance. They had made for a healthy diet, for she felt as fit as she had ever felt in her life, and the calisthenics she'd done during the long, boring hours on the raft had toned her muscles to an athletic hardness. She was as slim as a girl of eighteen, but with the flaring hips and breasts of a woman.

Dry! She was dry, and it felt wonderful. She walked a few hundred yards from the river through knee-deep, lush purplish-green grass. A small animal was startled out of a grassy nest at her feet and went leaping away on long rear legs, clearing the tall grass now and again to twist its rodentlike head to get its bearings. After her one attempt to eat flesh, the meat of the battering beast, she had no desire to try other animal flesh, but in the absence of the jungle fruit, she thought she might have no other option.

When she walked up a long slope, however, and gained the crest of the rise, she saw reddish-gold berries growing on low vines clinging to rocks. The berries were delicious. She cautiously ate a few and waited for some adverse reaction. When they did not make her ill, she gobbled double handfuls, then went back to the raft to stitch together four of the large jungle leaves to form a carrier. She picked enough berries to last a couple of days and put them into the carrier.

The view from the ridge was pleasant. Rolling, grassy plains extended far and away toward the mountains in the distance, and there were definitely, on the far horizon, taller mountains with snow-covered peaks. To the east the view was of rolling plains.

Since she had no desire to spend the rest of her life alone in the jungle, Theresita had two choices: one, to stick with the river, which would have to run into an ocean somewhere, with shoreline creatures and shallow waters; two, to strike out overland, either toward the mountains or the rolling plains. Since water was more regularly required than food for survival, she chose, quite naturally, to stick with the river.

The tall grass made her bed aboard the raft much more comfortable. She slept with the raft tied up to the bank and cast off next morning with her larder still stocked with the thin-shelled nuts, a couple of fruits, and the carrier of berries. The river water was drinkable, even more so than back in the jungle—when she put her hand into the river now, she could see it through two feet of the clearer water.

Just in case she had to try animal flesh, she spent most of the day fashioning long throwing spears, using the battering beast's scales for the spearheads. She saw the first grass-eating animals that day, goat-sized antelopes with silver-colored horns. Late in the day, when she took advantage of having drifted near the shore to ground the raft and search for more berries, she witnessed a kill as tawny-green animals as big as any Earth lion brought down one of the steer-sized grass eaters within a hundred yards of the riverbank and hissed and spat at each other while they gorged on the meat. She cast off. She didn't want to have to face one of those predators, with their long legs, tufted ears, and enough stamina and speed to chase down the grass eater.

The next morning, two things awakened her. First, she had started conserving the few remaining nuts, so she was hungry. Second, there was a difference in the motion of the raft. The river had narrowed considerably, and the constricted flow pushed through with a speed that pleased her. She didn't know where she might be going, except possibly to the sea, but she'd been drifting at a snail's pace for so long that the new speed of the current excited her, gave her a feeling of being on the verge of something

different. From being pleased, she quickly felt concerned.
To the west, the mountains were nearer. Weather on the
planet would surely follow the rules. If, as she suspected,
the clouds were bled of their moisture as they tried to
cross that range of high mountains, the result would be
semiarid or desert conditions. If there was a desert ahead
of her, and if it extended even a fraction as far as the
jungle had extended, she'd never survive crossing it unless
she could find a source of food.

The current was moving even faster now, the banks
constricted by the ridges to the south and rolling hills to
the north. She couldn't work her way toward shore.
Abruptly the river turned again, and the stream began to
cut its way through ever more rocky and ever more arid
land. It was growing late when she began to hear the
sound of low thunder, steady, frightening, for she was
caught by the swift current, unable to maneuver the clumsy
raft to one bank or the other.

Steadily the low thunder grew louder, and she realized that the stream, less than a quarter of a mile wide,
was rushing through a gorge with barren, rocky cliffs
rising fifty to a hundred feet on both sides.

"Well, Theresita," she said, "you're in for it. Nothing
to do but ride it out."

She took what precautions she could. She tied her ax,
spear, and bow and arrows into a bundle and lashed it to
her back with her remaining lengths of vine, then ate the
last of the nutmeats and the berries. No need to waste
food if that thunder came from what she was afraid it was
coming from.

With a suddenness that brought her to her feet, the
walls of the gorge dropped behind her and the river burst
out into a wilderness of exposed rock. It was going to be
worse than she had feared. She leaped to the sweeps, and
now it became a matter of survival for her to reach the
rocky, sandy bank fifty yards to her right. Water-smoothed
boulders were beginning to appear in the river, and the
swift waters swirled around them, piling up whitely. Ahead
of her the river was broadening, spreading out into a
boulder-studded, roaring, white-capped emptiness.

Now a large, smoothed boulder was dead ahead, and

Theresita pulled hard on the sweeps. One of them broke. The raft crashed into the boulder, and the sturdy vines parted. The raft broke up, and Theresita was hurled into the water. She went under, pushed herself away from the rock with her feet, and surfaced, gasping for air and swimming for shore.

Twice she narrowly avoided being dashed against boulders, and then she managed to fight her way to the slower-moving current along the bank and gained sandy footing, her chest heaving with the effort. Her leaf clothing and bundle of weapons were torn from her—and the last of civilization went with it, for the remnants of the waistband of her skirt had been torn off.

She lay prone on the pebbly shore, breathing hard. When she had her wind back she began to walk along the riverbank. There was a green belt near the river, mostly grass, a few low-growing shrubs. The river itself was quite spectacular, spreading for miles to the east, roaring and crashing past the protruding boulders.

Intrigued by the cloud of vapor sitting on the river and by the thunderous roar, she walked downstream. She began to bless the boulder that had destroyed the raft. She stood on a rock ledge and looked down five hundred feet over a sheer precipice. Ahead of her lay the true desert, a limitless waste of rugged, barren stone and gleaming sands. As the river appeared out of the mists below, flowing southward, it was wide and placid. Its banks were bordered in green, and there were tall, swaying trees, dwarfed by height and distance.

She scouted westward along the cliff. There were a few hours of daylight left when she found a place where she might be able to climb down. There was a steep, rocky slope, but good hand- and footholds on the barren rock. She made it down with only skinned knees, then picked her way over hard, pebbly, barren earth to the lower margin of the pool formed by the huge waterfall, her ears now numbed by the cascade's roar.

She was thirsty and lay on her stomach and drank from the pool. And as she lay there she saw movement in the water, froze, and watched as a large bluish fish with a white belly moved its gills lazily and flipped its tail only enough to hold itself motionless against the current. Theresita moved slowly, cautiously, and then, poised, lunged and grabbed the fish.

She flipped it out onto the bank. It was two feet long, had a streamlined, ovate body, and a skin that was slick and slightly slimy.

She found a sharp rock, chipped off a sharper edge with another rock, and cleaned the fish beside the pool. The meat was white and firm. Her mouth was watering with the thought of flesh after so many weeks of nothing but fruit and nuts. She would not have to eat this fish raw, for she had noted that there were, along the shores of the pool, lengths and pieces of driftwood bleached by the sun. She gathered wood and dry grass, then whittled very small, dry shavings from a piece of driftwood. She tried the friction method of making a fire first, whirling a stick between her palms, but although the end of the stick she turned between her palms would get hot, she couldn't quite make it hot enough to start a fire.

After she rested, Theresita walked along the rocky edge of the pool, saw stones that looked much like flint, and experimented until she had two pieces that, when struck together, made sparks.

It wasn't as easy as the survival booklets she'd studied in the Red Army made it sound. It was growing dark when, at last, her little pile of tiny shavings and dried grass gave off a tiny tail of smoke and, after three more false starts, glowed red. She blew on the grass gently and smoke rose to tickle her nose, and then, as darkness came, she had a briskly burning fire, which she fed with driftwood. She made a spit with two forked branches of driftwood that she stuck into the ground. She used a long, slender green stick to impale the fish, the ends resting in the driftwood forks. The smell of the cooking brought copious quantities of saliva into her mouth until she could stand it no longer. She ate the fish from the stick with which it was impaled, biting gingerly into the hot, sweet flesh, and saying, "*Mmmmm.*"

"If it poisons you," she said, the words drowned out by the mighty roar of the cascade, "it'll be worth it."

It didn't. She ate until her flat, muscular stomach was

distended, then kept what was left for breakfast, after a night during which she'd had to keep the fire going, for the temperature fell to a chilling coolness. She slept in a hollow in the sand near the fire, waking at times shivering to throw on more wood.

She set herself a goal to cover fifteen miles a day, which meant long hours of walking. She searched the riverbank, moving south, looking for logs to make another raft. She found wood but had nothing to lash it with. She made herself a new spear, however. Hull-less nuts formed in clusters on some of the trees, and although not as delicious as the jungle nuts, they were edible.

The water of the river was quite clear now, and Theresita enjoyed wading in the edge, plunging into the waters to cool herself as the sun warmed the day. Tuberous plants growing in the edge of the river had a bland, starchy taste, did not make her ill, and became a part of her diet. Now and then, in the green, grassy belt near the river, she found the same low-growing berries she'd eaten back on the plains. She was not going to starve, especially when she found that fish were plentiful, quite unwary, and relatively easy to spear.

She became quite accomplished at striking fire from her firestones, which she carried with her in case she would be unable to find more. Each night she shivered until she learned to dig a bed in the sandy soil and cover herself with a large blanket of grass. Even then she'd awake, chilled, and would start the fire up from its embers in the early dawn, squatting beside it to eat her breakfast of nuts and fruit, or fish when she had it.

Her shoes lasted only six days. They literally fell apart, and she reluctantly discarded them. The worn and frayed pieces of leather might have come in handy, but she had to carry her firestones and spear. She broadened her diet to include the eggs of waterfowl, cooked on a heated, flat rock, but found the flesh of the birds themselves to be very tough and stringy. Given a choice between bird flesh and fish, she chose fish.

Her adventure nearly ended one morning when she was standing in thigh-deep water, waiting for an unwary fish to swim within range of her spear. The wide river flowed lazily, the surface smooth and unbroken. At first she didn't notice the rippled surface twenty feet from her, for her eyes were on a two-foot-long fish which was browsing on the bottom, seen dimly through the water. When, out of the corner of her eye, the approaching ripples caught her attention, she almost waited too long. She saw that the ripples covered an area of several feet and, heart pounding, moved as fast as she could toward the bank, although impeded by the thigh-deep water. She ran with high steps through knee-deep and finally ankle-deep water, when a bellow of sound caused her to run wildly, looking over her shoulder as she raced up the gently rising bank.

The water behind her had erupted, and the thing that threw itself onto the bank in pursuit was legless, a mass of black, which ended in front in a T-shaped head, the bar of which was split open in a three-foot grimace of fanglike teeth. The thing moved onto the bank by vertical ripples of its long, black, slimy, flat body, and she outran it easily, going all the way to where the grass ended and the hot sands of the desert began.

Thus her pleasurable swims in the river became a swift dash to knee-deep water, where she quickly washed away the perspiration of the day's walking. Until the huge, flat, wormlike thing had almost caught her unaware, she had been lulled by the narrow valley and peaceful river.

The days became weeks. Her legs were hardened now, calf muscles pronounced. She often fancied herself to be undisputed master of a world, alone there, except perhaps for whoever had flown the aircraft she'd heard weeks ago. The distant memory of that sonic blast was dim, and there were times when she wondered if she had imagined it. She strode proudly, bronzed and naked, southward, ever southward, the desert around her extending endlessly on both sides of the river ever more barren and arid. Once a dust storm clouded the air, and her eyes and nose were tortured by it until she gave up, dug a bed in the sandy soil, and covered herself, head and all, with freshly cut grass.

With a fresh roar and much white water, the river narrowed into another cataract as it made its way down a sloping drop. The desert was the same, but below the cataract, the valley widened between two cliffs a full five miles apart. A herd of grass eaters watched her walk toward them, moved aside, heads all turned toward her in wary curiosity. She considered, briefly, an attempt to take one of the animals, but she would have had to get near enough to use the spear, and a nonlethal throw would, in all probability, cost her her best defensive weapon, so she continued to walk down the beautiful, wide valley, her daily goal now increased to an estimated twenty miles. She made her estimate by rule of thumb, known speed of a brisk walk, the hours estimated from sunrise to the time when the sun was at its zenith.

She knew that she was not getting enough to eat, for her ribs began to show in bony ridges, and she was more exhausted after a day's walking. And yet there was no end in sight, for when she detoured away from the river to climb to the top of the sun-heated cliffs, she could see the river, its green valley, and the desert, too, extending into infinity.

The carnivore began to stalk her as she angled away from the cliffs back toward the river. She saw it rise from the shadows under the cliff, stretch, and sniff the air as she hurried away. She didn't know it was following her until, almost back at the riverside, she turned and saw a movement in the grass, which stilled immediately. The animal blended so well with the grass that she could just make out the outline. She broke into a trot. There was a herd of grass eaters ahead, so she aimed for them, scattered them with her approach, and mingled her tracks with theirs, thinking that if the predator was following her, he'd lose interest in her as her spoor mixed with that of the grass eaters.

It seemed to work. As the afternoon shadows lengthened there was no sign of the carnivore behind her. She found a good campsite and was lucky to spear a fish quickly. Refreshed by the water, she built her fire and ate half the fish, saving the rest for breakfast, and dug her bed, lined it with grass, and piled up grass for a covering as the night grew chilly. She was so tired that she was asleep before the sun went down and, as darkness came, the fire had burned to a glowing bed of embers.

She awoke with the feeling that she was being watched. She threw fresh wood and dead grass onto the fire, and as it blazed up she saw the glow it reflected in the eyes of the carnivore. She threw a rock and yelled, "Get out of here!"

She stayed awake all night, keeping the fire going, thankful that she had gathered so much driftwood. She ate the leftover fish at daybreak. The carnivore was lying in grass fifty yards from the fire. She threw stones, and one small one hit close enough to make the animal rise and slink back into the grass.

She was using her spear to knock down the hull-less nuts from one of the riverside trees, having covered about three miles with no sign of the predator, when the beast decided it was time for its breakfast. She saw a slink of movement out of the corner of her eye. She held her spear in both hands and yelled, "I told you to get the hell out of here! Go eat a deer or something!"

His answer was a roar, which started low and raised itself in pitch to a scream as the animal launched itself on a thirty-yard charge toward her. Razor-sharp flakes of bark made it impossible for her to climb the tree—she knew; she'd tried it before, when she had had her shoes. The animal was closing the gap swiftly. She had an instantaneous understanding of its speed and knew it would be senseless for her to run.

She crouched, digging the butt of her spear into a hard spot on the ground, and aimed the spearhead in the direction of the beast's breast as it launched itself from the ground a full ten feet away, its huge, tawny-green eyes wild and its sharp teeth bared. It came at Theresita as if in slow motion, and she centered the spearhead, braced herself, heard the spitting snarl, and felt the jolt of impact on her taut arms holding the spear in place. The point buried itself, and she heard a scream and a sharp snap as the spear broke. The full weight of the animal came down on her even as she fell away, and pressed all the breath from her lungs. The beast's gaping mouth closed on her shoulder, and she felt a numbing shock as teeth pierced and crushed. But her spear had done its work, and the animal, in pain and dying, loosed her mangled shoulder, screamed, and began thrashing, its claws drawing a line of fire down the front of one of her thighs as Theresita rolled away to leave the animal clawing and twitching, its arterial blood spouting around the broken spear shaft in its chest.

She crawled away, her own blood reddening the sand. Her left arm was numb, and when she tried to move it, a terrible pain in her lacerated shoulder made her cry out. The blood spurted anew.

She fell onto her stomach and fainted. When she awoke, she was weak. Sand had clogged the teeth holes on the front of her shoulder, so the blood only oozed. She reached back with her right hand and could feel the tears in her shoulder there, and her hand came away wet with fresh blood. A darkness in the sand around her told her she'd lost too much blood.

She remembered the healing quality of the river mud in the jungle. A vague hope, plus thirst, gave her the strength to crawl to the water, where she first drank and then dug into the sandy mud and daubed the stuff on the wounds on the front and rear of her shoulder. She fainted again, then came to with her face lying partly in the water.

She knew she was not going to make it this time. She'd traveled so far, through jungle and desert, and it was going to end here, with her blood still oozing from the deep wounds left by the carnivore. The sun was hot on her back. She felt feverish. She drank more water, daubed more mud on her wounds, and seeking relief from the sun, crawled toward the tree, came into its shade near the dead animal.

"Killing," she said, shaking her head weakly. "Always killing. You must be a communist, my dead friend."

She knew, when next she awoke, that she'd made a mistake. Her throat was dry, her lips parched, and she was too weak to crawl back toward the river.

"Best," she whispered. Best because water would merely prolong the agony of dying. Best to lie quietly in the shade and sleep, letting the blood ooze until the sleep was permanent.

She heard flappings, opened her eyes. In the tree above her two of the scavenger birds perched, with their beady eyes and animallike teeth and leathery skins.

"Eat well, my friends," she whispered.

Between death and life she heard flappings, flutterings, and soft, ripping sounds. She opened her eyes to see the scavengers, a dozen of them, ripping and tearing at the body of the dead predator that had killed her. There was a certain element of justice in it, the killer killed, first to be eaten, with his slayer to follow. At least the scavengers were kind enough not to rip out her eyes and tear her flesh while she was still alive.

"Patience," she whispered, and there was a buzzing in her ears. She was dizzy; her head weighed nothing and seemed to float. She could hear the lapping ripple of the river at the bank, and she was desperately thirsty.

She closed her eyes, willing death to come. She felt so weak, the pain in her shoulder hardly felt. More scavengers were coming, these for her, coming with a swift clip-clop of wings. No . . . wrong sound . . . must be death, the pale horseman. Death was a blur of color and motion, and it towered over her, drawing closer and closer until, blurred and indistinct, it halted and, two-headed, looked down upon her. She closed her eyes, welcoming it. She had come so very far, and she was tired—tired to the death, having come over eleven light years on a ship of death, a dying, destroyed planet behind her, Ivan dead at the bottom of a jungle river, beasts seeking her, a long, black, fang-toothed horror coming for her in a blaze of many-hued, two-headed color.

She closed her eyes and felt only the tiredness, which faded, gradually, into nothing.

III

INGENIOUS TALENTS

SIXTEEN

"Wake up," Jackie Garvey said. She herself had dozed, and now it was past midnight. She put her hand on his shoulder and shook him. "Hey, sleeping beauty, wake up."

He sat up suddenly, the thin blanket falling away from his muscular chest. "Damn," he said. "What time is it?"

"I'm not sure," she said. "Sorry. I fell asleep." He had leaned out of bed to pick up his tunic and was looking at his button-watch with a frown.

"Jesus," he said, jumping out of bed to start throwing on his clothing, "you should have stayed awake."

Jackie sighed. That was exactly the comment she had expected him to make. It takes a long time to get to know some people, regardless of the degree of intimacy. With others, like Rocky Miller, you get to know them maybe a little too quickly.

"You'd better take a shower," she said.

"It's too late, damn it," he snapped.

She smiled with her lips. "I thought you said you didn't care if she did find out."

He looked at her angrily. "This just isn't the right time."

He paused before opening the door, turned, and winked at her. "I don't know about tomorrow night."

"I don't either," she said.

"What do you mean?"

"I think it's time we put the brakes on," Jackie said.

He grinned. She'd said that before. "We'll talk about it." He went out and closed the door behind him. In fact, she'd said after the first time that that was it, and then it had taken him only a few minutes with her to make her change her mind. Well, he knew what he was doing when it came to women.

Jackie, however, had no idea what she was doing. It had seemed harmless enough at first. And, to be fair, she felt she had some justification. She couldn't believe that Duncan was having an affair with Mandy Miller, not at first, but even if Rocky was a little boy in a lot of ways, he didn't seem to be a liar. And he *had* cried a little that first night when he told her about seeing with his own eyes Duncan and Mandy in a deep embrace. His tears had been quite manly, squeezing out of his eyes and sliding down to be swiped away quickly with the back of his hand, but his voice had thickened, and she had known exactly how he felt, even if she wasn't married to Duncan.

Jackie Garvey would never have characterized herself as being a vengeful person, yet she went into Rocky's arms with just a bit of vengeance in her heart, even though logic told her that she was hurting no one but herself. Then it had happened so quickly that there had never been a time when she could have stopped it. The guy was slick; in a contest, he could, she felt sure, be the champion woman-undresser of all time. Not that she'd resisted . . . she was definitely not promiscuous, but she *was* a healthy, normal young woman.

"Well, listen, Rock," she'd said, after they had made love, "I don't think you'd believe me if I said I didn't enjoy it."

He had laughed.

"But never again. It's a trip with a one-way ticket, and I'm not going along for the ride."

But she was so damned lonely.

"Rocky, this has gone far enough," she'd said, after the second night in her quarters.

So, here we are, she thought, a few weeks later, and

the lady has just had her bones pounced again, to her rather audible and obvious pleasure, and once again she'd said, "I think it's time we put the brakes on."

The difference was that this time she meant it.

Didn't she?

The door would be locked. The lady would not be in. It was over. Finished. And her body, remembering, regretted that decision. She groaned. "Well, Garvey," she said aloud, "you've had sex with the number-one and number-two officers. You can start on the juniors now."

She got out of bed and showered. Funny, she'd never felt the need to do that with Duncan. She'd wanted only to lie at his side, to feel the warmth of him, to let sleep come in a gentle kiss, and she had eagerly awaited the day when she would awaken and he'd still be beside her.

Whoever the hell said stolen fruit is the sweetest was a psycho.

Ah, Dunc, it would have been so good, the two of us together. Who could make a better service wife than a servicewoman? Who would make a better wife than a woman who thought that he, Duncan Rodrick, could be used as the perfect model in case the Maker wanted to recall the entire race for defects and start over?

And it made her angry to know that she'd given up without a fight. He'd simply pulled away, gone off somewhere by himself—or with Mandy Miller, as the case might be—and she, the dutiful lieutenant Jackie Yes-sir! No-sir! Garvey, had wilted away and pined. Too late now. But, damn it, why did she feel she'd been unfaithful to *him*? Stupid.

"You have only Rocky's word for it that there's something going on between him and Mandy," a part of her said. "Mandy is a decent person. She wouldn't play such games."

"Hell, Mandy is a *woman*. We're all constructed with the same built-in weakness."

"So, if you are going to feel like that, why don't you get into the competition with Sage Bryson for the admiral?"

Oh, hell, she thought, disgusted, she'd come a long way down to even be thinking such gossip as that. But women were funny creatures, weren't they?

She fluffed her pillow and tried to go to sleep, but her mind was in a rebellious mood. It gave her an image of Rocky going home with the scent of her all over his body. Perfume and woman essence. Women were very sensitive to smells, and because there were only four varieties of perfume in Hamilton, there were three out of four chances that Mandy wouldn't use the same one she'd selected. Had she deliberately let Rocky go without showering? Was there something deep in her subconscious that wanted the whole situation to blow sky-high so she'd be rid of him? But that said that she was too spineless to tell him, and mean it, that it was over.

She knew that she was a capable officer, an adult. She had always been near the top in any competitive effort. When the *Spirit* went back to Earth with a load of Omega goodies, she'd probably be promoted at least two grades in rank. She could see it now: Captain Jacqueline Garvey, commanding the good starship . . . *Unrequited Love*. But she didn't really want to be captain of a ship. She wanted to be the second mate—he'd been married once before—of Duncan Rodrick.

And if Mandy smelled strange perfume and the musky essence of woman on Rocky, the dumb bastard had it coming.

As it happened, Mandy did. As it also happened, it wasn't the first time. She didn't know who the woman was, and she didn't really want to know, but she knew her husband well and had sensed the change in him weeks ago. The lingering fragrance—not hers—on his shirts when she opened the hamper. A reluctance to meet her eyes. And above all, a new belligerence. She had not and would not confront him, nor would she match his belligerence.

When he came into the house, she was already in bed. She'd had to have Doc, the medical robot, prescribe reading glasses in the last month, and she'd chosen a pair with simple black frames.

"You're home," she said when he came into the bedroom, pulling off his shirt.

"Your thrill for the day," he answered, moving on through into the bathroom.

She went back to her reading. The scientific teams

were gathering so much information about the new planet
that it was a night-and-day job just to keep up. She was
going over the lab report on vegetables that had been
fertilized with the waste of the miners. She had made a
note that the colonists could cut their daily food supplements to one-third of the standard amount, for Amando's
vegetables were, if not rich, at least almost adequate in
vitamins and trace elements.

Rocky crawled into bed, said, "Good night," and turned
his back to her.

"You're putting in a lot of hours," Mandy commented.

"Someone has to," Rocky said, "with Rodrick off joy-
riding with his teenage buddy."

"Oh, Rocky—" She said it before she took time to
think, impatience in her voice.

"Oh, that's right," he said, "I mustn't criticize the
great hero."

"Good night," she said stiffly.

He was silent for a long time. She tried to concentrate on the reports.

"Look, could you turn off the goddamned light?"

She was tired. Her workload was heavy. Her marriage had gone sour. When she'd sensed that Rocky had
finally worked himself up to having an affair, she didn't
really care. Sex, although she enjoyed it, was not one of
the preoccupations of her life. She didn't miss it. When,
infrequently, Rocky initiated a sex act—she could no longer
think of it as making love—she made no protest and, by
habit, participated. But she felt relief, more than anything, when he found a release for his passions elsewhere.
Or, at least, that's the way she'd had it analyzed.

That one kiss she'd shared with Duncan under Omega's
two lovers' moons had caused her much pain. She had
never conceptualized herself as a cheating wife. Self-
disgust had been nagging at her from the time she first
recognized that the inexplicable, magnetic, and mutual
attraction between Duncan and her had become something more than just physical. It sometimes made her
furious to understand that there was a part of her that she
could not control. And when Rocky angrily told her to

turn off the light before she was finished reading, she felt belittled and immediately lashed back.

"If it's bothering you," she responded, "why don't you sleep on the couch?"

"Good idea," he shot back, throwing back the sheet violently and stalking to the door to the living room. There he stopped. His face was that of a stranger. "I haven't been sleeping too well in that bed anyhow. I never did like sharing my bed with another man."

Don't do it, she warned herself. *Don't be dragged down to that level*. But there was some guilt in her, and that guilt contributed to her reaction, for it is human nature to fight back more strongly if an accusation is based on truth.

"How dare you accuse me? You come home stinking of another woman, and you dare to accuse me?"

Rocky forced a hard little laugh. "Ah, Miss Purity. Before you get too holy on me, ask yourself who started it!" He slammed the door behind him.

She threw the stack of reports to the floor. "Damn!" she whispered. "Damn, damn." There was a basis, however slight, for his reasoning. She *had* started it. She'd found great and secret pleasure in those long talks with Duncan Rodrick in the observatory during the long trip out. She had kissed him in the moonlight. If a wife had that intuition that almost always told her when her husband began an affair, the husband could probably also sense when a wife's affections were altered.

Amanda Miller was the product of an old-fashioned home. Her parents had been very conservative, religious, and active campaigners in the effort to restore the stabilizing effects of the closely knit family unit to American life. She herself believed that marriage was a contract of honor, and that if a man and woman worked at it together, any problem could be overcome. It was a matter of pride to her that her father and mother had lived happily together all their lives, and when she had married Rocky, it had been with the intention of making her marriage as lasting and as beautiful as that of her parents.

But now she remembered something her father had said: "An extramarital affair, Amanda, is the world's worst excuse for divorce. The sex urge is a universal human weakness. I do not, of course, condone sexual promiscuity, but on the other hand, that most common lapse from the vows of matrimony is human, and forgiveness for it does not even approach the divine. When divorce results from one partner falling from grace, adultery is not the cause of the rupture of the marriage—the cause is false pride, for a person with a true sense of his or her own self-worth will realize that the spouse's adultery is not, in most cases, a personal, intentional blow. In fact, it usually has nothing to do with the way the erring spouse feels about his or her mate."

But Rocky is selfish and even cruel and callous, she thought, but as her anger began to fade, Mandy realized that she would have to be the one to do something to keep the marriage together—if she wanted it to stay together. Rocky, after all, had such poor self-image that he was always feeling persecuted by his commanding officers.

But he'd always put her on a sort of pedestal. He'd thought her to be the most beautiful, desirable woman in the world. And she'd known before she married him that there were aspects of his personality that were immature. Perhaps, if she'd given him more support . . . perhaps, if instead of spending the majority of her time with her own work she'd spent more time with him . . .

She got out of bed, threw a robe over her brief sleeping gown, and padded into the living room. "Are you asleep?"

"I'm trying to go to sleep."

"I'd like to talk. Just for a minute."

"It's late."

"Just for a few minutes?" she asked.

"What is there to talk about?" he asked sullenly, then rolled over to face her.

"Us." She sat down in a chair facing the couch. "I guess the first thing we have to decide is if we want to stay together."

He just grunted.

"You seem to have the impression, Rocky, that I've done something wrong. Will it do any good for me to tell you that I had never slept with a man until I married you and that you are still the only man I've ever been in bed with?"

"How'd you do it then, leaning against a wall?" he asked.

"I see," she said, holding her temper. "Do you want to file for divorce?"

There was a long pause. "I'm not sure," he said finally. He was looking at her as she sat, so calmly, so self-assured, with the light from the bedroom showing just one side of her face.

"When do you think you'll be sure?"

"I don't know."

"May I ask why you're so sure I'm being unfaithful?"

"That's one of the things wrong with you," he said. "You can't even call screwing screwing."

"All right, how are you so sure that I'm screwing somebody?"

"Not just somebody, love," he said angrily. "I saw you in *his* arms. I wasn't deliberately spying on you, either, if that's what you're thinking. I was on duty and things were dull, so when I heard that our dear captain was going outside, I turned on the night eyes just to see what was going on. It was a touching scene."

"All right," she said. "You saw me kiss him. I don't suppose you'll believe that that was the one and only time, that it hasn't happened again, hadn't happened before, and won't happen again."

To his surprise, he found himself wanting to believe her. He had always taken great pride in her. She was not only a respected scientist, she was one helluva lot of woman. Back on Earth he had always enjoyed the way men turned their heads to look at her when they entered a restaurant. For a long time he had felt that no matter how badly the world treated him, he could always count on this one person being on his side. He had missed that. But he hadn't realized just how much until she had started talking about divorce.

"You've never lied to me before, Mandy," he said.

"I'm not lying now."

"Why did you kiss him?"

"Because I'm human, I guess. Because the chemistry

is right between us. Because it just happened there in the moonlight."

"Did you enjoy it?"

She started to ask, *Why would you ask a thing like that?* But she was trying to heal a breach, not get back into an argument. "For a moment. If you were watching, you saw that it didn't last long."

"You're not lying?"

"No."

He sat up, pushed back his rumpled hair, looking very young and vulnerable. "It hurt me, Mandy," he said, because the thought of being without her was not pleasant. Because he needed to know that at least one person on the damned planet was on Rocky Miller's side. "I'm not in love with—the girl I'm—"

"I don't want to know who she is," Mandy said quickly.

"You want to try to patch things up?"

"That's the idea," she said.

"I'm going to take part of the colony south sooner or later," he said, watching her closely for her reaction.

"That can be called mutiny," she warned him.

He flopped onto his back. "So you're going to side with him against me."

"Right is right, Rocky. I'm not siding with anyone *against* you. Will you promise me that you won't do anything precipitous? That you'll let the matter be settled in a democratic way?"

"He'll never call for free elections," Rocky said. "You know that."

"He'll call for elections when the time is right, when there is no chance of being surprised by some unknown danger."

"Which will be never. Look"—he sat back up again—"you'll have to make a choice. I'm willing to forget—"

"Oh, thank you very much."

He frowned. "If you're going to be a smart-ass—"

"All right, let's both forget."

"You'll either be with me or against me," he said.

"I won't be a part of a mutiny."

"You must think I'm damned stupid," he said. "I have the support of a lot of people."

"If you want to be a politician, wait until the elections. Will you do that?"

"I'm not going to do anything dumb."

"All right."

"When the time comes, you'll have to make a choice, Mandy. You'll have to go with me or stay here alone."

"No discussion allowed? I won't have a vote?"

"Ever since we got married we've lived where *your* work demanded that we live. Our schedule has always been built around *your* work. I think it's about time I had a choice."

There was truth in what he said. "I reserve the right to discuss any plans that affect both of us," she said, "but, in general, I agree that you should have a choice. I would hope that you'd listen to and weigh my opinion."

"Haven't I always?" He sat up, swung himself around to face her, and took both her hands in his. "I've never stopped loving you, Mandy. I just have to know one thing: When the time comes and if I choose to move to the south, will you go with me?"

"Yes," she said, for she felt that most of the colonists were good, solid-minded people who would respect Rodrick's leadership and the ship's constitution. At worst, she would have months, perhaps years to try to change Rocky's mind about going his own way.

"Want to come back to bed?" she asked, rising. His arms closed around her, hands seeking out the thinness of her gown under her robe.

"Good idea," he said.

He made love to her with a vigor that assured her participation, and it was only when it was over and he was sleeping that she wondered if he'd pleasured his lover equally as well only a couple of hours earlier. She pushed that thought out of her mind. She had made her decision. She had loved Rocky and still felt a certain fondness for him and excitement when they were making love. She was no teenager, no young, star-struck lover. She was strong minded enough to overcome her infatuation with Duncan. To assure that, she would take one final, conclusive step at the first opportunity.

The opportunity came the very next day. Rodrick

came into her lab at midmorning, drew himself a cup of coffee, and said, "I was just talking with Jacob West. He got some impressive recordings of animal sounds during the night and wants permission to go down to the jungle floor and take a quick look around. I wish there were some way to get Mopro down there, but he'd be handicapped in the undergrowth."

"I think the admiral's armaments can handle most anything that comes along," she said.

"Did you see the film of those water things?"

"First thing this morning," she answered. "Big, aren't they?"

"Big." He smiled at her appreciatively.

"Explosive bullets killed the miners," she said.

"Yes." He leaned his hip against the side of a worktable. "I told Jacob to go ahead, but to take no chances."

She was going to miss these easy chats. She knew she had become Duncan's one confidant. Strong, private man that he was, he would never discuss his decisions and his reasoning with anyone else. But there was nothing for her to do but plunge ahead.

"Duncan, Rocky was using the ship's night eyes the night we went outside."

His coffee cup froze on the way toward his lips.

"Mandy, I'm so sorry."

It was just the right response, the perfect reaction. She felt her eyes mist. Infatuation? Hell, she was so much in love with the man that her entire being cried out to him.

"It wasn't your fault," she said stiffly. She smiled. "Or, at best, it was as much my fault as yours."

"That explains his change of attitude," Rodrick said glumly, for he, too, was feeling guilt. A good commanding officer never, never coveted the wife of a junior.

Mandy had the urge to tell him that Rocky's attitude toward him had started going bad before then, but she was silent.

Rodrick was thinking how badly he was going to miss these moments, innocent on the surface, not so innocent in his heart, for he made excuses to drop into her lab, found it delightfully easy to talk with her, felt that she understood his need to talk things over with her, if for nothing more than to have a pair of sympathetic ears, a sounding board.

"I have never loved a woman as much as I love you," Rodrick said, and his tone told her that his statement was the end of something, not a beginning. "If you want to leave him, God help me, I'll accept you with joy and with open arms, and worry about the consequences later."

"No," she said, putting her hand on his arm and withdrawing it quickly, for just being near him ate away at her resolution. "We can't do that. There's already a split, factions forming."

"Divorce him. Be my wife." Even as his heart formed the words, his mind was seeing the possible damage that could be done to the colony and the chances of completing his mission, but if she had said yes, he would have risked it all.

"Oh, Dunc, you know we can't."

"I know that you love me."

"Yes. I won't deny it. But we can't, and you know it as well as I know it. Don't you?"

Something inside her wanted him to protest, to argue, to be so forceful that she could not resist.

But in his mind's eye he was seeing President Dexter Hamilton's face, hearing the last, stirring words of Hamilton's speech just before the *Spirit of America*'s rockets blasted to lift her huge bulk into space. Duncan knew his own weaknesses, and that meant that their relationship would have to stop completely. Just being near her would tempt him.

"I will say just one thing more," he said, not able to look at her lest he seize her and squeeze honor and duty out of both of them and carry her to his quarters yelling, to hell with all of it. "I'll try not to think of you, but I will be thinking of you. I will want to be with you, to just talk with you, but I won't be with you."

"I understand," she replied, her throat tight and hurting.

"Oh, damn it all," he said, his voice husky as he spilled the remainder of his coffee putting the cup down so that he'd have two arms to reach for her, to draw her close, one hand going up to cup her face as he tried to put a lifetime of loving into one kiss.

She saw the tears forming in his eyes just before he turned away and rushed from the room, and she ran after him, but the door closed in her face. She locked it, then doubled over, her arms clasped to her stomach as if she were in pain, and let the agony of loss pour out of her in shuddering, wrenching sobs.

Rodrick was on his way to induce weeping in still another woman. Jackie was on morning duty. Rodrick sent a junior officer to relieve her and waited for her in his quarters. She came in, straight and tall and beautiful in her uniform, and, standing almost at attention, said, "You wanted to see me, Captain?"

"Sit down, Jackie. Coffee?"

"I'm floating now," she said. "You know communications duty, nothing to do but listen and talk and drink coffee."

"Jackie," he said, as she settled into a chair, knees together, long, nice legs in a ladylike, crossed ankles position, "I won't blame you a bit if you tell me to go to hell."

"Why, Captain," she said, startled, "a good officer would never be so insubordinate."

"I've had a lot of things on my mind, Jackie. To be open and frank with you, I decided that I wasn't setting a very good example." He grinned uncomfortably.

Jackie's smile was frozen on her face.

"You know, we've got to get that old bear down in the engine room married before he blows all his fuses," Rodrick said.

"What?" she asked, thrown off by his change of direction.

"Max and Grace. They've taken out papers." He rose, walked to her, placed three sheets of paper on her knees. Good old service red tape. A marriage license in triplicate. "Papers like these," he said, smiling down at her puzzled expression. "This may not be a very romantic proposal, Jackie, but I've signed, and if you'd like to put your signature just below mine, it would please me very much. If not, I'll understand."

She looked down quickly, saw the familiar scrawl of his signature, was stunned, looked up into his smiling face thinking, *Oh, you son of a bitch, why couldn't you have done this two months ago?*

"I thought, if you didn't object," he said softly, "that we'd make it a double wedding."

Yes, yes, all of her said. "A very businesslike proposal, Captain Rodrick," she said, but her smile was warm. "Worthy of the service. In the same businesslike spirit, I accept." She pulled out her pen, put the papers on the side table, and signed all three with a flourish.

"Thank you, my dear," Rodrick said. "I will do my best to see that you never regret it."

Just two months earlier, and there would have been no regret, no guilt, only happiness. She stood. He did not move back. Her face was close to his. He put his hands on each side of her face. "Lieutenant Jackie Garvey, you are a very beautiful woman," he murmured. He could not bring himself to speak of love, but he could speak the truth, and when her eyes suddenly filled with tears, he kissed her, lowered his arms, and drew her slim, tall body to him.

"I'll just go enter these legal papers into the log," he said. "We'll have dinner in my quarters tonight with Grace and Max and see if we can work out the details together, okay?"

"Yes, sir," she said, with a salute and a crooked little smile that left him slightly puzzled as she wheeled and almost ran from the room. She ran directly to her own quarters, not far away in officer country, slammed the door behind her, and threw herself across the bed to let the tears come, trying to seek out the happiness she knew she should have felt, knowing only that she'd listened to that bastard, Rocky, had bedded him, enjoyed it thoroughly, and all the time Duncan had been just biding his time, putting duty first. "Bitch, bitch, bitch," she said, through sobs, beating her pillow with both fists.

SEVENTEEN

Jacob West had positioned Renato's scout ship, *Apache Two*, according to directions given by the admiral, so that the ship's powerful winch cable would run freely down through the cut-out in the mesh of the jungle-canopy landing pad. The admiral was lowered first, standing with one foot in the big hook on the end of the cable, holding onto the cable with just one hand. Once on the jungle floor, he looked around and waved, and Jacob brought the hook back up, stepped onto it, and nodded to Renato. It was a long and thrilling ride down.

The cable with its hook was hanging just above the ground, ready to lift them up out of danger. In the event that the source of the big life signals showed up and had teeth, Jacob, with his soft and fragile human flesh, would be drawn up first while the admiral stood rear guard.

Both of the dauntless explorers were equipped with a laser weapon with an oversized power pack and a preset shallow beam. Jacob led, effortlessly slashing his way with the laser through the undergrowth. He had a camera-pack helmet mounted on his head, and now and then, as he noted some new jungle plant, he'd pause, point with his nose, and trigger the camera. He was headed in the direction of a tree that was as tall as the others but a bit more slender, with ladderlike limbs growing out at right angles from the trunk and fruit the size of a large grapefruit. Amando would always be interested in some new kind of fruit.

They reached the fruit tree quickly. The fruit smelled delicious, but Jacob wasn't going to sample it until it was cleared for human consumption by Amando.

"We'll get a couple of samples on the way back," he told the admiral.

They found a lot of life under the canopy. The birds were noisy, plentiful, brilliantly colored, and almost like those on Earth. Once Jacob and the admiral caught a glimpse of an animal high up in the foliage but could not see it well enough to know what it looked like. Three types of trees, with huge boles, predominated. Now and then there'd be an oddball tree, which bore either fruit or nuts. Jacob cut their pathway so they might conveniently gather samples of the potential food items on the way back.

It was hot, steamy work. They extended the path for a few hundred yards and saw nothing new, so Jacob stopped to rest and think things over. Hunting the source of the life signals wasn't going to be simple. He'd seen no trails, no clearings, no breaks in the dense undergrowth.

"Let's make a circle," he suggested, moving aside so that the admiral could cut the trail for a while.

Thus it was that the admiral was in the lead when he cut into a clearing. He halted, listening, then stepped out, shifting his laser to his left hand and drawing his weapon with his right. Jacob had his own projectile weapon in hand. The clearing was roughly circular. The undergrowth, matted and dead, had been pushed into a circle and piled up in the center to a height of about six feet.

The admiral started to walk; Jacob, alert, head jerking back and forth, followed.

"What do you think?" Jacob whispered.

"I don't think the underbrush cut itself and piled itself up," the admiral answered.

"Some kind of nest?"

"Big nest," the admiral said.

Jacob was a scientist, not an outdoorsman. Apache or not, he'd spent his life in well-heated or cooled houses, laboratories, or ships of the Space Service. He'd grown up in a new, high-rise factory-residential city in the New Mexico desert where the only green things were in irrigated gardens.

The brush pile was about twelve feet in diameter. They walked around it. There was nothing like an opening.

"Shall I cut into it?" the admiral asked.

"Why not?"

The laser cut away inches of dry brush at a sweep, the material disintegrating so swiftly that it did not ignite the pile. The cut was about two feet deep when Jacob said, "Hold it."

There was something inside the pile. He heard a chorus of piping squeaks.

"Perhaps we should desist," the admiral suggested.

The pile of brush was big enough to hide something quite large, *with* teeth.

"If there was something fierce in there, it'd have already come out," Jacob said. "How does it get in and out?"

"Perhaps the opening is at the top," the admiral guessed. He holstered his weapon, put the laser aside, and climbed up the side of the tightly packed brush pile.

"You will want to see this," the admiral said.

Jacob climbed up. The top of the pile was open, and it was now quite obvious that it was a nest. The piping squeaks were louder, and they were coming from three of the darnedest little animals Jacob had ever seen. They looked as if they had been designed by a cartoonist and finished by a maker of fine jewelry. The head of a comic dragon sported a beak, which was not quite comic. The neck was long and sinuous, the body arched, and then, supported by legs so long, the little animals seemed to totter around the nest on stilts. The legs ended in three-clawed clubbed feet, and the claws looked sharp and dangerous. But the crowning touch were dime-sized scales, extending from beaked snout to the end of the short, stubby tail, scales that caught the dim light and sparkled with all the colors of the rainbow.

"Cute little devils," Jacob said, grinning.

At the sound of his voice, the three young animals turned toward Jacob and the admiral, looked up, threw their mouths open to show a row of sharp teeth, and began to make that piping, whining sound. And to add to the decorative effect of the rainbow scales, a peacock ruff unfolded from just behind their heads to stand out in vivid blue.

"They think we're mama," Jacob said, his dark eyes dancing. "They're hungry."

The remains of various fruits littered the well-packed ground in the spacious interior of the nest. Jacob recognized the rind of the large fruit they'd seen. In fact, there was such a tree growing in the edge of the cleared area, but the fruit had been plucked to a height of about twelve feet. He climbed down and used his laser to cut a high branch laden with fruit, carried it back, climbed up again, and broke a fruit into small pieces with his hands at the expense of getting a sticky juice all over them. He tossed a small piece, aiming at a gaping throat, which, like the ruff around the little animals' necks, was a vivid blue. The piece was snatched quite expertly in midair while the other two jostled and piped their disappointment.

The three colorful little beasts piped and begged until Jacob had fed them all the fruit he had.

"Admiral," he said, "we've got to take one of these little dudes back with us. They're the cutest critters I've ever seen."

"I think it would be best to leave capture of native species to the zoologists," the admiral responded.

"But they're just babies. We can take one in a capture bag with no problem."

"Those teeth and claws look quite efficient," the admiral continued.

"And you're the man who wrestled a miner," Jacob said.

"And lost," the admiral reminded him.

"Look, I'll get some more fruit. I'll lure two of them over to the other side, and you can toss bits of fruit out to get one of them to your side of the nest. Then all you have to do is leap down, throw the capture sack over his head, and get back up before the other two start chewing on you."

"Perhaps," the admiral said, "I should lure two of

them to my side and let *you* leap down and capture the other."

"Come on, Admiral," Jacob said. "Your skin is replaceable. Mine has to *grow* back."

"Well," the admiral relented, "I think Grace would like to see one of them. They are quite unusual, and attractive in an alien sort of way."

"Good boy," Jacob said.

Jacob used his laser to shoot down another branch of fruit, and the deed was accomplished with a minimum of fuss, the admiral using his more-than-human agility and strength. The captive seemed to resign itself to its new surroundings quickly, so that it was immobile as they picked up their lasers and entered the trail they'd cut into the clearing.

"I want to come back and set up a camera here so that we can get a look at their mama," Jacob said.

"We'd just better make sure mama isn't home," the admiral said. "I doubt if she'd take kindly to our kidnaping one of her brood."

Jacob froze. "Do you hear something?" he asked.

"I do," the admiral said, handing Jacob the capture bag and drawing his projectile weapon as the sound of rustling came from the undergrowth on the other side of the clearing.

"Mama," Jacob gasped. "Let's get out of here."

Before he turned, he saw the creature and was very impressed with her size: legs fully eight feet long and the same long, sinewy body, but enormous, with scales seemingly radiating fires of color. He couldn't take his eyes off her. She crossed the clearing in a flash and simply stepped into the nest, from which came the sound of renewed pipings.

"Go!" Jacob urged. He moved rapidly, trying to be quiet. The admiral brought up the rear. "Admiral, don't shoot her. She's a mama, remember."

"I will have to shoot to protect your life," the admiral said. "That's the way I am."

"If she follows us, we can climb the fruit tree," Jacob panted, moving at a trot now, gripping the capture bag in one hand. The little animal in the bag suddenly emitted a very loud, very high-pitched call. There was an answering bellow from behind them.

"Run like hell!" Jacob shouted. They were within fifty yards of the cable dangling down from the landing pad.

"*Apache Two!*" Jacob yelled into his communicator.

"Yo," Renato answered.

"We want to come up fast!" Jacob gasped.

"Standing by." Renato's voice drifted down from over a hundred feet up, muffled by the canopy of foliage.

"Admiral, we'll both go up at once."

"Agreed," said the admiral, looking over his shoulder as a piercing, bellowing roar of rage came from the direction of the nest and then the thunder of feet and the cracking, crashing sound of Mama enlarging their pathway at high speed.

They were almost to the cable. "Stand by, *Apache Two!*" Jacob yelled, leaping for the hook, his foot going in first, the admiral's on top of it. "Oh, damn, Admiral," he groaned, "*my* bones have to mend, too."

The cable jerked and began to move upward slowly. The sound of snapping, crashing underbrush was much nearer, and the shrieking bellow told them that Mama was very, very angry.

"Faster!" Jacob yelled. The cable jerked and began to move faster, and there was Mama, peacock ruff fully extended, now a fiery red of anger, eyes the size of baseballs gleaming orange, beak open, teeth very impressive, the thick legs eight feet long, the neck six.

Renato, having heard Mama's protests, had cranked the winch motor to full speed.

"We are presently fifteen feet off the ground," the admiral said calmly, "moving upward at the rate of approximately ten feet per second. She will have to be able to jump twenty-five feet to—"

"*Yeooooow!*" Jacob yelped, as Mama leaped twenty-five feet into the air and missed doing him serious harm by a half inch as her teeth took the seat out of his pants and left bloody lines across Jacob's American Apache rump.

And then they were entering the vertical tunnel of the canopy and were being scraped severely by the vegetation. "Slow down!" Jacob yelled. "Slow down," he yelled again just as his head hit the grill with a thump. He saw bright lights and shook his head to realize that the upward motion had stopped.

"Take a look to see if my brains are oozing out," he joked to the admiral, who handed over the capture bag.

"I have made a decision," Jacob said to Renato as he was pulled up through the hole. "From now on any space that isn't climate conditioned and off limits to all animals and insects *is* off limits to all Apaches."

A few hours later he was lying flat on his stomach, embarrassing portions of his anatomy exposed to the ministrations of Dr. Mandy Miller, telling her that in the face of grave danger he, personally, the Apache brave Chief Sky Flyer, had captured what was probably the most beautiful and exotic animal on Omega.

"I'm going to have to put some stitches in this one," Mandy said. "Lie still while I get the local anesthetic."

"Me heap big brave," Jacob said. "Me hate needles. How about you weld-um rump."

"Be still," Mandy said, misting anesthetic and beginning to sew.

"You use-um red thread, of course," Jacob said.

"Of course."

"White-eyes woman heap handy with needle. As reward, you can play with Baby."

"Which baby?"

"My dragon. It is named Baby."

"I want to see it, of course," Mandy said. "As for playing with it, I can see what its teeth did to you."

"That was Mama."

Baby, Jacob's dragon with the technicolor scales, rapidly became the most popular resident of the new town of Hamilton. Baby was an omnivore. At first Jacob fed Baby fruit, then tested it on some table scraps, and soon food was no problem. Baby started growing at the rate of a full inch in height a day.

Within one week Jacob had Baby sitting up, rolling over, and begging for tasty tidbits, and nestling down, beaked head across his legs, for a soothing rub of the leathery, rainbow-hued scales. When pleased, Baby's peacock neck ruff was a brilliant blue. She came to like Jacob,

Clay Girard, Cindy, and Grace Monroe, who took time out from her wedding preparations to give Baby a quick intelligence test. Mandy's testing revealed that Baby was a female. Baby adored Jumper, the dog, who barked and frisked and finally became trusting enough of the dragon, twice his size at first and growing rapidly, to play tug the stick with her.

When Baby began to drop her scales, Jacob was concerned and called Mandy's Life Sciences group to see what was the matter, but then new scales began to form, which were larger and more brilliantly colored. The flexible, leathery scales that she had shed began to harden almost immediately into crystalline things of such beauty that everyone in the colony wanted one, and an amateur lapidary discovered that, when artificially hardened in a temperature approaching the cold of space, the scales could be faceted to gleam as impressively as the finest gemstones.

Among those who came to admire the rapidly growing Baby was Sage Bryson, and she was one of the first recipients of a dragon's scale. It came from the man who loved her.

"How very sweet of you," she said, touching his hand. "It's so beautiful."

"I wish I could give you more. I want to give you everything."

"Your company and your kindness are more than enough for me," she said. "I'm not greedy. I just wish there was something I could do for you."

She liked to tease him like that. She liked to strike flirtatious poses, liked to greet him in her quarters dressed in her skimpiest shorts and halter. She liked touching him, running her hand down his arm, or through his hair. And all the time she was laughing inside, laughing at all the men who, throughout her life, would have crawled on their hands and knees to get the same treatment.

"I hesitate to suggest it," he said, "but there is something you can do, Sage."

"All you have to do is ask."

"I'd like a name. I mean, my title is good enough for

use in my official capacity, but I think it would be nice to have a real name, one that only you and I know."

She smiled. Sometimes the game got rather interesting. "Let me see. The name of some famous admiral?"

"No, no, I think something a bit more personal."

"I've always liked the name Rhett. It's an old name. There was a Rhett in a classic cinema film from the mid-twentieth century. He was quite handsome, and brave, and devil-may-care."

"Rhett," the admiral said. "If you like it, I like it. Will you call me that when we're alone?"

She wrinkled her nose at him. "Want me to?"

"I'd like that."

"All right, Rhett."

"Yes, I like it," the admiral said. "There is something I feel that I should mention, Sage. I hesitate, because it might bother you, but—"

"You know you can say any old thing to me," she assured him.

"It has been noticed that we are spending time together," he said. "In fact, there is some talk about it, and some good-natured joking."

"I know," she said, taking his hand between hers. His hand was simply marvelous, she thought, so lifelike, and never damp and sweaty, the way *their* hands always got when they touched her. And she could hold it as long as she liked and be assured that he would never, never try to put it down inside her skimpy halter, or elsewhere.

"I know," she repeated. "Don't let it bother you. They just don't understand."

There were times when *she* didn't understand. It had started as a game. It was really funny the way he looked at her, adoration in his eyes, just as if they were real eyes. But then it was nice to be adored and have nothing demanded of her. She'd been thinking seriously of being seen more often with him in public. That would really be rubbing *their* noses in it.

"It doesn't bother you?" the admiral asked.

"Not in the slightest. You're more human than any man I've ever known."

"Sage, there are some things I wonder about."

"What?"

"You *are* human, with human biological processes and, presumably, human urges."

"You're not going to talk nasty are you?"

"Oh, no, please," he said quickly. "It's just that I can't—uh, give you anything, uh—"

"Hush," she said. "You can give me a massage."

"Yes, I can do that."

She'd taught him. She loved the feel of his gentle, dry hands. He was programmed to know the human anatomy perfectly, had tapped into the health and fitness material in the library to learn all there was to know about the art of massage. Back on Earth she'd been massaged, by women, of course, and none of them had even come close to the admiral's skill.

"Now?" he asked.

"Unless you have something else to do," she said, a bit petulantly.

"Oh, no." He lifted her gently from her chair. She liked that. He was so strong and so gentle. He had installed a massage table in her bedroom. It made things a bit crowded, but it was wonderful to be lifted, to be placed gently down on the padded top, to have her shorts and halter removed without even a hint of carnality, to have every muscle in her body massaged so thoroughly.

After a long, delicious time, he rolled her onto her back and began to work on her front thigh muscles.

"Do you know, darling, that no man has ever seen me like this?"

"I'm sure that they would find you as beautiful as I do," he said.

"Sometimes you're stupid," she said harshly.

"I'm sorry. How was I wrong in saying that?"

"Oh, forget it," she said. "Work on my rectus abdominus."

The admiral had never seen a naked woman before he'd started giving Sage massages, but he had seen pictures and anatomical models. He knew the biological purpose of the taut, pert breasts and the hotly moist vaginal area, which he never touched and had no desire to touch.

He knew, too, that it was not normal, human normal, this relationship with Sage, and he worried about her.

To him, she was beautiful in all detail, as beautiful in full uniform as out of it. His lips had never touched her. He had no desire to touch her with his lips. He merely wanted to be around her, to be able to look at her clothed or unclothed, to know that warm feeling that wasn't supposed to be a part of him, the feeling of being valued for himself alone, not because he was a first-class fighting man, a crackerjack computer, a deadly weapon, a dependable protector, a mechanical-electronic wonder.

"I'm going to keep you for always," Sage said contentedly, as he finished off his massage with her deltoids, coming down the front of the pectoral muscles to gently work the soft-firm sides of breasts.

"Do you really want to be with me always?" he asked.

"*Ummm,*" she said, with deep, comfortable sleep just a blink away. He covered her with a sheet and looked down at her. She was so beautiful, and she, even more than Grace herself, loved him, considered him to be a person. And she wanted to be with him always. Yes, it could be arranged. She'd said, hadn't she, that she didn't care about the gossip and the laughter?

It was simple for him to obtain the papers for a wedding license. He gave the central computer an order, and the papers, three copies, came from the word-processor printer.

To see Hamilton City from a distance as dusk fell was to see a multihued jewel. The translucent plastic walls of the dwellings, programmed in colors of individual choice, glowed softly against the background of the endless western ocean.

The well-traveled crawler approach-roads, worn into the plain by the treads of many vehicles, carefully avoided Amando Kwait's fields of grains and vegetables. Wheat was turning golden under the ideal growing conditions of the new Eden. The heavy evening air carried the smell of freshly dampened soil as Kwait's automated irrigation system released flows of cool water from the Dinah River to gurgle its life-giving way down the furrows between rows of giant Earth vegetables.

A regular shuttle of cargo crawlers brought ore from Stoner McRae's low-yield iron mine in the badlands. The metalwork shops, equipment removed from the *Spirit of America*, were producing the molds and machine tools needed to add copper-refining facilities and the equipment needed to separate the rhenium from the copper ore that was being delivered in small but regular quantities by miners all over Eden. An entire task force, under the direction of Paul Warden, spent time coordinating trade with miners. Even with the discovery during the outward voyage that the Shaw Drive would operate with a fraction of the rhenium that had been utilized originally, it would take decades to collect enough rhenium from trading with the sluglike miners to send the *Spirit of America* back to Earth.

The hydrogen separation plant was in operation, and there was plentiful fuel for the scouts. As a gesture of compromise to the concerned-citizens group, Rodrick cut back on exploration and mapping—other than of the continent of Columbia—and used the scouts to keep the colony supplied with a growing variety of fruit and nuts from the fertile southern zone. There had been no further attempts to penetrate the dense equatorial jungle. Curiosity about the jungle's huge life signals would have to be satisfied by watching the multihued Baby grow, something she did very well.

Baby had become the darling of the entire colony, and she had the run of the place. She followed Jacob West around like a dog—then like a pony. By early fall, when the good Earth produce began to come from Amando's fields and grace Hamilton's dining tables, Baby was the size of a horse. It took only one swat on Baby's beak for Jacob to get across the lesson that she was to stay out of Amando's vegetable fields. Of course, she'd put away a couple of hundred pounds of potatoes, digging them with her three-clawed feet, before she was discovered, but Amando's harvest was so generous that no one got too upset, and after that Baby would carefully avoid the fields, piping plaintively until someone would toss her a tomato or a potato or a head of cabbage.

Grace Monroe's concern for Tina Sells, the adolescent infatuated with the admiral, was soon replaced by concern for the amount of time the admiral was spending in Sage Bryson's company. Grace was frankly puzzled about Sage's motivation.

Max, growing a bit nervous as the date of the double wedding neared, coarsely brought the question of Sage Bryson and the admiral down to basics.

"Let's rip the skin off his crotch and implant a tool," he growled. "What that woman needs is a good screwing."

"You put it so delicately, dear," Grace said, making a moue.

"Or let one of Mandy Miller's shrinks at her," Max said.

"I'm not sure that it's Sage who will need a psychiatrist," Grace said.

"Grace," Max groaned, "he's a machine, a robot."

"In many ways he's like a teenager having his first crush," Grace said. She smiled. "Is that really all he is to you, just a machine?"

Max grumbled something unintelligible, and then grinned. "I know how you feel, honey. Hell, you can't help but be fond of him. Look, you want me to have a talk with that dumb broad?"

"No," she said quickly. "I'll speak with the admiral. It's fascinating, watching him develop qualities he should not, in all logic, have. He's discovered Shakespeare. And the twentieth-century lyric poets. He *feels*, Max. Thank God he doesn't know hate or jealousy or spite—at least not yet—but he feels friendship. He's big on honor, and now he's in love."

"You afraid he's going to blow a circuit or something?"

"I don't know," she said, frowning. "Just last week he and I ran every circuit in him and scanned his memory chambers. Everything's normal, except he's discovered a way to double-load his amino-acid memory chambers."

"Overload? Is that why he's going nuts?"

She touched Max's hand. "Falling in love is nuts?"

"I think you and Sage have the same problem," Max said, with a leer.

She leered right back at him. "I think you might have a point there, Chief."

Max swallowed, looked around. They were in Grace's lab. All was quiet. He asked, "Do you suppose, by any odd chance, that if I kissed you and maybe sneaked just one little feel, everybody and everything on this oversized mudball would stay away for just five minutes?"

"We won't know until we try," she said, going into his arms, lifting her lips. His kiss was tentative, and his hand stayed at her waist. He was open eyed, eyes moving back and forth.

"You're not concentrating," she whispered.

"I keep waiting for the door to get busted down or a general alarm to go off."

"Relax," she whispered, and as he did, Jackie Garvey burst into the room with a frothy something in white held out before her.

"Whoops," Jackie said, starting to back out.

Max sighed. "Come on in, Jackie," he said in total defeat and resignation. Grace giggled.

"It's finished," Jackie said, extending a wedding dress.

"Good-bye, Max," Grace said. "You don't see the wedding gown until the big day."

"Try it on," Jackie urged when Max had gone. And then, "Grace, you're beautiful."

"Well, I'm a little older than most women who marry," Grace replied, "but I managed to stay chaste, and to tell you the truth, I'm glad."

Jackie looked down to hide the quick expression of shame on her face.

"You're going to wow them," Jackie said.

"We'll wow 'em together," Grace said. "You're so young and beautiful, no one will notice the gray hair at my temples and all the crow's feet."

Jackie laughed.

Following Duncan Rodrick's surprise proposal and his suggestion to Max and Grace that they make it a double wedding, Jackie had come to be very fond of Grace. She loved it when Grace started talking about Max, because

Jackie had always felt that Max was a grouch, and to see him through Grace's eyes was a revelation.

"Jackie," Grace said as she began to remove the wedding gown, "may I ask you something in confidence?"

Jackie swallowed hard. Now and then her guilt and self-hatred for her affair with Rocky Miller sneaked up and hit her in the gut. "Sure," she said.

"How well do you know Sage Bryson? She's in the electronics section."

"Not all that well. She's a very beautiful woman, isn't she?"

"That she is," Grace agreed.

"Why do you ask?"

"Oh, just curiosity, I guess." Grace was not one to gossip.

"Are you getting a cupid syndrome?" Jackie asked with a smile. "Since we're getting married, you're wanting to play matchmaker for Paul Warden?"

"He's a nice man," Grace said. "I was just wondering why Sage is so cruel to him." But that, of course, was not her real reason for asking Jackie if she knew Sage. The admiral's newly found ability to experience emotions was a constant source of concern for her, but she put it aside for the moment because she and Jackie were scheduled to spend some time with the ship's supply officer and dietitian, making up the menu for the wedding reception to which the entire colony was invited.

Meanwhile, Grace's concern for the admiral was being shared by Duncan Rodrick, who was facing a situation that made him want to yell loudly for help.

The admiral, all earnestness, was standing at full attention opposite the captain in his office. "Sir," he said, "I realize that this is without precedent. That's why I wanted to talk with you about it before I get the signature of the bride-to-be on the marriage license."

Rodrick had come to value the admiral highly. His association with the lifelike robot, however, had always been in the line of duty, so that he had not developed, as had many members of the colony, a fondness and regard so complete that it was almost possible to forget that the admiral wasn't human.

"I have studied the ship's constitution and laws pertaining to the question, sir," the admiral continued. "And I find nothing to prohibit such a contract between robot and human, unless one draws a very literal conclusion and states that I am, after all, a minor, being less than five years old from my activation date. But since I have a large body of experience and knowledge, I feel that there is just cause to set aside that question."

"You have a point," Rodrick said, wondering if he should call Grace Monroe and let her handle the situation. The admiral was her "boy," after all.

"Now, I'll admit that I have not studied the entire body of the law," the admiral went on. "Do you, sir, know of any legal reason why this contract should not be made?"

"Well, I don't know of any law against it," Rodrick admitted, still at a loss.

"I had thought to ask Grace and Chief Rosen to allow us to join them in their ceremony," the admiral said, still standing at attention. "But Grace seems so happy and so busy, I decided not to add to her concern."

"Very considerate," Rodrick agreed.

"There's another matter, sir," the admiral said. "As the head of a family, I will have certain responsibilities. To date, it has been my pleasure to serve without set hours and without pay. In the future, when I am married, I think it would be only fair that I be allowed the same privileges as any other Space Service officer." He laughed. "Not at admiral's pay, of course. I realize that Grace has a certain quaint sense of humor, and that she gave me the name of admiral as a sort of a jest, or mild protest against the military mentality. My rank, sir, I will let you determine. If I have to start at the bottom, as ensign, that's fine with me. And it will not be necessary to make my service pay retroactive. I ask only that I be allowed the same terms of duty, and that I be given the right to make a claim to land, as all the others can."

"Admiral, have you talked this over with Grace?" Rodrick asked.

"Not in full, sir. As a member of the service, I thought it my duty to speak with my commanding officer first."

"The lady in question," Rodrick said, "has agreed to marry you?"

The admiral stood taller, smiling proudly. "She wants to be with me forever, sir."

Rodrick made up his mind. He had never been a man to dodge responsibility. "Well," he said, "I think the first thing we have to do is get that young lady of yours in here to sign the license." He was thinking that the admiral's lady was young Tina Sells, a minor, and that once that was pointed out to both of them, the situation would be defused long enough to have Grace poke around in the admiral's brain a bit and to have someone talk some sense into Tina.

"Sir, I'd rather have her sign the license in privacy, if that's all right."

"You do admit that the situation is rather unusual?"

"Yes, of course."

"In unusual situations, Admiral, we sometimes have to resort to methods not to our liking. I think it's best that I have a talk with both you and your young lady."

"Yes, sir, if that's the way you feel, sir."

"I think that's best," Rodrick said.

"May I use your communicator, sir?"

Rodrick handed over the communicator. He was thinking that he might as well get it over, although he himself had a lot to do. The admiral turned his back and spoke softly. Finished, he handed the communicator back. "She'll be here in five minutes, sir."

"I'm sure that you two have discussed the long-range implications of your marriage," Rodrick said.

"Oh, yes, sir," the admiral replied. "Our union will be purely platonic. She is in total agreement, which is fortunate, of course." His face was quite serious. "As it happens, sir, she has no desire to bear children. There are precedents for such a nonphysical union, sir, as I'm sure you're aware."

"Have you considered that you will be removing from the breeding pool one woman who is capable of helping to build Eden's population?"

"We have discussed that, sir. I realize that this is a fine point, but our casualties to date have resulted in a surplus of one female in the colony. The nature of the work will, by the laws of probability, produce a larger surplus of females as the development and exploration phase continues."

Rodrick didn't answer. He drew himself a cup of coffee and was stirring in the cream when his caller sounded and he said, "Come in."

"You wanted to see me, sir?" Sage Bryson asked, after casting a clouded look at the admiral.

Rodrick's shock must have showed on his face, because Sage's face went red, and she looked grimly at the admiral, who was smiling happily.

"The admiral tells me you two have plans," Rodrick began.

"I have been working with the admiral on certain aspects of field theory, sir," Sage said quickly. "I'm sure you're aware of his impressive capability as a computer."

"Yes, I am, Miss Bryson," he said. "The admiral is a very valuable member of this expedition."

The admiral stood taller, chest swelling.

From a look of tension on Sage's face, Rodrick had the feeling that there was something very wrong. His first impulse was to send the admiral out of the room and talk with Sage alone, but there was enough smoke present to indicate some fire. Better to get it all out in the open. He picked up the wedding license and handed it to Sage.

"What's this?" she asked, and then her face went red again.

The trouble is, Rodrick was thinking, *the admiral is too human*. He could understand how a woman could forget that the admiral's blood consisted of cooling and lubricating fluids, and, perhaps, Sage's flirtatious actions and words, which would have been understood by a man, had been misconstrued by the robot.

"And just who are you going to marry, Admiral?" Sage asked, her voice very cold and harsh. She had told him time and time again that one of the most beautiful aspects of their relationship was that it was totally private, known only to the two of them.

"Sage?" the admiral asked, his beaming smile fading.

"What has this, this, *thing* told you, Captain?" Sage demanded.

The word stung the admiral deeply. He realized that he had made a serious error. For a moment he felt the nearest thing to pain that he had ever felt, and then he was no longer thinking of himself. He stepped forward, holding out his hand. "Please forgive me, Sage, Captain. I fear that the experiment I have been conducting on double-loading my memory chambers has had an adverse effect. If you'll give me the papers, Sage, I'll destroy them and ask Grace to repair my memory chambers. We can't have erratic behavior, can we?"

Rodrick, filled with admiration, said nothing.

"What has he told you?" Sage screamed at Rodrick. "I demand to know!"

"I don't think it's anything to get excited about," Rodrick said soothingly. "I believe the admiral has made his explanation."

"Oh, no you don't." Sage raised her voice and waved the marriage license. "There's something going on here, and I demand to know what it is!"

"I believe that the admiral has become very fond of you during your work together," Rodrick said. "That's all, plus a slight malfunction, as he has explained."

Sage turned her blazing eyes on the admiral. Her fair skin was flushed and her mouth distorted. "What did you tell the captain?" She whirled to face Rodrick. Her voice took on a malicious edge. "I've been trying to decide, Captain, whether or not to come to you. This *thing*, this machine, has a filthy mind. He is a menace. He brought a massage table to my quarters because I'd been having stiff neck muscles from my work. I saw nothing wrong in having him massage my neck muscles, but then he—" She bent closer and whispered, "—tried to take off all my clothes. He—"

"Sage, you don't have to say anything else," the admiral said sadly. "I accept full responsibility. It is all a misunderstanding on my part."

"Are you calling me a liar?" Sage shrieked. "You filthy-minded pile of nuts and bolts?"

Now Rodrick felt a new concern. Sage Bryson had

passed a very thorough psychological screening back on Earth, but a lot of time and a lot of miles were behind them, and the danger, the strain—well, he'd been pleased that there hadn't been more adverse effects among the scientists and colonists. Sage's reaction was not the reaction of a well-adjusted woman.

"Miss Bryson, the admiral had the idea that you had agreed to marry him," he said gently. "Did you do anything to encourage that idea?"

She was very calm. She pulled herself together. She laughed. "I cannot be held responsible if Grace Monroe has allowed her creature to overload its capacity."

"No, of course not," the admiral said.

Sage laughed again. She looked at the admiral, and there were tears in her eyes. "I thought you were my friend."

The admiral started to speak, but he caught a motion of Rodrick's hand telling him to remain silent.

"I thought, surely, that I could be myself with you," Sage said. "All my life I've had to hide any friendly feelings I might have had for you men, because after one little smile, one innocent touch on my part, you become slavering animals." Her voice had begun to rise slightly. "You, you're not even a man, but, oooh, she did a good job on you, didn't she, planting into even a bionic brain the same filth and animal desires. And now you reward my friendship by telling the captain lies."

She whirled to face Rodrick. "I haven't told you all of it," she said, eyes flaring, lips making large, exaggerated movements as if each word was pain. "I suppose he has told you I willingly undressed, exposed my body to him." Her laugh now was high, on the verge of hysteria. "I guess you *men* had a great, big old belly laugh out of that. At last Sage has let her guard down. At last a man has seen Sage's body, and has touched it *all over*. I'll bet you laughed and laughed at that, didn't you, you sons of bitches, you filthy, mother—" Her voice rose, and the obscenities poured out, a sewer puking vileness.

"But you didn't get Sage, did you, you ball-less wonder, you animated junk pile, you—"

She fell silent. She lowered her head, and, somehow,

seemed to be very much younger. Her hand went to her mouth, and she covered her full lips with thumb and forefinger. "I'm so very tired. I think I will have to rest now."

She walked as if sleepwalking, smiling shyly, shoulders hunched, to slide down the wall and sit in the corner of the office on the carpet. "I don't want to play that game anymore," she said, in a soft, high-pitched, little girl's voice. "It's nasty, and I won't play. Leave me alone, Uncle Freddie. You're hurting me. I am tired." She leaned her head back and closed her eyes.

"Admiral, get a medical team up here on the double," Rodrick ordered. The admiral reached for the communicator as Rodrick came around his desk. "No, use a communicator outside," Rodrick said. The admiral left on the run. Rodrick stood over Sage, looking down. Her eyes were closed.

"Sage?"

"Tired," she whispered.

"Sage, get up. Come and sit in the chair. Dr. Miller is coming. She'll see that you get some rest."

He reached down and took her hands, thinking to help her to her feet, into a more dignified position in a chair. As he touched her, she went rigid and her eyes flew open.

"Get your hands off me," she screamed, neck straining, hands jerking away, then flying to narrowly miss scratching Rodrick's face. "Don't touch me, you filthy—"

The obscenities were still coming from her in a hysterical scream when two members of the medical staff rushed in, the admiral behind them. The doctors took in the situation at a glance, saw the set of Sage's face, the wide, staring eyes, and the grating, throat-injuring scream of words. Sage fought fiercely, but soon a tranquilizing mister was slapped against her thigh, and within seconds she quieted, closed her eyes, and was limp as she was lifted onto a stretcher.

"Admiral," Rodrick called, as the admiral started to follow the medical team. "I don't think you'll be needed."

The admiral's face was twisted in pain. Rodrick,

touched, put his arm around the admiral's shoulder. "I think she'll be all right."

"It's my fault," the admiral said softly. "I should have realized—"

"Son," Rodrick said, surprising himself, for he was not thinking of the admiral as a robot, "the seeds of that outburst, of her mental anguish, were planted a long time before she ever met you. Don't blame yourself."

"Captain, permission to be absent from duty for a while?"

Rodrick nodded. "You're not going to do anything foolish . . . ?" He felt foolish himself, worrying about a robot performing irrational actions.

"No, I just want to do some thinking," the admiral said. "With your permission, I'll check out a crawler and camping equipment and spend a few days in the Renfro Mountains."

"Permission granted."

When the admiral was gone, Rodrick called Grace on the communicator and told her of the scene in his office and of granting permission to the admiral to go off by himself.

"What has that woman done to him?" Grace asked, in quick, protective anger, then, just as quickly, "No, I don't mean that. The poor woman is sick."

"Maybe the admiral should see a psychiatrist when he gets back, too," Rodrick said.

"How long did he say?"

"A few days."

"He'll be back in three days," Grace said. "He won't miss my wedding."

Rodrick felt a quick little sadness. People had the most ingenious talents for messing themselves up. Poor Sage. Somewhere back in her childhood, it had all begun, but she'd repressed it all these years. He wondered who Uncle Freddie was, and what he had done to cause her to say, as a little girl, "I'm tired of playing that game."

But what was *his* excuse? In three days he was getting married to a woman he didn't love.

One thing for sure, he promised himself, as he went back to a cold cup of coffee, made a face, poured it out, and drew another. Regardless of what he felt, he would never give pain to Jackie. She would never know that he didn't love her. He didn't like seeing anyone in pain.

The admiral was finished with his packing when Baby came running smoothly past the vehicle park. Baby was carrying three healthy, whooping teenagers—Clay, Cindy, and Tina—without a sign of strain. She was still only a youngster herself, but she stood six feet tall on four-foot-high legs, and her entire body and tail length was reaching twelve feet.

"Whoa, Baby," Clay Girard yelped. Baby came to a stop, and the three youngsters piled off to surround the admiral.

"Where are you going?" Clay asked.

"North," the admiral said.

"What's the expedition?" Clay asked, always on the lookout for an interesting mission to try to get in on.

"Rest and relaxation," the admiral answered.

"All alone?" Tina Sells asked.

"Yes."

"Hey," Clay said, "I've been wanting to get up into the mountains to try for trout up there."

The admiral smiled. He couldn't help but feel a bit better in the presence of such youthful good spirits. "Give me a day or so, Clay, and then I'll call and let you know how things look in the way of trout streams."

"Locate a good one, Admiral," Cindy said, "and we'll get Dad to bring us up to have a real fish fry."

"I'll call," the admiral promised.

He watched as Clay and the two girls leaped onto Baby's back, while Jumper and Cat played chase-the-tail in and around Baby's three-toed legs.

He envied all of them with all his being.

EIGHTEEN

Earthlings had always been fascinated by the possibility of life after death, and this fascination was enhanced by civilization's advanced medical techniques. New drugs and new procedures enabled doctors to save patients who were very close to death, and pseudoscientific literature latched onto this and was full of accounts of individuals who had been "dead" and had come back to life with glowing stories of peace, bliss, and wonderful visions. Skeptics said that such feelings and visions were simply the results of the brain's temporary deprivation of oxygen, but such unbelief did not lessen the new faith of those who had experienced the visions, or those who were desperate for assurance that there was something beyond the grave.

Theresita Pulaski was mildly surprised to find that there *was* life after death, the death she had felt as she lay in the dust under a tree, without the strength to crawl to the river for a cooling drink of water. She felt an absence of pain. She saw visions: Her vision was blurred, as if seeing through vast time and distance, and there was a blur of vivid rainbow-hued movement, and death had two heads, one of them looking at her with kind eyes.

She floated without pain or worry. Her body had no needs. There was no time. From a high place she looked down on beauty and wonder and the warm sun and the wide, peaceful river. There were soft, soothing hands on her. If this was death, it had always been totally under-rated, even if she couldn't ever seem to bring anything into definite focus . . . not even the beautiful visions of being loved with a skill and intensity that reminded her of the nights she'd spent with Yuri. She was lifted, loved, and loved again, experiencing either endless orgasms or sweet, total sexual desire for it all to begin again. When she was no longer dead, she missed those times with a strength of yearning that caused her to shake as if with a jungle fever.

Rain pounded down on a thatched roof. Through an open window she saw the long stringlike fronds of a nut tree dripping in the downpour, and for an awful moment she thought that she was back in the jungle.

She sat up with a start. She remembered her wounds and tried to move her left arm. The arm felt slightly weak, but when she looked down, there was no blood, no gaping tooth tears, only barely distinguishable scars. And her skin was not bronzed, but was her natural Slavic swarthiness. There was a funny little dizziness in her head. She began to concentrate on her surroundings: walls of horizontal logs chinked with mud, open windows, a floor covered with a thickness of fresh leaves, a bed of fronds under her, a ceramic vessel on a wooden table beside the bed, water, and nothing much else in the small room.

She shook all over, and her body cried out for some-thing. She seized the ceramic jug and drank deeply, but the need was not satisfied. Sliced fruit beside the water container eased the shaking only a bit, and then she felt as if she wanted to scream and run, so she got off the bed, falling back to catch herself with her hand. She was very weak.

The doorway was covered by some kind of animal hide. She pushed it aside and looked out onto the muddy clearing surrounded by thatched-roof log huts. Nothing moved but the falling rain and the trembling fronds of the trees.

The rain was chill, but she walked into it, her bare feet sinking into the mud. Her nude body shivered with chill, adding to the other tremors, which seemed to come from deep, deep inside. She walked to the nearest hut and pushed aside the leather covering. An oil lamp was burning on a table, and by its light she saw a thin, sticklike thing rise quickly from a bed like her own and turn a hard-surfaced, gleaming head with yellow, faceted eyes the size of coffee cups toward her. A stream of clicks and whistles came from the thing's wide mouth, which opened in a slit below a shiny, visorlike beak. The being pointed a three-fingered hand and made sounds, and Theresita turned away, letting the covering fall back over the doorway.

She walked toward the open end of the village enclosure and emerged into a grove of broad-leafed trees. No one tried to stop her. She hugged her arms over her breasts against the chill rain and walked toward the sound of surf until, topping a dune, she saw an ocean with a broad sandy beach and, in orderly rows, huge, hulking, blunt-ended, cigar-shaped, lighter-than-air craft swaying ever so slightly on mooring ropes. She walked toward the airships, whose wooden gondolas rested on the ground, and a sticklike being reared up from a gondola. The thing made sounds and pointed a three-fingered hand back toward the village.

She didn't know why she was shaking so. She was in no mood to be ordered around by clicking, whistling, insectlike stickmen. She told the thing so in Russian, with appropriate profanity from her early days in the Red Army. Other heads popped up from the gondola. The first one leaped out and ran toward her. She held her ground. The stickman stopped in front of her, pointed back toward the village, and clicked and whistled.

She pointed toward the strand. "I don't know about you, Comrade Mantis"—for the thing reminded her of a member of that insectivorous hunter of Earth—"but I am going for a walk along the beach." She turned away and started walking. She felt a hard hand on her shoulder and was jerked around with surprising strength. A stream of sound issued from the slit mouth. In sudden anger she knocked the hand from her shoulder, and when the insect man made louder sounds and lifted one hand, three-fingered fist clenched, she went into a crouch and watched the blow coming, went under it, seized the arm, and sent the stickman tumbling over her shoulder.

A wailing sound came from the mouth, and a dozen stickmen came running from the nearest airship. She had no place to run. She stood her ground and sent three of them moaning to the ground before she was swarmed under by sheer numbers.

Scratched and bruised by the hard exoskeletons of the stickmen, she was carried, kicking and cursing, back to her hut and tossed bodily in to land on the soft floor. She leaped up, ready to fight, but the flap fell into place and she sat down on the bed, breathing hard. A few minutes later the flap was lifted. There was something different about the stickman who stood in the doorway—the abdomen was fuller, the rump rounder. This one held a braided leather whip in one three-fingered hand and used it to indicate that Theresita was to come outside.

It had stopped raining. She followed the stickman—or woman, she felt—to a wooden hut larger than the others at the center of the village compound and went inside. Other insects—she would begin to think of them in that term—were taking down squirming gelatinous-looking sacs hanging from pegs along all four walls. The one with the whip gestured, and Theresita duplicated the actions of the others, lifting two of the squirming sacs, which she realized were larvae, down by a looped handle at the top. She followed them outside and hung her two sacs on a pegged rack in the full light of the sun.

She was already turning away when the whip lashed across her calves smartly. It was not too painful, but she leaped toward the whip bearer, caught the lash in midair as it came at her again, and jerked hard, bringing the thing toward her so that she seized it by the neck, jerked the lash out of its hand, thrust the lash up against the yellow, glaring eyes, and said, "Do that again and I'll break every bone in your body." She shoved the thing away, threw the lash to be caught in the thing's hands, and turned to go back to the big hut for two more of the squirming sacs.

As soon as all the larvae were transferred from the hut to hang squirmingly in the sun, most of the females— Theresita could tell the difference by the shape of the abdomen and the bulging rumps of the stickwomen—started drifting away toward the beach. Theresita looked questioningly toward her guard, the one with the whip. "Shall we go get some sun, sweetie?" she asked, pointing toward the beach.

The female clicked, pointed. They walked together to the strand to find the others digging happily in the wet sand left behind by the outgoing waves, plucking out circular things that they cracked with their rows of solid, serrated teeth. The one with the whip pointed and whistled. Theresita walked to the edge of the surf, waited for a wave to recede, saw frantic movement in the sand, and picked up a round bivalve. She opened it with her fingers and saw a piece of white flesh the size of a peanut. She sampled it. It tasted like oysters.

The shellfish feast continued for a long time, and then the stickwomen sauntered away toward the grove, Theresita and her guard following, to pick fruit and nuts. Before the sun went down, the larvae were moved back into the large hut where a fire smoked, sending part of the column of smoke through a hole in the roof, but spreading most of it inside. The community's males joined them there, and the fruit and nuts that had been gathered were shared. Theresita thought she was beginning to pick up a word or two of the whistling, clicking language of the insects: A muted click and backward movement of the head meant yes. The muted click partly whistled, the head thrust suddenly forward, meant no. They called themselves Whorsk.

Three females began to sing. It sounded somewhat like crickets, but more melodic and varied. A male leaped to the center of the rough circle that had been formed. His movements were very graceful, slow, and sinuous. A female joined him. Others joined in the singing. The couple dancing drew closer. The female's rounded rump seemed to swell, and when a long, pointed protrusion appeared from the male's groin, the singing grew more frenzied. The dancing matched the music's pace until, with a sweet whistling sigh, the female leaped high, came down on her hands and knees, and displayed a rosy opening in her swollen rump. The male, with an equally sweet whistling cry, inserted his long, pointed organ there and began to sway ecstatically, while the singing softened and slowed. One by one, other couples joined, until Theresita was the only unjoined entity in the room.

She walked out amid the soft hummings and whistlings and clickings and went to her hut. Communal though the joinings were, as alien as they were, she was reminded vividly of that dreamlike state during which she herself had been joined with a male.

Question, comrade, she was thinking. *How can it be so vivid, that memory? How did these bug things heal you? You've seen enough mortal wounds to know that you were bleeding to death there beside the river. And what is this interior trembling, this all-body hunger that is not satisfied by food or water?*

She slept. The day following, and the day after that, and the day after that were much the same. She began to enjoy the sweet singing that prefaced the nightly communal orgy. She began to pick up words. Her attempts at reproducing the clicks and whistles of the insects' speech were greeted with what she came to know as laughter. One night two of the females with whom she spent the days pulled her out onto the dance floor and teased her good-naturedly into trying to duplicate their slow, sinuous dancing. Loud clicking, which indicated approval, greeted her efforts, and she, laughing, began to do a rather raunchy Earth-style bump and grind. A male leaped onto the dance floor and started trying to copy her movements, and when his organ began to extend and swell, she gave a series of laughing clicks and pushed him away, then took her seat, staying out of the circle until the first ritual coupling had been performed.

She had lost track of time. A group of Whorsk arrived, and there was a huge celebration. The newcomers had a variety of fruits, nuts, and nuggets of crude copper for trade. She gathered that they had come across a piece of ocean and was impressed. She climbed into a gondola and tried to pedal the wooden pedals, which drove the airscrews. She managed to make the four-bladed wooden propeller rotate, to the good-natured clicking approval of those who were watching. Then the trading visitors left.

Question, comrade. Where do they get the hydrogen to fill the bags? The only signs of technology she saw were wood-fired kilns for making pottery from a type of clay that the males brought in from the west and the much-valued bronze heads of spears, arrows, and axes.

One day she saw a group of males, armed, leaving, headed west. She suspected that the big river was in that direction, so she ran after them, thinking to join them, to see where the river reached the sea. After all, she'd spent a lot of time on that river. It was, in her mind, her River. The males, headed by the one she'd come to recognize as the village chief, formed a defensive group, pointed spears and arrows at her, and ordered her back to the village.

Her conversation had reached a point where she could ask a female, "Go men?"

"They go to the river."

"I go?"

"If you go, you will die," was the answer, with a rattling warning.

This, of course, made her more determined than ever to go to the river. She had concluded that her interior shaking had been a sure symptom of drug withdrawal. If so, that would explain those dreamy days and nights when she was "dead," when she was healing. Obviously, the insect people did not have the skills to heal her alien body. They had no drugs; they lived simply, except for the incredible airships; their food and drink came from nature; they had no organized agriculture. Somewhere, over on the big river, were beings who had a drug that would keep a human being in a dreamlike state for a very long time, long enough for some very severe wounds to heal, and yet not make that human too dependent on the drugs.

Theresita's first attempt to sneak away to the west showed her that she had underestimated her captors. She left just before dawn and had not gone two hundred yards before she was quickly and silently surrounded by a group of warriors, who escorted her back to her hut at spear point and admonished her in no uncertain terms, although she did not understand all the words.

But, damn it, somewhere there was a man, a real man, who had used her body so lovingly and skillfully that the memory was stronger than the drugs, which had, obviously, had the effect of making her forget everything but odd, inexplicable flashes of sexual ecstasy, rainbow lights, and an odd beauty.

One morning the door flap was lifted by the female who had been Theresita's constant companion. She was carrying a soft, well-cured fur, which she handed to Theresita. It was tawny green and had been fashioned into a simple sleeveless garment, open down the front. She slipped it on. The nights had been growing so cool, she had been pulling the fronds and leaves of the bedding atop her. There was a belt with the garment, made from the tail of a beast. The fur extended to midthigh. For the first time in a long time she was clothed. It felt rather peculiar, after so many months of nakedness.

"You killed a *kkkee*," the female told her.

"I kill?"

"You killed." The name of the beast she'd killed on the river was not translatable. It was a syllable like *kkkee*.

"Who fix me?" she asked.

". . . people."

Something people. What people? She did not have the words to pursue the question.

"You were brave," Theresita was told. "So you live."

She had been brave. She had killed a *kkkee*. So she was allowed to live.

By whom?

"I live because of Whorsk?" She could come fairly close to pronouncing the name the insect people called themselves.

"No . . . people."

"I see people?"

"If you see them, you will die."

Paul Warden sat in the waiting room of the ship's sick bay. He had forgotten to remove his service cap. He was a bit dusty, for he'd just returned from a trading route, which had taken him to the rugged foothills of the Snowy Mountains. He'd been told by one of Mandy Miller's staff that Dr. Miller was with Sage Bryson and would speak with him as soon as she was finished. In the meantime, he'd pulled a portable reader into his lap and was idly punching up possible titles and not seeing them.

He put the reader back on the table, rose, and began to pace. The corridor door opened, and Evangeline Burr, in white shorts and a middy blouse that showed her tanned midriff, smiled kindly at him. "Hi. I heard you had just gotten back."

"Hi, Vange," Paul said, remembering his hat and removing it, running his hand through his hair, which was still somewhat damp from his long ride in the hot late summer sun. "Do you know what happened?"

"I believe it was some sort of mental breakdown," Evangeline said.

"How is she? Have you seen her or anything?"

"No. She's been under sedation." She sat down, watched him pace for a moment. "Is it your intention to wear out the carpet, Paul?"

He gave her his lopsided grin, then sat down.

"Did you have an interesting trip?" she asked.

"Not bad. There's some pretty spectacular country out there beyond the badlands, and the closer you get to the Snowy Mountains, the more impressive they are. It rained on us a couple of times. I didn't know how much I'd missed rain."

"Yes," she said. She started to make a comment on the weather but held her tongue. Paul looked too worried for small talk.

Evangeline had changed in the past months. She had started playing tennis with some of the young married people. She no longer felt uncomfortable with her womanly curves, and she found herself thinking about Paul a lot. She remembered with great pleasure those beautiful nights under Omega's two moons when a group of them would be sitting around Paul's campfire and eating hot dogs. She wasn't sure she was in love, but she knew that she always took great pleasure from being around Paul, and she admired him greatly. On the other hand, her friendship with Sage Bryson had begun to cool for two reasons: First, Sage no longer seemed to have time for her, and second, Evangeline did not approve of Sage's cold, often rude treatment of a man who obviously adored her.

She was trying to think of something comforting to

say, when Mandy Miller, in white reading glasses pushed up into her dark hair, came into the waiting room. Paul leaped to his feet.

"How is she?" he asked.

"Well," Mandy said, "she's had a good rest. We kept her sedated until an hour or so ago."

"That doesn't tell me anything, Mandy," Paul said, with his little grin.

"Paul," Mandy said, looking grim, "there is nothing physically wrong with her. But she's a very disturbed woman. When she first came out of sedation, she seemed to think that she was back in New York, and that she was about ten years old."

Paul's face went white.

"Dr. Allano is with her now," Mandy said. "He's the best we have."

"Is it a nervous breakdown?" Paul asked.

"It's too early to speculate," Mandy answered. "From what she said to Captain Rodrick, and from what we've been able to get from her in the last couple of hours, I'd say that her problem has very deep roots, and that she has in the past been quite successful in compensating." She shrugged. "She was so successful in compensating for her, uh, problems that she fooled the selection board. Sometimes, when things are buried that deeply, when they do at last come out—"

"Bad, huh?" Paul asked.

"We just don't know yet," Mandy said. "Dr. Allano will have to work with her, to make a complete evaluation. I'm sure you're aware that we have fine tools to work with mental disturbances. Given time, now that she's come face to face with her . . . uh, problems, we'll be able to help her."

"Would it be a good idea for us to see her?" Evangeline asked.

"Not right now," Mandy said. "I'll keep you posted. She's going to need friends, and she's fortunate to have two like you."

Paul and Evangeline walked slowly down the corridor away from the sick bay.

"Why?" Paul asked, after a long silence.

"Paul, she's never opened up to me, but I think something traumatic must have happened to her very early."

"I'd like to be able to go back in time and—" Paul didn't finish.

"I know how you feel," she said.

Evangeline was feeling something that bothered her. Sage had never given Paul the least encouragement, but he was just the sort who would, ever faithful, ever hopeful, become the tragic figure, waiting for Sage to be cured of her psychosis. And she, Evangeline, had decided that *she* wanted him. She hadn't made much progress. Now that Sage was ill, would she take advantage of Sage's absence from the field of competition? In a way that was dishonorable, but, damn it, it wasn't right for a man like Paul to martyr himself for a love that had never existed.

Camped beside a clear mountain stream in a narrow, wooded valley, the admiral's eyes gazed into a dying campfire. He'd been sitting beside the fire all night, keeping it going with fallen limbs he'd gathered in plenty. He was looking inward, however, not at the glowing embers. He knew he was not unlike the humans. If anything, his brain, his mind—for there was more to him than his computer—was superior to the fleshy human brain. It could store more information. He had been exposed to, had more ready access to, more knowledge than any person alive.

He suspected that his emotions, his personality, all those little traits that gave him individuality had, in one way or the other, come from Grace. When he and Grace worked together, their thought processes were astoundingly similar. His opinions on almost any abstract subject mirrored Grace's.

Grace had fallen in love with Max Rosen.

He had fallen in love with Sage Bryson.

Was he, then, nothing more than an electronic copy of Grace Monroe? But he'd fallen in love with a sick human, whose fleshy computer was malfunctioning.

So robot, he thought, *you can win affection only from a human whose mind is confused. Second-class stuff? You're not even on the same rating list. True, you could kill an even dozen of them before the first human began to react. True, you have more knowledge in your man-sized brain than an even dozen of them. True, you are immune to physical pain. True, you are an animated pile of nuts and bolts, symbolically speaking, just as Sage said you were.*

Why, then, he wondered, were the patterns in the glowing embers so fascinating, the happy sound of the stream so pleasing, the Omega sunrise so spectacular?

But why, in your newfound emotion, does it seem so unimportant that what Sage Bryson felt for you was not the romantic love you've read so much about of late? Why is there no pain? Why is there only a sincere pity for the woman? What is your destiny, robot? What is your function?

The admiral, examining himself, talked aloud. "I was constructed to be a mobile, military, decision-making computer. My intended function was to direct fire, to position other robots for the most effective attack or defense, to kill humans in the form of enemy soldiers, or to destroy the robots of the enemy."

Protection of the humans was his primary function now, with his lightning-swift mind on call to aid any scientist with a problem that could be approached by computer.

And was that all?

Did some of the humans really enjoy his company, or were they merely being kind? A fish jumped in the stream, and he thought of his promise to let Clay know about possible fishing places. What about young Clay Girard? He seemed to be genuinely friendly. Clay was one of the several humans in whose company the admiral himself almost forgot that he was a robot. Stoner McRae was his friend. Of that he was sure. He could say the same about any number of people. Like Tina. He'd been foolish enough to think that the young girl had fallen in love with him, when all the time she'd just been fond of him. When he had been damaged, her tears and her "nursing" of him had not indicated love, but human concern.

Concern. Yes, that was what he felt for Sage. Concern, and some genuine shame for his own stupidity. And yet he would lay down his electronic life for Sage. Or for Clay, or Cindy, or Grace, or—for any of them. What was that if not a form of love? Yes, the protective instinct was programmed into him, but did that make it less?

He rose in the light of the early sun and walked upstream until, at the head of the valley, the stream foamed whitely down a hundred-foot waterfall. His eyes were attracted by the reddish tint of a layer of the exposed cliffs. The admiral climbed up, using superhuman strength and agility to do some rock climbing that would have made the most accomplished human mountaineer blanch. He examined the reddish layer from close up, broke off some samples, and made his way back to the camp. He used the communicator in the crawler, asking for Stoner.

"McRae here," Stoner said.

For a moment the admiral was mute. He'd started to say, "This is the admiral." He suddenly realized that he felt a bit uncomfortable about that title now. *The* admiral, with a capital T.

"Stoner," he said, "I'm in the Renfro Mountains, and I feel fairly sure that I've found a deposit of low-grade bauxite."

"Hey, great!" Stoner came back. "I don't need to tell you to record the map coordinates, I'm sure."

"I have them here," the admiral said, reading them off. "I thought perhaps you might like to fly up while I'm here."

"I'd sure like to," Stoner said. "But I've got to go out to the badlands."

"Would you please pass the word to Clay and Cindy that the streams here are full of trout?"

"I don't dare," Stoner said. "They've been after me for weeks to let them get up into the Renfros. If they know there are fish up there, I'll hear no end of it."

"All right, sir," the admiral said.

"Come to think of it, Admiral," Stoner said, "how long do you plan to stay up there?"

"I'll come back in time for the wedding, sir."

"If you wouldn't mind company, I can drop Clay and Cindy off in a couple of hours, and then they can come in with you on the crawler."

"I'd enjoy their company, sir," the admiral said. There was no doubt in his mind that the cool, crisp mountain air, the beautiful stream, and the sleek, fighting fish would give Cindy and Clay much pleasure. That, in turn, would give *him* pleasure. Sharing their enthusiasm would also be a great pleasure for him.

"So," he said, feeling better, "enough deep thoughts and self-doubts, robot." Some unforeseen quirk in the functioning of his brain made it possible for him to feel an emotion of gladness. He would guard and protect Clay and Cindy. He would enjoy. What more could he ask?

Jumper and Cat were the first out of the scout as it settled on hydrojets in a small clearing near the stream. Jumper licked the admiral's hand and barked a greeting, while Cat climbed to his shoulder and nestled there, glowing blue with pleasure. Then Clay and Cindy leaped out, all youthful energy and laughter. They shouted thanks to Stoner and their pilot, Jack Purdy, who piled bundles of camping gear and light fishing tackle on the ground. When the scout took off, the day blended into pleasant images: Jumper and Cat cavorting at the camp, Clay catching a large fish on the second cast and, for the humans and the dog, a lunch of fresh trout filets. Then exploration of the beautiful little valley, sunset, a glowing fire. Clay and Cindy growing sleepy, Jumper curled nose to tail near the fire, Cat on the admiral's shoulder—with an extension plugged into the admiral's chest computer as the admiral fed into Cat's smaller, less complex facilities basic information on the appearance of minerals and metals in nature. Cat could scale rocks and cliffs where not even the admiral could go, and while Clay and Cindy fished the next day, the two robots would do a survey of the exposed cliffs around the valley.

The admiral, with no vain pride and no feeling of superiority, did not envy the human need for sleep. He filled his nights with a form of introspection, choosing a subject at random from his doubly packed memory cells and examining it to the fullest extent of his reasoning powers. Sometimes the nights were not long enough. And as he sat back and examined the events of the previous few days, he believed he had truly made peace between his mechanical and emotional selves.

While Clay and Cindy slept soundly beside a campfire in the Renfro Mountains, Rocky Miller sat in a conference room aboard the *Spirit of America* with his growing group of conspirators, for they had, indeed, advanced to that status now.

Rocky was a little annoyed because Clive Baxter had been holding the floor for over ten minutes with a series of niggling little complaints. Baxter talked about Eden's summer heat as if it were just two degrees cooler than an old-fashioned Baptist hell. He bemoaned the lack of rainfall. He called the captain a fool for settling the colony in a semiarid wasteland. He complained abut the taste of the bread being made with Amando Kwait's new harvest of wheat. Not once did he touch on anything important, such as the basic human right to make one's own decisions, to fashion one's own life-style, to be in charge of one's own fate.

There were times when Rocky was tempted to tell Clive and his malcontented followers that they were overgrown children. But he always managed to keep his cool, because he needed the malcontents. Without them he would be unable to prove two things to himself and all of them, especially Duncan Rodrick: that Rocky Miller was a competent leader and was overdue for a command, a world of his own. There was plenty of room for it on Omega, even on the continent of Columbia. With some very basic equipment, which the Hamilton colony wouldn't even miss, a settlement much more pleasant and much more productive could be established in the southern areas of mild climate, sensible rainfall, and plentiful natural foodstuffs. He would be able to handle the grumblers once they had broken away from Rodrick's rule; they'd be helpless without him. He might have to take a hard-nosed approach at first, letting them know who was boss, but it could and would be done.

The other thing he had to prove was that his wife really loved him and not Duncan Rodrick. In spite of Rodrick's upcoming marriage to Jackie Garvey and Mandy's assurance that what she'd felt for Rodrick was merely a momentary attraction, there had been a change in Mandy, and in Rocky's mind the final proof of her love for him would come when she climbed into a crawler with him to build a new settlement in the south. Rocky snorted. He wondered if Rodrick knew that Jackie had been a cozy armful for *him* for the previous few weeks.

"I say we tell Rodrick that we've had enough," someone was saying, Baxter's monologue having ended. "I'm sick of this place, just as Dr. Baxter is. I say let's give Rodrick an ultimatum."

"Before we get too excited," Baxter said, "has the list of necessary equipment and supplies been compiled?"

The list had been ready for weeks. A plan of operation to gather the needed equipment and other items had been approved, the plan being mostly Rocky's work.

"Let's go over it once again," Baxter suggested.

"There's no need for that," Rocky said. "It's time we did something besides talking."

"What would you suggest, Commander?" Baxter asked icily.

"I suggest we set a date," Rocky said.

There was a stir of nervousness in the room. There were fewer than a hundred people there, but Rocky knew that that group influenced others. He estimated that he would be able to pull over three hundred people out of Hamilton.

"Setting a date might be premature," said one of Baxter's supporters. "There are too many things to be decided."

"The only thing to be decided," Rocky said, "is if we're serious, or if we just meet here to voice a few petty gripes."

"What about electricity?" a woman asked.

"We've known from the beginning that we're going to have to rough it for a little while," Rocky answered.

"We have only one doctor."

"We will have no air transport."

Mandy Miller's staff had been a tough challenge. And Rocky's cautious approaches to individual scout pilots had been met with blank stares, or worse. Mandy had, it seemed to Rocky, done one hell of a job indoctrinating her staff with loyalty to Duncan Rodrick, and the scouts were pure Service, who would consider any attempt to go against the captain's orders as mutiny.

"You've all heard the plan a dozen times," Rocky said, standing to take the floor. "Now do you want freedom and a choice of where you're going to make your permanent homes, or do you want to wait until Rodrick *chooses*, at some undefined time in the distant future, to have elections?"

There was a murmur of talk, and three or four of them tried to take the floor, but Rocky waved them down.

"We have two choices," he said. "To forget it and make the best of it here, or to present Rodrick with a fait accompli and then negotiate for our share of the facilities. No, we will not have electricity at first. We will be without the laboratories left aboard the *Spirit of America* for a while. We will be cut off from the production facilities that are already built. We will have no metals. But there are reasonable people who are not on our side, and once we're settled in the south, we'll be able to trade food with them—the good fruit that is always in short supply here, all the things that the south will produce so easily, for the things we need. We'll have all the resources of the equatorial jungles at our fingertips. And the reasonable people here in Hamilton will insist that the two separate colonies cooperate."

"It's too soon," Baxter declared. "Rodrick is still, in effect, a military dictator. Even if the others had goodwill for us, *he* would punish us by cutting us off. Two things are vital for the success of the new settlement—petroleum and electricity. Rodrick controls both. And he's going to continue to control all vital supplies until he has enough fuel to take the ship back to Earth."

"The *Spirit of America* will never lift off Omega," Rocky said.

"I'm inclined to agree," Baxter replied. "But I think we can be sure that there will be another ship from Earth here within a very few years. If we make Rodrick our enemy, we could be considered mutineers. When other people from Earth come out here and the colony grows, we'll be just a little splinter group and we'll have to come crawling back to take our punishment and beg forgiveness."

"The time for us to make our move is now," Rocky said. "There will never be a better time than during the captain's wedding. The entire colony will be celebrating the great event." He put heavy sarcasm on those last words. "We will be able to take our share of the crawlers, a couple of plastic-making machines, all the things we need and are entitled to, and be well on our way south before he realizes we're gone."

"And if he sends the robots after us?" a woman asked.

"Now really, can you see even Rodrick turning Mopro's weapons against us?" Rocky asked.

"No, he wouldn't do that," someone said.

"Either we make our move," Rocky said, "or we settle down to become good citizens of Rodrick's Eden. I'd like a vote on it."

After some discussion, the roll-call vote got under way and Rocky realized quickly that he was going to be defeated.

"Hold it right there!" he shouted, leaping to his feet.

"You are interfering with a democratic vote," Baxter said.

"To hell with your democratic vote," Rocky said. "It's quite clear that your democratic vote is going to leave us all under Duncan Rodrick's thumb. You're all voting to postpone a definite decision because you think, or hope, that the *Spirit of America* is going to lift off and go back to Earth for another load of colonists, or that Harry Shaw has another starship almost ready and that it will show up here within the next few years. Let me disillusion you. First, this planet will never yield enough rhenium to lift the ship. Paul Warden and his crew are feeding synthetic fat to every miner they can find in exchange for the low-grade copper ore, which contains minute amounts of rhenium, and I mean minute. They've gathered exactly two hundred and forty grains of rhenium to date. That's half an ounce. And as for another ship coming, there won't be one."

Rocky paused. He was on the verge of betraying every oath he had ever taken.

"How do you know that there will not be another ship?" Baxter asked.

Well, Rocky was thinking, *under Earth and Service laws, I've already committed treason and mutiny*. But there was no more Earth law. It had gone up in the nuclear war that had followed the naval war off South America as surely as night follows day.

He took a deep breath. "I know that there will be no ship, not in the next few years, not in millions of years, because I know something you don't know, something that Rodrick has kept from all but a few people because he doesn't trust anyone but himself to know the meaning of duty and honor. I have been sworn to secrecy, and that's bothered me, because I feel that everyone has the right to know that war broke out between the United States and the Soviet Union while we were firing our rockets to leave Earth orbit."

There was a stunned silence.

"I'm sorry," Rocky said. "I know that you're shocked, and I hate to break the news to you so brutally. Rodrick wouldn't put it on the viewscreens outside the bridge, but the United States destroyed the Russian fleet off the west coast of South America."

"The bombs . . ." someone began fearfully.

"In all honesty, we did not see the bombs begin to fall. When the hidden explosive went off in the communications-room area, we lost all contact with Earth. But I have no doubt that they did fall. The Russian fleet was being destroyed, and without the fleet, South America would have been lost to them. Do you have any doubt that they used their bombs?"

There was a sound of weeping. Everyone sat with downcast eyes.

"Do you want to continue to live under the military dictatorship, at the whim of a man who would keep such news from you because he's determined to waste the energies and resources of this colony simply to carry out his orders to take the *Spirit of America* back to an Earth where there will be no one left alive?"

"Goddamn it, no!" a man shouted. "I move that we strike the results of our balloting so far and start over."

When the vote had been taken, a satisfied Rocky Miller rose once again. "It's not going to be easy," he said. "We're going to have to work together. We're going to have to keep quiet that I told you about the war on Earth, because if Rodrick finds out that anyone other than his little elite knows, he'll know that we are planning something. We must prepare in the greatest secrecy. One by one the crawlers must be moved, the two plastic machines edged toward the south, and all the things we're taking loaded onto cargo carriers and trailers. We must be out of Hamilton, out of the immediate area, and headed south before the alarm is given. Are there any questions?"

There were, many of them. But before the meeting ended, the assignments were made and each of the dissidents was firm in the conviction that now, more than ever, they had a right to choose their own dwelling places on the planet that would be their home for the rest of their lives. Knowing Earth's sad fate made it even more necessary, in their minds, to exercise freedom of will and freedom of choice.

Time was short. Many of them went to their quarters and began to pack, to plan, and also to weep a bit, in some cases, for friends and relatives left behind on Earth, now dead.

It was important, they all felt, to break away from the tyranny of the ship's captain quickly and permanently. Theirs, they felt, was the true spirit of America. They were going to establish independence and freedom, just as President Dexter Hamilton had said that the colony would. They were all good Americans, all exceptional in their own fields, and each was secure in his or her own self-esteem. But because they were Americans, each felt that he or she knew better how to establish true freedom than any other person alive. In that respect, transporting a representative group of Americans over eleven light years into space and then telling them that they were the last Earth people alive hadn't changed the American attitude one iota.

NINETEEN

Max Rosen was ready a full two hours ahead of the start of the scheduled wedding festivities. He spent those two hours standing up, drinking coffee, and snarling at the well-meaning jokes of other officers and his engineering crew. He stood up because he was well aware of his extraordinary talent for wrinkling unwrinklable service material, and he wanted to avoid walking to the altar looking as if he had slept in his uniform.

"Nervous!" he yelled. "Why the hell should I be nervous?" He spilled a cup of coffee, narrowly missing soiling his white uniform, to prove how calm he was.

As Max opened drawers and slammed them, looking for something to mop up the mess, Stoner McRae winked at Paul Warden and said, "We'll do it, Max. You just take it easy."

It was a beautiful Sunday morning. Eden's late summer days were becoming a bit shorter, the nights a bit cooler. Rains had been recorded not more than two hundred miles to the north, and the weather scientists predicted that Hamilton would see its first rain with the beginning of the rainy season in a matter of weeks.

The entire colony was putting on its finest. Field teams had been bringing back representative samples of Eden's spectacular flowers for days, and Amando Kwait had been keeping the flowers fresh with infusions of some magical formula, which prevented wilt for weeks. The streets were decorated with the flowers and with native plants, which the colonists had been gradually planting. The Unified Meeting House, glowing, gleaming white plastic in a design by the Earth's finest architect, was bustling with people making last-minute additions to the masses of flowers there.

It was not just a double wedding that had put the colony into a festival mood: Amando Kwait's fields were still producing a large variety of good things to eat. The veld around Hamilton had bloomed with a crop of low-growing but very delicious berries. Fish was now a staple on all tables, with Allen Jones reporting glowingly that the western ocean teemed with edible varieties. In spare time—and there was some for the very energetic, due to Omega's long days—two sportfishing boats were being constructed in a shed by the beach. There were now three new real natives of Eden, three more babies having been born, a little girl and a set of male twins.

Only Rocky Miller's group of dissidents failed to see that things were just about as optimum as possible, that Hamilton had been built on what was probably the most beautiful site on the continent, and that just about everything was right in this new world.

But on that Sunday, even the minority led by Rocky and Clive felt a genuine excitement. It had been relatively simple to move equipment they would be taking into positions where departure would be swift and unnoticed, with all the colony crowded into the meeting house.

The only people who seemed to be worried were the two brides-to-be, although the worry was not a major one. It was just that the flower girl and ring bearer had not returned from their fishing trip into the Renfro Mountains with the admiral. Betsy McRae was helping Grace and Jackie get ready, as was Evangeline Burr—the McRae house was being used as a dressing room because it was near the meeting house. The two wedding gowns were spread out carefully on the beds in Betsy's and Cindy's bedrooms.

"The admiral will have Cindy and Clay back in plenty

of time," Betsy told Grace. "Stoner talked to them early this morning, and they were well under way."

The admiral had discovered that he was quite a singer. He had not spent too much time with music, but as Clay and Cindy blended their young voices, he analyzed the songs they sang, tried his own wave-generating voice box, and found that he could modulate his voice quite nicely and sing anything from tenor to bass. It came as no surprise to any of them. They belted out some nice rounds based on a children's song about an eency-weency spider. Jumper howled accompaniment when they hit high notes.

The sun was warm, the breeze cooling, as the crawler sped southward in the Renfro foothills. They were taking the most direct route home, and once they were out of the foothills and could bring the crawler up to full speed, they'd be in Hamilton well before eleven o'clock, giving Clay and Cindy a full hour to get ready. They both knew their roles in the wedding, thanks to a very thorough rehearsal on the night before they joined the admiral in the mountains.

Shortly after dawn, Clay had called control and been patched through to Stoner to report on their progress. Clay was at the controls of the crawler. He was a good driver—Stoner had seen to that. Clay was a responsible boy, not the sort who would endanger himself, his passengers, or valuable equipment through thoughtlessness or recklessness. The admiral was navigating.

The crawler sped down the valley beside a hundred-foot-wide river, which formed a lake just ahead of them in the broad, open end of the valley. Beyond the lake, down the gorge formed by the river, the rolling slopes of the veld began and flattened quickly, giving them a sixty-mile-per-hour driving speed to cover the last hundred and fifty miles into Hamilton. The lake, which blocked their southward progress, was long and narrow, spreading across the valley to a length of about three miles. Between the crawler and the exit gorge was less than a half mile of deep water.

"Hey, Admiral," Clay said, "we'd save maybe a half hour if we go straight across. What do you say?"

It took only a microsecond for the admiral to evaluate the choice. The crawler was amphibious. By activating hydrojets, it would move across the half mile of lake at a speed of thirty miles per hour.

"The sea is my element," the admiral said.

Clay didn't slow the crawler. It sped across the grassy verge of the lake and sent sheets of water splashing as it hit shallow water. The treads dug, and its forward speed took it to a point where it was afloat. Clay hit the hydrojets, and the speed was maintained.

They were less than two hundred feet from the far shore of the lake when a shadow passed over them swiftly, and Clay jerked his head up to see a winged figure, quite large, zoom past and bank off to the left, heading for the shore. Something hit the water within five feet of the crawler's side, and a second later the lake erupted around them, the water blinding Clay for a moment. There was a hollow explosion, and Clay's feet went numb as the floorboard of the crawler leaped up. A jet of water came directly up between his feet.

In those frenzied few seconds before the crawler sank swiftly, leaving them treading water, the admiral saw that a stream of large-winged things, quite manlike except for the huge, spreading wings, were arrowing down toward them from above the western ridge. He assured himself that Cindy and Clay were all right—they were stunned, and their ears rang with the force of the explosion, but they were treading water, and Clay was holding a laser rifle clear of the water with one hand. Jumper had already started swimming for shore. Cat had climbed swiftly onto the admiral's shoulder.

"Get to shore, quickly," the admiral commanded.

Clay and Cindy swam the short distance, Clay keeping his weapon dry. The admiral ran up onto the rocky shore and pointed toward an outcrop of rock. Jumper was barking excitedly. The winged figures were closing in swiftly, flying in a disciplined line. Clay raised his laser rifle and fired once, twice, three times, and fire lanced up to send two of the flyers tumbling limply into the lake. The others veered away after releasing a barrage of spears, which fell just short as Clay seized Cindy's hand and ran for the cover of the rocks. The admiral's laser pistol functioned, even though wet, but the flyers were quickly out of range.

The flying squad, about twenty strong, landed on the pebbly beach two hundred yards away, and quickly shed their wings, now giving the appearance of thin, almost sticklike humanoid shapes.

"Admiral," Clay said, "I think we've just met the people who built the dead city." He remembered the one representation of a flying man, the limbs mere straight lines, and other pictures from the city.

"Cindy," the admiral said, "I want you to crawl up under this overhanging rock and stay there. Take Jumper with you."

The admiral was blaming himself. He had not been alert. He'd let peaceful Omega lull him. He had been as surprised as any of them by the sudden attack. Now he had no communications. The crawler was sunk in deep water, and he hadn't even been careful enough to carry a communicator with him. He was not yet overly concerned for the safety of the humans in his care, but Clay and Cindy would miss the wedding, and the first contact with the intelligent race of Omega had, through no choice of his own, begun with violence.

The admiral knew his adversaries had explosives. That meant that any approaching flyer had to be shot out of the air before he got near enough to drop anything near them; the laser rifle that Clay had been alert enough to salvage would take care of that. His own laser and projectile weapon would handle those on the ground. He could see that a few of them had long spears, and others were unslinging bows from their shoulders.

The stickmen were falling into line two hundred yards away. The admiral said, "Stay under cover, Clay. Don't move from this spot." He stood, walked toward the stickmen, holding both his hands, empty, out in front of him. The stickmen went into a defensive formation, those in front kneeling, arrows strung, those behind ready to launch their spears. The admiral kept walking toward them, his hands out in front of him in peace.

Clay kept scanning the sky. He guessed that the

stickmen had launched themselves from somewhere high on the western ridge, using the huge wings like hang gliders.

"What are they doing?" Cindy asked, for she couldn't see from under the overhanging rock.

"The admiral is trying to talk to them," Clay said. "Come on out and watch. It's all right."

Now the admiral was nearing the group of stickmen. He halted a hundred feet away. "We do not want to fight," he said, amplifying his voice. He extended his hands, palms out. "We are friends."

From one of the stickmen came a barked sound, and with a strength and accuracy that surprised him, the spears were launched. He danced, jerked, leaped, avoiding the rain of spears, which whizzed past him with a speed that spoke of great throwing strength in the sticklike arms. A hail of arrows followed, and then the stickmen were rushing forward, drawing battle-axes from slings at their hips. He couldn't dodge all the arrows, but his tough skin shed them as if it were armor. He looked down and saw that there were several holes in his uniform. Then he sadly drew his laser and cut down the three stickmen who had taken the fore in the wild rush that was closing on him rapidly. He hoped that he would not have to kill all of them. When a fourth stickman went down, the others, with wild, grating screams, turned and fled.

The admiral hurried back to the rocks. "I didn't want to have to kill them," he said sadly.

"I know," Clay said. "I don't think they'll bother us anymore, though."

"Why would they just attack us without trying to find out if we were peaceful or not?" Cindy asked.

"They're quite humanlike," the admiral said.

The admiral had made his plans. He knew that as time for the wedding neared and there was no communication from them, Rodrick would send out a scout to look for them. Meanwhile, he saw no real threat from the primitive weapons of the stickmen as long as he exercised care and stayed alert. It was possible that the homing device in the crawler was still functional. He called Cat, who had joined Jumper in taking a snooze in the sun. He

gave Cat instructions, and Cat slinked across to the lake
and plunged into the water.

Something moved above the western ridge. The admiral saw just enough to worry him. It was big and smooth
and rounded and had caught his eye for only a moment
before sinking back down behind the ridge. A ship. It
made no sense. Stickmen armed with spears and bows and
one explosive bomb coming from an airship? Then he saw
the flyers, just clearing the tops of the trees on the distant
ridge.

"Clay, let me have the rifle, please," he said.

"Uh, oh," Clay said as the flyers zoomed down the
ridge in formation, a hundred strong.

Cat had disappeared. Cindy saw it surface and swim
rapidly to the bank, shake itself, and dash for them. It
climbed to the admiral's shoulder.

"Cat turned on the homer," the admiral said. "The
light came on."

"Good," Clay replied. He, like the admiral, had not
been too concerned about twenty or so stickmen armed
with Stone Age weapons. But a hundred?

"Here's my pistol," the admiral said. "Above all, we
mustn't let them get close enough overhead to drop explosives on us."

"Admiral, look!" Clay shouted, as something big—he
could tell it was big even at that distance—appeared over
the top of the ridge. Seconds later a new flight of the
stickmen were gliding down the slope.

"Stand by," the admiral said as the first flight started
across the lake. He looked for suspicious burdens, anything that might be an explosive device, and saw one of
the lead flyers with a bulky object in his hand. He aimed
carefully, and the flyer detonated in midair, wings shatter-
ing, the explosion throwing those near him out of control
to crash into the lake. Another flash and another explosion.

"Clay, wait until they reach the shoreline before you
begin to fire," the admiral ordered.

Clay had the short-range laser pistol. The admiral saw
no more bombs. He dropped a half dozen of the lead
flyers, and then the flight veered away to land out of range

down the shore. The second flight veered away, too, this time to the west, to land on the low ridge nearest them.

"They're surrounding us," Clay said.

A round, bulky projectile arched into the air from the group of stickmen on the ridge to the west and fell two hundred feet short of them, to explode noisily and harmlessly.

The admiral's projectile weapon held twenty bullets, and he had an additional fifty in his cartridge belt. The laser rifle and the pistol would fire one thousand times each before the charge and crystal were expended. It was nine o'clock, Omega time. If the homing device had not been damaged by the explosion, it was broadcasting an emergency signal. A scout ship could reach them from Hamilton in less than half an hour. If the homing device was not working, Stoner and the others would begin to worry when Clay and Cindy hadn't shown up by eleven o'clock.

No real problem, the admiral was thinking as he watched the newly arrived flight of stickmen form themselves for an attack. It meant slaughter for the attackers, but he could keep his party safe until help came from Hamilton.

The attack came from east and west. The admiral, incapable of missing with the laser rifle, whirled from east to west, slicing down the stickmen in the lead. Before they were within spear range, Clay's laser pistol began to have its deadly effect. The charge faltered and turned, and the admiral felt that surely, as intelligent beings, the stickmen would see the futility of attacking again. But they came again not fifteen minutes later, and the unthinkable happened. Just as he was turning the eastern attack force with his deadly laser fire, and Clay was causing a slowing of the western group at a range of about seventy-five yards, the laser rifle failed. He put it aside and expended ten rounds of explosive projectiles before the attack faltered and turned.

The ground to the east and west was littered with the dead. Individual stickmen dashed among the dead, salvaging spears and arrows. It was obvious that they would try again, and the admiral had only one laser pistol and sixty rounds of projectiles left.

Mandy Miller's moment of decision had come before she was prepared for it, or expected it. Actually, she had expected Rocky's resentment and discontent to fester, for in the past he had not demonstrated any great capacity for direct action.

He had not come home that Saturday night. She had spent the evening catching up on her report reading, for since Duncan Rodrick's engagement had been announced she'd had no desire to be with people. She was so intent on her reading that she didn't stop to analyze her feelings, but if she had, she would probably have breathed a sigh of relief that Rocky was staying out late. And if he was enjoying himself at one of the prewedding parties, that was fine, too.

She went to bed after midnight and was awakened the next morning by Rocky's hand on her shoulder. He was fully dressed. He had not been drinking. There were dark circles under his eyes, and he looked as if he had not slept. Her first thought was that he had found himself another lover, and that thought didn't even make her angry.

"It's seven o'clock," he said. "I have some breakfast ready."

That was so unlike him that she didn't dress, just put on a robe and joined him in the little dining alcove. The smell of coffee cheered her. It was going to be a typical Hamilton day, bright, almost cloudless, warm. She ate heartily, and he didn't speak until they were both finished.

"There are containers in the living room for your clothing," Rocky said. "You won't be able to take all your files. I'll pack the kitchen items."

"What are you talking about?" she asked.

He looked at her, eyes hard, lips compressed. "It's test time, baby. You told me that you'd go with me when the time came. It's come. We're pulling out this morning, during the wedding."

"Oh, Rocky," she said sadly.

"I'm going," he said, his voice calm. "And we're going to see what you're made of, how much value you put on this marriage. There are about two hundred people who'll be leaving just after twelve o'clock, so you have plenty of time to pack and make up your mind."

"Rocky, please don't do this."

"It's too late for that," he said. "The only undecided question is whether I go as a bachelor or with my loving wife."

She opened her mouth to tell him that she would not go, that she would not betray her oath, but through the open windows came the sound of the meeting house's bells, and soon those same bells would be ringing for the wedding of Duncan and Jackie, and if she didn't go, she'd be a woman alone, seeing him almost every day, seeing him with Jackie. Then, too, she had made certain vows to Rocky, vowing to love, honor, and cherish, for better and for worse.

"You're very quiet," Rocky said.

He looked scared, she realized. "Rocky, you don't really want to do this. You don't really want to cause this split. It can only lead to trouble. We're few enough as it is. How long do you think the others will be content living without the advantages of civilization? What will you do when they begin to crawl back to the colony, one by one, begging to be taken back?"

"That's not going to happen. We'll make it fine," he said.

"You're asking me to leave my work—to abandon my responsibilities."

"How many times did I ask for a transfer so that you could be near your work?" he retorted. There was a chill fear in his eyes. "What's it going to be, me or your work? It won't do you any good to stay, you know. Rodrick's not the kind to cheat on his new bride."

"You have a filthy mind!"

"What else am I to think? I'm your husband. You've assured me that you love me. If it's Rodrick you love, I think you'd better run to him now and tell him that you're ready for him, tell him not to marry Jackie."

She swallowed her shame and her anger. She felt just

enough guilt, for still loving Duncan Rodrick, to be vulnerable. "There's to be no fighting, no armed resistance if they try to stop you?"

"No one will be hurt," he assured her.

"I'll pack," she said. "I'll need a full medical kit from the lab."

"It's already on a cargo crawler. Two of them, as a matter of fact."

"You've been planning this for a long time."

"Since Rodrick set the date for the wedding," he said. "We'll be gone while they're all weeping and smiling happily at the wedding. They won't use force to bring us back."

"No, they wouldn't," she said.

"I have things to do," he said, rising. "We're taking camp beds. All we'll take from here are personal necessities, clothing, the kitchen equipment. We're taking the electrical appliances as well. When we're settled, we'll trade for one or two of the wind generators. We won't be roughing it for long."

She wept as she packed her clothing.

"I'm going to ground that young man for six weeks," Stoner McRae fumed. It was ten minutes after eleven. Betsy was looking worried. "Now, don't worry," he said hastily. "Nothing has happened to them. They're just running late. We've still got fifty minutes."

"But why haven't they called in?" Betsy asked.

Stoner had been wondering the same thing, but he wasn't going to let Betsy know that he was worried. "Communicator failed, most likely. It happened to us once, remember? They get a terrific jarring around on a crawler."

Stoner went outside, looked up across the veld toward the north. He saw only a herd of silver-horned antelopes and the shimmer of heat over the plains. He walked to the *Spirit of America*. Ito Zuki had volunteered to act as communicator on the bridge during the wedding. He'd heard nothing from the admiral. It was twenty minutes past eleven. "Who's on standby alert?"

"Jack," Ito said. "Want me to get him?"

Stoner nodded. Soon he was explaining the situation

to Jack Purdy. He suspected that Jack had volunteered to miss the wedding because he was still mourning the death of his wife, although he hid it well.

"Ito," Purdy said, "Renato Cruz is in line after me. Get him here to hold the fort while I take the scout for a little run up north."

It was eleven-thirty when Jack lifted the *Dinahmite* and started north at a speed that would give him visuals of the ground in case the crawler was somewhere on the veld.

Betsy, seething, drafted Tina Sells to wear the flowergirl's gown she so lovingly had made for Cindy. It took two tries to find a teenage boy who could wear Clay's suit. It was, by then, almost twelve. People were already seated in the meeting house. Others milled about outside in the pleasant sunshine, all dressed in their finest.

Recorded synthesizer music began to boom out of the meeting house. The stragglers hurried inside. Ito Zuki had the scene on one of his screens. He located Emi and thought she looked lovely in her best dress. Renato Cruz, just a little hung over, began to check all the detectors in weapons control. Shortly after twelve o'clock Dr. Robert Allano, the psychiatrist who was also a justice of the peace, took his place in front of the altar. The grooms' parties entered from a side room. Max Rosen's face was twisted up in agony. Rodrick was calm, handsome. He led Max to their assigned places, then let his eyes play over the audience, which filled the meeting house to standing room only. In that brief glance he did not see the face he was looking for. He didn't blame Mandy if she hadn't come. Perhaps she was somewhere in the back.

The music masked the muted sounds of hydrogen engines from the equipment park on the opposite side of Hamilton. Renato Cruz saw several lights go on and pushed buttons to see a caravan of crawlers begin to leave the park. He wasn't aware of any large-scale expedition scheduled to leave during the wedding, but he'd been on a weekend pass. He watched idly, seeing that Commander Miller was driving the last crawler to leave the park, and then Renato turned his attention to the wedding ceremony.

* * *

Rocky Miller was giving instructions on a seldom-used radio frequency. The caravan was straggling as it left Hamilton, and he kept coaxing and ordering until the gaps were closed, and then he had to contend with the fervent complaints about the dust.

The well-traveled crawler road to the south allowed for speed, and soon the entire caravan was moving along in a cloud of dust at just under fifty miles per hour.

Grace and Jackie had decided on a full orchestral arrangement of the wedding march, and it thundered out with the fullness of an entire symphony orchestra and a volume that made Max wince.

From his scout ship, Jack Purdy saw only empty veld. He had flipped on the homing-device detector and was getting no signal. The low, rolling foothills of the Renfro Mountains were ahead of him. He had the coordinates that the admiral had given Stoner by radio for the location of the probable bauxite deposit. He zoomed up and over the foothills and punched the coordinates into the navigation computer.

Max's Adam's apple bobbed when he saw Grace start down the aisle. She was so beautiful that it made his mouth go dry. His agonized expression became a look of such bliss that those who knew him well smiled and nudged others, and then turned to watch as Grace, smiling, swept down the aisle. There was a chorus of ohs and ahs and murmured approval. When she took her place beside Max, he had never looked quite as handsome, quite as at ease as he did at that moment.

A new chorus of ohs and ahs escorted another beautiful bride down the aisle—Jackie Garvey, in pink. And behind her, looking positively angelic, the flower girl and ring bearer, Tina, all smiles, and the teenage boy holding himself stiff and stern.

Only ninety families, just over two hundred people, had decided to join the group that was seceding from the colony at fifty miles per hour. That, Rocky Miller felt, was enough. If the others were too cowardly to make the break, let them rot in that desert in back of Stanton Bay. The caravan was still moving through the veld, and Rocky had steered his crawler to one side to be able to keep an eye on the entire column. He had to watch for rough ground and an occasional old miner trap.

It was Clive Baxter's wife, riding beside her husband, who first saw the airships.

"Clive, what on Earth?" she asked, pointing.

Baxter was negotiating a curve in the well-beaten crawler track and couldn't take his eyes off the road. "You should say what on Omega, dear," he said, feeling quite good, almost jolly. He'd had all the military rule he wanted. He was looking forward to freedom, to being able to carry on his work as he saw fit. He looked up just in time to see an apparition from the past, a lighter-than-air vessel, long, rounded on both ends. He threw on the brakes in shock, and the crawler behind him, its driver having also spotted the airship, slammed into the Baxter crawler from the rear at a speed of fifty miles per hour. Baxter, his head up at an unnatural angle, his mouth open, didn't expect the collision. His neck snapped, and there was one terrible moment of pain before a round, bulky object landed squarely on his stomach and blew bits of human flesh and shattered metals and plastics high into the air.

Two more crawlers slammed into the wrecked pair, and others steered wildly, shooting out at angles from the column, trying to avoid the wreckage.

"Weapons! Man your weapons!" Rocky Miller was screaming into a dead communicator, having forgotten to switch it on.

Mandy was looking at the airships that were converging on the halted column. She knew now what it had been that Allen Jones had salvaged from the bottom of Stanton Bay, because a boatlike gondola, open, long, and rounded, was suspended below each gasbag. And from the open gondolas a steady stream of winged things were leaping, forming up quickly in the air, swooping down toward the halted caravan.

Rocky flipped on the communicator to a confused

jumble of screaming voices. "Man your weapons!" he bellowed.

A vee of flyers swept over the vehicles at a height of about one hundred feet and dropped bombs. Several of the crawlers erupted in smoke and flames. The hydrogen tanks on one were breached, and flames reached out, charring screaming men, women, and children.

Paul Warden, sitting beside Evangeline, was thinking how beautiful Sage would look in a white wedding gown. The music was still thundering as Jackie swept down the aisle. He turned his head and cocked one ear. He thought he'd heard something but decided that it might just be Jack Purdy's *Dinahmite* going supersonic up toward the north. By the time the music stopped and Dr. Allano began to speak, the explosions had also ceased, and the screams of the members of Rocky Miller's separationists, several miles to the south, could not carry that distance.

Organized flights swept the length of the wrecked caravan. Spears lanced down with deadly accuracy. People ran to escape, only to be skewered by the long spears. A group of the flyers landed, quickly discarded their wings, and began to pick off the screaming, running survivors with arrows.

"We've got to go for help," Rocky said, his face white. He gunned the engine of the crawler, and the vehicle slewed in a circle, throwing dust, attracting the notice of a vee of flyers.

"Let me have your laser," Mandy said.

"Got to get help," Rocky panted.

She jerked the weapon out of his holster, turned in her seat, braced her hands on the back of the seat, and sent a lance of fire upward. One of the flyers screamed shrilly and tumbled, but others released spears, and she saw them coming, spelling death. She kept pulling the trigger to see another and then another of the flyers go out of control.

There was a sound like a dropped watermelon beside her, a gasping gurgle, and she felt the crawler swerve violently. A spear had entered Rocky's neck just at the base of his skull and the point had exited at his crotch to make a little hole in the plastic cover of the seat. She knew that he was dead. The spear held him in an erect, seated position for a moment, and then, as the vehicle swerved again, he toppled against her. The crawler was moving faster and faster; his foot was jammed on the accelerator. Spears fell around her, and she glanced up to see three flyers soar past to the front. She raised her pistol, and the crawler, at that moment, hit an old miner trap, the front of the treads dropping. She was thrown over the windscreen, taking a nasty bump on her knee. She saw the grass coming up and felt a thud, and then all was black.

Each bride and groom recited the ancient rituals. The teenage ring bearer had to scratch his ear and almost dropped the velvet-covered tray on which rested two double sets of wedding rings. Max said his "I dos" in a loud, almost belligerent voice. Grace squeezed his hand and winked at him.

A relieved ring bearer saw all four rings disappear from his velvet-covered tray and watched as the ring vows were mutually exchanged, couple by couple. And then the quiet voice of the justice of the peace was saying the old, beautiful words, and Max was grinning down at Grace as he heard, "I now pronounce you husbands and wives." Max and Grace were already lifting Grace's veil when the justice said, "Gentlemen, ladies, you may now kiss your spouses." Max had his lips puckered. He didn't care if everyone in the whole damned colony was watching. His eyes were on Grace's, then shifted down to her parted, full lips. He bent toward them.

"Red One. Red One. Captain to the bridge. Scouts to your ships. Mopro to vehicle park."

The words blasted out from Rodrick's communicator.

There was a single intake of breath in the meeting house, then an explosion of movement as the service personnel leaped to their feet and ran toward the exits.

For a second, Rodrick suspected a prank, but only for a second. Ito Zuki was not the kind of man to joke about anything as serious as a Red One alert, which indicated maximum danger to the ship or to the colony.

Rodrick grinned at Jackie. "I think, Mrs. Rodrick, you might be excused from your duty post long enough to change into more practical garments."

Jackie smiled back. "Aye, aye, sir," she said, and then he was gone, communicator in hand, his voice demanding information.

Max was bending toward Grace's lips. For a split second a look of pain came onto his face, and then the mild, pleasant smile was back and he kept bending until his lips touched hers. His arms went around her and lifted her. She tried to talk through the kiss, but it was muffled and he wouldn't let her go as people hurried from the auditorium to their assigned emergency stations. He held the kiss for long seconds, half a minute, a full minute. Grace ceased to try to talk, surrendering herself to his kiss. Then, with a sigh, he pushed her away. "Now, damn it," he said, with the old, pained grimace, "now I'll answer the damned Red One."

The admiral had been working on the laser rifle. "Doing any good?" Clay asked, looking over his shoulder.

The admiral shook his head. "About one in a million crystals will shatter," he said.

"Fine time to hit us with one in a million," Clay grumbled.

"Hey, you guys," Cindy said, "don't worry. There'll be a scout here any minute."

"Sure," Clay said uncertainly. He looked around. The stickmen on the ridge were hidden among the trees. To the east the other group had withdrawn into the shelter of the rocky area below the southern rim of the valley.

"How good are you with a projectile pistol?" the admiral asked.

"I'm better with the laser," Clay admitted.

"You've done well," the admiral said. "I saw no wasted shots. When I expend the remainder of my bullets, I'll take the laser—not because I'm a better shot than you but because my reaction time is faster."

"Okay," Clay said. "But I don't think they're going to

come at us again." He was saying that for Cindy's sake. He knew he was blowing smoke and knew that she knew it when a giant lighter-than-air ship nosed up over the western ridges and cruised to hover, almost motionless, over the far side of the lake. The airship was near enough for them to get an idea of its construction. The gasbag seemed to be fabric. The gondola was wood, like the thing they'd thought was a boat, and there was a curious contraption extending forward from twin airscrews at the stern of the gondola.

The admiral, having an advantage with his better-than-human eyesight, said, "They use muscle power, Clay. If you look closely, you'll see a series of sprockets and chains."

"I see. Like pedaling a bicycle."

"Probably hydrogen in the bag," the admiral said.

"If it is, then all we have to do is put one of your explosive rounds into it," Clay replied.

"I hesitate to destroy it," the admiral said.

"Take a look down there." Clay pointed. The stickmen to the east were grouping. "Let me see your gun for a second."

He aimed carefully, holding the heavy pistol in both hands. The recoil kicked the weapon high, and he waited for the flare of burning hydrogen. The round blew a hole a foot across in the fabric, but there were no flames.

"Helium?" the admiral guessed, a bit amazed. Hydrogen separation was enough to strain his belief, but the more technically difficult isolation of helium would be an incredible feat for a society that used spears and bows.

Winged warriors leaped down from the gondola while two others scrambled up to the gasbag, toward the rent in the fabric, holding onto lines that Clay couldn't see. Other stickmen leaped onto seats along the center of the gondola, and Clay guessed they were pedaling furiously. The ship, sinking all the time, moved toward the shore of the lake.

The reinforcements from the airship glided down to join the group to the east on the shore. The airship just made it to the grassy margin of the lake before settling.

The bag obviously had a rigid skeleton, because it was holding its shape.

The arrival of the new group seemed to postpone the attack. The stickmen to the east faded back into the rocks. Clay sat down beside Cindy. The admiral was at the outer edge of the rocks, on the alert.

"Clay, we're in trouble," Cindy said.

"C'mon, Cindy, I've gotten you out of bad spots before," Clay said, deepening his voice. He was thinking of the time he'd saved Cindy's life by killing the madman who'd held her captive on board the *Spirit of America*.

She reached for his hand. "Yes, you have," she said. "But unless someone comes, we're in trouble." She wasn't acting scared, Clay saw, just serious. "Clay, you know that my mother and father hoped we'd get married someday."

He blushed. "Yeah. I guess I'd rather marry you than anyone."

"Me, too," she said. "I've never asked you this, but when you first came to live with us, Mother had a long talk with me. I'll bet my dad had a talk with you, too, didn't he?"

Clay grinned. "Did he! He said if I ever laid a hand on you, he'd have my hide."

"Clay, I don't want to go against my parents, but I don't want to die without ever having kissed you." She was blushing, too, and was unable to look at him.

His first thought was that Stoner would skin him alive. "No one's going to die," he answered harshly.

"Well," she said, smiling, "isn't one excuse as good as another?"

"I guess so," he said, grinning.

"Do you know how?" she asked.

Clay had been twelve years old when he stowed away on the *Spirit of America*. He hadn't been interested in kissing girls back then. And since then, aboard the *Spirit*, Cindy had been his almost constant companion.

"You don't have to be ashamed," she said. "I've only kissed one boy."

He felt a flash of jealousy. "Yeah? Who?"

"I'm not going to tell."

"When was it?"

"Aboard ship."

He made a face. "Not that skinny Tom Blackman?"

"I only kissed him twice," she said. "Are you mad?"

"Naw," he said. Then, "What did you want to do that for?"

"Oh, just to see how it felt."

"How'd it feel?" he asked, his face glum.

"Funny. I kissed him the second time pretending he was you."

"That make it feel any better?" He was grinning in spite of himself.

"Not much." She smiled. "Are you going to kiss me or not?"

"I guess so, if you really want me to."

"I really want you to."

It took a while. He couldn't figure out how to hold his mouth. When their lips met, his lips were pressed tightly together, and when he felt the soft warmth of her lips, something lurched inside him.

"Just relax a little," Cindy said.

He relaxed his lips a bit and tasted sweet moisture and felt his heart pick up a few counts in beat, and then for the first time he closed his eyes and thought about what he was doing. His eyes popped open, and he said, "Wow, Cindy!"

"Wow," she echoed.

"Clay?" There was an urgency in the admiral's voice that jerked him to his feet, laser in hand. Both attack groups were in the open now, moving toward them silently. The eastern group had been reinforced by over thirty members.

"Open fire when they get in range," the admiral ordered. "Shift quickly from group to group. You have the greater firepower. I'll have to pick my shots carefully."

"Cindy, you get down and stay down!" Clay yelled. He saw her smile, felt a new sense of responsibility toward her, vowed that he'd tear five million stickmen apart with his bare hands before he'd let one of them touch her.

"Stand ready, Clay," the admiral said as the attackers broke into a silent, rapid run.

*   *   *

Mandy heard screams of agony. She lifted her head slowly. Her mouth was full of sand. She spat and raised one hand to wipe dirt from her left eye. She felt bruised, but not broken. She tried to move her legs, and they worked. She remembered the sound of the spear plunging into Rocky's neck with all the force and gravity behind it, then felt a dull ache in her stomach. The laser pistol was lying a few feet in front of her. She crawled to it, seized it. The screams were still ringing terribly inside her head, and she turned to look back toward the caravan to see stickmen hacking at a woman who, even as Mandy watched, fell bloodily.

She started crawling, staying as deep in the grass as she could, pulling herself along on her stomach. There were no more screams. Once she raised her head to look. The stickmen were plundering the unburned crawlers. Clothing, household items, all sorts of things were being tossed to the grass and trampled by the victors. She crawled, reached an old miner trap, and paused to rest. Ahead of her was nothing but open veld, and any enemy flyer would see her. She began to dig, using the butt of the laser, and in a while she had dug through the sod into the cavity below ground. She enlarged the hole, trying to keep the grass sod in as near one circular piece as possible. When she had the hole large enough, she lowered herself into it, stood on the platform that surrounded the miner's circular burrow, and pulled the sod to cover the hole she'd dug.

Her left knee began to let her know that it had taken a severe bump as she was thrown out of the crawler. Only a bit of light came in through her imperfectly concealed entrance hole. She shuddered, thinking of a miner suddenly appearing there.

Once she heard strange, high-pitched sounds, the voices of the flyers, and a party of them walked quite near, avoiding the trap. It seemed that she waited forever until she no longer heard the squabbling, high-pitched voices of the horde of stickmen who were looting the crawlers.

Mandy gave it what she estimated to be another hour. Then she stuck her head out of the hole, could see only the surrounding grass, and pulled herself out, her knee quite stiff now. She raised her head carefully and saw only devastation. The dead lay as they had fallen, all around the caravan. One crawler still smoked and smoldered. She turned and looked back toward Hamilton, and in the far distance she could see motes in the sky, a fleet of the airships, and they were moving in the direction of the city.

Hamilton City had to be warned. She started to run toward the tilted crawler nearest her but fell as the knee gave way and had to hop, then crawl the rest of the way, only to see Rocky hanging over the windscreen, his eyes open and glazed in death. She choked back a quick urge to vomit, or scream, or both. She crawled to the vehicle and pulled herself up. The hydrogen engine had cut itself off automatically. The ready lights still glowed on the electronic equipment. She flipped the transmitter switch.

"Hamilton control, Hamilton control," she said, and waited for a reply. When it didn't come she tried again, and again.

"What's happening, Ito?" Rodrick asked via communicator as he ran from the meeting house.

"Explosions and fire from the direction of that expedition headed south, sir," Ito responded. He gave the bearing and the distance.

Rodrick wanted to ask, "What expedition?" but he was not ready to confess ignorance, not until he found out what the hell was going on.

"Any scout," Rodrick called up. "Any scout."

"Cap'n, Jacob West," came a reply.

"Status?"

"Cranking up, sir," Jacob said.

"Armed readiness," Rodrick replied, still running for the *Spirit of America*. "Coordinates—" He gave the location of the smoke and fire to the south.

"Airborne," Jacob said.

Four more scouts were airborne before Rodrick pounded onto the bridge, panting from his run.

"Jack Purdy's on," Ito said.

"Yeah, Jack," Rodrick said.

"Cap'n, I'm hovering over a dead campfire at—" He

gave the position. "Crawler tracks headed south. I'm following."

"We're at Red One, Jack," Rodrick said. "Possible attack."

"I've had my ears on," Jack said.

"*Apache One* to control."

"Go, Jacob."

"You're being closed by a fleet of the damnedest things I've seen outside an aeronautical museum, lighter than air, about twenty of them in view to the south of you."

"Weapons control," Rodrick said, "do you detect?"

"On the scope," Renato Cruz responded. "Nineteen blips. Range twenty miles and closing at roughly fifteen miles per hour."

"*Dinahmite* to control."

"Go, Jack."

"I've got me one of those lighter-than-air ships on the ground in the valley at—" He gave coordinates. "No crawler in sight, but there's one hell of an attack taking place on the admiral across a lake in a pile of rocks."

"Take appropriate action, Jack," Rodrick ordered.

"*Apache One* to control."

"Go, Jacob."

"I'm over a halted column of thirty-two crawlers. They've been hit and hit hard. Dead all around."

"Hostile action?" Rodrick asked.

"None now," Jacob said. "I think they're all moving toward Hamilton. I don't know what they've got, Captain, but several of these crawlers are pretty beat up. Watch yourself up there."

"Mopro," Rodrick said.

"Screen two," Ito said as Mopro, voiceless, flashed his response through the computer.

"Position, Mopro?"

The TR5-A defense robot had chosen a spot on the cliffs where he would have an open field of fire in all directions.

"Mopro, you have permission to open fire against any hostile action," Rodrick said.

"*Apache One* to control."

"Go, *Apache One*."

"There is at least one survivor."

"Pick him up and get back here at speed," Rodrick said. "We'll call Mandy Miller and get a med team down there as quickly as possible. Take your position at the rear of that fleet closing on Hamilton and await orders. Fire if you're fired upon or if the fleet begins hostile action against the town."

Clay was beginning to think that his first kiss was going to be his last. He was firing as fast as he could aim accurately, and there were tears of anger and fear and frustration running down his cheeks and a feeling in his stomach of purely wanting to puke because he'd never killed anything in his life and now he was killing running, living, manlike things as fast as he could pull the trigger. Jumper was barking furiously, and the admiral's projectile pistol was making sharp little evenly spaced sounds. The masses of the stickmen were closing fast, too fast, their spears beginning to fly close by now.

"*Apache One* to control."

"Control."

"I have Dr. Mandy Miller here, sir."

Rodrick's heart lurched.

"Captain?"

How could that voice sound so dear to him? He had just said, "I do" to another woman. "Yes, Mandy?"

"They have an explosive device that they drop from either the airships or from wings, which they use individually. Don't let them get overhead."

"Roger, thank you, Mandy."

No time to ask what the hell she was doing outside Hamilton in a column of crawlers not authorized to be in the field.

"Fire control to bridge."

"Go, Paul."

"I have nineteen lighter-than-air vessels ranged. And I have forty blips to seaward, range five miles."

"Stand by, Paul."

"*Apache One* to control."

"Jacob."

"Dr. Miller says that aside from the explosives, which they drop by hand, these dudes are armed with bronze-tipped spears, which they throw on the wing, and with bows and arrows."

"That's roger, *Apache One*," Rodrick said. "We can slaughter them," he said to Ito, who was standing next to him on the bridge, "but do we want to?"

"Damned shame we have to fight the first alien intelligence we meet," Ito commented.

"All scouts," Rodrick said. "I want you to form a line between Hamilton and the fleet approaching from the south. The lighter-than-air ships apparently have nothing that can hurt a scout ship. My intention is to prevent the fleet from passing over Hamilton, since they seem to have the capacity to drop explosives. It is my wish to prevent further bloodshed if possible. Report when you're in position."

"The laser, Clay," the admiral said, and Clay knew that all the admiral's explosive projectiles were gone. The slaughter around them was sickening, and yet the flyers came on and on, screaming now, so close that he could see their odd, huge, faceted eyes—yellow, ovate protrusions on their upper heads. He passed the laser to the admiral and looked for Cindy. She was huddled back under the overhanging rock, Jumper in one arm, Cat in the other. Her eyes were wide. He wanted to go to her, but the stickmen were almost upon them. He stooped quickly and seized two baseball-sized rocks and cocked his arm, waiting for one of them to get close enough. And then, just as he threw and was looking right down the mouths of dozens of them, there was a frightful wail, and he recognized the alarm siren of a scout ship. The good old *Dinahmite* was fifty feet directly over them, with port and starboard lasers extended.

"Get down, Admiral," Clay yelled, just as the lasers blazed, the beams seeming to pass right over his head to cut down stickmen in heaped piles until the survivors could halt their rush, turn, and flee.

"Admiral," came an amplified voice from the scout,

"I'm coming down. Have your party ready to board in a hurry."

They didn't have to be told twice. They lifted Cindy into the scout first, then Clay, Jumper, Cat, the admiral. It was a bit crowded, but no one cared.

There was no time for lengthy talk or explanations. Purdy reported that he had the missing persons aboard and received orders to blast at speed for Hamilton to put himself between the city and a fleet of airships moving in from the ocean.

Jacob West was concerned about Dr. Miller. She had strapped herself into the second seat and was sitting as if frozen, her wide eyes staring at nothing, but he had his orders.

"I know you're not all right, Dr. Miller," he said, as he flew to join the others before reaching Hamilton, "but can you hold up for a while longer?"

"No, I'm all right," Mandy insisted, shaking her head to dispel the memory of the woman being chopped down with axes. "Do what you have to do, Jacob. Don't worry about me."

"We'll get you back to the *Spirit* as soon as possible," Jacob promised.

"We can't let these killers get into the colony," Mandy said. "If you like, I can handle communications for you."

That would give her something to do, he thought, and keep her mind off what she'd seen. He flew *Apache One* into a gap between two of the other scouts. "Tell control we're in position," he told her. She obeyed.

The fleet of lighter-than-air craft came to a halt and began to drift east on the prevailing wind.

"Why aren't you firing?" Mandy asked.

"Orders. We're to avoid bloodshed if possible."

"They killed over two hundred people," Mandy replied angrily. "Women and children among them."

"I guess they didn't know any better," Jacob said.

"Didn't know any better? They're savages." Mandy's voice rose. "They deserve to be wiped off the face of the planet."

"I know how you feel," Jacob said.

"*Apache One* to control." Mandy spoke into the communicator.

"Go, Mandy," Rodrick said.

"Are you going to let these savages get away to attack again without warning?" she asked.

Rodrick was silent for a moment. "How are you, Mandy? Are you injured?"

"I'm fine," she said. "Duncan, they killed over two hundred people. You must kill them. You must wipe them out totally."

"Mandy, I want you to relax. As soon as we can we'll get you back here," Rodrick said.

"Don't try to humor me," she hissed. "I saw it. I saw them ax down women and children."

"Jacob, will you please take the communicator from Dr. Miller?" Rodrick asked. "Control out."

Grace Monroe, still in her wedding dress, came onto the bridge ahead of Max.

Max took a look at the pictures being transmitted by the scouts, scratched his mussed hair, and said, "Must be hydrogen. One burst of fire, and they'd go up like blazes."

"Clay Girard put an explosive round into one up north," Rodrick said. "It didn't burn."

"Helium?"

"Or something we don't know about, Max."

"And spears," Grace said, shaking her head. "It doesn't make sense."

"That's why I'm not ordering them to be exterminated," Rodrick said. "We might have to kill a few of them, because there's a fleet of them twice this size moving in from the sea."

"Fascinating," Grace said. "Humanoid?"

"Arms and legs like sticks, like the illustrations from Stoner's Valley. Huge, protruding, faceted eyes. Almost like insect eyes," Rodrick said.

"We must contact them," Grace said. "They're an intelligent, alien race. We're the ones who have invaded their planet."

"I'm more than willing to talk," Rodrick said, "if we can find a way to make them understand."

"Capture one," Max suggested. "Let Grace have a go at him with her translation machine."

"I won't endanger anyone," Rodrick said.

"Fair enough."

"Let's find out what the fleet coming in from the sea makes of antiaircraft fire," Rodrick said. "Fire control and Mopro." Paul and Mopro reported. "When the fleet from the sea closes, put up a curtain of air bursts, high explosives. Do not shoot to hit. Just put a curtain of bursts in front of them."

It happened quickly. The fleet from the sea, riding the prevailing winds, closed fast, and there was a roar of sound as the *Spirit of America*'s weapons joined Mopro's.

"Well, they're not dumb," Max said, as the fleet veered northward, Jack Purdy's *Dinahmite* keeping between the fleet and Hamilton City.

"*Apache One*," Rodrick called. "We want live prisoners. Put a hole in a gasbag and bring it down. Then use stunners. Try to pick one close to the city. We'll send out a capture party by crawler."

"Roger," Jacob said. "I think I've got the leader spotted, Cap'n. His ship is all red. The others are painted blue and white, like clouds and sky."

"You should be putting explosive rounds into the gondolas," Mandy complained, as Jacob flew to the red airship and put a hole a yard wide in the gasbag. The ship quickly settled. Before it hit the ground, stickmen began to leave it on their gliding wings, and *Apache One* joined the other scouts in low-level runs to stun each of the flyers as he hit the ground.

The remaining ships of the fleet allowed the wind to blow them toward the west. Jacob kept *Apache One* in position until the crawlers from Hamilton reached the scene and began to load the stunned stickmen.

Duncan Rodrick helped lift one of the stickmen, who was light, weighing only about sixty pounds, with hard, scaly skin. The eyes were like the enlarged eyes of an insect. One had suffered a broken arm in landing, and a yellowish liquid oozed from the compound fracture.

Each captive was immobilized with many bands of tape around arms and body and legs.

"Skipper," Paul Warden said when the stickmen were all loaded, "it looks as if we're going to have to share this planet with a race evolved from insects."

IV

THE WHORSK

TWENTY

Grace Monroe had changed to slacks and blouse. Max thought she looked more beautiful than ever with her musing, thoughtful face bent toward a stickman lying, carefully trussed, on an examination table. Max had helped her attach the brain scanner on the pointed, hairless head. He took his eyes off Grace and watched the feedback being made by a marker on a roll of paper.

"High nodes," he grunted. "I think he's coming around."

Adam Hook, the colony's sergeant at arms, a short, round man with a bulldog face, was standing at the foot of the examination table, well armed, ready for anything. The strength of the stickman was not known. Max, too, wore a sidearm.

"I want to take a look at Mandy," Grace said. "Call me when he's conscious, will you, Max?"

"Happy wedding day," Max said, saluting, but he grinned. He knew that everyone was pitching in. His fellow groom, Duncan, was south of the city, with a medical party and a heavily armed guard, doing a distasteful chore. Over two hundred bodies, some of them in shocking states of mutilation, had to be bagged and returned for burial. Hamilton's cemetery was going to be well populated, and far sooner than anyone had imagined. One-sixth of the strength of the colony had been decimated in one hour.

Mandy's hospital bed was empty. Grace walked rapidly to the operating room, and there she was, in white, limping around, one knee swollen to twice its normal size.

"Mandy, what the hell do you think you're doing?" Grace demanded.

"We tried to keep her out," said Dr. Robert Allano.

"I feel better working, Grace," Mandy said. "I'm all right. Tired. That's all."

The stickman with the broken arm was lying on the operating table. "All we could do was put the break back in place," said Dr. Norman Jacks, the top bone specialist on the Life Sciences staff. "That stopped the oozing of fluid."

"Dr. Miller," a young lab technician said, "we've done some preliminary analyses on the fluid from this thing's wound. It's more hemolymph than blood. I think we're going to find that he breathes through his skin, taking in oxygen through many spiracles directly to the interior organs."

"Judging from that, Dr. Jacks," Grace said, "we should find no interior bone structure to speak of."

"We haven't had a chance to dissect one," Jacks replied, "but I did a little discreet probing while I set this one's broken arm. Apparently there's an exoskeleton only, with perhaps, I'd guess, some cuticular core in the larger, weight-bearing areas to give additional strength."

"They always said that insects, particularly the cockroach, would be the only survivors of a nuclear war on Earth," Allano said. "Here the insect kingdom didn't have to wait."

"They'll be bringing in the ones I killed when we were attacked," Mandy said, in a dull, matter-of-fact voice. "We'll know more about them when we can dissect one."

"Dr. Miller," asked the young lab technician, "you really killed some of them?"

"I wish I had had a laser cannon," Mandy said nastily. Her bitterness caused Grace to look at her, to examine her tired, set face. She knew that Mandy was a strong woman, but, after all, she'd lost her husband and witnessed terrible atrocities.

"It's taking them a long time to come out of stun," Allano remarked. "The exoskeleton is tough and hard to rupture, but inside they're apparently relatively fragile."

"Mandy," Grace suggested, "why don't you come on back to your room and let me give you a sedative. You're out on your feet."

"In a little while," Mandy said. "Thank you."

Grace went back to the other examination room. Max was listening to Adam Hook recount an interesting murder investigation from when he was a New York detective. The brain waves of the stickman were stronger. Before Hook finished his story, the eyes of the stickman began to glow, and suddenly the table shook as he tried to escape the bands of strong tape that had been wrapped all around him, pinioning his arms to his sides, immobilizing his legs.

Grace stood at a careful distance and saw the thing's mouth open to show bony, serrated ridges of teeth, and she leaned forward eagerly when sounds began to come from the open mouth. At first the sounds came loudly, and rapidly, then there was a silence. Facets of the eyes seemed to change color.

"I think he's looking us over," Grace said. The glowing eyes jerked from one side to the center, pointing directly at her. "Yes, we have his attention."

"Esseehavisatenshun," came from the stickman's mouth.

"Either he has natural ability to mimic sounds, or he's one smart bastard," Max said.

"Max, I want him freed," Grace said.

"Not a chance," Adam Hook said. "Sorry, Doctor."

"Then let's put him in a detention cell," she suggested. "We can talk with him through the grill."

"What do you think, Adam?" Max asked.

"He can't come through a steel grill," Hook said.

They eased the bound stickman onto a litter, and carried him to one of the never-before-used detention cells. They put the litter on the bunk, and Hook stood by, stunner at the ready, as Max cut off the tape, starting at the creature's feet. The stickman lay quite still, the glow of his eyes following Max's movements. When the tape was removed, Max and Hook backed out of the cell and closed the steel grill. The stickman sat up, stood, seemed to shiver, and then the yellow glow centered in his large, ovate eyes, and he kept that glow directed toward them as he pulled out the one chair with a three-fingered hand and sat down.

Grace had brought a plastic bottle of water with her. She took off the cap, poured water into her hand, and drank it. She extended the bottle toward the stickman.

"Water?" she asked. "Water?" She poured more in her hand and held her hand out.

"Water," the stickman echoed, extending his own hand. She opened a little door in the grill and handed the bottle through. The stickman sniffed, tasted carefully, and then turned the bottle up and drank deeply.

"Max, would you please get the translation computer?" Grace asked.

When the small black box was in place, she herself had found a slate board and chalk. She began with numbers, making diagonal slashes on the board and counting as she marked. She looked at the stickman, who had his hard-skinned, skull-like face pressed to the grill, yellow eyes glowing.

"Onetwothree," the stickman repeated for her.

"No," she said. She pointed to him. "You. You say." She turned on the computer to record and analyze his sounds.

The stickman made three distinct sounds, a mixture of clicks and whistles.

"Now we'll count to ten," she told him, turning up the recording volume.

"Hell, Grace," Max said. "It'd be faster teaching him English. He catches on fast."

"But we'd know nothing about his thought processes," Grace said.

"You just want to give your damned machine a workout," Max protested.

She smiled. "Well, maybe so."

"Let's work on this tomorrow," Max said, leering.

"Max—"

"I know. I know," he said, sighing.

Jackie Garvey Rodrick had also changed from her wedding gown and had reported to the bridge to relieve Ito Zuki. She was in touch with the team that was picking up the bodies at the site of the massacre and with the scouts who were keeping an eye on the airships, which had begun to beat their way toward the Renfro Mountains.

Clay and Cindy had been recounting their adventure to a thoroughly frightened Betsy McRae. Of course, neither of them mentioned that there'd been quite a kiss when things had looked very bad.

The medical team began to bring back the bodies of Rocky Miller and his unfortunate group. It was decided that there would be one ceremony for everyone, after interment.

Mandy Miller collapsed during the dissection of a dead stickman and had to be put to bed, where she slept soundly for hours and awoke screaming.

The scouts began a rotation watch on the air fleet, with half of them coming back to Hamilton to sleep and rest.

It was dark when Duncan Rodrick walked onto the bridge of the *Spirit of America* to find Jackie drinking coffee and chatting with Renato Cruz on radio. Cruz was circling the fleet of lighter-than-air ships, which was, he reported, in the process of landing on a sheltered plain. Jackie didn't see Rodrick come in. He stood in the shadows—she had turned on only one dim light—and listened to her, watched her graceful movement as she lifted her coffee cup.

Finally, he said, "Hi, Mrs. Rodrick."

She jumped. "Lord, I didn't know you were there."

"Jackie, I'm sorry. Not much of a wedding day, was it?"

"You're sorry?" She laughed. "I'm sorry. But we have a lot of days ahead, don't we?"

"Yes. Who's on tap to relieve you?"

"Well, we're a bit strung out. I told Ito I'd stay until midnight."

"I think a new groom should have some consideration," Rodrick said. He walked over and picked up the communicator. Ito's voice answered, husky, full of sleep. "Ito, the brand-new groom needs a favor," Rodrick said. "I'd like to borrow my brand-new wife for a while."

Emi was with her husband when he came to the bridge, Emi all smiles, saying that she hadn't had a chance to kiss the groom, then remedying that omission as Ito shyly kissed Jackie on the cheek.

The house that had been built for the captain and his bride was on the south ridge, one entire side giving an unobstructed view of the bay and the ocean beyond. Native stone had been worked in with the plastic building blocks, and Amando Kwait had, at Rodrick's request, filled a large atrium with some of the more attractive species of native flowers and plants. The entire house had a feeling of openness. Jackie dialed a soft, golden light from the walls after Duncan had carried her, laughing, over the threshold.

"Who's first for the shower?" Jackie asked, a little breathless after a very interesting kiss that had followed the act of threshold carrying.

"Who's captain of this ship?" Rodrick growled playfully. In the golden light she was more beautiful than he remembered. He felt almost shy, although he had known that tall, slim body, had loved every inch of it.

"We leave rank outside that door, Husband." Jackie grinned.

"Well said, Lieutenant." He reached for her, pulled her close. Perhaps he didn't love her, but she had always had the ability to heat his blood. It was more important than ever that he learn to love her now, because, when he'd learned of Rocky Miller's death, his first thought had been, "Now she's mine. Now it is possible." And the very fact that he had been pleased to hear of his first-officer's death had done more to put Mandy beyond his reach forever than anything that had gone before. Never would he sink so low as to betray the vow that he had made to this beautiful woman in his arms, looking up into his face with melting green eyes and inviting, moist lips.

"I have an idea," he said. "As a matter of fact, it did not just this minute occur to me. You yourself commented on the size of the shower I had installed."

"I said it was very big," she said, eyes widening.

"Big enough for two?" he asked.

"I think so. Why don't we find out?"

It was big enough for two.

Max came back to the detention cell just after midnight with sandwiches and coffee and a couple of the big, southern fruit with a figlike texture. The stickman saw the fruit, pointed, and made a whistling, clicking sound. Grace handed him a fruit, and he ate hungrily.

"Grace, it's after midnight," Max complained.

"Max, listen to this," Grace said, turning a dial on the translation computer.

Max heard Grace's voice counting from one to ten, and then a series of clicks and whistles. Then Grace's voice said, "My name is Grace Monroe."

Max listened to the clicks and whistles into which Grace's words had been translated.

"Grace, that's very impressive. But it's after midnight on our wedding night."

"Yes, but listen," she insisted. The machine clicked and whistled and then counted to ten. And more clicks and whistles and a mechanical voice said, "I am called Chingclonk."

"I have real martinis in the fridge at our new home," Max teased.

Grace sighed and turned off the machine. It was, after all, going to take a long time to translate the whistling, clicking language of the stickman. She clung to Max's arm. "Okay, buddy," she said. "I'm with you now."

"I made the house totally robotproof," Max said. "There isn't a communicator in it, and I'm going to turn the alarms off."

"Good idea," Grace said.

They were just ready to step out the main hatch of

the ship when Jacob West came running down the corridor behind them, yelling, "Hey, Max, Grace! Hold up!"

"I don't hear a damned thing," Max commented loudly. "I do not hear a eager voice yelling my name."

"I thought you two would like to have a look at this," Jacob said. He had a parchmentlike scroll in hand. "Just take a minute."

They went over to a worktable, and Jacob spread the scroll. "We found it in the downed airship," he explained. "It was in a box that looked as if it was filled just with arrows. On the bottom. No one noticed it until just a while ago, and since the captain is already at home in bed I had to show it to someone."

"If I don't say that I am eternally grateful, forgive me," Max said pleasantly.

Jacob grinned at Grace. "You're already being a good influence on this old bear," he said. "He's mellowing."

Grace bent over the table. The parchment was a very good map of the globe of the planet they called Omega.

"There's no writing," Jacob said. "Just as there was none at Stoner's Valley, but look at the pictures. Here's Eden."

The contours of the Eden peninsula were quite accurate, and at several spots there was a neat little drawing of a miner with his head and neck extending from a burrow.

"The jungle," Jacob said, pointing to a little drawing of a fierce beast in a vast area of green. "But here's what I wanted to show you." He pointed to the largest western continent, which looked somewhat like a diving duck. "Here, along the coast."

"Definitely a river," Max said.

"A river valley with buildings?" Grace asked, for the light was not all that good and the drawings along the river were tiny.

"There's a pyramid," Jacob said. "And there are other buildings here and there. You can see them pretty well with a magnifying glass. But look at this." He pointed. A slightly larger drawing showed a group of five figures, all sticklike except the one in the center.

"There's a difference in body shape," Jacob said.

"Stickpeople, but different. Females, maybe. But look at that one in the middle."

Grace looked and saw a creditable drawing of a woman, nude, tall and slim, big breasted.

"Is there any way one of them could have added that picture today after seeing human beings for the first time?" Grace asked.

"I doubt it," Jacob answered. "Besides, it doesn't look like new work. See? The wrinkles in the sheet run through it just like the others, the stickpeople."

"I think we should wake the captain," Grace said.

"Damn it, he is not asleep," Max growled.

"Max, that's definitely a drawing of a human woman," Grace said. "Think what that means."

"Grace, we are going, *now*, to our new home, where I am going to turn off all alarms—"

"Oh, Max," she said.

Max bent and put his arms around her thighs, just above the knees. He lifted her as she squealed and hefted her onto his shoulder.

"Mr. West," Max said formally, "at this time I am leaving the ship to take my wife to our new home. My wife will not be available to anyone until well after sunup tomorrow. Nor will I. You may pass the word that if anyone knocks on my door, he or she will be shot with a stun gun. We will be unreachable by communicator, and we will not hear any alarm that is sounded."

"You may put me down now, Max," Grace said calmly as he stalked out the hatch.

"I'll walk now, Max," she said, after a few paces.

"Oh, well," she said, after a few more paces. "I am rather tired. If you want to carry me—"

Mandy Miller awoke screaming. One of her nurses put a hand on her shoulder and eased her back. "Would you like another sedative, Dr. Miller?"

"Yes, please," she said shakily, for she kept seeing the spear running all the way from the back of Rocky's neck to his crotch, saw the woman being axed down, smelled the blood, and mixed in with that horror was a sadness that was as damaging as the horror.

She looked at the clock. It was after midnight, Omega time. She had not come out of sleep screaming because of Rocky, or the axed woman, or the blood. She had been dreaming that it was she who was now in that spacious, open house on the south ridge with Duncan Rodrick, and her unconscious mind had fed into her dreams the gladness that Rocky was dead, the happiness that at last she was free to love Duncan. And to know that even in her unconscious she could harbor such thoughts had jerked her up out of sleep screaming.

Grace Monroe drew a model of Omega's solar system on the board. Chingclonk, the Whorsk, stood beside her, sipping water. He had refused to take coffee, tea, or anything containing alcohol. He'd spent more time with Grace than her new husband had, much to Max's chagrin.

"We are here," Grace said, and the translating machine whistled and clicked, and Chingclonk nodded his head sharply backward. "This is the star we call 61 Cygni B," Grace said.

"The sun," Chingclonk said, through the translator.

"We humans come from far away," Grace said. "From so far away that it would take a Whorsk airship thousands of years to travel that distance."

Chingclonk jerked his head back as if in total understanding. "You come from—" The translating machine was stumped, but the name had an alien sound on Chingclonk's lips.

"We come from Earth," she said, and the translating machine made the word in Whorsk for Earth.

"You lie," Chingclonk said. He was not noted for politeness . . . or was it just the blunt, simple nature of his language?

"Why do you say that?"

He took a marker and drew a dotted line far and away from Omega, indicating great distances by drawing several parallel lines in spots. "You come from—" Once again the machine could not find an English equivalent. But it was obvious that Chingclonk had a conception of space. He knew that the bright points of light in the night sky were other suns, like 61 Cygni B, or, as he called it, the sun.

And such revelations were keeping people in the colony awake nights.

The translation machine had severe limitations, and Grace spent long night hours, the admiral or Evangeline Burr at her side, trying to improve it. The physical nature of Chingclonk's sound-making organ was a challenge. So far, Grace had not been able to program the machine to imitate all of the sounds of the Whorsk language. The name she applied to Chingclonk's kind was itself a compromise, for the Whorsk sound was more a whistle than a combination of dipthong and consonant, but at least a simple, basic communication had been established.

Duncan Rodrick was able to ask, "Why did you attack us?"

"You steal."

"Steal what?" Grace asked. Chingclonk tapped the steel grid, the metal bulkhead.

"Steal metals?"

"Steal—" Chingclonk said. He seized the marker and drew a recognizable picture of a miner and a Whorsk facing each other, thrust his head violently backward, for yes. Then he drew a fuller, manlike figure with the miner, crossed it out, thrust his head forward, no.

Rodrick showed Chingclonk a map of Eden. He drew pictures of two airships. "Your fleet is camped here," he said. "You are chief?"

A violent yes nod.

"Will you tell your people that we desire peace?"

"We will not fight," Chingclonk said. "Otherwise, you will kill us."

"Good thinking," Rodrick said. "Peace?"

"No choice," Chingclonk answered.

"We will trade with you," Rodrick said.

"Yes. We will trade food, furs, and metals for things that make the killing sun."

"No lasers," Rodrick said.

"We will return to our home," Chingclonk said, making a quick, obviously obscene gesture with one three-fingered hand.

"I think he just said 'up yours,' " Rodrick noted.

"Yes, up yours," Chingclonk said in English.

The other captives had made themselves comfortable in their detention cells, whistled and clicked for food and water, and ran their hands admiringly and greedily over all metal surfaces.

In one cell, where five of the Whorsk were being held, a fight broke out, and with swift and deadly malice four of the Whorsk killed the fifth. When the door was opened, they tossed the dead body out and turned away to whistle and click among themselves.

The incident shocked the scientists, who met for breakfast with Duncan Rodrick.

"From what we've been able to determine," the animal behaviorist, James Wilson, said, "they have no system of ethics as we know it. Death to them is no more than eating."

"I've been studying the one called Chingclonk, the chief," Dr. Allano, the psychiatrist, said. "He is chief because he can throw a spear with the greatest force, and he killed three rivals to earn his position. He shows absolutely no remorse for having massacred over two hundred people, women and children among them. He looks upon us as invaders of an area that is his by custom and right. He can't understand why we won't move out of Eden so that he can make his trades with what we call miners. If he had the chance, he'd kill all of us as quickly and with as little regard as he killed the Miller group."

After breakfast, Grace continued her observations in the detention area. Rodrick joined her.

"Chief Chingclonk," she said, "you seem upset today. What is bothering you?"

"You," he said.

"Explain?"

Suddenly Chingclonk thrust out his lower abdomen and his long, pointed organ was glaringly evident. "Must have female," he said. "When the two moons come full three or four times and we've had no female, we die."

"Do you want to go home?"

Chingclonk walked to the map, stabbed a finger at one of the islands to the northwest of Stanton Bay. "Go there."

"Is your home there?"

"Females there."

"Will you go in peace?" Duncan Rodrick asked.

"I have no choice."

"Please listen closely," Rodrick said.

Chingclonk jerked his head back. Yes.

"We are few," Rodrick said. "We cannot, repeat, *not*, allow the Whorsk to kill even one more human. Do you understand?"

"Yes—you need numbers to steal our metals." The last word was in English.

"Before we allow you to kill even one more human, we will be forced to kill all Whorsk."

"Give us things that make the killing sun, and we will share our metals."

"We will share the metals with you," Rodrick said, "but we will not give you the things that make the killing sun. We will have much more metal soon, more than you can ever gain in trade with the miners. We will share with you in peace, or we will have to kill you in war."

"I have no choice. How will you get more metals?"

Rodrick showed him pictures of Stoner's mining operations. Chingclonk nodded, impressed. "You will share?"

"In peace," Rodrick said.

"In peace," he agreed.

Before the captives could be released, there were some things that Rodrick had to know. "The gas that lifts your ships," he said. "How do you make it?"

"Magic," Chingclonk said.

"Where do you get the magic?"

"From you," Chingclonk said.

"Not from us," Rodrick replied.

Chingclonk walked to the board, drew the Omega system, and added the distance lines. "From you," he said.

"Do you trade for the magic?"

Head jerk back, yes. "Trade many babies."

"Your own babies?"

"Seed babies. We must go." He extended his organ. "Or seeds rot."

"Your females lay eggs?"

He drew a female on the board, posterior distended,

eggs coming out in a stream. Then he drew sacs hanging on a rack, making squiggly lines to show movement of the sacs. "You want babies. We want magic."

"Are you sure the translating box is functioning correctly?" Rodrick asked Grace.

"It's not perfected. But I think the trouble here is that we're not dealing with a being that has a thought pattern anything like ours. Did you ever see a praying mantis having his dinner? He eats his victim bite by bite while it's still wiggling and struggling, and he seems to do it not with enjoyment, but with cold necessity. I sense something of that in our friend here."

It was Grace who remembered the drawing on the map taken from Chingclonk's ship. She produced it, showed the Whorsk the drawing of the human. "Who is this?"

"You know. You were there," he said, tapping the map with a hard nail. "You tell us to keep this woman." He said woman in English.

"Could the Russians have landed somewhere in the western hemisphere without us knowing it?" Grace asked.

Rodrick shook his head. "Our sensors would have picked up something as big as the *Karl Marx* when it came into orbit."

"Would you agree that there's something very odd going on?"

"That I would," Rodrick said. "I think we'd better take a close look here." He tapped the spot on the map of the largest western continent. "Chingclonk, are there Whorsk here?"

Back jerked the head.

"We want to talk with this woman. How can we do it without having to fight Whorsk?"

Chingclonk drew back his head and gave a great whistling, wailing blast of sound. "The signal of Chingclonk."

"Record that, please, Grace," Rodrick said. "And then I guess we can let our guests go home. What do you think?"

"I'd like to work on the language more, but in the interests of possible future peace with them, I suppose we'll have to."

The Whorsk were taken by crawler to the area where

their lighter-than-air fleet was moored. They had not been overly impressed by any of the technology aboard ship, except for the plentiful metal, and it was the metal of the crawlers that caught their attention, as well.

Chingclonk, using his own maps, explained how they navigated the huge Omega distances by air. They had charts much like those used by sea captains in the days of sail, which marked the prevailing winds. To reach the islands to the northwest of Stanton Bay, they would have to pedal the airscrews to reach the northern and icy breath of the permanent icecap, and then drift on the icy winds to the west. To reach the large, southern hemisphere continent shaped like a diving duck, they quartered the northern hemisphere westerlies to the calm zones at the equator, leg-powered it, then drifted westward on the southern hemisphere easterlies.

"You have to admire them," Jack Purdy said as the gondolas lifted off. "How'd you like to try to steer one of those things around or through a tropical hurricane?"

"They seem to have made Omega their world," Rodrick agreed.

"With a certain amount of arrogance," Purdy commented.

"There are so many unanswered questions," Rodrick said, as the ships began to move slowly to the northwest.

"I haven't had a chance to read the section of Grace's report dealing with Chingclonk's statements about the dead city in Stoner's Valley," Purdy said.

"The more things change, the more they remain the same," Rodrick commented. "The city was built by a race of giants, the ancestors of the Whorsk."

"Ah, there were giants on Earth in those days," Jack said, quoting a verse from the Bible.

"So it seems. So it seems. And if we can believe our unfriend Chingclonk, there is at least one human on the big western continent. He gave us what is supposed to be a peaceful greeting. I'd like two scouts to buzz down there and find that Whorsk settlement. It's to the east of what Chingclonk called, according to the translator, the Great Misty River. I don't mind telling you, Jack, that I've been having some pretty spooky feelings about Omega ever since Stoner found his abandoned city. I don't know whether to be sorry that the race we've encountered is so savage, so alien, or to be relieved that they have only Stone Age weapons."

"And helium," Jack said. "Don't forget that."

"Magic," Rodrick said musingly. "I asked the chemists to run some tests. There's helium in the atmosphere here in just about the same ratio as on Earth, one part in about one hundred and eighty-six thousand. Separating the helium is a pretty complicated chemical process, involving washing with a couple of manmade chemicals, and then to get it pure it has to be cooled to minus three hundred degrees. Any way you look at it, that's pretty complicated technology."

"You'd think that a society that could produce helium would be advanced beyond bows and arrows in other ways," Purdy said.

"Who'd you suggest that we send to the Whorsk settlement?"

"I'd like to go myself."

"I hate to take all the joy out of your life, Jack," Rodrick said, "but I'd feel better if you'd ride herd on Chingclonk's fleet, just to be sure he doesn't decide to try to surprise us again."

"The wild bunch, then," Jack said, grinning. "The Injuns. Jacob and Renato."

"I flew across that continent one day," Rodrick mused. "I was letting Clay do some rocket practice, and we started at the west coast and came roaring across it about Mach three. It's all jungle, damned big, with wide rivers. Too bad we didn't fool around a little on the south coast. We might have seen the Whorsk's airships, and then we might have been able to prevent the loss of two hundred people."

"Yeah, I'd have thought we'd covered this globe well enough to spot something like those airships," Jack said, "but what we keep forgetting is the sheer size of it."

* * *

Jacob West and Renato Cruz welcomed the new assignment. "Hamilton control," Jacob said, "we're airborne."

"Roger on that, Jacob," Jackie Garvey Rodrick said.

"If we find this naked lady," Jacob said, "can I keep her?"

TWENTY-ONE

Theresita Pulaski was as drunk as a czar. All around the Whorsk village, berries of autumn had ripened, and the Whorsk had gorged themselves on a concoction that was delicious—berries covered with the sweet, sticky honey of the stingless Omega bees. Theresita had discovered that, if left covered in a jar for a few days, the crushed berries, sweetened by honey, fermented into a sweet but potent drink that hit her like a falling space station after so many months without alcohol.

She tried to share the goodies with some of the females, but they turned up their hard, shiny snouts in disgust, so she had it all to herself and lay on her bed, one bare knee crossed over the other, foot kicking in the air to the tune of a ribald Moscow drinking song. She suddenly leaped to her feet and did a little dance as she sang. She could hear the singing going on down in the big hut as the nightly party got under way.

"Bugorgy," she slurred, and it made her giggle, because they were bugs and because the males came on from the rear of the females. A bug orgy. "Bugorgy!" she shouted, giggling again.

Goddamn, she was as lonely as a dissident in Siberia.

"To hell with it," she said after considering joining the bugs at the bug orgy. At times it was interesting to watch the dancing, but in spite of the erotic aspects of

338

what followed, it soon got to be boring in its sameness, the whole village bug-screwing like crazy. And why were the males and females so perfectly matched in number? She was the only odd person out. For every bug there's a bug.

There flashed into her mind a vivid memory, or dream, of a large, clean-limbed man lifting her gently, easily, to place her, with her legs opening of their own accord, on a clean, firm bed.

"Watch it, Theresita," she said, "or you'll be playing with yourself."

So real. And yet it could not have happened.

She staggered out into the compound. The singing of the Whorsk females was sweetly shrill, exotic, erotic, and alien. She heard little peeps of sound from the big hut where the larvae were hung, and stepped in. The fire was a glow, giving enough light to show that the sacs were really jumping, as if they, too, were stirred by the increasing frenzy of the singing. They'd be ready to hatch soon, and then the population of the village would be more than doubled. What the hell would a young, freshly hatched Whorsk look like?

In spite of herself, she was drawn to the communal hut. Standing in the doorway watching the slow, ecstatic couplings, she finished off her container of honey beer, and decided that during the bug orgy would be a grand time to escape and sneak off to the west, to find that great river where the male Whorsk had gone that one time, and see if there had been any substance to her dream-memories of sex. But not tonight. She was too drunk.

And the next day brought change. She knew something was going on when she awoke. She went out, her fur draped over her shoulders against the morning chill, to find the females carrying the squirming larvae sacs toward the tethered airships. She ate her breakfast, fruit and nuts, as she followed along. There was a different type of singing from the females, a sort of sad little song, which repeated itself over and over.

Her command of the language was growing. She sought out the stickman who was chief. His name was a combination of a short, shrill whistle and a swallowed click.

"You go to sky?" she asked.

"Yes."

"I go?"

Violent forward thrust of head. *No*.

"You bug-juice pip-squeak. I could rip you apart."
She had a terrible hangover and was irritable. "You go
where in sky?"

"River," was the only word she understood.

"Why take babies?"

The word he used meant either give or trade; she
wasn't sure. "Give/trade for magic."

"Magic?"

He whistled, "Enough," and turned away.

While the fleet lifted and disappeared with the larvae
sacs toward the west, the females sang sadly, and then,
the ships out of sight, they picked up the tempo, began
dancing on the sands, and started back toward the village.
Theresita joined the female who had once struck her with
the whip.

"Where go babies?"

"Great Misty River."

"They come back?"

Negative thrust of head.

"You were sad. Now you're happy."

"I'll make more babies." And an expression, a suck-
ing, which indicated eating goodness.

"What will happen to the babies at the river?"

"They will grow, eat well, live joylife, build joyhouse
to Great Ones."

Interesting. "Who Great Ones?"

"Ones who come from far away and make magic."

"The magic that makes the ships fly?"

"That magic and other magic. For they are truly
Great Ones."

Theresita was getting an idea. She felt that she was
beginning to get some answers to questions that had been
haunting her.

"Whorsk admire Great Ones?"

"We have no choice. We must admire—"the word
could also mean obey"—or they will kill."

"Babies blessed by Great Ones?" Theresita asked.

"Yes."

The vague memories of the dream returned unbidden. It would not be unusual, judging by Earth's history, for a backward race to be ruled by a caste of priests. So they were trading their babies to a damned bunch of priests in exchange for helium and security. Probably the babies would be enslaved by the Great Ones of the Great Misty River.

"Trade babies for magic, then," she said, and got a yes. Theresita was satisfied she had the answer.

They had reached the village. The females were still singing and dancing, and one by one, pair by pair, they entered the hut where the sacs had hung. Theresita went with them. A female lay on her stomach, singing, making crawling motions without moving, and from her distended posterior there issued a quick stream of pulsating, golf-ball-sized eggs, a dozen, then more until the steaming pile held perhaps fifty eggs. The wife of the chief, ClickClick-Swallow, stirred the pulsating eggs with her hand, selected two, consulted with other females, tossed one of the eggs back onto the pile, and with her teeth nipped the other egg sac to form a hole. She carefully hung the egg on a peg on the wall and, with a cry, leaped back toward the pile of eggs and seized one in each hand. The other females, whistling and clicking gaily, fought good-naturedly over the others and popped the pulsating eggs into their mouths and chewed with muffled whistles of pleasure.

Theresita felt her stomach turn.

Another female went into the crawling, singing ecstasy of egg laying, and another egg was selected for life by the chief's mate. This time there was a surplus, so Theresita was offered an egg, which she politely declined. Then she got the hell out of there; other females started laying, and the sound of joyous chewing and feasting was too much for her.

She walked to the beach and was wading in the edge of the sea, fur open, firm breasts thrusting out, when she heard the sound of jets and looked up to see a scout coming low from the east. She waved her hand, screamed with a joy that strained her throat.

Oh, damn, damn, damn, he was moving too fast. He was only five hundred feet up, but he was moving too fast

and wasn't going to see her. She ripped off her fur and
waved it, and the scout did a cute little maneuver; in the
space of seconds it went from traveling at three hundred
miles per hour forward to hovering. Then it was lowering,
hydrogen jets hissing, and she was shouting in Russian
and dancing out of the surf with joy, waving the fur crazily
and then threw it on the shore. Oh, no more bug orgies
and leaf beds! Maybe a good, oh, yum, synthasteak and
baked bread and—

The scout landed. She ran to it, and the hatch opened,
and a man, a real, live man, stepped out, and she threw
herself into his arms and cried tears of joy. The dark-
skinned man was saying in English, "Hey, hey, take it
easy, honey. Take it easy."

She gained control, sobbing happily, and pulled herself
up to attention. "I am Marshal Theresita Pulaski, and I
thank you from the bottom of my heart."

Jacob West's eyes were on the verge of popping. She
was almost as tall as he, and during the past months, her
healthful diet had honed her down to perfect physique of
rounded hips, taut, thrusting breasts, and powerful but
shapely thighs and legs.

Renato, hovering overhead, was getting an eyeful,
too, using the optics to enlarge the scene.

"Lieutenant Commander Jacob West, U.S. Space Service," Jacob said, extending his hand. She took it in a grip
that won his respect. "I have a million questions, but
they'll have to wait. First, are you alone?"

"There is only me," she said, and thought about all of
the dead for the first time in a long time.

"Are there Whorsk about? We don't want trouble."

"The males are gone. The females are otherwise engaged, but if you're ready to leave, Commander, don't let
me hold you up."

"Marshal," Jacob said with a grin, as he let his eyes
feast on that tall, powerfully slender figure just once more,
"may I suggest that you might want to put on your, ah,
garment?"

She laughed. "How thoughtless of me," she said,
retrieving the fur. "It's just that I've been alone so long.
I've grown quite accustomed to nudity."

"I think I could learn to like it myself," Jacob said, as he took her hand and helped her into the scout.

She felt the thrust of the jets and was suddenly in contact with civilized things—merely the plastic of the seat on her thighs made her feel wonderful as the scout lifted.

Jacob asked, "Are you fit for a ballistic ride?"

"Commander, I could ride this bird through a ballistic trajector while hanging onto the rocket tubes with my teeth."

He laughed. "Hang on, then."

She felt the beautiful thrust, was driven back into the seat, yelled, "*Whee*," as the rockets stopped firing and the sudden weightlessness made her float. "Beautiful," she said. "And you, Commander West, you're the most beautiful sight I've seen since I landed on this planet."

"I've seen a lot worse sights than you," Jacob said, laughing. "I think I'll fall in love with you."

She laughed, too, but the laughter turned into sobs.

"Are you all right?" he asked.

"Yes, fine. It's pure hysterical happiness."

"You speak English very well."

"It's mandatory for everyone above the rank of major," she said. "Are you an American Negro?"

He laughed. "No, I'm an American Indian."

"Really! As in cowboys and Indians, the Wild West?"

He laughed again. Then he said, "Whoops, I forgot to report in." He flipped on the transmitter and got Jackie, in Hamilton control. "I think the skipper will want to greet my passenger," he said. "We have here a genuine marshal of the Red Army. And, Jackie, the lady is a bit underdressed. She's about your height. I think she'd appreciate a stretch skirt and tunic." He was too diplomatic to say that this Russian woman was built a bit more substantially than Jackie.

There was no more time for talk. Theresita saw the beautiful city, Earthlike but alien, the deep purple bay, the spreading veld. She was weeping again. *Apache One* kissed the pad without the slightest jar. *Apache Two* landed seconds later. Jacob opened the hatch and took a bundle of clothing from Duncan Rodrick, then hopped out to give her room. She pulled on the skirt and service tunic. The tunic was a bit tight across her breasts. She dismounted, barefoot, stood at attention before the impressive-looking American, and saluted.

"Welcome to Hamilton," Rodrick said.

"Thank you," Theresita answered, her voice husky. "Named for your president?"

"Yes. Do you need immediate medical attention?"

"No," she said. "I have never been in more perfect health."

"Then if you're not too tired, Marshal, I would appreciate a few minutes of your time in private."

"Of course," she said. She turned, thrust out her hand to Jacob. "Commander West, once again my heartfelt thanks. I want very much to see you again, to talk with you."

"Come to think of it, Jacob, you'd better come along also," Rodrick said. He didn't know, after all, what they'd talked about during the flight. They had had time to compare notes. She could have already told Jacob the answer to the question that was burning inside him.

"Aye, sir," Jacob said happily. He helped Theresita into the crawler and sat beside her. Rodrick parked at the main hatch. A curious group of people applauded as Theresita took Jacob's hand and dismounted. She, in the Russian fashion, applauded back. Then they were inside. She thought of the *Karl Marx* and couldn't stop the quiet tears. Jacob took her hand. "Are you sure you're all right?"

She squeezed his hand hard in gratitude for his concern. "I'm fine," she said. "Happy. Release of tension."

She did not, however, turn loose his hand. Rodrick didn't seem to notice. He led the way to his quarters, motioned Theresita into a comfortable chair. "I don't know exactly where to start, Marshal," he replied.

"With a drink of vodka," she said.

Jacob sprang to the bar, Rodrick nodded affirmation, and he mixed three vodkas with orange juice.

"I have dreamed of this," Theresita said, taking a deep, deep drink. That caused Jacob to laugh, but she continued drinking, then held out the glass. "Just one more, and I will nurse it slowly."

"I'm turning on the recorders," Rodrick said, pressing buttons.

"I understand," she said. At last she was able to stop the quiet flow of tears. The vodka was warming her stomach.

"I assume you are from the *Karl Marx*," Rodrick said. "Are you the sole survivor?"

"Of that I am almost certain," she said.

That was not the question he wanted to ask. Nor was it her chief concern at the moment. Each of them was thinking that, because of the early loss of the ship's communications, the other would have more recent news from Earth, two years more recent, for the outgoing ships could have been in radio contact for the entire two-year period of sublight cruising out of the solar system.

"The Earth . . ." Rodrick began, dreading the answer.

"My question to you!" she responded in surprise. "We lost all communication only days into the journey."

Duncan Rodrick laughed bitterly, not knowing whether to feel relief that he would not know the worst or disappointment that he would know no more than he already knew.

"When we fired our rockets the naval war was coming to a climax off the western coast of South America," he said. "Then we, too, lost our communications. You left a few weeks later?"

"Yes," she said. "The Russian fleet had been destroyed. The Red Army, in retaliation, moved armor to the French channel ports in thirty-six hours."

"And?" Rodrick asked, holding his breath.

"All Russian radio and television stations went off the air," she said. "The Americans were still broadcasting. The captain of the *Karl Marx* received orders to turn back, to take up positions of attack on the American space stations. At that time I instituted a mutiny against the captain and the crew, and in the fight the communications room was destroyed."

"Then you don't know if the bombs fell," Rodrick said.

"No."

"Damn," Jacob said softly.

"Sorry, Jacob, to give it to you this way," Rodrick

said. "There are only a few of us, Marshal and Commander, who know that the situation had worsened. I wanted to keep it that way for a while, for reasons I'm sure you'll understand."

"If people think that the bombs fell, they will not want to spend all their time and energy getting the ship ready to go back?" Jacob asked.

"Yes."

"I know that you left with only enough fuel to make the outward journey," she said.

"Marshal, we have a lot to talk about," Rodrick said. "Before we allow you to rest, is there any chance that there are other survivors?"

"The ship died in space. Only one scout left it. The pilot was killed upon landing in the jungle. I estimate that our landing took place approximately three thousand miles north of the point where Commander West found me."

Jacob whistled. "Three thousand miles? You have quite a story to tell, lady."

"I'll be happy to tell you," she said, with a smile that radiated warmth toward Jacob. "I've had no one to talk with for so many months—except the Whorsk, who are not the best of conversationalists."

"I think we can take pity on the marshal," Rodrick said. "Just one more question. We've had an encounter with the Whorsk. In your contact with them, have you learned anything that I should know quickly, perhaps some hidden capabilities? We were quite surprised to find that they filled their airships with helium."

"I, too," she agreed. "No, I think that is the only unexpected thing about them, other than their total alienness. They are of no danger to a force with modern weapons."

"Thank you," Rodrick said. "Now I think you should see our medics—or would you like some food first?"

"Captain," she said, "I ask only two things: a bottle of this excellent vodka and a real bed. Give me four hours' sleep on a mattress, with a clean sheet—oh, with a shower and soap beforehand—and I'll talk my head off."

"It's a deal," Rodrick replied. She'd held a fantastically high rank in the Red Army, and yet she seemed to be just another human being. "I'll call one of our female officers. She'll show you to, uh, well, Jackie's quarters are vacant, Jacob."

"Will *you* show me to my bed?" Theresita asked Jacob, rising. She looked at the captain with a laugh. "The commander is the first human face I've seen. And he saw me in my uniform of the past few months. I feel as if we're already fast friends."

"Be happy to," Jacob said. He took a bottle of vodka from the captain's bar and showed her out the door. They walked in silence side by side down the corridor. He opened the door to Jackie's former quarters.

"Ah, sheer luxury," Theresita said. "Please. Stay and have one drink with me."

"My pleasure," Jacob answered, moving to the kitchen for glasses.

"And no orange juice, please."

She sat on the couch, looking down glumly at her stained, somewhat splayed feet. "My feet have spread two sizes bigger," she announced. "Your American people will call me Big Foot."

"You walked three thousand miles?" Jacob asked in total awe.

"Oh, no. Most of it was by raft on a river through the jungle."

"I've done a bit of exploration in the jungle," he said. "How in the world did you manage to survive?"

"With luck and stubbornness," she said. "Keep talking to me. It's been so long since I've heard a human voice."

"Maybe you'd better get some rest," he suggested.

"No, please." She shivered. The thought of being alone frightened her for some reason. Tears formed and slid down her tanned cheeks. "Don't mind me," she said, wiping them away. "All of a sudden I've become quite emotional."

"Let me get you some food," Jacob said uneasily.

"No. Do you know what I need more than anything else at this moment?"

"No. What?"

"Just the touch of a human hand. Just to tell me that

my eyes and ears are not deceiving me, that I am not alone."

He sat beside her on the couch and gently took her hand between his two.

"If they could see me," she said, tears hanging on her lower lashes.

"Who?"

"The old men of the Kremlin. They would laugh. The great Polish marshal asking a man to hold her hand because she fears being alone."

"It must have been rough," Jacob said.

"It didn't seem so at the time," she said musingly. "I was alone, and that was the situation, and there was nothing to do, short of giving up, but go on." She sighed shudderingly. "My mother told me when I was just a girl, 'Theresita, don't try to be a boy. You are a girl, and you should act like a girl.' And now, rather belatedly, I feel very girlish and weepy and—" Her eyes went wide. "I'm taking advantage. Your wife—"

"I have no wife," Jacob said.

"Please don't think—"

"I'm thinking nothing. If I'd been alone in the jungle for months, then with those Whorsk things, I'd probably be yelling for pain pills and the nearest psychiatrist and hanging onto your skirt screaming."

She laughed, hiccuped with a sob, and burst into a very unfeminine spasm of giant, racking sobs.

Jacob whispered soothing sounds into her ear, enfolding her, holding her tightly. "Hush, now. You're safe with us."

It went on for perhaps a full minute, then she swallowed hard.

"All right," she said, straightening. "That's that. Thank you for your shoulder."

"Any time," he assured her.

"Now I am going to see if this great American settlement has gallons and gallons of hot water."

"Okay. Sounds reasonable," he said, thankful she had gotten herself under control. He was afraid he'd have to send for a medic.

"Where do they keep the towels?"

He went into the bath and opened the linen cabinet. There was a stock of neatly folded towels. In a drawer beside the cabinet Jackie had left some plain, serviceable nightgowns. He selected one, handed it to Theresita, and turned to leave.

"Commander?" she said, panic in her voice.

"Yes?" he asked, turning.

"I'm not going to cry anymore."

"Good."

"May I ask you to do something very silly?"

He grinned. "If it's not too silly."

"I'm not really trying to seduce you. . . ."

He waved one hand at her in negation.

"Stay until I'm out of the shower?"

"Sure."

He mixed a drink. He was remembering how she looked there on that beach as she ran toward him—lithe, a big woman, big woman's body without an ounce of fat, long-legged and graceful, and how she had felt in his arms. Oddly enough, he felt no heat, no desire, only a musing appreciation of beauty.

The shower ran, a roar of distant rain. And he grinned as she suddenly burst into song, singing a Red Army marching cadence in Russian.

After a while the shower stopped and then, five minutes later, the door opened. She had fluffed up her short, chopped hair and was wearing one of Jackie's gowns, which failed totally to conceal her slim waist, her outthrust of hip, her proud breasts. She seemed to be suddenly aware of her body. The gown, thin, showed the browner areolas, the thrust of nipples, the prominent vee of her pelvic bone. She walked swiftly to the bed and threw back the coverings. "Ah, clean sheets." She slipped in, and pulled the sheets up to her neck.

"All snug?" he asked, standing.

"Very." She nodded in the manner of the Whorsk without realizing it.

"Okay. Look, there's the communicator on the table. Just press the red button, and you'll get the duty officer. If you need me, my quarters are still here on the ship."

"Thank you."

"Have a nice nap."

He had opened the door and turned around to look at her. Her eyes were wide, and there was an odd look on her face.

"Not yet, huh?" he asked. He walked back to the bed, pulled up a chair, and reached under the cover to take her right hand in his. "All right, I'll stay right here until you're sleeping."

"I feel so stupid." Tears welled up in her eyes.

"Close your eyes."

"Yes, sir."

He looked at her. Her round face was deeply tanned and totally unlined, yet she had to be at least in her late thirties to have attained such high military rank. As he looked, she started shivering.

"Are you cold?" he asked.

She didn't open her eyes. "Once we jumped by parachute into the snow on a training exercise," she said. "The drifts were ten feet deep in places. The temperature was twenty below. *Then* I was cold."

"And now? Want me to get another blanket?"

"How far will your patience last with me?" she asked with a sigh, opening her eyes. "No, no blanket. We slept in arctic tents. The small heaters we carried in our packs were almost worthless. We had only one way to keep warm in the night. Two crowded into one arctic sleeping bag, then we were warm."

Now ain't that a kick? he thought. *I'm actually jealous.*

"I was a captain then," she continued. "My second in command was a young lieutenant from Orel. We had to give signals when we wanted to turn over, for there was only room to sleep spoon fashion. He had the hottest body I have ever touched. And he was so polite. He would say, 'Comrade Captain, may we turn now, please?' And once in his sleep he put his arm around me and woke up and spent the next ten minutes apologizing. It was so cold." She laughed. "The poor boy would have been shocked had he known *my* thoughts."

"Horny old soldier, huh?" Jacob asked.

"Only in my secret mind," she said, looking at him. "As now."

"Now are you trying to seduce me?"

"No." She was still shivering. "In my secret mind I am imagining your warmth pressed against my back."

"And if I'm not as trustworthy as your lieutenant from Orel?"

She shrugged.

There was one amazing thing about women, Jacob thought, as he lay, stripped to his service shorts, with his arm around her waist and his body curled, spoon fashion, pressed against her back, her rump, her legs. They can be as athletic as all hell, not an ounce of fat, all muscle and tendons. And yet, if they're not totally emaciated, they're so soft. He felt and heard her breathing deepen. He could not have gone to sleep with a bottle of sleeping pills. He let his hand flatten on her stomach, soft-hard, rising and falling with her breathing, smelled her clean, fresh hair in his face.

Lady, he thought, *things must be one helluva lot different in Russia.*

He felt himself becoming aroused and pulled away so that he wouldn't press against her. She murmured in her sleep, turned, threw one arm across his chest, one heated, soft thigh across his thighs just below that evidence that he was not as cool as a Russian soldier in a sleeping bag. He ground his teeth and bit his lip to keep his body from trembling. Her gown had ridden up. He could feel, against his bare thigh, below his shorts, a heat that was greater than any other body heat. He ached. He itched. His every muscle wanted to move, but she was sleeping so soundly, so peacefully, so trustfully.

He awoke with a feeling of something missing. He put out his hand, and the bed was empty and the lights were on. She was sitting, in the borrowed skirt and tunic, in the chair beside the bed.

"Thank you," she said, when his eyes found hers.

"No problem," he said, wondering how he had ever managed to fall asleep with the most beautiful leg in at least two worlds thrown across him. "Line of duty."

She smiled. "Really?"

He sighed. "I'm going to see a lot of you, you mad

Russian, but don't you ever, ever ask me to get in bed with you again without *very* serious intent."

"All right," she agreed.

A small group of video technicians were waiting with the captain for her. She told her story with great animation, weepingly as she described the mutiny and the destruction of the *Karl Marx*, musingly as she spoke of her time on the river, a bit proudly as she told of killing the *kkkee*, with puzzlement as to her recovery, quickly and quite businesslike in regard to her time with the Whorsk.

Then she answered questions about the life habits of the insect people, and there was a proper amount of interest and a bit of shock at her description of what she had once thought of as the bug orgies and the ceremony of the selection of the egg that would survive and the eating of others. Duncan Rodrick was most interested in the other society of people along what the Whorsk called the Great Misty River, and she gave her opinion, that the River People were merely a ruling class, a class of priests, demanding and receiving gifts and obedience from the other Whorsk.

Her knowledge of the native Omegans, plus what the Americans already knew, convinced most that there was nothing to fear from the Whorsk as long as the natives were prevented from obtaining deadly modern weapons.

"They are so different that we will never be able to live with them in complete harmony," she said. "But from what I have learned, this is a big planet. Perhaps, with much study and much patient effort, we can coexist with them."

The story had been heard, with avid interest, by the entire colony. When the cameras and microphones had been turned off and the technicians had gone, Theresita turned to Rodrick. There were only three of them in the room—them plus Jacob.

"Captain," she said, "perhaps I am, perhaps I am not, the only Russian alive. Whichever it may be, this Russian asks you for a place in your wonderful colony. If you will have me, assign me where you will."

"I think, Marshal, that you will be a valuable addition to our group," Rodrick said.

"Not a marshal. No longer," she said. "May I be just Theresita?"

Rodrick smiled.

"I'm going to show her around," Jacob said, "with permission to skip my duty standby."

"Permission granted," Rodrick said.

Everyone wanted to meet the Russian lady. She remembered a few names, among them that of a pale, thin, and beautiful woman named Sage Bryson, who, sitting on the beach between Paul Warden and Evangeline Burr, smiled and showed a great deal of curiosity about how it felt to be alone in the jungle for so long. And Theresita was pleased and made happy by the bubbling enthusiasm of a handsome boy named Clay and a lovely girl named Cindy who clung to Clay's hand all the time they were talking.

A Space Service beautician trimmed Theresita's hair, evening up the chopping she'd given it, and the ship's tailor shop ran her off a plain, white uniform with matching shorts, skirt, and slacks. She ate a huge synthasteak, drank a quart of fresh orange juice, couldn't believe that the admiral was an android, fell in love with Cat, and found herself walking, at dusk, beside Jumper's Run with a thoroughly exhausted Apache.

"Such wonderful people," she said. "Are all Americans like that?"

"We have our bad apples, too," he replied.

"So many of them are happily married," she said. "And the children! The young ones! How beautiful." She reached out and took Jacob's hand. "Not many singles, Jacob," she went on. "I heard an expression. Someone said that someone else had chosen. Is that what it is called?"

"Yes," he said.

"And you have not chosen?"

"Not until yesterday, when I saw a certain Russian soldier naked on a beach."

"Be serious," she said.

He stopped and turned her to face him. He leaned to

kiss her, and she pulled back and put her hand over his mouth. "Do you know what I feared most when I was naked and alone?"

"No," he said.

"I was afraid my teeth would decay and fall out. I brushed them with twigs, and sometimes with fine sand, and with salt after I was with the Whorsk."

"That's an odd subject to bring up to keep from being kissed," Jacob said.

"Not to keep from being kissed," she said, "but to let you know how happy I am that my teeth didn't decay and fall out. Then you wouldn't have looked at me the way you're looking at me now."

"I'm not so sure," he said. "I think you'd be beautiful even without teeth."

She laughed. "No one has ever, ever accused me of being beautiful."

"You're guilty nevertheless," he said.

"You know the trouble with you American Indians?"

"I could name several."

"You talk too damned much when there's kissing to be done," she said.

They could see the lights of Hamilton from where they stood. A game of tennis was going on under the lights, and there was a sound of young voices. The entertainment robot, Juke, was wheeling around and playing music, a waltz. The strains floated up to them, and down across the bay, which was rippled by a light southeast wind. The night was cool, and from the southern horizon came the flash of lightning and the rumble of distant thunder.

"Do you first want a chance to look around to check out the other singles?" Jacob asked.

"Why do you ask?"

"Because I have chosen. And because it's only fair. You may think you care about me only because I rescued you. What if another man had flown that scout? Would we still have fallen in love eventually?"

She removed her hand from his, and turned away.

"What's wrong Theresita?" he asked.

She faced him. "I have decided. I am yours if you want me. But you know nothing of my past."

"The only thing I want to know is what happened in that arctic sleeping bag," he replied, grinning.

"Seriously," she said, "I am not a young girl, Jacob."

"And I'm no kid, myself," he said. "I've been a pilot for twenty years, a good one and a hot one in a glamorous service."

"Oh, a lady killer."

"I thought we were trying to compete with each other for who had the most sordid past."

"I haven't been all *that* bad!" she exclaimed.

"Just tell me what went on in that sleeping bag."

"Nothing. Only an older woman thinking very heated thoughts about a handsome young officer."

"That's all?"

"Truth. That's all."

"Then I think I'll keep you," he said. "After all, I'm the one who found you."

"I agree; it is your duty."

He took her hand, and they walked back down the slope, through the town. "Would we be accused of immorality if I asked you to warm me again tonight?" she asked.

"Do you remember what I told you this morning? About having serious intentions before asking me to do that? And would you still feel immoral?"

"No," she said. "Well, maybe a little."

"Enough to bother you?"

"How will I know unless we try?" she asked.

TWENTY-TWO

As far as Captain Rodrick was aware, the group of Those Who Knew had been depleted by one with the death of Rocky Miller, and increased by two, Jacob West and Theresita Pulaski. But then Rodrick did not know that Commander Miller had told his group of dissidents about the imminence of nuclear war. But his group had perished in the Whorsk ambush. Mandy, the only survivor of the attack, already had known about the possibility of nuclear war on Earth.

The captain had called a breakfast meeting. As they ate, Evangeline tried her Russian on Theresita and was complimented on vocabulary and advised on accent. Mandy Miller, still hollow eyed, was mostly silent. Jackie sat on Duncan's right and had trouble keeping her eyes off his face, just now beginning to believe that she was married to him, and that he was everything, and more, than she'd ever dreamed of. Emi and Ito Zuki completed the group.

"I just wanted to talk things over," Rodrick said, as people helped themselves to another round of coffee when the meal was finished. Theresita had discovered that her stomach was not yet ready for heavy foods after months of fruit, berries, and nuts. Two days of glutting herself on bread, sweets, and synthasteak had made her stomach feel distended, and, indeed, there seemed to be just a bit of roundness there. She'd returned to her diet of nuts and fruit for the time being.

"Does anyone have anything pressing?" Rodrick asked.

No one spoke. Theresita had a medical examination scheduled. It was going to be performed by Dr. Miller and her staff, and since Mandy didn't offer any information about it, neither did Theresita.

"Recent events have presented us with some information to consider," Rodrick said. "I've asked two more members to join our little group." He looked at his button-watch. He'd asked Max and Grace to breakfast, and Max, grinning, had said, "Duncan, after a long and pleasant bachelorhood, I've just discovered the pleasure of looking at my wife across the breakfast table."

"They should be here any minute," Rodrick told the group, just as the caller sounded. Rodrick said, "Come in," and Max and Grace entered. Grace snagged two coffee cups and fixed, then handed, Max his coffee. Neither she nor Max was surprised to hear that the situation on Earth had been much worse than was general knowledge.

"You all know the mission with which I was entrusted," Rodrick said. "I've been doing a lot of thinking since Marshal—excuse me . . . *Theresita* told me what she knew. We know only that over three years ago, when Theresita had her last contact with Earth, the bombs had not yet started to fall. My thinking is this: The situation was grim, true, but the United States and the Soviet Union have been nose to nose for a hundred years now, with bombs available for most of that time, and they had always found some way to avoid the final confrontation. We know that the greatest threat was Premier Yuri Kolchak's determination to see the world converted to communism before his death, but he died before he realized that ambition, and, presumably, men who were a bit more sane were in power in the Kremlin."

Theresita felt her heart lurch at the mention of Yuri's name. No one here, she decided, could ever learn that she had been Yuri's lover—and then his murderer, in hopes of staving off the final confrontation between the United States and the Soviet Union.

Rodrick continued: ". . . personally believe that there's

a very real chance that the two big powers found a way to avoid nuclear war. Any comment?"

He looked around the table. Everyone was silent.

"Stoner tells me that the deposit of ore he's working, although it wouldn't be considered worthwhile on Earth, is promising. Fortunately—this is probably going to come as a surprise to you, Theresita—our discoveries during the outward voyage mean that we didn't have to mine tons of rhenium, only pounds."

"Pounds?" Theresita asked. "Then we wasted enough with the *Karl Marx* to power a fleet of starships and explore the entire galaxy."

"That's right," Ito Zuki said. "We did the same on *Spirit*."

"Stoner says that if the ore deposit keeps looking more promising as he goes deeper, he will be able to give us a power load for the ship in two years, perhaps less," Rodrick said. "I'm sure that all of you know that I fully intend to take the *Spirit of America* back to Earth."

"Of course," Max said.

"What about rocket fuel, Max?" Rodrick asked.

"We've got the raw materials," Max reported. "It'll take a year to build the manufacturing facilities. We've got a lot of scrap metal now. The crawlers the Whorsk blew up can be reclaimed, and we can use the metal from the bulkheads of the portable quarters."

"Good, Max. Keep in touch with Stoner, and if he finds more rhenium than he expects and can accelerate his program, be ready to keep up with him."

"No problem," Max responded.

"The return cargo of the *Spirit of America* will be foodstuffs, growing stock. Amando has a few Omega plants that he thinks will help green up the arid areas of Africa and Asia. He's very interested in having a talk with you, Theresita. He's very impressed that you are so fit and healthy after living on Omega's natural foods for a year. Apparently we have something to learn about diet and nutrition. If you can look the way you do eating fruit and nuts—"

"And fish," Theresita said.

"—the Omegan fruit and nut trees transplanted in the

tropical and subtropical areas of Earth will greatly increase the food supply." He paused. "Too bad we don't have fabulous treasures to take back."

"The jewelry made from Baby's discarded scales would be a sensation," Jackie remarked. "If we had a way of getting enough—"

"That is *some* animal," Max said. "I timed her the other day, with Clay and Cindy riding on her back. She was doing a smooth thirty miles an hour all the way to the Dinah River. Beats the hell out of a horse. Anyone ever think of breeding those things as transport animals?"

"Just don't ask me to be the one to capture them," Jacob said.

"I've been trying to think of some way I could be of value to the colony," Theresita said. "I'm probably more familiar with the jungles than anyone."

"Hush," Jacob said.

She smiled and winked at him. "Don't worry, Sky Flyer, I'll take care of you."

"Russians are pushy," Jacob complained, but with a grin of affection and pride.

"Jacob, I hereby appoint you and Theresita to explore the possibilities of adding—have we named that species yet? No? Well, of adding more Babies to the stock and to look for a source of discarded scales."

"Thanks a helluva lot," Jacob grumbled, again grinning at Theresita.

"All right," Rodrick said. "Until we keep our pledge to Dexter Hamilton and take the *Spirit of America* back to Earth, we'll have to deal with some situations we had not foreseen. First, our strength has been reduced by a full sixth." He could not bring himself to look at Mandy when he spoke of that. "And not even the pleasant surprise of having Theresita join us can make up for that. We've lost valuable skills, and we've lost valued friends and relatives. However, I'd like to ask Dr. Miller—if you think you're up to it, Mandy—to do a survey regarding the skills and knowledge of those who were killed, and to report the results to Max, who is now first officer. That way we'll know what we're lacking and we can start making plans to have others cover in the areas of need, and think long term of, perhaps, training some of our youngsters to fill the gaps."

"I'm quite ready to work, Captain," Mandy said.

"Thanks, Mandy." He rose, got a coffeepot, and came back to the table. "Anyone?"

"I've had better-looking waitresses," Max growled.

"I'd like to use you now as sort of a brain trust," Rodrick said. "Let me state a couple of things that have been keeping me awake nights: First, we suffered great losses in our first contact with a culture that is in only one respect advanced beyond the Stone Age. I take some responsibility for that. We were simply not alert. I also take responsibility for not being aware of the morale of the colony. I knew that there was some desire among a few to move the colony, or to at least establish a settlement in those fabled paradises of the south. The wholesale defection caught me completely by surprise, and the fact that I was rather distracted"—he put his hand on Jackie's shoulder and smiled at her—"is no excuse."

He looked around, looked into each of the faces. Mandy couldn't meet his eye. If he felt guilty, how should *she* feel, having known of Rocky's plan? If anyone alive was to blame, it was she.

"I want to start a regular series of community meetings," Rodrick said. "I want them to be informal, not a forum for open discussion of every minor gripe, but open enough to bring up concerns to the entire colony. Grace, I think you've got just the right amount of charm and good sense to run the meetings. Any objections?"

"We're not finished with our honeymoon yet," Max said quickly.

"Objection overruled," Rodrick said, grinning. "Bite the bullet, Max." He sat down. "Here's where I want your input. We're shorthanded. We've lost some irreplaceable equipment. We're going to be very busy just doing the necessary things to keep our life-style from regressing, and to refuel the ship. The question is, what are to be our spare-time priorities in regard to exploration, scientific study, and interaction with the native race? Keep these questions in mind, and I'll be interested in hearing your opinions on them. First, how do the Whorsk get helium when the limit of their technology, as we know it, is to make a presentable ceramic pot and hammer out bronze weapons? Second, was it just the limited capacity of Grace's translation computer that brought out some interesting statements from Chief Chingclonk? He kept calling both us humans and some group from along what he called the Great Misty River *you*, as if he considered us one and the same with those unknown people on the big western continent. Then he insisted that we had originated outside the Omega system, among the stars, in a direction almost opposite the direction of Earth. Or, again, did we simply misunderstand?"

"Primitive societies on Earth had an understanding of the heavens," Ito said. "They knew that the stars represented distance, and they had legends about gods who came from the heavens. The Whorsk, being able to fly in their airships, should have some conception of the stars."

"To know that each of them is a sun like 61 Cygni B?" Grace asked. "That's pretty advanced reasoning for Stone Age people."

"Lastly," Rodrick resumed, "there's the matter of Theresita's having been healed of what she is sure were some very severe wounds. With those points in mind, what should be our policy toward the Whorsk during the immediate future, when we're going to need all our time and energy to accomplish our primary mission?"

"As to Theresita's healing," Mandy said, "remember the jungle mud, which seemed to have healing properties. I know that raises the question of how the Whorsk would know such mud would heal human flesh. I'd like to have some samples of that mud, incidentally."

Jacob took the floor. "We can solve the mystery of what Theresita thinks is a society of priests or a Whorsk ruling class by a few quick, low runs of the river valley. I volunteer."

"As soon as possible, Jacob," Rodrick said.

"We could send an anthropological team to study the Whorsk," Emi Zuki commented.

"It's a worthy idea," Rodrick said. "Theresita, in your opinion, having lived among them, would they cooperate with such a team?"

"I'm not sure," Theresita answered. "And I question the value to be derived within any reasonable length of time. I don't think it's going to be possible for anyone to learn to speak the Whorsk language with any degree of proficiency, simply because we don't have the right sort of sound-originating mechanism."

"I haven't had a chance to tell you this, Duncan," Grace said, "but I was going over the voice recordings I made with Chingclonk, toying around with them. You remember how there seemed to be pauses in his speech at times? Those pauses are actually filled with sound at a frequency above our range of hearing."

"Maybe we'll have to train Jumper to listen for that," Ito Zuki said, and Emi giggled.

"I think we should find out how those bugs isolate helium," Max suggested. "That's about all I care to know about them."

"There's something else that bothers me," Rodrick said. "Why wasn't Theresita more of a curiosity among the Whorsk? From listening to her story, I got the idea that they accepted her without too much question, just as if they were familiar with humans."

"And they didn't seem to be surprised to find us here in Eden," Emi said. "What do you think, Theresita?"

"They never showed surprise, or any sort of emotion, at anything," Theresita remarked. "They just seemed to take everything that came as a matter of course. For example, one of them fell from a gondola one day and was killed. The airship didn't even turn back but just went on with its flight, and when it returned that night they picked up their fallen member by the arms and legs and carried him about a quarter of a mile from the village and threw the body into the surf."

"It'll be a long time before we even begin to understand the Whorsk," Grace said. "This is the first alien intelligence we've encountered. Human values are based on having evolved on an entirely different planet, with a code of behavior based on a lack of understanding of death. We could be the only beings in the universe who concern ourselves with death. We're like the English poet who said, 'Any man's death diminishes me, because I am involved in mankind.' It seems to mean nothing to the Whorsk when anyone or anything dies. That makes them so alien that we can't get beyond that one difference, much less all the others."

"I agree that we must avoid a campaign of extermination," Jacob said. "The Whorsk are savage and different, but they were here first, and just like the Apaches—another race that was there first—I think they have a right to continue to live just as they've lived in the past. Certainly this planet is big enough for all of us."

"I agree," Rodrick said.

"They're no threat to us," Max said, "if we stay alert and avoid surprise attacks. I'll tell you this, and back it with everything I've ever learned—there's no high-tech society over on the Great Misty River or anywhere else on this planet. Hell, if anyone was burning fossil fuel, even, we'd have detected it in the atmosphere, and all we've found is an almost undetectable amount of combustion residue from burning wood. Forest fires, most likely, maybe forests caught in lava flows in the volcanic belt down in the islands or in the western hemisphere or on the east coast of Columbia. I say let's go full blast on what we need to do, and if we have time to diddle around studying the Whorsk, okay. If not, that's okay, too. As soon as we have some spare copper and tin to trade, they'll be hanging around and Grace can use the translation box on them."

"I gather," Rodrick said, with a rueful smile, "that none of you is imagining some of the things that keep me awake nights."

"I've got something that keeps me awake nights, too," Max said, grinning, putting his hand on Grace's.

"Not even a little bit of wondering if we're the first humanoids the Whorsk have seen?" Rodrick asked.

"Dunc," Max said, "I'll start dreaming science-fiction dreams when I find a functioning helium separation plant in operation."

"The giants who built the city in Stoner's Valley?" Rodrick asked.

"Hell, even modern Cambodians feel that a race of giants built the temples at Angkor Wat," Max said.

"Theresita," Rodrick said, "in your opinion, was the

abandoned city I showed you pictures of built by ancient Whorsk?"

"It's possible. They have the manual dexterity. They do fine work in tanning hides and scraping them thin for the covering of the gasbags on their airships. They work wood well with basic metal tools to build the gondolas. They have, with the exception of the airships, a basic hunter-gatherer society, doing only the minimum work required to build the ships and their log huts."

"It wouldn't be the first known instance of regression of a society," Mandy said. "It could be as simple as this: The development of the lighter-than-air craft freed them to roam a pretty interesting and very large world."

A silence fell.

"Any further comment?" Rodrick asked.

There was none.

Jacob had a companion as he flew in from the mouth of the Great Misty River on the western continent, only to find dense fog covering the valley for about fifteen hundred miles. He flew *Apache One* on up the river, saw the huge cascade that had so impressed Theresita, and then she was remembering a lot of things as he traced the wide, brown river northward into the dense jungles. According to Theresita's estimate of time and river-current rate, she had crashed almost in midcontinent over three thousand air miles from the coast, even more miles when one considered the curves and windings of the river.

Flights over the river on three other days had the same results. "Now we know why they call it the Great Misty River," Jacob said. The dense fog that hung over the river valley was, they decided, some sort of local natural phenomenon. Surveys of Whorsk settlements on that continent and the two in the northern hemisphere in the west showed nothing new about the Whorsk.

Four days after being picked up by Jacob, Theresita finally kept her appointment for a medical examination. She came to like Mandy Miller immediately and, knowing the story now, felt that Mandy's smudged eyes and distracted attitude were signs of mourning for her dead husband.

The examination took place late in the day, and when Theresita was finished, she met Jacob at the clubhouse, an attractive, multihued plastic-stone building that someone had found spare time to build on the rocky headland at the mouth of Stanton Bay, a five-minute crawler ride from Hamilton and the *Spirit of America*. Juke, the entertainment robot, and Makeitdo, the RD-77 repair robot, had installed large screens and a sound system, which, if it were ever to be cranked up full blast, would shatter stone. Juke had decided that he'd become a nightclub host and, if anyone would ever listen to him, a nightclub comic. That last had not yet been realized because every time he started to tell his jokes, people yelled, "Not now, Juke!" But they did appreciate his selection of music.

On a Saturday night a representative group could be found at the club, filling the three tennis courts and the swimming pool, cooking on the grills in the picnic areas, lounging on the ocean beach, or just sitting on one of the open balconies and watching the gloriously colored Omega sunset.

Grace had finally convinced Max that it was time for a night out. Theresita found Jacob at a large table with Max and Grace, Duncan and Jackie Rodrick, and Paul Warden, who was escorting, as usual, two women, Sage Bryson and Evangeline Burr.

Juke had not yet met Theresita. He saw the newcomer and rolled hurriedly to the table just as she leaned to kiss Jacob on the cheek.

"Who's the beauty?" Juke asked, in his slightly flat, mechanical voice.

"What's this?" Theresita asked.

"Ignore him and he'll go away," Sage said. Her treatment under Dr. Allano was going well. She was learning some things about herself that frightened the hell out of her, but she was coping.

"I, madam, am Juke, the invaluable source of all things entertaining."

Theresita sat down, smiling happily at the canlike robot.

"Ah," Juke said, "I see that the newlyweds are out in force tonight. That reminds me—"

"Not now, Juke," several of them chorused, and then burst into laughter.

Juke, encouraged, said, "I haven't been married long myself, you know, but my wife's been giving me the cold shoulder so much lately that I'm thinking of buying her a thermal shawl."

"What?" Theresita gasped, before she broke into laughter.

"For God's sake, don't encourage him," Max moaned.

"I don't know what happens to romance after marriage," Juke said, playing directly to Theresita, "but the most I get from my wife these days is a passionate nudge."

Theresita laughed. She had an infectious, hearty laugh that was irresistible. The others laughed in spite of themselves. Juke's eyes glowed with pure happiness.

"My wife is wild about the lean, hard, vicious type. I guess that's why she's always spending time with her mother."

"And to think I was considering marrying this woman," Jacob said, as Theresita caught his shoulder and leaned against it, laughing so hard that even Max chuckled.

"Before we got married my wife said, 'You're only interested in one thing.' After being married to her for a while, I can't even remember what it was."

"Oh, stop!" Theresita begged through laughter.

"Second the motion."

"I thought it was the English who were supposed to have a weird sense of humor," Jacob said, grinning at Theresita.

"He is *so* very funny!" Theresita gasped.

"Now you've done it," Grace groaned. "He'll be here all night." She herself thought Juke was very funny, too. She'd had a hilarious time using some spare memory chambers to hold the jokes of all the old comedians on Earth.

"Did you read about the woman who divorced her husband for habitual adultery?" Juke said. "I don't see how you can call adultery a habit, but if it is, it sure beats nail biting."

Grace winked at Juke and motioned him away. He

rolled off, chuckling tinnily to himself. He hadn't been able to hold an audience for so many jokes in a long time.

"He *is* funny," Theresita gasped.

"I always knew Russia was behind us," Jacob said, "but a hundred years behind on jokes?"

"I will show you who is behind," Theresita threatened, giggling and beating Jacob on the shoulder. Then, after a couple of residual giggles, she said, "And speaking of funny things, Dr. Miller gave me the most thorough going-over I've ever had in my life."

"Aside from your sense of humor," Jacob said, "did she find anything wrong?"

"No. I am as healthy as a horse. This is the funny thing: She told me that I am three months pregnant."

Jacob straightened up with a start.

"Isn't that funny?" Theresita asked.

"Very," Jacob said, his eyes questioning.

She hit him on the shoulder again. "Don't be silly, Sky Flyer, not even *you* are that fast. No," she continued, her face serious. "There is nothing to worry about. She ran the test as a sort of afterthought, when it was getting very late. There is something wrong, of course, with the test itself."

Jacob was still looking at her questioningly.

"Jacob," she said, "three months ago I was with the Whorsk, and I assure you that I did not join in their nightly play."

"I'm sure it was just a faulty test," Grace agreed.

"Oh, sure," Theresita said. "Impossible, you see." She laughed heartily. "If I am pregnant, it means that I missed something that I certainly would not have wanted to miss."

Jacob laughed with her.

But a month later, after Theresita's flat stomach had swelled noticibly, no one was laughing.

EPILOGUE

Dr. Mandy Miller sent her request for a private conference with the captain through channels. The memo was seen and initialed by the captain's semiofficial secretary, Mrs. Duncan Rodrick. A time was set at the end of a workday; the place was the captain's office, which would eliminate any temptation to make personal contact, for official meetings in the captain's office were automatically recorded.

There are, however, finely shaded emotions capable of being passed from person to person without detection by audio or visual recorders. The camera, for example, could not pick up the soft glow of love that came into Mandy's eyes as she entered the office after knocking, nor the immediate, heart-stopping reaction that look had on Duncan Rodrick.

Duncan had anticipated the meeting with a mixture of doubt and pleasure. He had thought he could control his emotions regarding Mandy and had convinced himself that he'd been doing the colony a disservice by avoiding her completely. She was, after all, the head of the Life Sciences section and, as such, an important official whose continuing service was vital to all.

"Come in, Mandy," Rodrick said, standing. "Have a seat."

"Thank you," she responded, taking the chair in front

of his desk. "I asked for this meeting, Captain, to discuss several things."

The tone was set—it was to be strictly business. Duncan resisted his inclination to grin, for just to look at her was pleasing.

"First," Mandy said, "there is no doubt that Theresita Pulaski is pregnant. The fetus is quite well formed, and it looks and tests to be quite normal."

Duncan rubbed his chin and said nothing, for it was obvious that Mandy was not finished.

"Which brings up some questions," she went on. "It is biologically impossible for Theresita to have been impregnated by a Whorsk. Due to the time she spent journeying down the river, it is equally impossible for the father of the child to have been one of the Russians aboard the *Karl Marx*. And since she was three months pregnant when Jacob West rescued her, it can't be his child. That, of course, leaves one possibility."

"I agree," Duncan said. He had been procrastinating on that matter. He'd sent a half-dozen scout flights to the area of the Great Misty River, but their reports were all identical: nonvisibility and no life signals emanating through the fog that hung over the river.

"I won't presume to make suggestions," Mandy said, "but—"

"I know," Duncan cut in. "We're going to have to send a ground party to explore the river."

"The problem is that we don't know what kind of child Theresita is carrying," Mandy said. "It tests normal. There's just one strange thing—"

"Yes?"

"For a four-month-old fetus, the brain seems too well developed."

Rodrick felt a chill, as if a sudden draft had swept into that climate-controlled office. Perhaps he should have taken charge of the situation sooner. "Have you discussed abortion?"

"We have. I talked with Theresita again today. She will obey an order to terminate the pregnancy, but she will not choose to abort voluntarily. At first Theresita seemed inclined in that direction, but we procrastinated too long for an abortion to be emotionally acceptable to her. She's now experiencing the maternal syndrome." Mandy chuckled without mirth. "Furthermore, she is curious about the fetus. As am I. Jacob, incidentally, has told her that the decision is hers and hers alone."

Rodrick drummed his fingers for a moment. "For the good of the colony, should I order her to terminate the pregnancy?"

"I don't know," Mandy admitted. "How can there be men—beings—so much like us that crossbreeding is possible? It's a bit frightening."

"I've studied the recordings of Theresita's debriefings," Duncan said. "It's not wise, of course, to draw conclusions based on such scanty information, but do you agree that it seems that someone with pretty advanced medical techniques healed some very severe wounds on Theresita's shoulder?"

Mandy nodded. "The scars are there."

"And she's convinced that she was kept under the influence of drugs for a considerable period of time," Duncan continued. "Her description of her symptoms when she regained consciousness in the Whorsk village seem to indicate classic drug withdrawal. Her memory is only a vague blur. She remembers making love with a handsome man. Shall we assume that that man is the father of Theresita's fetus?"

"I think we have to," Mandy answered.

"And that makes an expedition to the Great Misty River a high priority," Duncan said. "And yet we can't afford to lose any more personnel. Our original group of a thousand colonists was a minimal assurance that this colony would not, due to the lack of qualified people, revert to pre-industrial primitivism. We're dangerously overextended as it is. The loss of even one more person would be critical."

"Yes," Mandy agreed, feeling her cheeks getting hot from her ever-present guilt and remorse.

"On the other hand, we can't afford any more surprises like the Whorsk attack," Duncan said. He spread his hands and smiled. "It's a nasty situation: Send an expedition now and risk conflict and loss, or do nothing and risk a surprise attack from an enemy about whom we know nothing."

"If it will help you in your decision," Mandy said, "we can watch the baby very closely as it develops, without endangering its health or Theresita's. Perhaps we can learn something of the nature of the father in that way."

"Yes, do that," Duncan said. "Keep me posted."

"Now," Mandy said, opening a file folder, "there are some more routine matters."

For another half hour he listened, nodding in agreement or making suggestions as they discussed various aspects of policy regarding the health and well-being of the colony. Finished, Mandy rose, closing her folder.

"Thank you for your time, Captain," she said.

"I think, Dr. Miller, that we should schedule a conference such as this on a regular basis—say every two weeks?"

"I would appreciate that," she said.

He came around his desk and opened the door for her and, on impulse, stepped out into the hall, out of range of the recording instruments.

"How are you, Mandy?" he asked, and she realized that his question was deeper than the casual, often-used words.

"I have my work," she answered.

"I've never taken the chance to say how sorry I am about Rocky."

She shrugged.

"I hope you don't blame yourself for what happened."

"I could have come to you about Rocky's intentions."

He looked at the floor. Yes, she could have come to him, and if she had, perhaps two hundred people would have lived, but he couldn't find it in his heart to hold her responsible.

"Mandy, I want you to know that, regardless of what has happened or will happen, you have a friend."

"Thank you," she said, her eyes misting. She put out her hand, and he took it. "That's all it can be, Duncan."

"I know," he said sadly.

He watched her walk away, then went back into his office, sat down behind the desk, and ran his hand through his hair. Things were complicated enough, uncertain enough, without that unexpected welling up of emotion he'd felt when she walked into the room and when she shook his hand. He had his Jackie—a wonderful, beautiful woman—and there were still a few unattached men left among the single personnel. It would be best for Mandy to make a new attachment, once a suitable period of time had passed, for the needs of the colony made personal loss and unhappiness secondary considerations.

He had a job to do, and he would put Mandy Miller out of his mind in order to get it done. He had some decisions to make. At the moment his inclination was to concentrate on the important task of accumulating enough fuel to send the ship back to Earth. That was the overriding priority, but it presented problems. When the ship was ready to leave Omega, how could he leave with it, knowing that the mystery of the Great Misty River still hung over the colony?

In his mind there lingered a picture, a carving from the dead city in Stoner's Valley. Among the images of the sticklike Whorsk, there had been one other humanoid representation—a winged creature with full, muscular limbs.

Although Theresita's baby showed all indications of being a normal human fetus, would it also sprout wings? It was beyond logic.

That one inescapable fact was to dominate his thoughts for hours, until he joined Jackie in their bright and airy home overlooking Stanton Bay. Jackie's warm kiss of greeting caused a moment of sadness, but it didn't last long as his hands went to rest on her hips and he drew her to him.

"How was the meeting with Mandy?" Jackie asked with no apparent guile or suspicion.

"Interesting," he said. "Events are pushing me to make a decision I'd rather postpone."

"It's not like you to be reluctant to face anything," Jackie said, pride in her voice. "I know you'll make the right decision at the right time."

He grinned. It was heady to have a woman who felt

that he could do no wrong. With support like that, he would make the right decision, and even as she took his hand and led him into the dining room for the evening meal, he knew which decision he would make.

Coming in 1987 . . .

AMERICA 2040 SERIES

Volume Three

Little is known about the master race that lives along the Great Misty River, except that they possess astounding medical skills and are enough like Homo sapiens to have impregnated an Earth woman. Captain Duncan Rodrick, whose small American colony has suffered a devastating attack by one native Omega group, decides to send a small expedition to the Great Misty River. He will not be caught unaware again.

The expedition is met by the River People, a superrace with nothing but disdain for the Americans. They demand that Captain Rodrick stop mining rhenium, the scarce, precious metal needed to power his starship. Rodrick's reply is to launch an offensive against the River People. Too late he learns that they control a vastly superior war technology, capable of annihilating every American on the planet Omega . . . and they intend to use it.

Read the exciting sequel to AMERICA 2040 and THE GOLDEN WORLD, on sale in February 1987 wherever Bantam Books are sold.